As Brenda turned and walked back to the sink, her gaze shifted past the mirror when she caught a hint of motion beyond her reflection.

Seated on the edge of the bed, no more than ten or twelve feet behind her, was a small, dark figure. Even before Brenda's eyes adjusted, she realized it was a person and, in that instant, she also realized that it was not her husband. The figure was distinctly female, small with narrow, slouched shoulders. Even in the darkness, Brenda caught a glimpse of the flowing hair that draped like smoke around the figure's shoulders. As vague as it was in the mirror, the figure looked frighteningly real and very much like her now-dead mother.

Brenda didn't dare turn away from the mirror and look at it directly—she sensed it would disappear instantly. She couldn't shift her gaze away from it, either.

"Are you . . . *who are you?*" she asked, her voice cracking . . .

LOOKING GLASS

Praise for A. J. Matthews's debut thriller,

THE WHITE ROOM

"A suspense thriller with a dash of the supernatural . . . builds to an exciting and satisfying conclusion."

—Cemetery Dance

looking
glass

A. J. MATTHEWS

BERKLEY BOOKS, NEW YORK

This is a work of fiction. Names, characters, places, and incidents either
are the product of the author's imagination or are used fictitiously, and
any resemblance to actual persons, living or dead, business
establishments, events, or locales is entirely coincidental.

LOOKING GLASS

A Berkley Book / published by arrangement with
the author

PRINTING HISTORY
Berkley edition / January 2004

Copyright © 2003 by Rick Hautala.
Cover design by Jill Bolton.
Interior text design by Kristin del Rosario.

For information address: The Berkley Publishing Group,
a division of Penguin Group (USA) Inc.,
375 Hudson Street, New York, New York 10014.

ISBN: 0-425-19099-4

BERKLEY®
Berkley Books are published by The Berkley Publishing Group,
a division of Penguin Group (USA) Inc.,
375 Hudson Street, New York, New York 10014.
BERKLEY and the "B" design
are trademarks belonging to Penguin Group (USA) Inc.

PRINTED IN THE UNITED STATES OF AMERICA

10 9 8 7 6 5 4 3 2 1

With love to Holly . . .

my "Alice"
(who took me "through the looking glass"),
my "Josie"
(who is the "singular determinant of
the rest of my life"),
and my enkeli
(who hides her wings . . . sometimes).

"It's a poor sort of memory that only works backwards."

—Lewis Carroll,
Through the Looking-Glass

"Life is eternal; and love is immortal; death is only a horizon; and a horizon is nothing save the limit of our sight."

—Rossiter W. Raymond

ONE

housewarming

"**ARE** we having fun yet?"

Brenda Ireland chuckled softly and turned her head to one side so she could see her husband. He had stepped up close behind her and was pressing himself against her hip. His hands grasped and massaged her waist lightly, and his breath was warm in the cup of her ear. Brenda caught the bitter aroma of beer on his breath but decided not to say anything about it.

Not now, anyway.

Let him enjoy himself, just for tonight, she thought.

Raising one hand, she ran her fingertips along the edge of his jaw and slumped back into his supporting embrace. She sighed and nodded as he squeezed her tightly.

"Umm, yeah . . . I'm having a great time," she murmured.

"Seriously?"

The pressure of his hands around her waist grew stronger, and his breath heated her neck. She was suddenly flushed. In other circumstances, she would have turned around and melted into his embrace.

"Yes," she whispered. "Seriously."

She turned and surveyed the gathering of friends, neighbors, and business associates who milled around in their living room. Conversations and laughter, ice clinking in glasses, and muted music filled the house. Brenda couldn't deny a stirring of pride as she glanced around at the living room's decor, all of which she had picked out. The floral-print sofa and chairs, the rustic stenciling that ran along the top of the walls, and the rich, colonial blue wall paint had all come together even better than she had thought they would.

Once again—as she had so many times tonight already—Brenda wished it was just the two of them here tonight, alone . . . together. The housewarming party had been Matt's idea. Brenda thought they could easily have waited until later in the year, maybe after Thanksgiving, to celebrate moving into the new home. But Matt had insisted that they do something as soon as possible, and Brenda couldn't fault him for that. He worked hard at the law firm, and they both were very proud of everything they had accomplished. She felt a twinge of guilt—and worry—that her job at the bank had been downsized so soon after they committed to this new house, but Matt assured her things would be fine as long as the market didn't take another nosedive.

"You might consider going a little easy on the beer, darling," Brenda whispered, unable to stop herself from saying something. She knew Matt was a little tipsy just by the way he leaned against her, as though he needed a little extra support. And she could feel the solid bulge in his pants, pressing against her.

"I'm fine, hon. Honest," he said.

And, truth to tell, he did seem fine. His speech wasn't slurred, and his brown eyes looked clear and focused. It was just his breath.

"Oh, you're better than fine, darlin'." She twisted around in his embrace and raised her face to kiss him lightly on the lips. "You're . . . incredible." She breathed the last word in a gusty exhalation.

"I know I am," Matt said, sniffing with laughter as he ran his hands slowly up her sides, tickling her ribs and smiling wickedly. Brenda loved seeing her joy reflected in his face, and for just a few seconds, she forgot all about the friends and neighbors milling around them she gazed deeply into her husband's eyes. She knew how easy it was to get lost in those eyes.

Matt grunted softly as he crushed her against him. The stiffness of his erection pressed against her lower belly. The message was clear. Closing her eyes, Brenda kissed him passionately, opening her mouth to let her tongue dart playfully between Matt's teeth.

"Hey, hey, hey! Get a room, why don't you?"

They broke off the embrace and turned to see Ed Lewis, one of the senior partners and Matt's boss at the law firm, approaching them. If Matt had had a beer or two over his limit, Ed was perfectly lit, and with whiskey, if his past performances at office parties were any indication. His bulging blue eyes looked like large marbles coated with oil, and his face was so flushed he looked like a front-runner in the Who's Going to Have a Stroke This Week contest.

"Damned beautiful place you've got here, m'boy." He clapped Matt on the shoulder hard enough to stagger him. "Damned beautiful. See what working in a partnership will get you? Much better than wasting your time and energy working in the state DA's office, wouldn't you say?"

"I'll drink to that," Matt said, raising his beer bottle high.

Ed sloshed some whiskey on his hand as he took a sip. He seemed dangerously unsteady on his feet, and Brenda tried not to imagine the mess he would make—or how angry she would be—if he spilled anything on their brand-new carpet. Accidents were bound to happen eventually, especially with two children in the house. The place wasn't going to look like something out of *House Beautiful* for long. Maybe Matt had been right to have the party now, before the wear and tear of family life took its toll, but Brenda certainly didn't need Matt's boss to initiate it.

"You and the missus will be more 'an comfortable here," Ed said, nodding sagely. "More 'an comfortable."

When he took another gulping drink, Brenda noticed with some disgust that the white gunk in the corners of his mouth seemed to thicken.

"What say you 'n me take a little stroll," Ed said, clapping Matt on the shoulder again and pulling him away from Brenda. "I'm dying for a cigarette, and since I don't see any ashtrays lying round about, I'm guessing you want us social pariahs to smoke outside. 'S that right?"

"You're absolutely right, Ed," Brenda said, stepping forward before Matt could reply. "It's the back deck for the likes of you." Realizing she might have overstepped her bounds as hostess, she quickly added, "There's a nice view of the woods out back. You know, I've already seen more deer than I can count since we moved in."

"'S that a fact?" Ed said. His focus wavered a bit. "So you're holding up okay, living out here in the willie-whacks?"

"Oh, I absolutely love it," Brenda said, casting a quick glance at Matt. Apparently Ed didn't realize—or mind—that she had taken him by the elbow and was guiding him through the crowded, noisy living room and into the kitchen, where the sliding glass door opened out onto the deck. Matt followed along behind, and Brenda noticed that he snagged a bottle of Sam Adams from the refrigerator before following her and his boss out onto the deck.

The night was warm, especially for late April. A soft breeze whispered high in the dark pines that bordered the backyard. The land sloped gently down to a small pond, which the local fire department had designated an emergency fire pond, so it was fenced off. The steady song of spring peepers rose in the night, sounding like jingling silver bells in the distance. Light from the waxing moon cast a powdery blue glow over the scene, making the shadows under the trees deep and dimensionless.

Once out in the open air, Ed seemed even more unsteady. Brenda wished she could tactfully take his drink away from him before he embarrassed himself in front of everyone. Maybe he had judged that he'd had too much, too, because he rested his glass on the railing and, gripping the rail with both hands, tilted his head back, closed his eyes, and inhaled deeply. When he exhaled, a thin mist came from his nostrils.

"Well," she said, "I suppose you two want to talk about *guy* things."

Keeping his eyes closed, Ed fished a pack of Marlboros from the pocket of his suit coat and shook one out. Before he had it in his mouth, Matt flicked a cigarette lighter and held the flame so he could light up.

"Thanks," Ed said, exhaling a billow of gray smoke.

Brenda didn't go back inside immediately. She was curi-

ous if Ed had anything important to talk to Matt about, or if he
really did just want to fill his lungs with nicotine. She had just
decided that Matt's boss was too tipsy to talk serious business
and was about to return to the party when she noticed something in the woods: a faint glow of diffused light that angled
through the pine boughs.

"What the—" she started to say, then stopped herself.

Matt appeared to have noticed the light, too, because he
was shifting his gaze back and forth between his boss and the
woods. Brenda wanted to ask him what he thought it might
be, but she remained silent and strained to watch the light. It
was so faint, it disappeared now and again in the dense brush,
swallowed by the darkness.

Could it have been a flashlight? she wondered as a slight
feeling of foreboding took hold of her. *Or was it Saint Elmo's
fire or swamp gas?*

"I know this probably isn't a good time to mention something like this," Ed said.

Matt turned his full attention to his boss, his eyebrows
raised in silent question.

"You must've heard somethin' about it on the news today."

Brenda stiffened. It was a conditioned reflex, she knew, but
it seemed like she was always expecting the worst, especially
since losing her job. Almost a year ago, a bank from Massa-
chusetts had bought the local bank she worked for in Augusta.
Her job as a loan officer—along with plenty of other jobs—
had been consolidated with the home office. Since they had
just started building the house at the time, which had seriously
drained their finances, Brenda seemed always to be waiting
for the second shoe to drop even as she tried to convince herself that it would all work out for the best. During the con-
struction, she had been able to oversee and approve or modify
all the final details for their new home and shop for the deco-
rative touches that made the house so pretty. Better still, she
had been able to stay home, like she had always wanted to, to
raise Emily, her fifteen-year-old stepdaughter from Matt's
previous marriage, and John, the son they had had together
right after they'd been married, seven years ago.

But she was unnerved by the tone Ed had adopted. His
forced casualness signaled imminent danger.

I hope he's not thinking about letting Matt go, she thought. It had been a big step, moving from public legal services to a private practice, but Ed was right: Matt was tired of seeing the absolute worst side of humanity as a state ADA.

She couldn't help but cringe as she waited for whatever bad news Ed was about to deliver. Maybe the settlements they'd been waiting for hadn't come through, and Matt wouldn't be getting the raise he'd been promised over a year ago. Whatever it was, it was something bad. Brenda knew that.

"No," Matt said with a slight tremor in his voice. "What news was that?"

Brenda sensed that her husband was expecting some kind of bombshell, too. She could see it in his eyes, in his tensed jaw, and in the tight grip he maintained on his beer bottle.

No, she told herself. *If it's really bad news, Ed wouldn't drop it on us tonight, not during our housewarming party. Would he?*

"You didn't hear 'bout your old friend, Jeromy Bowker, huh?" Ed asked. "He's filed another appeal on his conviction. That makes—what?"

"Three," Matt said.

"Says he's got new evidence that absolutely proves his innocence, and he's gonna be out of jail by Christmas."

Obviously relieved, Matt snorted with laughter and shook his head before taking a sip of beer.

"He didn't happen to mention *which* Christmas, did he?" he asked, still chuckling.

Although her initial panic had subsided, a teasing chill still danced up and down Brenda's back like a cool whisper of wind. It wasn't the night that was making her feel uncomfortable. She knew that much. They had lived out here in the country for more than six weeks now, and not once had she felt lonely or threatened.

Maybe it's because of that glow of light I saw in the woods, she thought. *Could there really be someone out there in the dark? What the hell would they be doing out there? Or was it something else?*

Shivering, Brenda looked out across the backyard to the trees again, but the light was no longer visible. She might have imagined it, but even if she hadn't, the woods were dark now, the trees like black lace against the starry backdrop of the sky. Except for the steady sound of the spring peepers and the noise of party conversation coming from inside the house, everything was peaceful and still.

Stepping away from her husband and Ed, Brenda walked to the far end of the deck so she could be alone for a few minutes. She inhaled deeply and looked up at the night sky, wondering why she had suddenly felt so . . . vulnerable.

Everything was fine. She should be feeling great now that they were celebrating their new home with all of their friends.

Maybe it was the mere mention of Jeromy Bowker that had unnerved her so, Brenda thought. She remembered all too well the hideous details of the case her husband had prosecuted for the state. A man like Jeromy Bowker deserved to be in prison for what he had done. For what he had done, he deserved the death penalty . . . if only the state of Maine had one.

But Bowker was safely locked away in the Maine State Prison in Warren. Whoever might or might not be wandering around out there in the woods at night, it sure wasn't Jeromy Bowker.

So why am I feeling all nerved up? Brenda wondered.

It wasn't like her to react like this. Then again, ever since she and the family had moved out to this little bedroom community of Three Rivers, just outside of Augusta, she hadn't felt completely like herself. It wasn't a bad feeling. In so many ways, this house and the new life she was leading were exactly what she had always dreamed about. True, they were feeling some financial strain at this point in their lives, but she was happy.

Her life was good now.

Better than good.

It was great.

She loved her husband and her son, and even though there had always been a certain amount of tension between her and her stepdaughter, that was to be expected. After all, Brenda had come between Emily and her dad, who she had pretty much all to herself until she was eight years old. Matt and his first wife had divorced when Emily was just over a year old. Unfortunately, John's birth had only added to the problem.

Brenda had been disappointed that Emily had never displayed much of the excitement and joy they had expected her to show about having a new baby brother. All in all, though, the family was doing fine.

So why do I feel so uneasy right now?

The sounds of the party inside the house seemed to distort and recede as she stared out at the dark woods and tried to convince herself to calm down.

There was nothing—absolutely nothing—to be upset about.

She glanced over at her husband and his boss. Ed had finished his cigarette and was nursing his whiskey again. Thankfully, there wasn't much left in his glass. She hoped Matt had the sense not to offer to refill it for him. Matt looked more relaxed now. His arms were folded across his chest, and he had his beer bottle in one hand as he leaned back against the deck railing. Brenda still thought she detected some slight tension in the way he held his shoulders, as if he wasn't entirely comfortable talking with his boss in this kind of situation.

Or maybe the news is bad, she thought. *Maybe talking about Jeromy Bowker trying to get his life sentence overturned had just been Ed's preamble before he dropped the bomb.*

She had just decided to leave the men outside and rejoin the party when the sliding glass door opened, and Emily stuck her head outside. Light from inside the house illuminated her from behind, making her dark hair glow like polished amber. She had the portable phone in one hand and looked around until she spotted Brenda and then held the phone out to her.

"Phone call for you," Emily said tonelessly.

Brenda started toward her, wondering—as she did pretty much every day—when and if Emily would ever refer to her as "Mom."

Probably never.

"Who is it?" she asked. Pretty much everyone they knew and loved was in the house, except for Brenda's mother, who was in a nursing home.

"How should *I* know?" Emily said, giving Brenda a standard teenager's *whatever* shrug. "She sounds all official and stuff. She asked for *Mrs.* Ireland."

Their hands touched, briefly as Brenda took the phone from Emily and pressed it to her ear. She opened the sliding glass door and entered the kitchen where there were only a few people standing around the food-laden table.

"Hello," she said.

Her voice sounded thin and tinny to her. The plastic receiver was slick in her hand, and she realized that her hands were sweating as though . . .

As though what? As though I'm expecting—

"Yes, I'm trying to reach Denise Swanson's daughter, Brenda Ireland."

"Yes. Speaking."

"This is Hillary Milford at Austin Place."

—something terrible to happen?

Brenda's breath caught like a small stone in her throat. The back of her neck suddenly went cold, as if someone unseen had lightly grazed her skin, teasing the hairs at the nape of her neck. She couldn't repress a shudder because she knew . . .

Something bad has already happened. It's too late to stop it or change it.

"Yes?" she heard herself say. Her voice was so weak in the receiver it was like listening to someone speaking from the next room.

"I'm afraid I have some rather bad news for you about your mother," the woman said.

Brenda sucked in a breath, but the air in the kitchen seemed too thin to fill her lungs. She gasped and tried to speak but couldn't.

"She apparently was attempting to get out of bed when she fell," Ms. Milford continued. "She's suffered a quite severe head injury. We're not sure of the full extent, but we've had her transported by ambulance to Maine Medical Center in Portland."

"I . . . I see," Brenda finally managed to say, surprised that she could speak at all.

Involuntarily, her gaze drifted around the kitchen. Her eyes were stinging as tears filled them, making her view of the room turn into a gauzy, yellow glow. She had the distinct impression she was looking through an inches-thick sheet of plate glass. The sights and sounds of the party receded. Even the brand-new kitchen appliances and table and chair set seemed oddly and frighteningly distant. A few of their guests were staring at her, obviously having picked up that something was wrong.

"The doctor on staff here tonight, Dr. Heitz, can speak with you, if you'd like," Ms. Milford said. "Of course, I'd expect you'd want to drive down to the hospital in Portland and—"

The woman's voice cut off so sharply Brenda thought for an instant that the phone had been disconnected, but then she heard the woman's breath catch as she tried to continue.

"What? What is it?" Brenda heard herself ask.

She shook her head as though to clear it, struggling against the disorienting feeling that some vast distance was opening up between her and everything around her.

"The injury to her head is quite severe," Ms. Milford said with a trembling, hesitant voice. "She . . . when she left here, she was—" Ms. Milford took a steadying breath, which Brenda could easily hear over the phone. "If you would like to speak with Dr. Heitz, I can page him for you."

"I . . . ah, no. No thank you. I—we can leave for Portland right now. I'll call the hospital on the drive down. But thank you. Thank you for calling and telling me."

Brenda vaguely realized how ridiculous she must sound, thanking the woman for informing her that her mother was seriously hurt.

How serious is it?

Brenda pulled the phone away from her ear and flicked it off with her thumb.

Is she dying? Is she already dead?

Her hands felt like lead weights, and her shoulders slumped as she leaned back against the refrigerator and tried to absorb what she had just heard. As she looked around the kitchen at all of her friends laughing and having fun, a sour, aching sob gathered strength deep in her stomach. She struggled against the terrifying feeling of complete isolation that swept over her. It was almost as if she were somehow outside of her body, floating near the ceiling and looking down at everything—even herself—with a peculiar detachment.

The slight grinding sound of the sliding glass door opening drew her attention like a distant rumble of thunder. A warm gust of the evening air carrying the song of the spring peepers brushed against her face. Turning her gaze to the door, she saw her husband enter the kitchen. His eyes darted back and forth as he looked around until his gaze stopped on her. He smiled at her and gave a quick thumbs-up.

Brenda could only stare at him, her expression flat and frozen, her eyes wide and staring. Matt frowned as he looked at her, cocking his head to one side in a silent question.

His lips were moving. He was saying something, but Brenda couldn't hear him over the party noise. She guessed it was something like, *"Are you okay?"* When she didn't respond, a rush of concern darkened his eyes.

All Brenda could do was stare back at him and shrug. She raised her dead-weight arms as though to hug him, barely aware that she was still holding the useless phone in her right hand. Matt started toward her, but in the hollow concussion of her shock, it seemed to take him forever to cross the kitchen floor. When he was finally beside her, he whispered, "What's the matter, hon?"

She looked at him, fighting back the feeling that invisible fingers were gripping her throat and steadily tightening. Tears filled her eyes, blurring her vision. Unable to take a breath, she gasped so hard her chest ached with a cold, raw sensation.

"Bren . . . What is it? Tell me."

"That . . . that was the nursing home."

She was amazed by how distant her voice sounded to her.

"My . . . my mother. There's been a . . . an accident."

"An accident?" Matt said, echoing her. "What do you mean?"

When Brenda tried to say more, her voice cut off, and she leaned forward and pressed her face hard against her husband's shoulder. Deep, wrenching sobs racked her body, and she felt as though she was getting smaller, dissolving into her husband's all-encompassing embrace.

"Is she—? Where is she? What do you want to do?"

"We have to go to the hospital in Portland," she said.

Tears smeared her face, and her body shook violently.

"Yes, yes. Of course we will."

Matt's breath was warm on her neck. The mixed smells of his deodorant and the beer he'd been drinking filled her nose.

Those smells and the warmth of her husband's body seemed like the only real things in the world. Everything else—even her own thoughts—seemed impossibly far away as she stared into the darkness behind her closed eyes. She desperately tried to deny the single, clear thought that was echoing like a lonely chime inside her head, but she couldn't deny it.

All she could think was, *My mother's probably already dead, and there's not a thing I can do to help her.*

TWO

encounter

"**YOU'LL** do it because I say you will, and that's final. End of discussion."

Matt's voice was slightly slurred from the beer he'd been drinking, and he was still a bit unsteady on his feet as he stood in the doorway, looking into Emily's bedroom. He had his hands on his hips, and an angry flush colored his face as he glared at his daughter.

"This wasn't a discussion," Emily said, her voice twisting into a high-pitched whine. "You're telling me."

"All right, then. Yes. I'm telling you. That's the way it's going to be."

"But why *her?*"

Emily pouted like someone a lot younger than fifteen as she plunked down on her bed and swatted several of her stuffed animals onto the floor.

"I don't even *like* Mrs. Elroy. She . . . she *smells* funny, and she's always mean to us. Besides, I'm old enough to be a baby-sitter myself. Why can't I—?"

"This is different."

From behind, Brenda lightly tapped her husband on the shoulder to get his attention, but he ignored her as he took another step into the room. Still pouting dramatically, Emily folded her arms across her thin chest, squared her shoulders, and raised her chin in defiance.

"Look, Em. Your mot—Brenda and I are worried enough as it is about Grammy Swanson. We don't need to be worrying about you guys, too."

He was struggling to keep his voice down, but Brenda could tell that his patience was wearing thin.

"Do you understand that? This is really serious. Grammy Swanson had an accident and she's—" He hesitated and cast a worried glance over his shoulder at Brenda, then looked squarely at his daughter. "She could be seriously hurt, and we have to go help her if we can."

"She's not *my* grandmother!" Emily said, her voice tight with anger. Looking past her father, she locked her gaze onto Brenda, who was hanging back in the hallway. "She might be *John's* grammy, but she's not *mine!* So I don't *care* what happens to her! And I certainly don't need Mrs. *Elroy* baby-sitting me."

Matt sighed heavily as he walked over to the bed and sat down beside Emily. He placed an arm around her shoulder and, pulling her close, kissed her on the forehead. She seemed to shrink away from him, not wanting or allowing his affection to get to her.

"It's not like we're going out to the movies or something," Matt said, his voice lower now, and patient. "We have to drive to the hospital in Portland, and there's no telling when we'll be back. I want someone—an adult—here to watch out for you and John."

"You don't think I can handle it?" Emily said, sounding hurt. "I've baby-sat for both the Costellos and the Bishops."

"I know you have, and it's not that I don't trust you. I know you could do it."

Matt pulled her even closer, but Brenda could see that Emily was still holding back, resisting his embrace.

"But we might not be back till morning, and you guys have to get ready for school in the morning. I want an adult here to make sure you and John are covered."

Emily's forehead furrowed as she looked up at her father. A look of concern crossed her face but quickly vanished.

"Yeah," she said, looking down at her feet, "but why Mrs. Elroy? She—"

"I don't want to hear any more about it. She offered to stay and help us out, and that's all there is to it. And *please*—keep your voice down. She's right downstairs. I don't want her to hear you."

"I don't *care* if she can hear me," Emily said, but Brenda noticed that she had lowered her voice to a whisper. She held her body stiffly for another few seconds, then—finally—let herself be pulled into her father's embrace. He raised his hand and twirled her hair between his fingers.

Clearing her throat as she took a single step into the bedroom, Brenda signaled to Matt that she wanted to speak with him in private. He nodded his understanding as he stood up and walked with her out into the hall.

"Look, why don't you stay here with the kids?" Brenda whispered. "I can drive down there by myself."

"Nope. No way."

Matt shook his head sharply. The sour smell of beer on his breath blew into Brenda's face, making her wrinkle her nose. He'd finished his last beer over an hour ago, so she knew he wasn't really looped; but all things considered, she thought it might be best if she drove down to Maine Med on her own.

The truth was, from the sounds of things, her mother was in really bad shape. As much as she appreciated Matt's support, she felt she needed to face this ordeal alone . . . especially if she got down there and found out that her mother was already gone.

"Look, hon, you've had a bit more to drink than you're used to," she said, running her hand along the side of his face. "I'd really rather not have you driving anywhere."

"Fine. You drive," Matt said, "but I don't care what you say. I'm going with you. Besides—"

He jerked his head to one side, indicating Emily's open door. Through the doorway, Brenda could see her stepdaughter sitting on her bed, pretending not to be trying to overhear what they were saying. Matt dropped his voice to a whisper.

"If she gets her way on this, we'll regret it later. She's made it an issue, and I can't back down now. You understand, don't you?"

Brenda considered for a moment, then nodded her agreement. "All right, then. But I'm driving."

"Absolutely."

BRENDA and Matt talked almost nonstop on the drive to Maine Medical Center, but Brenda felt as though she just kept repeating the same things, over and over. She could hear the worried edge in her husband's voice and fought hard to keep focused on what they had to do.

"We won't know until we get there," she said for the umpteenth time. "We have no idea what her condition is, right? So we can't be jumping to conclusions."

Matt nodded his understanding and reached out to touch her, to rub her arm and shoulder, but Brenda couldn't stop feeling as though she was all alone in this.

"But what if . . . what if she's really bad off?" she asked. "She has a living will, and I have power of attorney and can sign a DNR."

"A do not resuscitate order."

Brenda sighed and nodded, keeping one hand firmly on the steering wheel as she wiped the tears that were gathering in her eyes.

"Remember? You drew up the paperwork and I signed it when Mom went into the nursing home last winter."

Talking to Matt like this, focusing on such practical-sounding matters, was making it all too real for her. For all they knew, this was it—this was the end of her mother's life.

"We'll just have to see. She may not even be as . . . even be as bad as we think."

Her voice choked off with tears, and Matt gave her shoulder another firm, reassuring squeeze.

"If there's no hope of recovery," he said, his voice sounding a bit distant and hard, "then you'll have to do what you have to do and pull the plug. Let's wait until we get there."

"Do you have to put it like that? 'Pull the plug.' God, you make it sound like she's a—an appliance that doesn't work anymore or something."

"You know what I mean," Matt said.

Brenda glanced over at him and saw the look of sympathy in his glance. She sucked in her breath and held it, struggling to focus on the road ahead.

Up ahead, the headlights illuminated the sign for Exit 8, which was the quickest way she knew to get to Maine Med. Brenda slowed the car and snapped on her turn signal. She slowed for the turn onto the exit ramp, her foot shaking as she applied the brake. A cold, downward spiraling sense of dread filled the pit of her stomach.

Brenda had no idea what she might have to face over the next few hours, but she braced herself for the very real possibility that, when she got there, they would find out that her mother was already dead.

BUT her mother wasn't dead.

It was worse than that. Much worse.

While Matt paced back and forth across the floor behind her, occasionally stopping to rest his hand on her shoulder and pat her, Brenda sat hunched in a padded chair in a small hospital office. The room was little more than a converted storage closet with a single desk, which was cluttered with half-empty coffee cups and assorted charts, files, medical books, professional magazines, and old newspapers.

She could feel herself drawing in upon herself, trying to make herself smaller, as if that would help ease her pain and confusion. A few doors down the corridor, her mother lay in a coma. A respirator was the only thing keeping her alive, and digital monitors charted all of her vital functions, which they could see were gradually lessening. Brenda didn't have to be told. For all intents and purposes, her mother was already dead.

How can she be gone . . . just like that?

Dr. Stiles, the chief neurologist on duty, was a young man with sandy brown hair and clear, green eyes. He seemed too young to be a doctor—a neurologist, no less—but he had a quiet, calm demeanor that instantly engaged Brenda's trust. Still, there was no way he could soften the seriousness of her mother's condition. He sat on the edge of the desk with one foot on the floor and his hands folded on his lap. His eyes were narrowed with sympathy and concern.

"Essentially," he said, "the impact from the fall dislodged your mother's brain stem from her brain. In effect . . ." He shrugged as though helpless. "Her brain was unplugged." He made a slight motion with his hands like he was disconnecting an electrical plug. "Life support is the only thing keeping her alive right now. We can do that indefinitely, but there's really nothing more we can do medically."

He paused and took a sharp breath, allowing Brenda and Matt time to let what he had just said sink in. Then, leaning close and lowering his voice, he said, "Your mother is not going to recover, Mrs. Ireland. I hate to be the one to tell you this and to be so blunt, but that's the simple truth."

Brenda started to speak. She wanted to say something . . . anything, if only to cut through the terrible rushing sound that was roaring inside her head. The only sound she could make was a low, strangled gasp. Her mind was an absolute blank. She felt numb and only distantly aware of Matt's hand on her shoulder, squeezing gently, reassuringly. She looked up at him, but he seemed impossibly far away, like she was peering at him through the wrong end of a telescope. She wanted desperately to stand up, turn around, and gaze straight into his eyes, but she was too drained to move. The hot pressure behind her eyes was almost too much to bear. Tears made the light in the room shimmer like quicksilver. Everything went out of focus, the lights fragmenting into brilliant, glasslike splinters.

"Ultimately," Dr. Stiles said, sounding far, far away, "it's your decision what to do." He paused, but only for a moment. "You said your mother has a living will . . ."

Dr. Stiles stopped talking, letting what he had said hang between them. Brenda blinked her eyes, but the visual distortion didn't stop. It only got worse as she looked up at the doctor's face until it blurred into a colorless smudge with her gathering tears. Hot pressure filled her head.

"I know this is a very difficult decision for you," Dr. Stiles said softly. He got up from the desk and stared toward the door. "If you'd like, I'll give you and your husband some time alone to discuss it."

Brenda opened her mouth to speak again, but this time nothing, not even a puff of air would come out. She couldn't breathe. Tears were streaming down her face and dripping from her chin. Her chest felt like it was constrained by ever-tightening metal bands. Turning around slowly, she watched the doctor as he opened the office door and stepped out into the corridor. Everything except the racing thoughts in her head appeared to be moving in slow motion. Beyond the doctor, she saw motion in the hall as a gurney was wheeled by with a sheet-draped figure on it. She caught a fleeting glimpse of an elderly man, his thin, white hair waving in the breeze like goose down as the attendants wheeled him to . . .

Where? she wondered. *The operating room . . . his room . . . the morgue?*

She caught Matt's glance, and their gazes locked. Shivery tremors ran like tiny earthquakes inside her. Dr. Stiles hesitated in the doorway a moment, then stepped out into the hallway, gently closing the door behind him.

Once they were alone, Brenda said, "I don't—" but that was all she could get out before her voice twisted up and cut off.

"I know . . . I know," Matt said, kneeling beside her, his grip tightening on her shoulder. His eyes were shimmering with tears, and seeing him close to losing control filled Brenda with a terrible sadness. She struggled to find a modicum of strength.

"I think we have to—" she said.

She cleared her throat, fighting back the hot waves of emotion that welled up inside her and threatened to carry her away. As desperately as she wished she could extend her mother's life, she knew it was futile.

What's the phrase? "Quality of life?" Well, what would Mom's quality of life be after sustaining an injury like this?

Brenda squeezed her eyes closed and pressed her face against his shoulder. After taking a deep breath, she said, "I know I have to sign the papers now and get it over with." Her voice was strained and husky with emotion.

Matt patted her on the back. "It only makes sense," he said.

Brenda opened her eyes and stared at him. His eyes were glazed, and his lips were pinched and pale and trembling. He looked somehow diminished, as though her mother's impending demise had reduced everyone and made her truly see how fragile and vulnerable they all were.

"I mean—"

Brenda closed her eyes again and leaned forward, her head in her hands, covering her eyes. Her pulse throbbed painfully in her neck. She took a shuddering breath and bit down on her lower lip, struggling hard to keep her emotions in check. When she opened her eyes again, she stared blankly at her husband.

"We don't have a choice, do we?"

"You know we don't," Matt said, lowering his gaze. They looked at each other for a long time, and Brenda found herself getting lost in her husband's eyes. She was glad that he didn't say anything more. There was nothing he could say. There was nothing anyone could say. There was no comfort, no solace for what she had been called upon to do. Ultimately, it was her decision. She was the only person who could sign the papers and let her mother die naturally.

She had been entrusted with this terrible responsibility but had never seriously considered that she might actually be called upon to use it. She might have thought or *wanted* to think that her mother would live forever, but this was it.

This was the end.

The worst that could happen had happened, and now she and she alone held the power of life or death.

Matt looked as though he couldn't quite believe any of this was happening. Brenda saw his shoulders shaking with pent-up emotion as a chilly emptiness slid open inside her. This was just the beginning of her own grief, she knew: grief for losing her mother, grief for feeling as though she had—in so many ways—let her mother down, grief for all the time that had passed that could never be recaptured.

It's all gone now. For better or worse, my mother has reached the end of her life.

"Call Dr. Stiles back in," she said simply. The decisiveness in her voice surprised her.

Matt locked his gaze on her for a lengthening moment. His eyes were wide and watery, and he looked surprised. She wondered if it was because she had reached a decision and accepted it so quickly.

But not easily.

Her body shook as a powerful shudder ran through her.

Her words echoed in her head, and she couldn't dispel the impression that someone else—certainly not she—had spoken them.

"We have to do it," she said, focusing past her husband so she wouldn't have to look at the pain and grief in his eyes. When she swallowed, a thick, burning taste filled her mouth and throat, almost gagging her. "There's no other choice, but I . . . I want to spend the night with her, first."

Matt regarded her with a blank stare as though he hadn't quite heard or understood her.

"I want you to go home," Brenda said, gaining assurance as she spoke. "I want you to be with the kids tonight, and I'm going to spend the night with her."

"Bren, do you think that's a—"

She made a quick chopping motion with the flat of her hand to cut him off, then turned and stared blankly at the wall in front of her.

"I'll sign the papers in the morning," she said. "But first . . . I have to talk to her."

"Bren, she's in a coma. You can't even be sure she can hear you."

Brenda raised her hands and wiped away the salty tears that were streaming down her face. She bit down hard enough on her lower lip to break the skin, but she didn't care if she bled.

It doesn't matter. Nothing matters anymore.

She knew what she had to do, and no one—not even her husband—was going to talk her out of it.

Before they stopped the life support, she was going to spend one last night with her mother—alone—so she could at least try to tell her some things she should have told her when her mother could have heard her.

late night visitor

THE drive home to Three Rivers late that night—early Monday morning, actually—was difficult for Matt for a lot of reasons. Throughout, he had to fight back waves of emotion. The buzz he'd gotten at the party earlier had long since dissipated to be replaced by a headache that felt like burning embers were lodged behind his eyes. The lights of oncoming traffic only made it worse.

Worst of all, though, was leaving Brenda alone at the hospital. He didn't like doing that and wouldn't have if she hadn't insisted.

Matt had never been very close to his mother-in-law. Marrying Brenda so much later in life, he had never felt comfortable calling his mother-in-law "Mom," preferring to call her Denise instead of Mrs. Swanson. Now he regretted that he and Denise had never developed anything more than a cool relationship, keeping each other at a safe distance. He wasn't entirely sure she liked him all that much, and Brenda had told him several times that Denise had been critical of both of them for her pregnancy. The fact that it had worked out and that they loved each other didn't seem to tip the scales. Whatever the situation, any possibility of making it better was now irretrievably lost.

"I guess that's just the way it goes sometimes," he whispered as he raised his hand and rubbed his eyes. The burning behind his eyelids was getting worse.

He wished to God Brenda was with him now or—better—that he was with her, because mostly he wanted to be a support for her. He wanted her to know that he would help her in every way he could. Of course, his wife had several close friends—particularly Cheryl and Deb—but if she needed someone to talk to or a shoulder to cry on, he felt obligated to be there for her. Most of all, he wanted to make absolutely certain that she was going to be able to handle the terrible decision she had to make because sooner, rather than later, his mother-in-law . . . Brenda's mother . . . Mrs. Swanson . . . *Denise* . . . was going to die, and they were going to have to face all the tangled emotions and upset that would evoke.

Since they'd gotten married, things had been going great. He'd gone into private practice, John was born, and now the new house. This was the first major tragedy they'd had to face together, and he wasn't quite sure how to handle it. Although Brenda had told him repeatedly how much she loved him and appreciated his desire to stay with her, she had felt it necessary to do this alone, on her own terms, and he had to respect her decision.

But he didn't like the idea of her being there alone with her dying—or already dead—mother.

As he drove, he realized he was squeezing the steering wheel. He shuddered whenever he recalled how Dr. Stiles had compared his mother-in-law's injury to unplugging a power cord. In the end, though, it really was as simple as that. The impact had pulled the plug on her brain.

"Jesus Christ," he whispered, shaking his head as he blindly fiddled with the radio, trying to find a station that didn't irritate him. He couldn't settle on anything and kept switching from classical to oldies to classic rock to some half-assed late night talk show then back to classical again. Finally, in frustration, he snapped the radio off and continued the drive in silence, dwelling on his mother-in-law's impending death and funeral.

Taking shallow breaths, he stared at the pale yellow wash of his headlights on the road in front of him. The night was warm and overcast. The steady hissing of his tires on the dark pavement was soothing. Matt tried to unwind, telling himself over and over that there was absolutely nothing he could do for Brenda or her mother. Calling her on the cell phone would probably only make things worse. She wanted to be alone. His only obligation was to get home and make sure the kids were settled and that they got off to school in the morning.

To help himself stay awake, Matt rolled the side window halfway down and let the slipstream of cool night air wash over him. He inhaled deeply several times, relishing the fresh, earthy smells of the spring night, but his pleasure disappeared with a jolt whenever it hit him that his mother-in-law would never experience something as simple and pure as breathing the moist night air.

Tears welled in his eyes as that simple, terrible thought wormed deeper into his mind. He had already dealt with the deaths of both his parents: his father from alcohol when Matt was twelve years old, and his mother a few years later from breast cancer. But the finality of his mother-in-law dying— *She's already dead!*—hit him hard. In some ways, it cut even deeper than the loss of his own parents because of the unresolved issues between him and Denise. It pained him to be on the outside, watching Brenda struggle with her grief, and it hurt him that she had asked—no, demanded—that she deal with this alone.

It made him feel so useless. All he could do was take care of his own thoughts and emotions and let the rest of it slide so he could be strong for Brenda. Like anyone else, he had to face, as best he could, his own intimations of mortality, and that was never easy to do . . . especially alone on the road so late at night.

And the kids, he thought. *How are the kids going to handle this?*

Denise wasn't Emily's grandmother, and she had never developed any kind of attachment or affection for the older woman, no matter how much they had encouraged it. Even John, who was her only grandson, had always been distant from her. Maybe it was because Denise had been so much older when John was born, but maybe he also picked up on the emotional distance between his father and his grandmother. Only Brenda had visited her regularly while she was in the nursing home. Which was just one more thing to add to his list of guilty feelings and opportunities missed.

As he slowed for the turn off Route 202 onto Burnt Mill Road, Matt noticed that another car had suddenly appeared out of nowhere and was following close behind him.

Too damned close, Matt thought, as the headlights loomed like baleful eyes in his rearview mirror.

His first thought was that it might be a cop. He automatically eased up on the accelerator, slowing the car until he was going almost ten miles per hour under the posted speed limit. It had been hours since his last beer, but he wondered how much alcohol might still be in his system. Wouldn't do his practice much good for the local lawyer and former state ADA to get stopped for an OUI.

"Come on. Get off my goddamned ass," Matt whispered heatedly as he glanced at the bright lights that filled his rearview mirror.

Does this asshole have his high beams on, too?

It sure looked it.

Matt flipped the rearview mirror to night vision, but the reflection from the side-view mirror still caught his eyes, making his headache spike all the more. He shielded his face from the glare as the car loomed even closer, looking like it was only a couple of feet from his rear bumper.

Matt chuckled, remembering a bumper sticker one of the secretaries had on her car that read "If You Can Read This, I Can Step on My Brakes and Sue You," but he pressed down on the accelerator, speeding up a little. The car stayed right behind him.

"What do you think you are, a goddamned hemorrhoid?" he whispered heatedly to the twin lights in his rearview. "Get *off* my *ass!*"

One thing for sure, it wasn't a cop. If it was, and they were going to pull him over, they would have done it before now and not followed him like this.

So who the hell is this, and why's he driving so damned close?

His frustration was rising steadily, but he held himself in check, not wanting to get swept up in road rage. When they came up to a straightaway, Matt slowed down to well below the speed limit, almost coming to a complete stop as he rolled his window down and waved the driver past him.

But the car slowed down with him, keeping pace and hanging back on his tail, not even trying to pass.

"Okay. You want road rage? I'll give you road rage," he said. He debated slamming on the brakes and letting the car hit him, but he knew that would be foolish. This wasn't the time or place to be playing games. He didn't know who was in the other car or what they were capable of doing. Instead, he reached into his jacket pocket and clasped his cell phone, ready to call the cops and report this jerk.

After the straightaway on Burnt Mill was the turn onto Collette Road, a mile or so ahead. Matt hoped that his unwelcome shadow would just keep going straight when he made the turn. Gripping the steering wheel tightly with one hand, the other hand squeezing the cell phone, he was ready to hit speed dial to call the cops as he approached the turn.

"Come on . . . come on! Just pass me," he whispered angrily.

Collette Road was just over the next rise. Matt slowed even more, hoping the driver behind him would finally lose patience and pass, but no matter how slow he went, the car remained right behind him, edging even closer to his rear bumper. Matt could feel the heat from the headlights on the back of his neck. A sheen of sweat sprinkled his forehead.

"Up yours, asshole," he whispered as he pressed the button on the cell phone to turn it on. He glanced down at the lighted screen, his thumb poised and ready to dial 911.

A tight trembling gripped his stomach when he crested the hill and snapped on his blinker.

What's he gonna do? he wondered.

If the creep just drove on by, then that was the end of it.

But what if he doesn't? What if he follows me onto Collette? What if he stays right on my ass until I pull into my driveway?

Jesus, who is this guy?

Matt tried to convince himself that he was just wound up and that this wasn't really anything out of the ordinary, and certainly nothing dangerous. He wasn't thinking straight because of what had gone on at the hospital. Like him, the driver behind him was someone out late at night, impatient to get home, and leery of passing on a country road.

There was a slight chance, Matt knew, that it might be one of his clients who had recognized his car and wanted to talk to him. Or maybe it was someone who felt wronged by something he had done professionally and was out to harass him. That didn't seem very likely, but it could happen, although he no longer really handled the kinds of dangerous nut cases he dealt with working for the state. And most of those unfortunates were either locked up in jail or at least had the sense to stay away from him and not do anything overtly threatening.

Still, someone was following him, and Matt was filled with tension as he accelerated into the turn onto Collette Road. His tires squealed on the slick asphalt, and he muttered a low curse when the car took the turn, too, staying right behind him, now less than ten feet from his rear bumper.

"You don't want to be messing with me, I can tell you that," Matt whispered out loud.

His thumb hovered above the speed dial button, ready to press it as he slowed to less than twenty miles per hour. The car behind him slowed, too, still keeping pace, looming large in his rearview.

Matt navigated the curvy road but felt no better when he saw his house up ahead on the right. Soft moonlight bathed the front of the house and the woods that surrounded it, casting everything with an icy blue glaze. Without signaling, barely tapping the brakes, he jerked the steering wheel sharply and lurched to a stop in his driveway so fast the car skidded, spinning a little to the left and leaving twin black marks on the asphalt. It came to a stop, angled behind Mrs. Elroy's car.

The car that had been following him went past the head of the driveway and then braked on the side of the road in front of the house. Its red brake lights illuminated the night like the glow of a blazing furnace.

Throwing the cell phone down onto the passenger's seat, Matt killed the ignition, swung the car door open, and leaped out. Fuming, muttering under his breath, he cut across the front lawn, heading straight for the car that was now stopped on the road.

"What in the *Christ* do you think you're *doing?*" Matt shouted, shaking his clenched fists with rage.

Through the side window, Matt could see a dark silhouette outlined by the dashboard lights, but the driver didn't move. Matt had no idea who it was or even if it was a man or a woman. The closer he got to the car, the more he slowed down, realizing this was a potentially dangerous situation. When he was less than twenty feet from the car, the dome light inside came on, and the driver's door swung open.

"I don't know what you think you're doing, but I—"

He caught himself when the driver turned to face him. The interior light of the car underlit her face, but even in the dim light, Matt recognized her. It had been almost fourteen years since he had last seen her, and the years hadn't been kind to her, but there was no mistaking his ex-wife.

"Jesus Christ, Susan! What the *hell* are you doing here?"

His voice echoed in the night as he stood frozen, staring at the woman he had divorced in what seemed like another lifetime.

"Hello, Matthew," Susan said, her voice low and mild but still fragile sounding.

Matt took a quick breath and held it, trying to think of something—anything—to say.

After everything he'd been through this evening, after all those things he'd been thinking about on the drive home while being followed, his ex-wife was the last person he expected to see. Shoulders tensed, he took a few tentative steps toward her as she·swung her car door shut, killing the interior light. Her shoes made an odd scuffing sound in the roadside gravel as she came around the back of the car toward him. He shuddered, recalling how she had injured her leg in an accident, driving drunk, several months after Emily was born.

"Surprised to see me?" Susan asked.

Matt let out the breath he'd been holding and tried to relax the tension that was bunching up his neck and shoulder muscles. He shook his head, forcing a humorless chuckle.

"You might say that. I figured you were still in Iowa with your mom."

"I was," Susan said softly, "until last week." She took a few

awkward steps closer to Matt, her left leg giving out noticeably beneath her.

Still feeling threatened, Matt took a quick step back, looking to see if she held a weapon . . . or, maybe, a summons.

"I decided it was time to come back East," Susan said.
"Time for me to see Emily again."

"What?"

"I want to see my daughter."

"Are you—?"

Matt couldn't finish the question. His voice faltered as cold
rushes ran up his back and shook his shoulders. An awkward
silence fell between them until Susan finally said, "Am I
what? Am I crazy? Is that what you were going to say?"

"No, I was . . . I was . . ." Matt stammered.

"Well it doesn't matter what I am except that I'm her
mother," Susan said, "and it's time for me to see her. Long
past time."

Matt could hear her struggling to keep her voice low and
under control, but there was that edge—that same, shaky edge
in it that had always frightened him. Looking over his shoulder, Matt followed her gaze as Susan stared down the gentle
slope at the house. All of the windows were dark except for a
single light that shone in one upstairs window. Matt knew that
was John's bedroom. John still slept with a night-light.

"Looks like you've got quite a nice place here," Susan continued. "Nice, big, beautiful house . . . and in such a fancy
neighborhood. You can't even see your neighbors on either
side."

She tisked and shook her head, her eyes glistening in the
ambient moonlight. Matt noticed that she cocked her head to
one side as though listening to something he couldn't hear.

"We never had anything this nice when we were married,
did we?"

Matt's breath caught like a needle in his chest, but he managed to say, "No. We never did." He rolled his shoulders, trying to ease the tension that was winding up inside him.

"Too bad, don't you think?" Susan said, her voice sounding distant and wistful, almost sad. "Maybe if we'd been able
to afford something like . . . this . . ." She swept her hand to

include the house and yard. ". . . we might have been able to hang in there. Do you think?"

"Honestly, I doubt it," Matt said simply.

He knew that his words would hurt her, but he didn't care. He didn't want to think about things he had thought were long since over and done with. He was surprised at how unnerved he was, seeing her unexpectedly like this, but he knew what he would have said if she had called first. Just as he had worked through all the emotional distress he'd had to face and gotten on with his life, he had assumed—or wished—that Susan had finally gotten the help she had obviously needed and moved on with her life.

Bottom line was, he didn't care. It didn't matter what she did, not after what had happened when Emily was not quite two years old. Susan had had some kind of mental breakdown right after Emily's birth that may or may not have been triggered by postpartum depression. It didn't matter because it had only gotten worse with her drinking, and—finally—he could never forget or forgive her for what happened that terrible night.

Over the years, they had been in touch a few times, but they had never been able to talk on the phone without one or both of them losing their patience within a few seconds. They hadn't actually spoken in at least seven or eight years now, certainly not since John had been born, and it was a genuine shock for Matt to realize that Susan hadn't moved along.

And now, here she was—back and, apparently, wanting to mess things up again.

"Look, Susan. You gave up custody of Emily a long time ago," he said. "There's no way you can—"

"She's my daughter, too, Matthew!"

The harsh edge in his ex-wife's voice made Matt take a quick step back. Caught off guard like this, he tried to collect his thoughts. After everything else that had happened today, being surprised like this was simply too much to handle.

"You—ah, you forfeited your rights to see her when you left fourteen years ago," he said, keeping his voice as firm and steady as possible. That was the only way to deal with her so she wouldn't flip out. "And I . . . I don't think . . . I hope I don't have to go over all of it with you again. It was very painful for both of us, and I, for one, don't even want to think about it."

"I want to see her, Matthew. She's all I have left."

The pleading, almost pathetic tone in her voice touched Matt, but he knew he couldn't yield. If he didn't draw the line now and stop this, he was sure to suffer for it later.

"Look, Susan, I don't think you've thought this all the way through. Have you considered how Emily might feel? What she might want or need? Have you thought about what this might do to her?"

"What do you mean, might do to her?" Susan's voice took on a sudden dangerous tone again as she stepped forward, her fists clenched at her sides. "She's my daughter, and I have every right to see her."

"No, you don't," Matt repeated. "You gave that up in the settlement."

As much as he regretted the lack of emotion he heard in his own voice, he knew he couldn't cave in. Not under these circumstances.

"You signed all of your rights away in the divorce agreement, and—" He shook his head, trying to calm himself. "I don't want to rehash any of the crap we went through, all right?"

"I'm clean and sober now, Matthew. I really am. I've been working my program really hard, and I'm making a lot of progress. I'm not the same person I was."

"I'm sure you aren't, Susan, but that doesn't change our legal agreement. If you want to go back on it, then it's going to cost you, and I suspect you don't have the money to engage in a custody battle."

"I was hoping you'd see reason," Susan said mildly.

Neither of them said anything for several seconds. Matt stared at his ex-wife's moon-shadowed face while listening to the steady chorus of spring peepers from the woods and the heavy hammering of his pulse in his ears.

Finally, Susan broke the silence. "I thought you might be willing," she said. "I thought—"

"No," Matt snapped, cutting her off with a sharp chopping motion of his hand. "You didn't think. If you had, you would have called first, not just shown up and opened old wounds like this." He took a deep breath. "It's obvious you weren't thinking by the way you were following me just now. And do you really think you can just waltz back into Emily's life now and . . . and announce that you're her mother?"

Susan was silent again, her face no more than a ghostly white blob, floating in the night. Her shoulders collapsed inward, and she sniffed loudly.

"What do you mean, announce that I'm her mother?" she asked with a trembling edge in her voice. "She knows I'm her mother, doesn't she? She might not remember me, but she knows I'm her mother, right?"

Blinking his eyes rapidly and bracing himself, Matt shook his head slowly from side to side.

"She never even mentions you," he said softly. "Never. She—" He took a deep breath. "She doesn't even know you're alive."

As soon as he said it, he knew how deeply his words would cut her, but he didn't care. In the back of his mind, he had always feared that something like this might happen eventually, but he had always avoided thinking about it and had gone on with his life as if it never would.

And now, here it was. And he had to deal with it.

"What . . . what are you saying?"

Susan's voice sounded like ripping paper in the night. She was trembling violently as she stepped forward. Her left leg almost gave out beneath her. She clenched her hands into fists, and Matt tensed, squaring his feet and preparing to defend himself if he had to.

"Are you telling me . . . are you saying she thinks that I . . . that I'm dead?"

Matt nodded, positive that the motion wasn't wasted in the darkness.

"But you . . . you . . . why you lying piece of shit! I sent her birthday presents and Christmas presents every year. Every goddamned year since I left! Do you mean to say she never got them?"

"Oh, she got them, all right," Matt said tensely, "but I never told her they were from you."

"You *bastard!* You lying, cheating bastard! You stole her. You stole my daughter from me!"

Susan's voice rose shrilly in the night and echoed from the surrounding woods. Matt hoped that Emily and John didn't have their windows open.

"How could you? How could you do something like that?" Susan wailed. "How in the name of God could you go and . . . and erase me from my daughter's life like that?" Her voice was ragged with tears, and the high, keening wail was something Matt found all too terrifyingly familiar, even after fourteen years.

"I didn't do it," Matt said, struggling to stay calm and dreading that this was going to get out of hand. "You did. You were responsible for what happened, and you knew exactly what you were signing when you signed it."

"I'd just gotten out of the hospital then, from the psych unit! What could I have possibly known?"

"It doesn't matter. The agreement still stands, and you can't change it on a whim."

"A whim? Do you think I'm here on a whim? Do you have any idea, even the slightest clue what I've been through since . . . since then?"

In the moonlight, Matt could see the tears streaming from her eyes, glistening on her cheeks like quicksilver.

"You never even *tried* to understand what I was going through, and you sure as hell never gave me any credit for the work I did to get better."

Matt took a deep breath and let it out slowly between his teeth.

"We can go back and hash it all over again if you want," Matt said, "but after fourteen years, it won't do either of us *or* Emily any good."

"You don't understand," Susan said, her voice now nothing more than a pained moan. "I'm not the person I was back then. I've suffered over what happened, and I'm ready now. I really am. I'm clean and sober, and I've been in therapy, and I want to spend time with my daughter. I want to see how she's grown up."

"You can't," Matt said, steeling himself. "It's as simple as that."

"You can't do this! You have no right! No right to tell me that I can't see my own daughter!"

"Yes I do, and I can," Matt replied evenly. "And that's exactly what I am telling you. As much as I'd hate to do it, I'll get a judge to issue a restraining order on you if I have to. I swear I will."

"Why do you have to be such a bastard?" Susan raised her arms, her fingers outspread like a religious suppliant. After a lengthening moment, when Matt didn't say anything else, her voice shifted to an icy tone. "After all these years, you're still nothing but a power-tripping bastard. That's all you are."

"You can't say anything to hurt me, Susan. Not anymore."

Matt could see that she was trembling as she struggled to suppress or channel her rage. He didn't think he was in any real danger, but he couldn't be sure. She was as angry and hurt as he had ever seen her.

"As painful as this is, you have to accept it." He tried to keep his voice as mild and calming as possible but knew he wasn't doing very well. "It's over and done. I know it must have been terrible for you—just like it was terrible for me— but it's done now, and as far as Emily is concerned, you don't even exist. You can't expect her to just . . . just open herself up to you. Think of the hurt and confusion it would cause."

"Think how good it might be for her to know her mother . . . her *real* mother."

Matt didn't say a word, trying not to think of the problems between Emily and Brenda. He simply stood there, shaking his head from side to side, making sure he was between her and the house in case she tried to make a dash for the front door.

But Susan didn't move, and she didn't say another word. The silence crackled between them like heat lightning. Matt took a long, deep breath of the fresh night air, hoping to calm himself, but he was still on edge.

Finally, Susan exhaled noisily and turned to go back to her car. Matt watched her limp away, her head bowed and her shoulders slouched. She looked utterly defeated, but he knew Susan, and he sensed that this wasn't over. With or without money, she would try to figure out a way to fight him or wear him down. Even with the law on his side, he wondered how safe he and Emily were.

Susan hesitated before getting back into her car. She

seemed to be struggling to say something. When she slammed the door shut, the sound echoed like a gunshot in the night, making Matt jump. She started up the car, revving the engine until it whined before shifting into gear and peeling out. A hundred yards down the road, she did a wide U-turn and headed back toward where Matt was standing. The headlights wavered back and forth, and Matt got ready to dodge to one side if she actually tried to run him over, but she didn't. She stopped the car across the road from him and rolled the driver's window down.

"This isn't over, Matthew," she said.

Now her voice was low and controlled, but Matt could hear a tremor in it.

"She's my daughter, and you can't keep me away from her."

"Don't push me on this, Susan," Matt said, but he had no idea if she heard him as she stepped down hard on the accelerator. A loose belt whined loudly as the car took off with a loud, squealing chirp that left behind a thin veil of exhaust that hung suspended in the air, wavering in the draft of the departed car.

Matt watched the taillights disappear over the crest of the hill. The sound receded steadily, but he could still hear it in the distance as she raced down Collette Road and took the turn toward town. Long after she was gone, Matt stood by the side of the road and listened to the peepers. The night breeze hissed in the trees overhead. His hands were trembling, and he knew it would be a while before he calmed down. He jumped when the lights by the front steps winked on, bathing the front yard with a warm, yellow glow. The front door eased open, and Emily stuck her head out into the night.

"Daddy?" she called out. Her voice sounded frail and frightened in the dark.

"Yeah babe," he called back. "I'm right here."

He started down the walkway to the front door, feeling the wire-tight tension between his shoulders. When he reached the steps, he peered into his daughter's eyes, smiling reassuringly as he wondered how much—if anything—she had heard.

"Who was that?" Emily asked. Her eyes twitched as she looked past him to the road in front of the house.

"Huh? Oh—no one," he replied as he eased into the house and swung the door shut, making sure to lock the dead bolt behind him.

"What'd she want?" Emily said, pressing.

"Nothing. Nothing at all," Matt said. As he reached out and touched her lightly on the shoulder, he couldn't help but notice that Emily had said *"she,"* so she knew he'd been talking to a woman. Glancing at his watch, he saw that it was past two o'clock in the morning.

"What I want to know is, what are you doing up so late on a school night? You should have been asleep hours ago."

"That lady's car woke me up," Emily said. "And I didn't like the way she was talking to you."

Matt tensed, his blood suddenly chilling.

"Why? What did you hear?"

"Nothing much," Emily replied with a simple, honest shrug of her shoulders. "Just her yelling. She sounded kinda crazy."

"Well, you don't have to worry a thing about it."

He took her in his arms, holding her close for several seconds before pulling back and giving her a kiss on the forehead.

"Where's Mrs. Elroy?" he asked, looking past her into the darkened house.

"She fell asleep watching TV," Emily replied. "I turned it off before I went upstairs so it wouldn't bother her." She hesitated, then added, "She's not much of a baby-sitter. I did all the work."

Matt kissed his daughter gently on the forehead again.

"I'm sure you did. I'll wake her up so she can go home," he said. "Now get to bed. You have school in—" He looked at his wristwatch. "Five hours."

He watched her trudge up the stairs to her bedroom, smiling to himself because he could sense her unspoken relief that he was home. It was almost like it was before, with just him and her.

FOUR

reflections

IT was well past two o'clock in the morning, and Marcus Card was sitting on the closed toilet seat in a bathroom in the Motel 8 just outside of Augusta. Pain throbbed through his entire body as he leaned forward with both elbows on his knees, cupping his face with his hands. He inhaled slowly, feeling and listening to the cool air as it rushed between his fingers. He hoped that breathing like this would dull the pain and help him clear his head, but the fiery tightness behind his eyes hadn't gone away yet, and the sour trembling in his gut was getting steadily worse. Even after a steak dinner, a couple of beers, and a futile attempt at sleeping on the first really comfortable bed he'd experienced in five years, there was no way he could relax.

Worse than the pain, he was convinced that something was terribly wrong with him. and it wasn't just that he was having trouble trying to adjust to being out of prison after five years.

Five goddamned long years in the state prison in Warren, and now a free man, for all that was worth. He'd been released just yesterday, but here he was with nowhere to go and nothing to do. There wasn't anyone he felt compelled to call or go see. His wife, Penny, had divorced him shortly after he'd begun his stint in Warren. He hadn't contested it, even though she got full custody of their two-year-old son. That meant Kevin was seven now. No doubt he wouldn't even recognize his daddy if Marcus showed up at Penny's place . . . that is, if he even found out where she had moved.

So where do I go? What the hell do I do?

Although he still had friends and a handful of relatives back home in Belfast, he had no desire to visit his hometown.

He sure as hell couldn't see himself slinging burgers at McDonald's or pumping gas at the 7-Eleven for minimum wage. And no matter what, he knew he couldn't take seeing familiar surroundings after being locked away for so long. The prison psych had told him it would take a long time to readjust, especially after what happened to his cell mate the night before Marcus was released. Plus, he wasn't sure he could show his face in town, knowing that everyone knew that he'd been sent away for trafficking coke.

His testimony had shortened his time, but he knew that some of the people he ratted out hadn't been convicted. He was fairly certain that they—or the people they worked for—might want to look him up and have a little chat if he returned.

When the chance had come along to traffic a few kilos of cocaine into the state for a guy he'd met at a bar in Boston, the money had been too good to pass up.

How was he to know it was a sting operation?

"Goddamned stupid moron, is what you are," he muttered into the darkness of his hands that covered his face. He could feel himself tearing up but choked back the emotion.

I can figure this out! I can handle it! I have to!

Lowering his hands, he twisted around to one side in spite of the pain. He blinked in the sudden glare of the light above the sink as he turned on the tap and let the water run until it was lukewarm. Cupping his hands, he splashed his face several times, snorting and sputtering loudly. He didn't care if water dripped into his lap or onto the floor. He needed this. He had to do something so he could begin to feel human again. It was so strange, being out in the world again. He felt like he had been to another planet or, like Rip van Winkle, had fallen asleep for twenty years instead of just five.

The sudden rush of warm wetness rolling off his face and

dripping from his chin revived him some, but it didn't remove the peculiar feeling inside. There was no way water could penetrate down deep enough to wash away the clinging, oily darkness, the scum and sour stench of where he had been for the last five years.

And there was no way he was ever going to forget what his cell mate had done the night before Marcus was released. He wondered if the guards knew what would happen and didn't stop it. One of them had been fired because of him—he'd reported the bastard for taking bribes from the cons to get them extra phone time or even private time with their ladies. Marcus had hoped to get time off his sentence for that. But it hadn't worked. Instead, it had just made all the guards and the cons hate his guts.

Over the past five years, he'd kept low, kept to himself. But after hanging tough for so long, now that he was out, he had no idea who he was or what he was going to do.

The investigation into his cell mate's suicide had been relatively simple and fast but still terrifying, considering that— for a few hours, at least—Marcus had been under suspicion of murdering the guy. An analysis of the splash patterns the blood made on the floor, walls, bed, and—especially—Marcus's back quickly convinced the investigators that the man had, indeed, killed himself by slicing his own throat. The slash across his throat was consistent with a self-inflicted wound and, more importantly, Marcus didn't have any blood on his face and chest.

After a brief visit to the prison infirmary to make sure he wasn't seriously hurt, Marcus had been given a test for any possible STDs, including AIDS, which they told him would have to be repeated in a couple of months; had a session with the prison psych; and been put through for release. He was a free man as of noon today, so all he had to do was figure out what in the name of Christ he was going to do now.

He had no idea. And despite what he'd been told, he was convinced there was something wrong inside him.

Remembering the fear and pain, the humiliation he'd experienced made Marcus's skin crawl like the nest of snakes had moved out of his belly and were now slithering underneath his skin. He had never felt so corrupted, so unclean before in his life. Even the embarrassment of being busted and the realization that he had been set up was easy to handle compared to the feeling he had now that his body and soul were stained.

Without looking down, he ran the tap water and filled his cupped hands, then splashed his face again and watched in the mirror as the water streamed like a gush of sweat from his nose and chin. The icy, writhing feeling reached deep beneath his skin, sliding like cold sludge along his muscles and bones.

"Something wrong inside," he whispered.

His eyes widened. The voice he heard was not his.

THE streetlights outside the hospital window made the slats of the venetian blinds glow like an array of fluorescent orange tubes, casting striped shadows across Brenda as she lay curled up in a fetal position in the stuffed chair by the window. She had dozed fitfully throughout the night, always within arm's reach of the bed in which her mother lay unconscious. She awoke every couple of minutes to look over and try to accept what was happening. Time and again, she would reach out and clasp her mother's fragile hand. The cool lifelessness of it terrified her, like she was holding a skeleton.

"I love you, Mom," Brenda whispered over and over as tears flooded her eyes, blurring her vision. A hot, stinging sensation filled her nose and touched the back of her throat.

She had no idea if her mother could hear her or not. The woman certainly didn't register any reaction, and it was only the steady but weak spikes on the monitors and the hissing of the respirator that convinced her that her mother was still alive. There was no movement of her thin chest beneath the clean, starched sheet and blanket. No feeling of life within her.

The truth Brenda was trying to face was simple but harsh.

It probably doesn't matter if she can hear me, she thought, *because for most of her life, she never listened to me—especially when I was trying to let her know that I loved her, no matter what.*

There were too many years of hurt feelings, too many senseless arguments and misunderstandings between them to bridge now, and Brenda was becoming convinced that it was useless even to attempt to reach her mother.

But she still had to try.

If her mother was going to die tomorrow, which the doctor had assured her would happen within half an hour of removing life support, Brenda was going to have to live the rest of her life with the heavy guilt of their unresolved conflicts.

"Sometimes there's just no time to say good-bye," she whispered.

Still, acknowledging that didn't ease the pain of parting. If anything, it made it worse because of the harsh fact that now there was absolutely nothing she could do to extend her mother's life or to settle anything between them. The only decision she had left to make was exactly when to tell the doctor to stop the respirator. Brenda accepted that she would have to live the rest of her life, knowing that she and her mother had lost their chance to make amends. The best she could hope for was knowing that she would make greater efforts to communicate with her son and her stepdaughter.

Sometime early in the predawn hours, one of the nurses came into the room and offered to get Brenda a cup of coffee or tea and something to eat. Brenda declined, even though her stomach was empty and rumbling. While the nurse went about her job, checking her mother's vitals, Dr. Stiles entered the room. Brenda knew what this meant. He was going to ask her how much longer she wanted them to keep her mother alive. As hard as it was going to be, it was time to let go.

No matter how much I wish this weren't happening, this is it, Brenda thought with a twisting deep in her gut.

"Are you ready?" Dr. Stiles asked, his voice low and sympathetic.

The apprehension rising inside her spiked as she shifted her gaze from the doctor to her mother's motionless form. She looked so relaxed, like she was merely asleep, but this was a sleep from which she would never awake.

"You . . . you're absolutely sure there's—"

She cut herself off, knowing the answer. When she leaned forward and grasped her mother's hand, it felt so thin and unnaturally light in her grip.

As light as a bird, Brenda thought, finding it almost impossible to imagine that life-giving blood was still pulsing, however weakly, through her mother's veins.

Dr. Stiles nodded, his expression sympathetic.

"We could sustain her life functions indefinitely, but you have to accept that there is absolutely no hope of recovery."

Brenda nodded her understanding.

"Could I—? I want just a few more minutes with her," she said, her voice almost breaking. She took a deep breath and braced herself. "I want to . . . to say good-bye."

"Take as much time as you need," Dr. Stiles replied.

He made brief eye contact with the attending nurse, indicating that they should both leave. Once the door swung shut behind them, Brenda shifted the chair closer to the bed and clutched her mother's hand desperately as warm tears slid down her cheeks.

"I—I know you can't hear me, Mom," she whispered. Her voice caught painfully in her chest, and she had an odd sensation that someone else was speaking for her. "And I know it's too late to say . . . to tell you I . . . how sorry I am. I know you did your best, and in the end, that's all anyone can ever do, right? I can't fault you for . . . for not always seeing things my way or being there for me. I know that now. Especially after having a child of my own. And I know I let you down in ways I won't ever completely understand. I know you didn't approve of my marrying Matt, but I hope you came to understand that he's a good man. And I . . . I know you loved me. I know that you had your own problems to deal with. I just want you to know that I . . . that I—"

Her voice cut off with a gasp that hurt her throat. A burning sensation filled her chest, and her vision blurred with her tears as she pressed her mother's limp hand against her cheek and rubbed it. For a moment, the delicate coolness relieved the flush of heat inside her that felt like it was strangling her.

"I love you, Mom. I know I had a strange way of showing it to you sometimes, but I really did . . . I do love you."

Tears coursed down her face as she reached blindly down to the floor for her purse and fished around in it until she found her cell phone. Her fingers tingled as she flipped it open and prepared to dial home. But then she hesitated and dialed her friend Cheryl's number instead. The palm of her hand was slick with sweat as she listened to the phone ring once . . . twice . . .

"Come on, Cheryl. Be there."

She glanced at the clock and realized that it was a little before five o'clock. She'd lost track of the time and almost hung up when she realized that Cheryl no doubt was still asleep. Before she could, though, Cheryl picked up on the third ring. From the sound of her voice, Brenda suspected she had been awake most of the night, waiting for her to call.

"Hey, it's me," Brenda said.

"Oh, Bren," Cheryl said. "Where are you? How are you holding up?"

As much as she tried not to let it show, Brenda knew the agony and torment were evident in her voice. She took a deep breath, struggling for control.

"I'm still at the hospital with my mom," she said.

She realized she was whispering and wondered why. It wasn't like her mother could hear her or would be disturbed if she could.

"How's she doing? How are you doing?" Cheryl asked.

"I haven't done it yet," Brenda said. "I haven't had them stop the respirator." As she spoke, she stared at her mother in the dim light. It bothered her, the way her mother looked so indistinct in the diffuse light of the room.

Like a puff of smoke that's going to be blown away soon, she thought with a shiver.

Cheryl sighed. "Do you want me to come in?"

"No," Brenda said, perhaps a bit too quickly. "I'm doing all right."

"You know what I mean, Bren," Cheryl said. "If you want me there, I can be there in half an hour."

Brenda exhaled to release the tension that was bunching up her shoulders. She sighed as she eased back in her chair. In the soft light, everything looked dreamy and unreal, like the room was underwater. Even this conversation with her best friend had a surreal tone, like it wasn't really happening.

How can any of this be real? How can I be sitting here, trying to decide when to let my mother die?

"No. I'm set. You don't have to come out," she said, once she had gained a slight measure of control. "You sound like you've been up all night, wondering and worrying—"

"True. I haven't slept much since I got home from your housewarming party."

The party and the joy Brenda had been feeling now seemed so long ago it was less substantial than a dream.

"Umm . . . I'll bet," Brenda said.

"This has gotta be so hard on you," Cheryl said.

"At least she isn't in any pain. I have to remind myself that she's not here. My mother isn't in this room . . . in this bed."

"Isn't Matt there with you?" Cheryl asked, and Brenda heard a slight note of accusation in her friend's voice.

"No. I—uh, he went home last night. I wanted him to be there to help the kids get off to school in the morning." When she took a breath, her chest felt like it was restrained by tight, invisible straps. "I guess I'm going to ask the doctor to come in and . . . and do it now."

"Oh, God, Bren. Are you sure you don't want to wait until I can get there?"

"No, I . . . I really don't want to do this, but I . . . There's nothing more we can do. There's nothing more anyone can do, and me waiting for you to drive down here wouldn't change a thing."

After listening to the long pause at the other end of the line, Brenda shifted her gaze once again to her mother's immobile face. She looked so at ease it seemed impossible to think that she was already as good as gone. Brenda tried to comfort herself with the thought that, for her mother, at least, all the struggles, all the sadness and joys of life were over.

This is just an empty husk. Her soul is already gone.

If there was some kind of ephemeral, eternal part of a human being, Brenda was positive that it no longer resided within her mother's body.

She's already dead!

Overwhelmed by her sadness, Brenda squeezed her eyes tightly shut until tears ran down her cheeks. Her face was flushed and warm, but an icy hollowness filled the cavity of her chest and stomach so much they physically hurt.

"She's already gone," Brenda whispered. "This is just her . . . all that's left is the shell. What made my mom who she is is already gone."

She could hear her friend sniff back tears on the other end

of the line, and the sadness cut her so deeply that words failed her. Blinking back her own tears, she stared at her mother so intently she could easily imagine the old woman suddenly reviving, her eyes snapping open as she lurched upright in the hospital bed with a dry rustle of starched sheets. The illusion was so powerful and convincing, Brenda had to turn away. As she did, she caught a fleeting glimpse of something—a vague, white, fluttery motion—behind her. She was so surprised she let out a scream.

"What is it?" Cheryl said. Her voice was little more than a tinny buzz from the cell phone. Brenda barely registered it as she stared, wide-eyed, at what had drawn her attention.

The orange sodium glow from the streetlight outside the window illuminated her face and cast a dim reflection of her features in the window. Bars of light and shadow rippled across her features, slicing her image into dozens of wavering strips that blurred from her tears. Her eyes were lost in the depth of shadow.

"Brenda? What the hell's happening?" Cheryl shouted.

Brenda's heart was racing high and fast, throbbing painfully in her neck as she stared at her own reflection in the window. The dim image of her shaded eyes held her riveted. She couldn't accept that this was something as simple as her own reflection she was looking at. Although she couldn't say what it was, she was positive she had felt or sensed—something else—a presence in the room with her.

Shivering uncontrollably, she wondered if it was possible if, even now, her mother's spirit was hovering, unseen above the bed, caught in some strange limbo where she was unable to let go of her body and her life, unable to move on to the next level.

What if her soul's drifting around here in the room, trying to communicate with me just as desperately as I want to communicate with her?

At this moment, the empty space Brenda had always felt between her and her mother in life seemed all the more unbridgeable.

She knew that all she had to do was call Dr. Stiles into the room and give him the word to shut off the respirator.

"Brenda? Are you there?"

Finally, Cheryl's voice snapped her back to reality. Her elbow was stiff and cold as she raised the cell phone to her ear and—somehow—managed to say, "Yeah . . . yeah . . . I'm still here."

"What the heck's going on?" Cheryl asked. "Why'd you scream like that?"

"I thought I saw . . ."

Brenda inhaled slowly in spite of the sharp pain that lanced her chest. It was impossible to look away from her reflection in the window. The dark hollows under her eyes gave her face a lifeless cast that made her wonder if *she* might not be the one who was dead in this hospital room.

"It was just . . . This isn't easy. . . . I wish you—"

She took a deep breath. The pain in her chest was gradually subsiding, but it was still strong enough to make her wince. Her view of her reflection in the window wavered in a watery blur as tears spilled from her eyes.

She knew what she should do. She should tell Cheryl that yes, she wanted her to get into her car right now and drive to Portland. If Matt couldn't be there with her, she needed someone to help her, even if it was only to hold her hand. She wondered if she should hold off on giving Dr. Stiles the word to terminate their mother's life until her friend got here.

Blinking her eyes, Brenda looked down at her mother's unmoving form.

There was so much that would be forever left unsaid, so many words and thoughts and feelings. Even if she could pour them out now, even if she had another hour or another day or another week, it wouldn't do any good.

"She's already gone," Brenda said again, her voice rasping in her ear through the phone. "I can't let her linger her like this. I can't do it."

There was no reply from Cheryl, and the phone was absolutely silent—no static hiss or anything. For a moment, Brenda thought the connection had been lost.

"Cheryl? You still there?"

After another lengthening silence, her friend answered softly, "Yeah . . . I'm here."

"I've been up all night at her bedside, and I'll need to get some sleep, but I'll start making the funeral arrangements to-morrow afternoon."

"Don't think about that now," Cheryl finally said, her voice low and subdued. "You just take care of yourself."

"This is—what? Monday morning? I guess we'll have to have the funeral on Wednesday or Thursday. I guess we'll have to shoot for Wednesday."

A sudden jolt hit her like electricity when she glanced over at her mother and realized that, for a few seconds, at least, while had been talking with Cheryl, she had actually forgotten that her mother was still alive in the room with her.

What if she can hear me? What if she knows I'm talking about her funeral? Is she afraid and can't tell me, can't talk about it? Or is she already so far gone it doesn't matter?

Turning away quickly, Brenda glanced once again at her reflection in the window, and this time she saw it for exactly what it was: nothing but a pale image of herself, hunched in a chair by the bed with her cell phone pressed against her ear.

"Be careful driving home," Cheryl said, her voice crack-ing. "If you want me to, I can drive down and pick you up."

"I'll be all right. Matt's coming down after he gets the kids off to school."

"You don't have to be a martyr, you know, Bren. You can ask other people for help."

"I know that," Brenda said, feeling the tiniest edge of anger flare up inside her.

"See you soon," she said. "Love yah."

"I love you, too, Cheryl. Bye for now."

And with that, she pushed the Off button on the phone.

A heavy sigh escaped her as she slumped back in the chair. For the span of several heartbeats, she just sat there, the cell phone clasped tightly in her hand. She was so lost in grief she didn't even bother to try to wipe away the tears that were streaming down her face.

What good will it do? There will just be more.

She raised her hand and stared numbly at the cell phone. She knew she should call Matt and tell him her decision, but something told her to let go of that. Matt was probably still asleep, unless he, too, had spent a restless night. The kids would still be asleep, though, and he'd be waking them up in a little more than an hour to get ready for school.

"Let it be. . . . Let it be," Brenda whispered, and as the tune to the Beatles' song started running like a tape loop through her mind, she got up and walked slowly over to the window and looked out at the first faint streaks of dawn in the sky. Then she turned and walked to the door. Determined to deal with it now and be done with it, she started down the corridor to the nurses' station to have them page Dr. Stiles so they could do what had to be done.

FIVE

watched

"**'S** that your mother over there?"

"Huh? . . . Where?"

"In that car."

Emily Ireland jerked to an abrupt stop on the grassy side of the road and looked to where her friend Amanda Simoneau was pointing. It was a warm, May morning, but when she saw the car that was parked at the intersection on the opposite side of the road close to where they would catch the school bus, a chill ran up her spine.

The car wasn't stopped, waiting to turn onto the main road. That much was obvious. There were no cars coming in either direction, and the driver could have easily pulled out and driven away. Instead, the car just sat there idling, a thin, blue veil of exhaust spewing from its tailpipe. Sunlight glinted in sparkling daggers off the windshield, making it impossible for Emily to see who was in the car.

But there's someone there.

She was sure of that. A dark, indistinct form that might be a woman . . . but then again, maybe not . . . was sitting with both hands on the steering wheel, hunched forward as though she was looking up the road.

At me!

Emily was sure of one thing. It wasn't her stepmother.

"Nope. That's not Mom's car." The sound of her younger brother's irritating voice was like fingernails being raked down a chalkboard.

"No kidding, retard," Emily snapped as she spun around and faced John.

It was bad enough that her father made her let him tag along with her and Manda when they walked to the bus stop. It wasn't her fault none of John's friends lived this far out of town so he didn't have anyone to walk to the bus stop with in the morning. He should know better than to speak to her and Manda, but it was just like him to irritate and embarrass her in front of her new best friend. Emily still hung out with the same kids she'd always been friends with at school. The only difference was, she no longer lived near any of them, and she'd started making friends with Manda because they rode the same bus to and from school every day. She and Manda would probably start hanging out together a lot more now.

Doing her best to ignore her brother, Emily settled her L.L.Bean backpack on her shoulders and started walking again, but she was still tense. Every step brought her closer to the parked car and the person waiting in it.

I'm sure I've seen that car before, she thought, but she couldn't quite place it.

The sun was shining directly in her eyes, making it difficult to see anything. All she knew for sure was that there was something about that car and its driver that made her nervous. So nervous, in fact, that she was considering turning around and going back home as fast as she could. Her father hadn't left for work yet. Maybe he'd give her and Manda a ride.

Emily found herself wishing the driver—whoever it was— would pull out onto the road and drive away. She knew well enough not to accept rides from strangers and all, but she had always thought those were just things parents told kids to scare them and make them behave. Until now.

As she and Manda and her brother got closer to the bus stop, Emily tried to convince herself that she was overreacting. The real problem, she knew, was that she hadn't really wanted to move away from downtown Three Rivers. She was nervous about living out here in the country, "the sticks," as the kids called it. Emily had grown up used to having everything—schools, stores, and friends' houses—all within easy walking distance.

She felt more vulnerable out here. It was easier to be noticed in the country. There were fewer people around, and Emily didn't like feeling as though she stood out so much. She felt like everyone was watching her. That was silly, she knew, but it didn't seem so silly now, because that's exactly what was happening. She was sure of it.

Cut it out, she cautioned herself even as the hairs on the back of her neck stood on end like tiny, electrified wires. *You're getting all freaked out about nothing!*

The woman—yes, Emily could clearly see now that the driver was a woman—was sitting there, staring at her.

Emily wanted to believe that she had just dropped her kids off at the bus stop and was waiting to make sure they got onto the bus without any problems.

Please let that be all it is, Emily thought, but she wasn't going to take any chances. She didn't know how or why, but she got a really bad feeling about the car and its driver. Even though it was parked on the opposite side of the road, she was ready to turn and run if there was any trouble.

What if she pulls out real quick and tries to run us over? What if she's got a gun or something, and is waiting for a chance to hurt me or Manda or John?

Yes, if John was threatened, Emily knew she would try to protect her brother. He might be a pain in the butt most of the time. All of the time, in fact. Still, he was her little brother, and there was no way she would let some crazy lady do anything to hurt him.

Manda noticed that Emily was lagging several steps behind. She turned and urged her to hurry when the bus appeared in the distance, its bright yellow side shining like a huge insect in the slanting morning sun.

Still nervous, Emily picked up her pace, keeping her head tilted downward as though she was carefully watching where she stepped. She kept glancing at the car, hoping . . . praying . . . that, now that the bus was in sight, the woman would drive away. She realized she was holding her breath and let it out in a long, slow hiss.

"Something the matter?" Manda asked, her narrow face scrunching with concern. Her bangs almost covered her eyes.

"Uh-uh," Emily replied, shaking her head. "I'm fine."

She could hear the lie in her voice and hoped Manda didn't hear it as well.

No matter how much she tried to push it aside, Emily realized that something was very much the matter. She had no doubt. She could see the lady in the car turn her head, watching her closely as she walked past where she was parked.

Go away. Leave me alone, whoever you are!

Even after she had walked past the car, Emily could feel the woman's gaze boring into her back. She slowed her pace even more in an effort to look unafraid.

The school bus pulled over to the side of the road and slowed to a stop at the pickup point. A cloud of pollen-yellow dust rose in its wake. Manda and John dashed ahead to meet the bus. The loud squealing of its brakes set her teeth on edge, but she resisted the sudden urge to run, knowing that if she did, the woman in the car would know that she was aware of her and was afraid of her. She didn't want her to know that.

After the bus came to a complete stop and the hydraulic doors opened like an accordion, Emily broke into a run, convinced that it wouldn't look at all suspicious now. It would look like she was worried that the bus would leave without her. That thought filled Emily with fear because then she would be left behind . . . alone . . . on the roadside with this woman watching her.

Panting and out of breath, Emily mounted the steps, the last one to enter the bus. She smiled weakly and nodded to Mr. Wight, the driver. The lingering smell of diesel exhaust made her stomach do a little flip, but Emily knew she was safe.

For now, at least, she thought, still perturbed that she had gotten so freaked out. Even out here in the country, she was pretty sure no one would mess with her with a whole school bus of kids as witnesses. Besides, it probably was all in her imagination, anyway.

Still shaking, Emily moved down the aisle of the bus and plopped onto the seat next to Manda just as the bus started moving again. The last three rows of seats on both sides were filled with boys who were hooting and jumping around until Mr. Wight glared at them in the rearview mirror and shouted, "Hey!" They all settled down.

The bus engine roared so loudly Emily couldn't hear the radio station Mr. Wight usually had on. As they started down the road, she took a short breath and, shifting around in the seat, glanced out the back window.

The car was nowhere in sight.

It was gone as if it had never even been there.

The bus seat creaked loudly beneath her weight as Emily turned around and settled down beside Manda. A trickle of sweat ran down her side, tickling her, and she was suddenly very self-conscious, fearful that her deodorant might not be working.

She wanted to believe that, for whatever reason, she had made it all up, that she hadn't been in any real danger, and neither had John nor Manda. She was just overreacting, maybe because she knew that her father and stepmother were so upset because of what was happening with Grammy Swanson.

Still, throughout the four-mile drive to school, Emily found herself turning around from time to time and looking out the side and rear windows, tensed and ready to see that car following the bus. She didn't know why she felt so much in danger, but a prickling sensation tingled at the base of her neck whenever she thought about the car and the woman in it. The fear and sense of danger she had felt had been real, but now it all seemed vague and was fading like a dream she couldn't quite remember in the morning.

Every time she looked to the back of the bus, she noticed that several of the boys—especially Kevin Normand, who she thought was kind of hot—would notice her. She didn't want any of them—especially Kevin—to think she was looking at them, so after a while she tried as best she could to get the car out of her mind. She wished she had memorized the license plate number, just in case there was trouble later.

"So did you get that math done for Mrs. Drake?" Manda asked.

Still preoccupied with what had just happened, Emily barely registered what her friend had said. After a few seconds, once it sank in, she shook her head and said, "Huh? Oh, yeah. Most of it. I'm gonna finish it in study hall."

"She is such a bitch, making us work so hard so close to the end of the school year."

Emily smiled thinly and nodded, but she still couldn't stop thinking about the car and the sense of danger she had felt knowing that woman was watching her.

Was she really watching me, or am I just making it up?

The air in the bus reeked of diesel fumes, and Emily was feeling a little light-headed. When she turned around one last time and looked out the back window, tiny white spots trailed like shooting stars across her vision.

"Forget about it," she whispered to herself.

"Huh?" Manda said, raising one eyebrow.

"Oh . . . nothing," Emily said as she settled back in the seat and closed her eyes. The last few flickering white sparks danced in the darkness behind her closed eyes. She took a shallow breath and started to feel a little better.

"What'd you mean, nothing?" Manda asked.

Her friend's voice seemed to come from miles away. Emily realized in a vague, dreamy way that she was drifting off to sleep. Her head rolled from side to side with the motion of the bus. She listened to the creaking sounds the seat made. It sounded like a string of firecrackers going off inside her head.

She didn't answer her friend, and she didn't open her eyes again until the bus slowed down as Mr. Wight downshifted for the turn into the high school driveway before dropping the younger kids off at Hillside Elementary. The boys at the back of the bus started getting rowdy again as they anticipated getting off the bus and starting another dreaded school day. Opening her eyes, Emily sighed and looked around, feeling like she was waking up in her bed at home, and that the walk to the bus stop, the car she had seen parked by the roadside, even this bus ride had been nothing more than part of a very vivid dream.

The bus lurched to a stop, but Emily stayed in her seat as the boys pushed to the front of the bus. Once the aisle was

clear, Emily slung her backpack off her lap and onto one
shoulder, then started for the door. She was still feeling a little
disoriented, but a sudden jolt of electricity slammed through
her when she glanced out the front window of the bus and saw
the same car. It was parked across the street in the dappled
shade of one of the maple trees in front of the town library.

"No way," she whispered.

Mr. Wight turned and glanced at her, but Emily stared past
him, focusing on the parked car.

It's the same one. She had no doubt.

In the shade of the tree, it looked darker and more dangerous. The woman sat behind the steering wheel, and although
Emily couldn't see her clearly, she knew with a dread cer-
tainty that she was watching every move she made.

Why is she following me? Emily wondered as genuine
panic raced through her. *Does she want to hurt me? Why
would she want to hurt me?*

This didn't make any sense, but whatever was going on, it
scared her. She couldn't make herself not stare at the car as
she stepped off the bus into the harsh glare of the morning
sun. Shielding her eyes, she tried once again to see the driver's
face or to catch a glimpse of the license plate number, but the
car was too far away.

The schoolyard rang with the sounds of laughter and
shouted greetings and conversations as the kids drifted slowly
toward the front door. Most of them seemed reluctant to go inside on such a beautiful day. To Emily, the world around her
looked far away. All the schoolyard sounds were muffled.
Once again, she had the unnerving feeling that she was
dreaming all of this and that any minute now she would wake
up at home in bed.

What scared her most, though, what made her weak in the
knees, was feeling as though the only *really* real thing in the
world was the cold, steady stare coming from the woman in
the car.

BRENDA was seated at a small corner table by the windows in the hospital cafeteria. The view looked out over the
visitors' parking lot to a few buildings on the Portland skyline

and a line of hills beyond. Half an hour ago, she had bought a large cup of coffee, but it had long since gone cold as she sat staring out at the sunny spring morning. The ceiling lights were still on overhead, and they reflected off the glass, looking like long, distorted bars of ice.

Focusing on the window and staring at her faint reflection, she had an odd, dissociated feeling that she was looking at someone else. In fact, everything around her—even simple things like the table where she was sitting and the people seated at other tables—had a weird cast of unreality. The ordinary sounds of activity in the cafeteria—people talking softly, dishes and silverware clattering, the low hum of the air conditioner—were distorted as though heard from a distance.

You're not dealing very well with this, are you? she asked herself.

She was wrung out, exhausted, her nerves and emotions shot. Lack of sleep made her eyelids feel like they were crusted with sand. She shifted her gaze up to the arch of blue sky above the hills but had trouble focusing because the reflection of the overhead lights and her own pale face skewed her perspective.

A thin raft of gray clouds hovered on the horizon. She chuckled to herself, remembering how, when she was a little girl and her mother would make her go to church and Sunday school, she had conceived of Heaven as being somewhere "up there." Any other time, she might have laughed out loud at such a naive idea; but once upon a time, she had actually believed everyone who died went "up there," wore a white robe, and floated around on puffy, white clouds while playing a harp.

Having seen her mother die in a rumpled bed on the fifth floor of the hospital, Brenda couldn't help but wonder where her mother was now—or if she even "was" any longer.

And you did it. The thought sent a wrenching shudder through her. *You signed the papers and sent her to . . . wherever she is now.*

Tears gathered in her eyes, but she sniffed them back and wiped her nose on the napkin she had grabbed from the dispenser. She had used up all the tissues in her purse the night before in her vigil with her dying—*No, dead!*—mother.

Matt had phoned a while ago to let her know that the kids had gotten off to school all right and that he was driving down to Portland to pick her up. Brenda's mind was numbed from her all-night vigil, but she realized that she didn't feel any desperate need to be with her husband. She supposed she ought to feel . . . something, considering what she had just been through, but she didn't.

She couldn't.

She simply had no urgent desire to be with Matt or anybody else. No one, she felt, was capable of giving her what she needed right now.

I guess I have to find it in myself.

That was one of the few conclusions she had drawn from last night's vigil. Surprisingly, it still made sense in the clear light of day. Her usual experience was that thoughts and ideas she got during late, sleepless nights didn't make nearly as much sense in the morning. Like dreams, convictions and insights faded with the daylight, but this idea seemed, if anything, to get stronger in the clear light of day.

The bottom line was, she had faced her obligation by herself, and somehow she had gotten through it.

Now she could begin grieving.

She had no doubt that what she needed was time to let her loss sink in. It would be a long time before she would be finished with her grieving.

If ever, she thought with a shiver so deep it made her chest ache.

Her talk with Cheryl early this morning, and knowing how much Matt loved her would help, but whatever unresolved issues there had been between her and her mother, they would stay that way. She had to accept that.

It was all part of life, and she was grateful that she felt strong enough to acknowledge that she could and would get on with her life. She could handle whatever she had to handle, any guilt and regret as well as the memories of the love and good times, as few as they were.

A sudden sense of her own impending mortality grew strong enough to wring a small whimper out of her.

Right now, she thought, *all I want is a hot shower and a chance to lie down in my own bed at home.*

Alone.

She knew Matt was working on some important cases, one of which was coming to trial soon, so he would probably have to go to the office later today. He might even leave soon after they got back to the house, and that was just fine with her.

Matt had told her several times how guilty he felt about leaving her alone at a time like this, but she wanted—she needed—this time by herself to let it all sink in. With the kids off to school and her husband at work, she might be able to scrounge up at least a few hours to be alone.

"And think about what you've done," she whispered as she glanced at her thin reflection in the window.

Yawning into her cupped hand, she figured she could start making the funeral arrangements this afternoon or the next. She was so lost in thought she didn't realize Matt had arrived until she saw him striding up the walkway to the front door. She stood up so quickly her knee bumped the edge of the table and spilled some of her cold coffee. With one hand, she hurriedly blotted it up with the napkin she had used to blow her nose while she rapped on the window with her other hand.

Brenda could tell by the look on Matt's face that his night hadn't been any better than hers. Dark smudges ringed his eyes, and his face—especially his cheeks and around his mouth—was pale and slack. He apparently didn't hear her knocking and kept walking toward the front door, so she tapped harder on the glass, still to no effect.

Feeling suddenly helpless and isolated, she watched her husband through the window. The sudden realization that she wasn't getting his attention filled her with the frightening feeling that she would never be able to communicate with him, no matter how hard she tried. Reflected in the glass, her face floated before her, looking ghostly and insubstantial. For an instant, she had a dreadful fantasy that, like her mother, she was fading away from this world into some other plane of reality. This wasn't just an ordinary pane of plate glass that separated her from Matt. It was an invisible, absolutely impenetrable barrier that had come between them, and she no longer had the strength to cross it or break through it.

Once that idea took hold, a feeling of panic rose inside her like a gush of icy water. It swept through her stomach and chest with frigid fingers, shaking her insides. She couldn't take a deep enough breath, and her vision was distorted, making everything look like it was rippling underwater. Whimpering softly, she fumbled her key ring from her purse and used it to bang on the window hard enough—finally—to draw Matt's attention, along with the attention of several people in the cafeteria.

Matt was almost to the front door, but he paused in midstride, looked around, then finally saw her. A mirthless smile tightened the corners of his mouth as Brenda waved him around to the side door of the cafeteria. She wanted to go over to the door and meet him there, but her legs didn't feel strong enough to support her, so she sat down heavily in her chair and waited.

She knew she should feel relieved, but that odd feeling of dissociation still gripped her. The fringes of her vision were cloudy as she slumped forward in her chair, resting her elbows on the table for support. She cupped her chin with her hands and turned her head only as much as was necessary to see her husband as he entered the building. He was still smiling tightly. As he wended his way over to her table, an intense feeling of vertigo swept over her.

"Hey," Matt said, pulling a chair out and sitting down across from her. He leaned forward and kissed her lightly on the forehead.

Sighing softly, Brenda shook her head from side to side, then closed her eyes and covered her face with both hands. The darkness behind her hands that filled her vision was a relief.

"Honey, you look terrible," Matt said.

His voice came to her as if from far away. His touch lingered on the back of her hand, but even that seemed oddly distant, as if her hands had lost all sensation.

"It was . . . horrible . . . absolutely horrible," she whispered into her cupped hands. The stale smell of her coffee breath made her stomach churn.

"I know . . . I know," Matt said, his hand moving up and down her arm, massaging her gently.

Brenda didn't say a word.

What is there to say?

She was alone with her decision to terminate her mother's

life. There was no other word for it. *Terminate.* She could try
to convince herself that the doctor had advised it and even that
her mother would have wanted it this way, but in the end *she*
was the one who had done it.

She had been the only person in the room, right up to the
end, watching as her mother slowly faded away, her vital
signs dropping lower and lower until, just as dawn was light-
ing the sky a pewter gray, her mother breathed her last. A
nurse tiptoed into the room and switched off the audio on the
heart monitor so Brenda wouldn't have to listen to it.

"She's gone," the nurse had said, and then withdrawn from
the room, leaving Brenda alone with her mother's lifeless
body.

A cold hollow slipped open inside Brenda's chest as she
ran all of this through her memory. Over the next several days
and weeks and years, she knew she would replay it repeatedly.
She also knew that, no matter how she tried to describe it to
her husband or anyone else, no one would ever fully grasp
what she had been through because they hadn't been there.

Taking a steadying breath, Brenda took her hands away
from her face, opened her eyes, and looked, squinting, across
the table at her husband. With the sunlit window behind him,
her vision shattered into thousands of piercing diamonds. His
face was lost in the sudden, stinging glare. She could only see
his silhouette, and for a heart-stopping moment, she wasn't
sure she even recognized him.

"Let . . . let's go home," she said, her voice a ragged
whisper.

Matt tightened his grip on her shoulder as he stood up and
came around the table to help her to her feet. Once he slipped
his arm around her waist, Brenda felt the last of her reserves
ebb away. Leaning her full weight against him, they started toward the door.

"FOR God's sake, Alice! I feel like my ass is on fire!"

Susan Ireland took a breath and listened to the heavy silence in the earpiece of the telephone.

"Well, it's no wonder."

Alice Ulrich, her therapist back home, always maintained

a calm, quiet tone of voice, but Susan thought—or imagined—that she could hear a slight judgmental tone behind it. A rush of anger pulsed like heat lightning inside her.

"Have you stopped to consider what your motives really are in doing this?" Alice asked. "Have you thought about the timing?"

Susan was sitting on the bed in her motel room, just outside of Augusta. The edge of the mattress was pressing painfully into the backs of her thighs, so she shifted to relieve the pain.

"My *motive*—that's singular, not plural—is simply to see my daughter again. Nothing else." Susan struggled to maintain control, but she could feel it slowly slipping away.

Would a drink help stop the slide?

"It . . . it's not fair that Matt, that my ex-husband, controls the situation the way he does."

"You're absolutely right," Alice said. "It isn't fair, but it certainly is legal. You told me when you first started seeing me that you had willingly signed the divorce agreement giving him custody of Emily."

"Yeah, but I was a drunk back then, and I—I'd been hospitalized."

"Are you taking your meds?" Alice asked calmly.

"Yes . . . of course," Susan snapped, wondering if Alice could hear the lie in her voice as clearly as she could. The truth was, she'd stopped taking her medication during the drive to Maine because she didn't want to be drugged up when she saw her daughter again after fourteen years. The drugs made her slow-witted and unemotional, she thought. Not how she wanted Emily to see her.

"I—I wasn't thinking straight back then, but I—I'm fine now. Besides, all I'm asking is for him to reconsider the agreement. He can't prevent me from seeing my daughter."

Unable to stand the pain in the backs of her legs any longer, Susan stood up and began pacing back and forth across the floor as far as the telephone cord would allow.

"But you said you've already seen her," Alice replied mildly. "You said you saw her this morning at the bus stop, and then a little while later when you watched the kids getting off the bus at the high school."

"That's not what I mean, and you know it!" Susan shouted.
The anger was like poison inside her. "I want to spent *time*
with her. I want us to be . . . to get to know each other."

Immediately, a wave of guilt for losing her temper at her
therapist hit her.

*Why am I getting mad at her? It's not Alice's fault I'm in
this predicament.*

Susan regretted that—as usual—her anger was coming out
sideways. When would she ever learn?

"Yes, I realize that," Alice said, "but I also realize—and I
hope you do, too—that seeing Emily may not be the only reason you've gone back to Maine. I want you to think this
through a bit more carefully. What results are you looking
for?"

Susan huffed with frustration and closed her eyes for a moment, trying hard to collect her thoughts. She found it difficult
to swallow, as if unseen hands were clasped around her throat,
squeezing tighter.

"I . . . I've had plenty of time to think it through on the
drive out here, okay?" she finally said. She didn't like hearing
the tremor in her voice, but at least she wasn't yelling.

"I know absolutely what *result*—also singular, not plural—I want. I want to be with my daughter. And I want to be
here to watch her grow up. She's already fifteen, and I don't
know who she is, what kind of person she is. And I want her to
know that I'm her mother and that I love her. I want to be part
of her life."

"That sounds like more than one thing," Alice said. "And
you haven't been a part of her life for a long time."

"I know that . . . I know that," Susan said heatedly.

"So then . . . why now? Why didn't you contact her in all
that time? And more importantly, what are you trying to accomplish now?"

"I already *told* you what I'm trying to accomplish! And I
did try to contact her. Lots of times. But Matt—that son of a
bitch—stopped me."

"I understand you're angry, and I can tell how much it
hurts you," Alice replied. She still sounded absolutely calm
and collected, so much so that it irritated Susan.

Can't she see how desperate I am? Susan thought. She

paused and stared so intently at the drawn curtains the colors started to vibrate and shift like melting wax.

If she's really the friend she says she is, if she's really doing what she's supposed to do, she should be trying to help me figure out what to do next, not make me feel guilty or question my motivation in coming to Maine.

"So you're taking your meds, and have you been to a meeting since you got to Maine?" Alice asked.

For an instant, Susan considered lying again and telling her that yes, she had been to a few meetings, but after a short pause, she let her breath out and said, "No, I . . . I haven't had a chance yet. I've only been here a couple of days."

"It sounds to me like you might benefit from a meeting. You're having trouble managing this alone. You must realize that."

"All I want is to see my daughter."

Tears sprang from her eyes, and the whining tone she heard in her voice made her cringe.

"I know I've made a big mistake. Hell, I've made lots of mistakes, but I want to fix this one at least."

"And you think you can do that simply by reinserting yourself into your daughter's life, without any advance warning or preparation?"

Susan couldn't respond to that, and silence hung between them for a lengthening moment.

"Have you even thought about how this would affect Emily? I mean, have you *really* considered it?"

"I . . . I would think that she . . . she'd be happy to see me again. She knows Brenda isn't her real mom."

"In many ways she has been. You have to admit that it'd be pretty disruptive to her on a lot of levels."

She balled her hand into a fist and punched her thigh hard enough to make it hurt. "I have no *idea* what Matt's told her over the years," Susan moaned.

"You can't know how she'd react, then, can you?"

Alice's voice cut into her like a razor blade. A deep, stinging sadness welled up inside her when she considered the possibility that Emily wouldn't be thrilled and overjoyed to see her after all these years. She punched her thigh again, harder, and thought fleetingly of hurting herself in other ways.

"She was—how old when you left?"

"Eighteen months," Susan said. The note of defeat in her voice irritated her, but she knew Alice was making sense.

"Not quite two years old," Alice echoed. "So she doesn't even remember what you look like. She's isn't going to recognize you, you know."

Susan blinked her eyes rapidly, trying to hold back the tears as she stared up at the ceiling, transfixed by the swirling patterns of the yellowing acoustic tiles.

"Two years old," Alice repeated.

"I know! I know, but—you know, I do think she'd recognize me. On some level, she would have to. I'm her mother, for God's sake!"

"Yes, you are. And you left her the same time you left your husband. Fourteen years ago, you walked away from both of them, and that included the job of being a mother."

Alice took a breath, and Susan cringed, knowing what was coming next.

"So why did you call me?"

"I . . . I'm not sure."

Susan trembled as she inhaled. Her shoulders slumped, and she was feeling weak in the knees, so she sat back down on the edge of the bed. Her thigh throbbed with pain.

"I called you because I . . . wanted your advice," she said.

"Susan, I think you should make sure you keep taking your medication, and you have to get to a meeting. This afternoon or tonight at the very latest. I'd suggest you come back here, too, but I doubt you'd listen to me. But you need some clarity right now. You need to look at what you're doing and how it will affect everyone involved, not just yourself."

"But what I think—what I *feel* . . . it's important . . . to me, at least," Susan said.

"And it's important to me, Susan. It is. But you have to do what's right. Your mother didn't leave you enough money to hire a lawyer and fight your husband for joint custody. Your ex is a lawyer. You don't think he'll throw everything he can at you to stop you?"

"Of course he will. He told me as much last night that he would." The admission burned inside Susan's gut like she'd swallowed a burning coal.

"Then do what I tell you. Get to a meeting, and just think this through a little more. Get some serenity and some perspective. You're still grieving, you know."

"Okay," Susan said, although she didn't believe it. A charge of anger as clean and bright as chrome shot through her as tears filled her eyes, blinding her. She extended her right arm and looked at the twisting scars on her wrists. No matter what Alice thought, her mother's death had nothing to do with this.

"You know what, Alice?" she said, surprised by the sudden strength she heard in her voice. "I don't care what you say. I don't care what anyone says. I'm going to talk to him again. I'm going to see if I can reason with him. And—yes, I'll go to a meeting today. I promise. But I'm going to see Matt, too, and I'm going to *demand* that he let me talk to my daughter."

"Susan, think about what you're saying. We both know that would be a mistake, at least right now."

"No it isn't. And even if it is, the biggest mistake I made was fourteen years ago, when I—"

Her voice hitched painfully, and the sour taste of vomit filled the back of her throat. "—when I left her behind. I shouldn't have done it. I know that now, but come hell or high water, I'm going to correct it now."

"Listen to yourself. Listen to what you're saying. Maybe you can change it, and maybe you can't. But what if you only make things worse for yourself *and* for Emily?"

Susan closed her eyes, sucked in a breath, and held it for a count of five. Tiny white lights danced across her vision, and a voice as clear as if someone was in the room with her speaking said, *Don't listen to her!*

After exhaling slowly, Susan swallowed and said, "I'm willing to take that risk, Alice. I really am."

Alice said nothing. All Susan heard was the low hiss of the phone in her ear, and she wondered briefly if she had imagined this entire conversation.

She's right, you know. You should listen to what she's saying, another, fainter voice whispered close to her ear.

Susan tried desperately to silence that voice because the other one, the one that spoke even louder to her, the one she had been listening to for fourteen years and had gotten steadily louder and stronger over the years was screaming at her that she had to see Emily again.

"I'm going to see her, Alice. I'm going to see my daughter. I have to talk to her."

SIX

grieving

BRENDA hadn't expected to drift off to sleep, but after drinking a glass of orange juice and eating a piece of toast with honey, she wandered into the living room and plunked herself down on the couch. Staring at the phone, she considered calling Cheryl again, or maybe Renee or Deb, but she decided what she needed most was rest. She might even get to sleep, if sleep would come.

But it didn't. Not easily, anyway.

She settled down on the couch, nestling her head on one of the throw pillows and pulling the afghan from the back of the couch over her shoulders. Her mind was whirling with thoughts and images of what she had been through over the last eighteen hours. Tears welled in her eyes again, and she cried with wrenching sobs so deep they hurt her ribs. After wanting so much to be alone, she now found herself wishing she had someone to talk to, but she was emotionally drained and couldn't rally the energy or heart to call anyone. Soon enough, her friends and neighbors would find out about what had happened, and then she would have all the company she could stand. Before any of that started, she needed at least a brief time to sort out her feelings on her own terms.

As she slipped off to sleep, her thoughts distorted and

blended into vague half-dreams. A few times she thought she heard faint footsteps upstairs and assumed the kids were already home from school; but when she opened her eyes, she realized she was alone. She strained to hear, but she noticed nothing unusual until she closed her eyes and settled down again. Then the soft scuff of what might have been footsteps and a faint creaking of floorboards upstairs intruded on her rest.

Is this what it's going to be like? A shiver ran up the base of her neck, prickling the flesh behind her ears. *I'm going to jump at every little sound and end up afraid to be alone.*

She didn't kid herself. She knew her grief would last a long time, especially since it was mixed with generous doses of guilt and regret. But she was confident that she was strong enough to handle it, even if a few things went bump in the night . . . or in the middle of the day.

Keeping her eyes tightly shut, she willed herself to relax and luxuriate in the warm, scented breeze wafting through the open living room windows. Late morning sunlight played across the walls, giving the blue paint a deep, rich tone. Somewhere in the distance, a neighbor's lawn mower was roaring, almost out of hearing. The simple thought that anyone—probably Old Man Rideout, a retiree from the phone company who lived far down the street—was doing something as ordinary as mowing his lawn while her mother was dead filled Brenda with ineffable sadness.

The wind sighed through the screen, making the curtains rasp on the sills as they swayed gently back and forth. Brenda dipped in and out of sleep, the droning of the lawn mower lulling her deeper but still keeping her near the edge of awareness. She toyed with the idea that, from time to time, she opened her eyes and could see a face, forming and disappearing in the gauzy folds of the white lace curtains, but she could just as easily have imagined that or dreamed it. She had the peculiar feeling that somehow she could see through her closed eyelids. Whenever the wind gusted, it whistled with a high-pitched, wavering note. Brenda imagined or dreamed that the face in the curtains was back, and that now its lips were moving. It was speaking to her, whispering words she couldn't quite hear, much less understand.

A little before noon, the phone rang, startling her awake. Surprised that she had actually dozed off, she leaped off the couch and scrambled for the receiver before she consciously knew where she was or what she was doing.

"Umm, yeah . . . yeah . . . hello," she said, her dry throat thickening her voice.

"Hey. Sounds like I woke you up."

It was Matt, and as foggy as she was, Brenda couldn't help but notice that she wasn't all that happy to hear from her husband. It wasn't that she didn't want to hear his voice; it was just that right now she didn't care one way or the other if she talked to him. The vague sense that someone else—someone she couldn't see—had been whispering to her still lingered in her mind, but she couldn't remember who they were or what they had been saying.

"Ahh—no. Not really," she replied, swallowing noisily and licking her lips to moisten them. "I was just kinda dozing on the couch." She glanced at the window curtains, almost surprised to see that there wasn't a face there. "So—umm, what's up? Are you in the car?" She could clearly hear the sound of the motor in the background.

"Yeah," Matt said. "Just wanted to see how you were doing and let you know I'm on my way home. Figured I'd have lunch with you, if that's okay. Heard something interesting today."

"What was that?"

She wondered if Matt could pick up on the vibe that she didn't particularly care one way or the other if he came home for lunch. She couldn't help but question why she was feeling like this. It wasn't as though there was any tension in their relationship. The truth was, they got along better now than when they'd first gotten married.

I just want to be alone right now. There's nothing wrong with that. That's entirely normal, considering what I've just been through.

"Remember Jeromy Bowker?" Matt chuckled tightly, drawing Brenda's attention back to their conversation.

"How could I forget?"

"Well, he was filing another appeal, but he's never getting out of jail, no matter what."

Matt paused, and Brenda found that she had nothing to say until he said, "He killed himself in his jail cell the other day."

"Really."

Brenda knew quite a bit more about the case than what had been reported in the newspapers because six years ago, shortly after she and Matt had gotten married, Matt had been working for the state and had been the prosecuting attorney who had sent the man to prison for life. She knew more than she wanted to know about Bowker and what he had done to his girlfriend and her one-year-old child.

"So I thought I'd swing by the house and grab a quick lunch with you if you're up for it. I still have plenty of work to do, but Ed told me to take off whatever time I needed for the funeral and all. I can pick up some Italian sandwiches on the way if you'd like."

"Sure. If that's what you want," Brenda said tonelessly. She wasn't feeling the least bit hungry.

Matt didn't reply right away, and she listened as he took a deep breath.

"I—uh, I don't know what to think about this Bowker thing, though," he finally said. Brenda heard the quaver in his voice. "I mean, he certainly was one sick son of a bitch, but I . . . There's something about the whole thing that makes me feel . . . I don't know." He paused and heaved a deep sigh. "Ahh, screw Bowker. He's gone for good. How you holding up?"

Brenda blinked as she looked around the living room. Early afternoon light filtered through the curtains, casting thin, gray shadows across the floor. They looked like smudges of charcoal on the carpet. The lawn mower she'd been listening to in the distance had stopped, and now she was left with the impression that she hadn't heard it but had dreamed it. Through the open window, she could hear a steady chorus of birdsong and a few frogs in the hollow.

"I guess I'm doing all right," she said. "I mean, it's not like this was a real surprise or anything. People who go into nursing homes generally don't get any better."

"True . . . true," Matt replied, "but they don't usually die from severe head injuries, either." He hesitated, but only for a second. "I was wondering if you thought maybe we should consider pressing charges against the nursing home for negligence."

Settling back on the couch, Brenda closed her eyes and rubbed them with the tips of her fingers to stop the sudden burning sensation of unshed tears. She didn't like feeling so emotionally raw like this.

"No," she said simply, "Definitely not. I—all I want to do right now is get through the next few days."

"I hear you. It's not gonna be easy."

There wasn't much Brenda could say to that, so she took a deep breath and whispered, "Okay, then. See you in a bit."

"Buh-bye, honey. Love you."

Brenda clicked the phone off before replacing it on its base. Her legs felt like they might not support her if she stood up, so she eased back down onto the couch as a powerful wave of grief swept through her. A warm, salty taste flooded the back of her throat, making her chest burn deep inside, but no tears came this time. Numbed by grief, she stayed where she was until half an hour later when Matt pulled into the driveway. She got up and, wiping her red-rimmed eyes, went to the door to greet him, smiling as best she could.

SOMEHOW—she had no idea how—Brenda got through the afternoon and early evening. Throughout the rest of the day, she had run on automatic pilot. By the time supper was over, she didn't have any real clear memories of anything she had said or done all day. All she knew was that she and Matt had an appointment with Gordon Chadbourne, the funeral director at Chadbourne and Sons, tomorrow morning at nine o'clock to select a casket. Later, Reverend Hayne from First Lutheran was going to drop by to help them plan the funeral service.

Word got around quickly about their loss, and as Brenda had known it would, the phone started ringing after lunch and never seemed to stop all afternoon as Brenda's and Matt's friends called to offer their condolences and whatever help they could provide. Cheryl and Deb offered to bring over some casseroles so Brenda at least wouldn't have to worry about what they'd eat. Holly and Jack, their friends from the old neighborhood in town, said they could stay with the children if Mrs. Elroy wasn't available so Brenda and Matt could go out and make whatever preparations they needed to make.

When Emily and John got home from school at two-thirty, they both went straight up to their bedrooms. Brenda had the impression that Emily in particular seemed like she wanted to talk about what had happened, but Brenda waited until Matt was back from the office before sending him upstairs to talk to her. As always, Emily clammed up around Brenda. Maybe because of the unresolved issues with her own mother, she sensed the gulf between her and her stepdaughter widening. She promised herself that, as soon as the funeral was over, she would make a greater effort to connect with Emily.

The phone finally stopped ringing around ten o'clock that night as they were getting ready for bed. Matt had already washed up and brushed his teeth and was tucked into bed by the time Brenda went into the bathroom. Her eyes were burning from crying for so much of the day, and she felt emotionally and physically wrung out as she leaned over the sink. She adjusted the water so it was running nice and warm, then leaned over the sink and splashed her face a few times, sputtering as the water dripped down her face and off her chin.

As she bowed her head over the sink, she had a sudden, unnerving feeling that she was being watched. A cold prickling that began at the base of her neck spread out like an unseen hand to clasp the back of her head. Shivering wildly, she wiped the water from her face and straightened up quickly to look around.

The bathroom light was bright, and the part of their bedroom she could see through the half-open bathroom door appeared much darker than she thought it should. She blinked a few times, but the pupils of her eyes wouldn't adjust. She seemed to be having some kind of muscle spasm in her eyes.

"Matt?" she called out, her voice a soft, trembling whisper. No reply came from the bedroom.

Brenda tried to convince herself that there was nothing to be worried about. Matt was already asleep. Her nerves were overwrought from the day. Still, she couldn't deny the chilly rush that moved across her back or the slight stirring of hairs at the nape of her neck. She looked down at her bare arms and saw the sprinkling of goose bumps on her forearms.

Moving slowly, she took a few cautious steps toward the bathroom door, all the while peering into the dark bedroom. She was looking for . . . something . . . she didn't know .what . . . anything out of the ordinary. Focusing on the bed, she stared long and hard at the slumped form of her husband. Turning her head slowly, she looked all around at the darkened room while listening to the low, steady rasp of Matt's breathing. She started to call out to him again but checked herself, not wanting to disturb his sleep.

It's nothing, she told herself, even though she didn't quite believe it.

There was nothing out of the ordinary to see or hear, but something . . . something most definitely was *different.*

A clutching pain stabbed her chest when she took another deep breath and held it for a moment, then let it out slowly. The fringes of her vision vibrated in the darkness, casting faint ripples in the corners of the dark room. The air seemed to have changed. Not so much the temperature as the pressure. Like it was charged with a pulsing current of electricity. She could practically hear the whoosh of air as it pressed against her eardrums.

Another shiver ran through her, stronger this time. She rubbed her forearms with both hands, trying to drive away the chill that gripped her.

After standing by the bathroom door for a long time, Brenda finally found the courage to turn and walk back to the sink to finish washing up for bed. When she leaned over, her gaze shifted across the mirror where she caught a dark hint of motion behind her reflection. She gasped as the cold pressure inside her chest intensified.

Seated on the edge of the bed, no more than ten or twelve feet behind her, was a small, withered figure.

Even before her eyes adjusted, Brenda realized it was a person; and in that instant, she also realized that it was not her husband sitting up in bed.

What—? Am I seeing things?

The figure was distinctly female, small and hunched with narrow, slouched shoulders. Even in the darkness, Brenda caught a glimpse of the flowing hair that drifted like smoke around the figure's shoulders. A weird internal light illuminated the woman's face.

A cold knot formed like a tiny fist in Brenda's stomach as she stared at the reflection, unable to believe that she was really seeing it. She wished she dared turn around and face it directly, but there was no way she could bring herself to do that. She knew the figure would disappear the instant she looked straight at it, but she couldn't tear her gaze away from it, either. Her throat made a tight gulping sound whenever she swallowed. The air around her grew suddenly cold, raising goose bumps across her legs and arms. The searing pain between her ribs intensified.

"Mom?"

The word came out of her without conscious thought, but when she heard herself speak out loud, she realized that had to be who she was seeing.

Brenda knew that she was emotionally drained, that her nerves were on edge, but the figure on the bed, as vague as it was reflected in the mirror, looked frighteningly real and very much like her recently deceased mother. The same slouched shoulders; the same thin, shoulder-length, gray hair; the same blank expression she'd had while lying in bed unconscious, only now her eyes were wide open and staring with the blank eyes of a marble statue. She caught a glimpse of a tear, flowing like a bead of quicksilver down one cheek.

Bracing both of her hands on the edge of the sink, Brenda leaned forward until her nose almost touched the mirror. Her breath left ovals of moisture on the glass. Afraid that the image would disappear like smoke, she didn't dare even to blink. Opening her eyes wider, she stared at the shape, willing it to become clearer.

"Is that . . . is that really you, Mom?" she whispered tenuously.

A cold clutching feeling took hold of her heart when she saw the shape on the bed slowly shake its head from side to side. Brenda imagined that she could even hear the bedsprings squeak from the shifting weight.

Brenda bit back a scream. The figure's cold, steady gaze bored into her back like a knife between her shoulder blades.

Her legs started shaking wildly, and her teeth were chattering.

"Are you? . . . Who are you?" she asked, her voice cracking.

She was tempted to reach behind her and turn off the bathroom light to see if the illusion—*Yes! That's all it is! It's an illusion!*—got any clearer.

This can't be real. There's no way my mother's ghost can be here!

Brenda had never really believed in ghosts and spirits. But still, she could see in the mirror that *someone* was sitting in the dark bedroom on the edge of her bed.

"No," she whispered. "Go away. You're not real."

She tried to find strength in the thought that this was merely an illusion. It had to be just something she was imagining from the darkness and her exhaustion.

To prove it to herself, she turned around quickly and took a single step forward, toward the open doorway. The sudden darkness after staring at the bright lights reflected in the bathroom mirror sucked in around her with an almost audible rush. The cold sensation tightened around her throat and chest. When she tried to take a breath, it seemed as though her entire body was constricted by something huge and unseen that was crushing her in its powerful grasp.

There's nothing there! she thought, and she was right.

The bedroom was absolutely silent and empty. The only person on the bed was her husband, who was lying on his left side with his back turned to her. The blankets were pulled up over his shoulder, and the soft, rhythmic sounds of his breathing filled the room.

That's all there is.

Looking directly into the bedroom, Brenda was surprised how the illusion—*Yes . . . it had to have been an illusion*—had changed.

It wasn't just that everything was reversed in the mirror image. There was something else. The bedroom looked brighter, and there wasn't even a hint of anything that could have created the image of someone sitting on the edge of the bed. Even the air seemed strangely changed. Ignoring the pain, she took a deep breath, luxuriating in the cool rush of air that filled her lungs.

"Mother of God," she whispered as she ran her hands

down the sides of her face. She wished desperately that she could quiet her racing pulse, but it was throbbing painfully behind her eyes.

What is going on? Am I so stressed out that I'm imagining things? Am I creating more problems for myself?

All she needed, she told herself, was a good night's sleep. Tomorrow was going to be tough enough as it was, dealing with the funeral arrangements and coping with all the family and friends who would be in touch.

Brenda acknowledged that she was going to have to watch herself closely. If there really was something wrong with her, she should be aware of it and make an appointment with her doctor or a therapist right away so she could deal with it before it got too out of hand. No sense letting things get any worse than they already were.

Screw it, she thought as she turned back to the sink, ran the water until it was warm, and started washing her face again. She blubbered and sputtered loudly, and for the short time she couldn't see, a wild, winding tension filled her as she imagined that the shape had returned to the bed . . . and was now standing up . . . and moving toward her.

Choking back a whimper of fear, she grabbed a towel from the bar beside the sink and swiped it across her face. She didn't quite trust it when she opened her eyes and saw that everything was back to normal, the way it should be. No ghostly figure lurked on the edge of the bed. She kept rubbing her face with the towel, enjoying the rough texture of the cotton against her skin. The fresh-washed smell stung her nose as she covered her face and once again had the unnerving feeling that as soon as her eyes were closed, the figure somehow materialized and was sitting there . . . unseen . . . watching her.

Another low whimper escaped her. She told herself that it was foolish to let her imagination get carried away like this.

That's all it is.

It took her a heart-stopping moment to realize that she wasn't the only one who was making a sound. A soft whimpering was coming from one of the kids' bedrooms.

Sudden fear shot like a lightning bolt up her spine. She dropped the hand towel onto the floor and dashed out of the bathroom, through the bedroom, and into the hallway. A night-light lit the hall with a faint orange glow. Her heart was pulsing painfully in her neck as she looked at Emily's and John's closed doors. She held her breath for a moment and waited for the sound to be repeated.

When it came again—a low, strangled cry—she realized that it was coming from Emily's room. Her legs weak and trembling, Brenda raced down the hallway, pausing at the closed door for only a moment. When the sobbing cry came again, louder this time, she rapped lightly on the door as she reached for the doorknob.

"Em? You all right?" she called out.

She tried to keep her voice low so she wouldn't disturb Matt and John.

No answer came from behind the door.

The sobbing stopped the instant she spoke, leaving her with the distinct impression that she had imagined it like so many other things she had imagined. She was just about to turn around and go back to her bedroom when she had the sudden, inexplicable feeling that Emily was in danger and too frightened to speak.

"Emily?" she called out louder as she turned the doorknob. The *click* of the latch seemed unnaturally loud in the gloom of the hall. Holding her breath, Brenda leaned forward and threw the door open.

Emily's bedroom was deep in darkness, illuminated only by the ambient light of the moon and stars that filtered through the windows. Both of her windows were halfway open. A warm breeze scented with damp earth swirled in the air. It took Brenda's eyes a few seconds to adjust to the darkness, but then she saw Emily sitting up in bed.

"I heard you," Brenda said, moving closer to the bed but not sitting down on the edge of it to comfort her the way she would if this were John. "Everything okay?"

Emily was so quiet Brenda had the impression she hadn't heard her.

"What's the matter, Em? Can't you get to sleep?"

Emily still didn't say a word. Brenda moved a little closer, watching as Emily's face resolved like a slow-developing photograph out of the darkness. Her eyes were wide open and staring straight ahead.

"Are you sad about what happened? Do you want to talk about it?"

Brenda heard the trembling edge in her voice and hoped Emily didn't notice it, but she couldn't help but feel unnerved herself. All she wanted was to hear Emily say something to convince her that she was all right.

Quivering inside, Brenda finally sat down on the edge of the bed. It sagged beneath her weight with a loud squeaking of bedsprings. Reaching out, she took Emily's hand in hers and squeezed it. She was surprised how cold it felt.

"You're freezing," Brenda said. "Want me to close the windows?"

Emily didn't say a word. A thrill of panic ran through Brenda as she listened for but didn't hear the sound of the girl's breathing. Leaning closer and reaching out with one hand, she started to stroke Emily's hair, lifting it away from her face.

"Why don't you lie back down?" Brenda said softly. "I'll stay with you until you fall asleep, if you'd like."

Still, Emily said nothing.

As Brenda peered into the darkness, the young girl's features resolved more clearly. For a dizzying moment, Brenda couldn't believe what she was seeing, but before long, she realized that she wasn't looking at her stepdaughter. The face staring back at her from the darkness was old and wrinkled and had cold, pale skin edged with traces of blue moonlight. And Emily's eyes were wide open and staring. An odd blankness filled the girl's gaze. Once again, Brenda thought of the solid eyes of a marble statue. Thin, bloodless lips were curled into a frozen smile that showed no humor whatsoever. As the lips parted, exposing small, flat, white teeth that glinted in the darkness, Brenda saw a dark, jagged gash running down the side of Emily's face.

"What happened?" Brenda whispered, each word catching like a thorn in her throat. Her voice echoed in the darkness from several directions at once. As the rumbling, pulsing sound in her ears intensified, Brenda, numb with fear, watched as the girl's face—*No! This isn't Emily!*—resolved more clearly.

Brenda found herself staring directly into an old woman's face. Deep lines ran like black veins across her pale forehead and cheeks. The hair that had appeared so dark and luxurious moments before now was a stringy, white mass that looked like a thick clot of cobwebs. The scar on the left side of her face twisted and writhed like a fat-bodied snake across her cheek. And her eyes . . . her eyes stared blankly straight ahead while at the same time piercing through her like knives.

Brenda groaned as she twisted her head from side to side, trying to break free of the hold those steady, unseeing eyes had on her. With a jolt, she found herself sitting up in her own bed, her fists clenched tightly, covering her mouth to stifle back the scream that threatened to burst out of her.

"What! Jesus, Bren! What is it?"

Brenda shrieked and pulled violently away from Matt when he touched her. Her breath burned in her chest, and the rancid taste of vomit filled her mouth. She couldn't say a word. Cold sweat bathed her body, making her shiver as she hiked her knees up and scrambled backward until her back pressed against the headboard.

"No . . . no . . . no!" she wailed.

When Matt reached out and took hold of her arm, she tore violently out of his grasp. She swatted viciously at him but missed and smacked the mattress instead. Matt shifted closer to her, grabbed her, and held her close to him. She could feel the sleep warmth of his body.

"Wake up. Jesus, Bren. Take it easy. You were having a nightmare."

Fear and anguish almost overwhelmed Brenda as she at first resisted him, then let herself collapse into his embrace. Violent sobs shook her shoulders, making her feel weak and light-headed. The sour taste in her mouth was fading only to be replaced by a warm, sickly saltiness.

"I was . . . I saw . . . Oh, my God! It was *terrible!*"

Her voice was muffled against Matt's shoulder, and she couldn't stop shaking as the image of the old lady's face burned like acid in her memory. She wished she could find reassurance in Matt's embrace, but the memory of the nightmare—*When did it begin?*—especially the woman's staring, blank eyes, filled her with a terrible sense of being utterly alone, no matter how close he held her.

"You want to talk about it?" Matt asked after a long while. He gently eased himself away from her but still gripped her arms just above the elbows.

Brenda sucked in a shallow breath and shook her head. The image of that horrible, mutilated face drifted in front of her closed eyes, filling her with unspeakable dread. The only sound she could make was a funny noise in the back of her throat.

"Man, I was sound asleep," Matt said, but even before he finished speaking, she felt his body stiffen. Brenda froze, too, and listened. Then, very faintly, she heard a low sob from out in the hallway.

"Ahh, shit. Sounds like Emily's awake," Matt muttered.

The mattress sagged as he released her and shifted around to get up. Brenda finally dared to open her eyes and look at him, amazed by the harsh reality of actually seeing things after the surrealism of her dream.

That's all it is, she told herself. *It was just a dream.*

"Be right back," Matt said. "I just want to check on her. Make sure she's all right."

"Yeah," Brenda said, surprised that she could say anything at all.

Feeling numb all over, she watched as her husband got up and made his way out of the bedroom and started down the hall. He moved without turning on any lights. Once she was alone in the bedroom, Brenda tried to hold back her panic. All she could think was that, the instant Matt opened Emily's door and went inside, he would see that it wasn't his little girl there in the bed.

She might look like a girl of fifteen, at least at first, but if he looked closely, if he turned on the light and really looked at her, he would see that beneath the surface, she was an old woman with a terrible jagged scar distorting the left side of her face, and that she had blank, staring eyes that could slice clean through him.

Still unable to move but terrified of being alone in the darkness, Brenda sat up in bed with her back pressed against the headboard and her knees pulled up to her chest as she watched and waited for her husband to return.

waiting

IN the eerie hush of predawn darkness, Susan Ireland eased the door to her motel room closed as if there was someone else in the room to disturb. As she started down the hall to the front door, a sudden pain throbbed in the stump of her left ankle where it connected to her prosthetic foot. It set her teeth on edge.

Looking down at the prosthesis, hidden from view in her sneaker, she was filled with disgust and remorse as she recalled the accident more than fourteen years ago that had claimed her left foot just above the ankle. It didn't help to think that, even if she hadn't been drinking that night, she probably couldn't have prevented what had happened. She was stopped at a red light when the van slammed into her from the side. She ended up losing her foot and, once the officers who responded to the call realized how intoxicated she was, her driver's license. The ultimate cost was her marriage and, at the bitter end of her drinking, her daughter.

Usually the pain wasn't much more than a distant memory, except for an occasional pulse like now to remind her. She was seldom bothered by any phantom limb sensations of itching or burning, but the guilt and shame and regret were as constant and permanent as the loss of her foot. She knew she would carry those feelings for the rest of her life. The only thing she was truly grateful for was that no one else had been injured or killed, and that the accident had been her wake-up call. Finally, she couldn't avoid getting sober.

And what I'm doing now—is this part of my recovery or part of a relapse?

She stepped outside into the unusually cool spring morning and exhaled. Her breath came out a white mist that quickly melted into the still air. A thin coating of dew covered the parked cars. Feeling in her purse for her keys, she started across the parking lot to her car when a voice, speaking suddenly behind her, made her jump.

" 'Mornin'."

Susan let out a little squeal and turned to see a middle-aged man of unremarkable appearance seated on the bench outside the front office door. He was wearing a dark jacket and pants, which may have been why she hadn't noticed him immediately. He had short, dark hair, a thin face, and an odd expression.

Susan wondered what he was doing out in front of the motel at such an ungodly hour. Maybe he worked here and had forgotten his keys and was waiting to be let in . . . or, more likely, he was a customer who was waiting to meet up with someone or who maybe had insomnia and couldn't sleep. He certainly looked like he hadn't slept. There was something about him—a dark cast to his eyes—that unnerved her.

It didn't matter to Susan as long as he left her alone. She sensed that he was dangerous but probably not to her. With a curt nod, she barely acknowledged the man's greeting as she fit the key into her car door and unlocked it.

You don't have to be doing this, you know, she told herself.

She didn't have to look to know that the man was watching her, his eyes steadily boring into her.

What if he's an undercover cop Matt's hired to follow me?

She knew she was hyperventilating and told herself to calm down.

You can go back inside, she told herself. *Settle the bill, pack up, and get the hell out of here. Drive back to Iowa and forget all about it.* She could sell her mother's house, rent herself a smaller place . . .

Matt wasn't going to give in on *anything* without a fight, especially on her wanting to visit Emily. No matter how much she wanted to or thought she deserved to, she knew his pride wouldn't let him yield. Being a lawyer, he could muster any resources he might need to stop her from revising their custody agreement. He had money as well as prestige and position in the community. If she took him to court, he'd crush her in the preliminary hearing simply because he had the law on his side. She had signed away her custodial rights. Just because she had been a drunk when she did it, wasn't going to change a damned thing.

"But she's my daughter, too, goddamnit," she whispered, clenching her hands until her palms began to ache. She stared out across the parking lot, her vision focused on the mist-shrouded trees in the distance.

"No," she whispered.

The bottom line was, no matter what Matt did legally, one way or another, she was going to see Emily. She had to find her and talk to her at least once before admitting defeat and heading back home to Iowa. She was trembling so much inside, her stomach hurt.

"This is home! Home is where my daughter is!"

She swung the car door open and shifted into the driver's seat, gripping the steering wheel with both hands for support until the wave of dizziness that swept over her passed. She cringed when she glanced at her reflection in the rearview mirror.

You look like shit, she told herself.

Her eyes were a network of tiny veins that looked like red-hot wires across the yellowed whites. Her skin was sallow, and her lips were thin and bloodless. The reflected glare of the dome light made her wince.

"Get a grip, get a grip," she said aloud, looking herself straight in the eyes.

Her hand trembled as she slipped the key into the ignition and turned it. The car had needed a new starter for months so, every time she started it cold, it didn't turn over on the first few tries. With each twist of the key, the solenoid made a faint clicking sound, but that was all. She impatiently kept cranking it and cranking it until, finally, on the ninth or tenth try, the engine sputtered to life.

"Thanks a lot, you piece of shit," she whispered as she swatted the steering wheel with disgust.

The plugs were bad, and the car chugged unevenly, threatening to stall out at any second, but Susan pumped the gas to keep it going. Behind her, a cloud of gray exhaust spewed into the still air, enveloping the car like morning fog.

Shifting into reverse, Susan slowly backed out of her parking slot. It was fifteen miles or so to Matt's house. Her stomach felt empty, and although she wasn't sure she could actually eat anything, she decided to swing by the Dunkin' Donuts on Route 22 before driving to Three Rivers.

As she pulled out of the hotel parking lot, she glanced at her rearview mirror. There was no sign of the man in the dark jacket outside the motel office. He had vanished, leaving her with the feeling that he had never been there at all.

FORTY-FIVE minutes later, with a plain donut sitting like a lump of clay in the pit of her stomach, Susan pulled to a stop in the same place she had parked yesterday, across from the school bus stop. The clock on her dashboard indicated it was still more than half an hour before the bus was due. Sighing with frustration, she settled back in the car seat and took a slurping sip of her still too hot coffee. It was bitter and made her wince.

She settled down to wait. She didn't have a clear idea what she intended to do, but she hoped she'd think of something.

Her first thought was simply to wait until Emily showed up and just walk across the street and introduce herself.

Will that work?

She trembled with a feeling of excitement and expectation. She certainly didn't want to frighten Emily, and she realized that there could be all sorts of trouble with the bus driver or any other parents who showed up if she, a total stranger to all of them, suddenly appeared and tried to talk to Emily.

What the hell else can I do?

She was feeling cornered and desperate. Matt hadn't left her many options.

The sun was rising slowly behind her, breaking through the morning mist and casting a warm, golden glow over the trees across the street from her. The day was warming up fast. Susan rolled her window down and listened to the chorus of birdsong from deep in the woods.

The more she imagined how she might actually initiate talking with her daughter, the more nervous she got. Before long, her body was tingling as if a subtle electrical current was running through her. Her hands and foot started to lose sensation, and she found it difficult to breathe. Sticking her head out the driver's window, she took several deep breaths, but her anxiety only got worse, finally spiking when she saw a group of kids coming down the road, heading toward the bus stop.

Is Emily one of them?

Susan sat bolt upright in the car seat, staring ahead, but she soon saw that Emily wasn't with them.

Groaning softly, she slumped in the seat, wishing she could disappear as the children—three boys and two girls—approached. All of them appeared younger than Emily. Once they got to the bus stop, the girls stood off to one side and talked quietly while the boys started goofing around, swatting at each other and laughing.

Susan kept staring up the road, expecting to see Emily appear at any moment along with her younger brother and the girl she guessed was her best friend. The dashboard clock was moving so slowly she became convinced it was defective. Every minute seemed to stretch out for five or ten. She counted a slow, measured cadence while waiting for the digital numerals to switch. Her anxiety rose steadily. Her pulse made soft, feathery sounds in her ears, and her throat felt constricted. She found it almost impossible to swallow.

She glanced at her wristwatch to make sure time hadn't stopped cold. Yesterday, the bus had arrived a few minutes past seven. It was already five minutes late, and there was no sign of it. It didn't matter that the kids waiting seemed unconcerned that it might be late today. On a beautiful spring day like this, with summer vacation only a few weeks away, the last thing on their minds was getting to school on time.

No, Susan thought, *what matters right now is, where is Emily? She should have been here by now. Has something happened?*

Susan began to fidget, wishing she had a bottle in the car. It wasn't that she *wanted* or *needed* to get drunk. Not in the least. All she craved was a sip—just one, tiny little sip to help steady her nerves.

"Is that so wrong?" she asked herself, looking at her reflection in the mirror.

Yes, it is! she told herself. *I have to be strong. If not for myself, then at least for Emily.*

But what would steady her nerves? What would take that terrible constriction from her throat so she could swallow normally?

She was heating up inside, her belly radiating heat like a blast furnace. Even with cool air wafting in through her open window, she was bathed with sweat and couldn't stop the tremors deep down in her body.

Where is she? Where is my daughter?

Her eyes strained as she stared up the road, waiting and wishing for any sign of Emily, but she was nowhere in sight. Susan's heart felt as though at any second it might stop beating. A wave of chills washed through her when, far up the road, she saw the school bus rounding the corner.

She's not going to make it!

The tightening around her heart got so bad she actually gasped out loud and put a hand over her breast. She bit down on her lower lip so hard a razor-fine pain shot through her. White spots danced across her vision. She was suddenly afraid she was going to pass out.

Something's happened to her, and she's not coming!

Susan's first thought was that Matt probably suspected what she was up to and was driving Emily to school. She hadn't been expecting that, so she wouldn't have noticed if Emily and Matt had been in one of the cars that had gone by in the past half hour.

That's what it must be, she thought.

And even as that conviction worked into her mind, Susan came to a harsh realization.

If Matt isn't going to play by the rules, if he's going to be a

*prick, then I'm not going to play by the rules, either. If Matt
thinks he's going to keep her away from me, I'll have to find a
way to take her away from him. It's that simple.*

In fact, it seemed so simple and obvious that Susan started
to laugh. Before long, she was laughing so hard tears filled her
eyes, blurring her vision so she couldn't see clearly when the
bus came to a stop. Its brakes squealed, and a plume of exhaust rose into the sky as the handful of kids climbed aboard,
the boys shouldering the girls out of the way to get on first.

Once everyone was settled in the bus, the driver took off.
Within seconds, the bus had disappeared down the road. Susan waited until she was calm and then shifted into gear and
took off. She crossed the intersection and then drove the short
distance to the turn onto Collette Road.

You've got a lot to think about, she told herself.

She knew, from now on, she would have to plan things out
carefully. The first thing she wanted to do was drive by
Matt's house just to see what—if anything—was going on,
how many cars were in the driveway and who—if anyone—
was still home. Then she'd head back into town, find a meeting to attend, and think things through. She had to be careful
now because her next move—whatever it was—would take
plenty of thought and planning if she was going to pull it off
successfully.

*And if it doesn't work, if I don't get away with it, what do I
really lose?*

"I've already lost everything that matters to me," she whispered to her reflection in the mirror. She had a fleeting thought
of her mother's funeral, but she pushed it aside.

As she slowed for the left turn onto Collette Road, Susan
was filled with a new sense of direction and confidence, something she hadn't felt in years.

She was in such a good mood that she actually started
humming softly to herself.

It was moments of clarity like this, she told herself, that
made her realize just how far she'd come, how much healthier
she was than she was when she left Matt. It thrilled her to
think about how much she had grown, how much more together she was psychologically and emotionally than she had
ever been.

She knew what she had to do. She knew what she was going to do. It was just a matter of planning it out so nothing would go wrong.

"I didn't sleep very well either," Brenda said, smiling at Emily as she closed the family room door, and they walked out into the two-bay garage. "At least John got off to school on time. I hope you have a good day at school."

"Umm—thanks," Emily muttered.

She barely made eye contact with her stepmother as she opened the passenger's door of the Honda Civic and got in. Once Brenda was settled behind the wheel and had the car started, she hit the button on the remote control clipped to the visor. The garage door rattled open with a loud, steady grinding of machinery. Early morning light poured into the garage like liquid gold.

Twisting around, Emily wedged her backpack into the backseat. Before Brenda could remind her, she snapped on her seat belt and, folding her arms across her chest, stared straight ahead as Brenda slowly backed out into the driveway and did a quick three-point turn.

The rising sun was shining directly in their faces as the car pulled forward. Emily squinted and looked out the side window to avoid the glare and her stepmother. Before they pulled out onto the road, though, she caught a glimpse of a small, dark car coming up the road toward them. Emily was convinced the driver was slowing to stop at the top of their driveway to block them in.

As soon as she saw the car, she stiffened. A short gasp escaped her.

I've seen that car before!

She didn't know what make or model it was, but she was convinced it was the same car that had been at the bus stop yesterday morning . . . the same car that had followed the bus to school and been parked out in front of the school when she was getting off to go inside.

"Is that—?"

Emily stopped herself. Her fists tightened in her lap.

Brenda shot her a quick glance. Apparently she either

hadn't noticed the car or didn't think anything was out of the ordinary now that it was creeping slowly past the house, heading down the street.

"What?" Brenda asked, turning to her, her eyebrows arched.

Hoping her stepmother didn't notice, Emily shifted her eyes to track the car. It had rounded the corner down the street and was already out of sight. It left behind a thin cloud of exhaust that lingered in the air before dispersing.

"Huh?" Emily said with a tight shrug.

"You were going to say something?"

Emily took a short breath, aware of the funny little click it made in the back of her throat. She was convinced that had to be the same car she had seen yesterday. Now that it was out of sight, though, she had the curious feeling that she had imagined seeing it.

There isn't anyone following me, she told herself. *How could there be? Stuff like that doesn't really happen . . . not in real life. It's only on TV and in movies and books that people get stalked. If that even was the same car . . .*

In a matter of seconds, Emily convinced herself that it wasn't—it *couldn't* have been the same car—or if it was, it was just a coincidence that she had noticed it two days in a row.

Still, that didn't prevent her from feeling that something was wrong. In the harsh glare of morning sunlight, she realized that she had only barely caught a glimpse of the driver, leaving her with the crazy impression that the car might not even have a driver, that it was moving on its own.

Maybe that's what's creeping me out.

A car without a driver, like some supernatural thing in a horror movie or something, was following her. She decided that, if she ever saw that car again, she would at least make sure she got a good look at the driver.

Then maybe I won't be so afraid of it.

Afraid? she asked herself.

Her mind was racing as she tried to think this all through and not let on to Brenda how upset she was.

Yes, that car had upset her. No question about it. She didn't know why, but it did.

"Huh?" Emily said again, blinking her eyes and glancing over at her stepmother.

"Oh, nothing," Brenda replied. "I just thought you . . ." She heaved a sigh and paused at the top of the driveway before pulling out onto the road. "You know, Em, if you ever have to talk to me . . . about anything . . . you can. I'm willing to listen."

"I know," Emily said, not caring how insincere it sounded.

Biting her lower lip, she shifted her gaze out the side window again. As Brenda started down the road, she watched as the woods along the side of the road slipped past her. She couldn't stop wondering why, after seeing that car, everything looked so . . . different now. In her heart, she knew she should say something to Brenda. If the person in that car—*If there even was a person in that car!*—was dangerous, she should tell an adult so they could handle it. She wasn't trying to be a big girl about this and handle it on her own. She was scared. It was just that she wasn't ready to talk to Brenda about it. If she was with her dad, it would be different. It wasn't that she didn't like Brenda. She was fine, as far as that went. She just preferred not to talk to her about how she really felt about things.

They drove the rest of the way to school in silence. Emily felt a twinge or two of guilt for not being honest with Brenda, but what she was more worried about was what she would do if that car—*That car without a driver!*—ever showed up again.

"**SOMETHING'S** wrong," Brenda said, cupping the cell phone in the palm of her hand and turning so she was looking out over the woods that backed the Chadbourne Funeral Home parking lot. "Something's really bugging her, and I don't know what to do about it."

"There's not much you can do," Matt replied, "except be there for her so when she finally decides to talk, you can listen."

"I know, but . . ."

Brenda heaved a sigh, not sure what to say next but aware that she might be projecting a lot of her own feelings onto Emily. She thought she had a pretty good idea how tough it was for Emily growing up with a stepmother. The distance between them had only gotten worse after John was born, but

Brenda had always worked hard to be fair and keep the sibling rivalry to a minimum. Still, even after all these years, she wasn't sure how to reach out to Emily, how to connect with her. It seemed like, no matter what she tried or how hard she tried, Emily always kept her at a distance. Maybe that was just Emily's personality, she thought, but it still bothered her.

Stretching out her left arm, she glanced at her wristwatch and saw that it was almost nine o'clock.

"Our appointment's in fifteen minutes. You heading over soon?"

The slight pause at the end of the line made Matt's reply obvious before he spoke. She stiffened at the thought of facing this ordeal on her own.

"Look, Bren, I—uh, I have a client coming by in half an hour. I'm really sorry, but I don't think I can get over there and back here in time."

"Matt, please . . ."

"I know I promised I'd be there, but this case is really important. You know, the firm hasn't had a lot of business lately, and our fiscal year-end numbers aren't looking so good."

"We're talking about my mother's funeral, for God's sake."

Brenda struggled to keep her voice from breaking, but the anger she felt was deep and genuine.

Matt exhaled noisily. "Look, Bren. If you can reschedule for later today—this afternoon, maybe, I might be able to make it."

"You *said* you'd be here with me."

The recrimination in her voice surprised her, but she didn't regret it. Many times in the past, her husband had put his job before her, but she couldn't help feeling that something was different this time, that he was keeping something from her.

"I want to get this over with as soon as I can, and I'd like you to be here with me."

"I know that," Matt said, sounding chastened. "But I can't let my work slide."

"Not even to plan my mother's funeral?" Brenda said bitterly.

There was an awkward moment of silence on the other end of the line. She could feel her husband squirming.

"Look," he said, "if you *really* want me there—"

"No. Don't bother. Forget it."

There was a snap in her voice. She felt a renewed strength inside her, and the truth was, she was confident she could handle this with or without him or anyone else.

"It's no big deal," she said. "It's just my mother's goddamned funeral."

"Jesus, Brenda!" Matt heaved another sigh.

Brenda swallowed, but the burning lump in her throat didn't go down.

"Jesus yourself," she said. "I'll do what I have to do."

She reached for the door handle and snapped it open. The sudden rush of warm air hit her like a gush of water. As she stood up, she feared her legs would not be strong enough to support her, but she swung the car door shut and started across the parking lot toward the front door of the funeral home.

"Brenda . . ." Matt said, his voice pleading. "I'll leave right now. I'll be there in twenty minutes."

"Too late," she said, trying not to shout into the cell phone. She hated it when people talked on their phones in public without making any attempt to keep their conversation private. "I'll be fine. I'll see you tonight."

Matt was silent for several seconds, then sighed and said, "Fine, then."

He might have had more to say, but Brenda broke the connection and slipped the cell phone into her purse as she walked around to the front steps of the funeral home. She opened the front door.

What's the big deal, right? she asked herself.

In the foyer of the funeral home, the thick perfume of flowers nearly suffocated her. She got light-headed, and tiny white lights flickered like fireflies across her vision. She took a breath and held it for a moment, forcing a smile as she nodded a greeting to the young man who was walking toward her.

"Mrs. Ireland?" the man said, extending his hand for her to shake. His grip was cool and surprisingly strong. "I'm Gordon Chadbourne. I'm so sorry for your loss."

Brenda nodded, repressing a deep shudder. She exhaled, then inhaled again slowly, trying hard to ignore the cloying aroma of flowers. She knew it was there to mask the smell of other, more noxious chemicals they used on the bodies.

"Thank you," she replied, hearing a curious flatness in her voice. "My husband can't make it."

Gordon nodded understandingly and indicated the open door of his office.

"Well, then," he said. "If you'd just come with me, we'll get through this as quickly as possible."

Brenda grabbed a tissue from her purse and blew her nose as she walked the short distance to Gordon's office. The high flutter of her pulse filled her ears like muffled drumbeats, and she desperately wished the drifting white spots in her vision would fade.

You just have to get through this, she told herself. *Just focus on simple, practical things.*

But the harsh reality was, her mother was dead and—even now—was somewhere down in the basement of this building on a cold slab. Even worse was the knowledge that those foul-smelling chemicals that the flowers didn't quite mask were replacing the warm blood that had once flowed in her mother's veins. But as terrible as the next hour or so was going to be, she braced herself, knowing that somehow she would find the strength to handle this.

I don't have a choice, she thought.

EIGHT

passing strangers

So far, it had been one hell of a day for Marcus, and as far as he could tell, it was going to be an even longer and weirder night.

Late in the afternoon, a little after four o'clock, he was sitting in the booth farthest from the front door in the Dunkin' Donuts on Route 22, in some Podunk town just south of Augusta. He'd been here since sometime after lunch, more than three hours ago. Leaning forward, he folded his hands as if in prayer as he clasped a large cup of gradually cooling coffee. It was his fifth or sixth cup since breakfast. He'd lost count, but he had no doubt he'd down a few more before the day was over.

And night began.

He was sure that tonight sleep wasn't going to come any easier than the night before. It wasn't the caffeine that was keeping him awake. He knew that much. Sometime after midnight last night, unable to sleep, he had gotten out of bed and just sat in the dark motel room, chain-smoking cigarettes and drinking whiskey straight from the bottle until it was gone. He was so desperate for sleep that he had actually prayed—something he hadn't done since he was a child. Even during the worst times in five years in prison, he hadn't prayed. But now he had.

His prayers hadn't been answered, and still sleep hadn't come. He feared he might never sleep again. How long could he last without sleep?

Sometime before dawn, he'd gotten dressed and walked outside to sit for a while on the wooden bench by the motel office door. Just for a change of scenery. Maybe the fresh air would make him drowsy, but still, he hadn't been able to stop the flood of crazy ideas that filled his head. The predawn darkness had been peaceful—at least as peaceful as he could have hoped for—until that woman had come out of her room.

What was there about her that bothered me so much?

Throughout the day, he kept turning that thought over in his mind.

As soon as he had seen her face, he had felt—something— some sort of connection, like he might have known her long ago, before he went to jail. There was a strong sense of familiarity about her, an intense feeling of déjà vu, like he'd known her in a previous life or something.

Then again, after spending time in prison, he did feel as though he'd died and been born again into a new and totally unfamiliar world.

He couldn't begin to figure out what this feeling was, but whatever it was, hours later he still couldn't get that woman out of his mind.

He had spoken to her, no more than a simple "Good morning," as friendly a greeting as he could muster, but she had all but ignored him. She'd been trembling so badly he could see her shaking even in the early morning darkness. Then she had gotten into her car, started it up after a few tries, and driven away, peeling out of the parking lot as if she was terrified of him.

What did she think, I was going to hurt her?

The thought sent a shudder through him because that was one of the thoughts that was worming up into his consciousness.

He *did* want to do *something* to *someone*.

He wanted to hurt someone, but it wasn't just anyone. He felt as though, deep inside, he had a purpose, like he was looking for someone in particular he wanted—he *had*—to hurt!

He had no idea where such sadistic thoughts were coming from, but he felt anger deep inside him, a powerful urge to get even with . . . someone . . . for something. . . .

The simple truth was, he didn't want to have anything to do with that woman, and he wished he could forget about her. She hadn't been the least bit attractive, other than being a woman; and in spite of some of the things that had happened to him in prison, he still considered himself fully a man.

No, it wasn't companionship he wanted. He preferred being alone.

So what difference did it make if he felt something about that woman or not? Judging by how he'd felt since getting out of prison, he was going to be spending a lot of time alone. And that was just fine with him.

He didn't know where or how to start, but he knew he had a lot to figure out.

Gritting his teeth, Marcus pressed his hands hard against the sides of his head. Heated pressure was building up inside him, making him feel like he was going to explode. There was something—something he couldn't even begin to identify, but it was dark and secret and ugly—churning deep inside him, making him feel nauseous and . . .

And what?

"And dirty."

He said the words aloud, cringing as he clenched his fists so hard against the sides of his head it hurt. Ever since prison—especially that last night—he hadn't really felt like himself. No, not at *all* like himself.

Of course, he had clear memories of who he had been before his jail sentence, but since his release, everything about the world and about himself seemed different, sometimes subtly different, sometimes powerfully different. The way he thought and felt about things, even smells and tastes, were strangely distorted from the way he remembered them. His sense of confidence had been replaced by feelings of revulsion and humiliation and a terrible self-loathing.

The sun was still several hours from setting. He knew it would be futile to go back to the motel and try to sleep now. Sleep simply wasn't an option. It was a luxury he could no longer afford. The thought crossed his mind that he might never sleep again, that he was going to stay awake until he finally lost his mind or died.

Maybe he should go for a drive.

He had no idea why he had driven to this town from Warren. Maybe, if he drove around the area some, he'd get a better idea of why he had come here and what he wanted or was supposed to do.

A slick, oily blackness vibrated at the fringes of his vision. No matter how much he tried, he couldn't block out the constant voice inside his head. At times, it seemed like someone was whispering into his ear, the voice hissing like a snake inside him, but he could never quite make out what the voice was saying. On some deep, unfathomable level, it might be making sense, but all he knew consciously was: *I have to do something!*

That much was clear.

But what? Where can I go? What in the name of Christ can I do?

He couldn't answer those questions, but the burning ache deep in his stomach made him feel as though he still had some unfinished business. He had no idea what it was, but it wouldn't let go of him.

"Accounts aren't balanced," he whispered out loud, his voice rasping like metal scraping against metal.

"You need something there, hon?"

Marcus jumped when the waitress, standing at the far end of the counter, shot him a quizzical look. Tightening his grip on his coffee cup, he shook his head sharply.

"Nope. All set," he said, but when he turned and caught a glimpse of his reflection in the plate glass window, he could see that he was anything but "all set."

Stroking his beard-stubbled chin with one hand, he stared at his reflection, wondering how that could really be him he was looking at. Then his focus shifted past his image, beyond the view of the Dunkin' Donuts parking lot and the wooded hills across the road. His mind went blank, and for the longest time he was lost somewhere inside his own head, in a place where he could almost make out what the voice inside his head was whispering to him, telling him, *commanding* him to do.

Maybe, Marcus thought with a bone-deep shiver, *maybe . . . with time . . . I'll figure it out.*

* * *

THE sun had set, and a deep indigo tint lingered on the horizon, gradually deepening to dark blue in the east. The evening air was warm, but just the same, Emily grabbed a sweatshirt before going out the front door. So far, the spring had been much cooler than usual, and she thought even if she didn't need an extra layer now, she might want it on the walk home from the corner store.

Her father had called an hour before supper and asked her to tell Brenda that he was running late and wouldn't be home in time for supper after all. That bothered Emily more than she would have admitted to anyone, even her best friends. Her father was the only family she had, and lately it seemed like he wasn't around as much as he used to be.

Maybe that wasn't really what was happening. Maybe it just seemed that way because he was always so busy now that he had his new job. She liked it much better when she was a little girl, before he'd married Brenda and they'd had John, back when she'd had her father all to herself.

Or maybe, now that they were living so far out of town, her father didn't bother to come home as often as he used to.

Or maybe, Emily thought, she was seeing and feeling differently about things. Could anyone blame her?

Leaving behind the house in town, the only home she had ever known, and moving out here had been a lot harder than she imagined it would be.

But it didn't matter. None of it mattered.

Whatever the reasons, either she or everyone else in the family had changed a lot since moving into the new house.

"I'm going to Sofia's," she called out over her shoulder as she opened the front door.

She hadn't asked for permission to walk up to the corner store, but she knew Brenda wouldn't stop her. She'd probably enjoy having her out of the house for a while. Besides, it would be a relief not to have to listen to her stepmother go on and on about how sad it was that Grammy Swanson had died.

"Wait for me!"

John's excited shout echoed in the stairwell from upstairs. A moment later, the rapid stomping of feet sounded on the steps as he ran down from his bedroom. Going to the store for after-supper snacks was about the only thing that tore him away from his PlayStation 2.

Emily started to protest. Just once, she wanted to go to the store without him tagging along, but she knew—especially to-night—that Brenda would insist that both of them go.

"Hurry up, twerp," she snapped, keeping her voice low enough so Brenda wouldn't hear her.

She jumped down from the front steps, swinging the door closed in his face behind her. She was halfway up the walk-way to the street when John burst out the door and ran to catch up with her.

"Thanks for waiting, jerk," he said, panting.

Doing her best—as always—to ignore him, Emily didn't say a word. Without slowing her pace, she continued up the road, the steady crunch-crunch of their feet on the roadside gravel echoing loudly in the gathering night. The only other sound was the steady chorus of spring peepers coming from the pond behind the house. Spring had always been Emily's favorite season, and hearing the peepers was one sure sign that warmer weather was on its way, but right now, she was cold. Shivering in the rapidly cooling night air, she was glad she had her sweatshirt. She slipped it on over her head without missing a step.

It was a little over a mile from their new house to Sofia's corner store. Once they got to the end of Collette Road, they had to cross Route 22 and walk another half mile or so along the busy road. Emily wasn't nearly as worried about the dan-ger of oncoming traffic as her father and Brenda were, but they had obviously drilled their worry into John. Whenever he tagged along, he slowed her down by walking on the rough shoulder of the road instead of on the gravel breakdown lane.

"If you don't keep up, I'll leave you behind. I swear I will," Emily said over her shoulder.

She listened to her brother huffing as he struggled to keep up with her and smiled, thinking how a fast walk like this might do him some good. Brenda was right about one thing. John spent way too much time playing video games, and with all the snacks and junk food he ate, he was getting a little chubby.

"Come on," she called. "Shake off some of that baby fat."

"I'm not fat," John shouted.

Only a few cars and trucks went by. The speed limit on Route 22 was fifty-five miles per hour, but almost everyone whizzed past, going much faster. Emily particularly hated it when the eighteen-wheelers went by, the roar of their diesel engines so loud they made her ears hurt. The gust of wind they made in passing was enough almost to knock her over.

"I hope you got your own money," she said as they neared the store.

Bright, warm light spilled like liquid metal onto the front steps and parking lot. Two cars and one pickup truck were parked out front. Emily was relieved to notice that none of them looked like the dark blue car that had been following her. The front door and windows of the store were plastered with homemade flyers and advertisements that waved in the chilly spring breeze.

"I got what I need," John said, shooting her a sour look as he patted the pocket of his jeans. The coins in his pocket jingled. He automatically stepped back, out of habit rather than politeness, as Emily swung the door open and entered the store first.

The bright light made Emily squint as she nodded a greeting to the young woman at the cash register. Emily didn't recognize her and was surprised that Sofia, who always worked afternoons and evenings, wasn't around. She went over to the cooler and grabbed a Mad River Iced Tea after surveying the choices.

John stood at the candy rack, obviously having trouble making up his mind. Emily paid zero attention to him as she moved up to the counter to pay.

The woman at the register smiled as she rang up the sale. Emily noticed how she hesitated as though unsure of what she was doing. She must be new.

"That'll be—umm, lemme see . . . with the deposit, a dollar sixty-seven." There was a slight tremor in her voice.

Emily dug the money from her jeans pocket and handed it to her. She looked around when the door whooshed open. A woman entered, blinking strangely as she looked straight at

Emily. There was an odd expression on her face, like she was scared or confused by the lights. It bothered Emily.

John suddenly appeared behind her, bumping into her as he plunked two candy bars and a bag of Doritos onto the counter. Moving deliberately, the woman rang up the sale.

"That'll be three dollars and twenty-three cents," she said, sounding proud of herself for doing the calculation so quickly.

John reached into his pocket and pulled out a handful change, which he scattered onto the counter.

"Lemme see . . ." He flattened out the two dollars, then started counting as he sifted through the change. "Twenty-five . . . fifty . . . seventy-five . . . eighty-five . . ."

Emily watched as he slid the money across the counter, but she couldn't stop herself from glancing at the woman, who was still standing by the door behind her. She hadn't moved, and Emily thought she was watching her like she had something important to say but either had forgotten it or hadn't worked up the nerve to say it.

"You're fifty-three cents short," the woman at the register said. She sounded apologetic, as if it might have been her fault, not John's, that he didn't have enough money.

"Em? Can I borrow fifty-three cents?"

Emily turned and glared at him. For some reason, the woman behind them was making her feel really nervous, and all she wanted to do was to get out of there.

"Can I?"

"You could put something back," the lady at the register offered when Emily didn't respond right away.

Emily's scowl deepened. Biting her lower lip, she faced him.

"I *asked* you if you had enough money when we left," she said. She had to struggle to keep her voice low and steady. She didn't know why, but she didn't want the woman by the front door to overhear her. Something about her really bothered Emily. She looked so confused or scared or something.

Maybe she's drunk or on drugs . . . or just plain crazy. Maybe she's dangerous.

"I thought I had enough," John said just short of whining. "Com'on. I'll pay you when we get home. I have the money on my desk."

"I'll bet," Emily said as she slid her hand into her jeans pocket. All she came up with was two dimes and three pennies. She dropped them onto the counter, knowing it wasn't enough.

"You're gonna have to put something back like she says," Emily said, cringing with embarrassment. Wasn't it just like John to do something stupid like this?

"Here you go."

The voice coming so suddenly from behind her made Emily jump as she turned and saw the woman smiling at both of them. She no longer looked scared. She was smiling widely, like she knew them. Still, her hand trembled slightly as she opened her purse and took out a dollar bill and placed it carefully on the counter beside John's treats.

John barely glanced up at her, frowning deeply.

"We—uh, we're not s'posed to take anything from strangers," he said quietly.

Emily couldn't stop wondering why she was so afraid of this woman. There was something about her she didn't like, but she didn't dare look at her long enough to try to figure it out. All she knew was, she didn't like having her standing so close to her. It made her skin crawl. She could practically feel the woman's breath on her neck, and it sent a cold, icky feeling up and down her back.

The woman laughed, but it was a tight, unnatural-sounding laugh. Emily knew she didn't really mean it at all. She chanced a glance at the woman but quickly looked away, afraid to meet her cold, steady gaze. She could feel it, drilling into her back.

"You're not really *taking* anything from me," the woman said. There was a strained quality to her voice that set Emily's teeth on edge. "I'm just helping you out. It's not like I'm offering you a ride or anything."

"Yeah . . . well . . . I guess so," John said.

He still didn't look at all convinced that it was all right for him to take money from a stranger, even if it was just fifty cents. Emily wanted badly to poke him to let him know he should refuse it. No matter how innocent or nice this woman pretended to be, she had a really strange vibe. Emily instinctively didn't feel safe near her.

"Go on," the woman said, indicating the dollar with a casual wave of her hand. "You can even keep the change."

The young woman at the register looked confused. She glanced back and forth between John and the woman, her hand poised over the money on the counter as if she felt guilty for taking it. Finally, she scooped up the money, completed the sale, and counted the change out of the drawer, which she handed to the woman.

"Uhh—thanks," John said.

Emily noticed that he kept his head turned to one side, as though he didn't dare look directly at the woman. He pocketed his treats and started for the door, pushing past Emily.

"Have a nice evening," the woman said with forced cheerfulness. "Both of you."

Emily hurriedly followed her brother outside, but all the while, she could feel the woman's eyes fixed on her.

That's her! That's got to be her!

Fear flooded through her, and all she wanted to do was run down the road as fast as she could, but she knew she shouldn't do that. It would only let the woman know—for sure—that she was afraid of her, and somehow she knew she shouldn't let her fear show.

But why? Emily wondered. *What is it about her that's so upsetting?*

Night had fallen as they started back down the road for home. Far off in the distance, Emily could hear the chorus of spring peepers, but now the sound set her nerves on edge. She wanted desperately to run or fly down the road and be safely away from the store and that creepy woman. She didn't want to be anywhere in sight when she left the store.

But she knew that wasn't possible.

Emily was convinced the only reason that woman had even come into the store was to see her. She wasn't sure how she knew this, but she did.

John was several steps ahead of her. He stopped and turned to look back at her.

"You coming?" he called out, waving her on. "What the heck are you doing?"

Before they crossed the road, Emily glanced back at the store. In the parking lot was a third car. It hadn't been there when they had first gone into the store. She was sure of it. She admitted to herself that she had been looking for it.

But now it was there, parked at the far end of the lot near the trash Dumpster. It was a small, dark-colored car, either dark blue or black.

Emily recognized it immediately, and the recognition sent an icy jolt through her. Whimpering softly and clutching her bottle of iced tea to her chest, she broke into a run. She passed John and quickly left him in the dust. He yelled at her to wait up, but Emily kept running. Her brother's voice gradually faded into the night behind her as she ran and ran.

Wind tore at her face and burned in her lungs. The only sound she could hear was the rapid slap-slapping of her sneakers on the roadside.

And she ran and ran, convinced that she was running for her life.

"SHIT! God*damn* it!"

After the children had left the store, Susan had driven a short distance down the road toward Matt's house before pulling over and parking. Clenching both hands into tight fists, she repeatedly banged the steering wheel so hard the steering column vibrated like a huge tuning fork. Tears squeezed from her eyes, blurring her view of the road as she stared down the stretch of road where, just minutes ago, Emily—*My daughter!*—had disappeared around the corner.

Tremors racked her body like invisible hands that had a hold on her and were shaking her. She felt so weak and help-less and terribly alone.

Damn it, I blew it! I had my chance, and—goddamn—I blew it! She was right there, and I let her slip away. Maybe forever.

Susan took a long, steadying breath to calm herself, but it didn't do any good. Hot pressure filled her head.

"What could I have done?" she asked herself as frustration and pain raged inside her. Emily had been right there in front of her. All she had to do was say something—*anything*—to her, but she hadn't been able to do or say a goddamned thing.

What could I have said? "Hello, Emily. I'm your mommy, and I'm here to take you home with me."

Of course that wouldn't have worked.

Alice was right. She hadn't thought this through, and she was paying the price. But Susan knew it couldn't have worked, not with witnesses right there to see her and identify her later if—*No, not if . . . When!*—when she finally took Emily.

Her nerves crackled like overloaded electrical wires. It was almost impossible to take a deep breath, and all around her, she saw things moving in the dark. Through her misery, there was only one thing Susan was positive of now.

That's what has to happen.

She realized it had been a mistake to follow Emily to school and into the store. It was a mistake to be seen anywhere near her until she had it all figured out and was ready to do what she had to do. She also realized that it had been a colossal mistake to contact Matt in the first place. She should have known he'd be a prick about it. He would never let her see her daughter.

He stole her away from me, and he plans to keep her!

Susan was seething with rage so powerful it ached like a weight deep inside her chest. Things were getting bad, and maybe she should start to take her medication again, but that might cloud her mind. Maybe the meds were what made her do these wrong things. She was better off without them.

Something like that isn't going to happen again, she told herself. *No goddamned way.*

First thing, she was going to have to calm down and get control of herself. She had to think. She had to anticipate anything and everything that might happen because nothing—absolutely nothing—was more important than getting her daughter back.

It was perfectly clear to her now. She had to take Emily away from Matt, by force if necessary, and bring her . . .

Where?

As soon as Emily disappeared, Matt would know she had taken her, so she couldn't do anything or go anywhere predictable. Maybe she would go to Florida or Montana or someplace where Matt would never think to look for them.

Money would be a problem.

She had worked back in Iowa, and she had saved a substantial amount. Her mother had died just before she left for Maine. There was some life insurance money, but not a whole lot. What she had wasn't going to last indefinitely.

If money was a problem, though, guessing how Emily would react to all of this was an even bigger problem. Susan had to consider that her daughter might not want to go with her. She might try to get back home.

But only until I earn her trust and love, Susan thought.

At first, it was understandable that her daughter would be frightened of her. She had seen it in her demeanor tonight in the store. Emily had been terrified of even looking at her, as if she already knew.

"But I'll change all that," Susan whispered heatedly. She gritted her teeth so hard they made a low, grinding sound deep inside her head. Her hands were trembling, almost out of control, as she stared down the long, dark stretch of road where her daughter had gone.

She must be home by now, Susan thought, and a cold pain stabbed her heart.

Did she even recognize me? Will she say anything to her father about the strange lady who paid for her brother's treats? Will the boy say anything?

Even if they did, Susan decided, what would it really matter?

There was no way Matt would know it was her, not unless he got the cops or a private investigator involved, and they questioned the cashier.

And then, what can Matt do?

He'd threatened to get a restraining order against her, but that wasn't going to stop her. No half-assed court order was going to keep her away from Emily.

Not now.

Not after everything she had been through: the hospitalizations, the therapy, the medications, the AA meetings, her mother's gradual death from lung cancer. She had survived it all, and she was working hard to get herself together in spite of the diagnosis. She wasn't crazy. The doctors could use all sorts of fancy terms like *borderline personality* and *paranoid tendencies*, but those were all just ploys to keep her away from Emily.

Now nobody and nothing was going to get in her way.

With her headlights off, she sat parked on the side of the road for the better part of an hour, staring down the dark road as she thought about what she was going to do next. After a while, very gradually, the voices in her head quieted, and the tension seething inside her slowly ebbed away. She didn't remember when she started breathing evenly and deeply again and when the trembling in her stomach finally stopped. It was just that, at some point, she felt better. She could think clearly again.

From now on, she would plan everything carefully so she could get her daughter and get out of Maine before Matt suspected a thing. Once she and Emily were together, once she could talk to her daughter and make her see what was going on, how her father and other people had worked so hard to keep them apart, she was positive she could make Emily understand how important it was that they be together as mother and daughter.

"I'm trying my best, baby," she whispered. "I really am, and I'm not going to let them stop me."

The evening air was cool, and her breath made faint puffs of steam that drifted like smoke in front of her face before melting into the darkness. Her throat burned, and her eyes ached with a deep, hot, steady pressure. Worst of all, she found herself thinking about having a drink.

What would it hurt? Just one little drink to help me steady my nerves so I can think this through.

Inhaling sharply, she licked her lips, imagining the sharp sting of whiskey or the sweet taste of wine or beer on her tongue. She anticipated the slow, soothing rush as the booze flowed like syrup down her throat and hit her stomach like a warm, velvet glove. She didn't need any medication. It clouded her mind. Alcohol would help her see things clearly.

"What I wouldn't give for a drink."

Her voice sounded like someone else's in the dark car.

How bad could it be? she wondered. She could go back to the corner store and buy a six-pack of beer . . . maybe just a single bottle. She didn't need much.

"What difference would it make?" she asked aloud.

A deep tremor ran through her. The scratchy rawness of her voice surprised her in the darkness of her car. She jumped when a blast of headlights flooded the car, illuminating her from behind. Squinting and shielding her eyes with her hand, she dropped down, lying flat on the car seat and waiting for the car to pass by.

Was it the cops, coming to arrest her?

Panic almost choked her as she raised her head just enough to see a mud-splattered pickup moving past her. The brake lights flashed for an instant, but—thankfully—the truck didn't stop. Susan waited until the red taillights had dissolved into the darkness ahead before sitting back up. Her breathing was fast and shallow as she gripped the steering wheel with both hands.

She knew she should leave before anyone else noticed her parked on the side of the road like this. She couldn't stop her hand from trembling as she shifted into drive.

Go back to the motel, she told herself. *Don't do anything stupid, now. Get some sleep and think it all through, every bit of it.*

She knew that what she was planning to do was a crime, a federal offense as soon as she crossed the state line, but she didn't care. What did it matter? There were things more important than laws about so-called kidnapping.

She knew she could go to jail for it if she got caught. A small corner of her mind told her that it might be smart to forget all about Emily. After all these years, her daughter was a stranger to her, so why not let her be?

Why not go back and live the way you did without Emily in your life?

Now that it is too late for Emily to ever know her grandmother, why not let her live her life without knowing her real mother is still alive?

"Why? Because I love her and miss her," Susan answered herself.

As she stepped down on the accelerator, Susan knew that she wasn't going to listen to that tiny voice in her head. She drove down the road toward Matt's house, telling herself that she was just going to swing by the house once to check things out.

And after that . . . Who knew?

NINE

visitor

"**YOU** owe me at least half of that."

"No way. You didn't pay for it."

"The heck I didn't! I gave you all the change I had!"

"So what? That lady paid for it anyway!"

Sitting in the living room, Brenda squirmed on the couch as the faint voices coming from the family room steadily rose in volume. She glanced over at Cheryl, who seemed to be trying her best to pretend not to hear Emily and John squabbling. She raised her glass of wine to her lips and took a sip.

Brenda took a deep breath and, angry about the distraction, tried to remember what she had just been talking about. Reverend Hayne was due to come by in a few minutes to help her plan the funeral service. It was tough enough facing that without the quarrelling going on in the other room.

"Don't worry about them," Cheryl said with a wave of her hand. "They're just being kids."

"I know, but . . ." Brenda shook her head. "It's just . . . I had this terrible dream last night, and I didn't sleep well afterward . . ."

Cheryl nodded but didn't say anything as she held her wine up to the light and studied the burgundy color.

"I—dreamed—about my mother. I don't really believe in ghosts and stuff like that," she continued, "but it was . . ." She shook her head and made a low, whistling sound. "It was really weird."

"Are you sure it was her?"

Brenda thought for a moment, then shrugged. "No. Not really."

She shivered and stared blankly ahead as she tried to recall every detail of what she had experienced last night in her bathroom, and later in Emily's room. With a little distance, it did seem more like a half-remembered dream than anything real, but there also was an edge to it that seemed much *too* real.

"You're upset," Cheryl said. "Bad dreams are to be expected."

Brenda nodded. "But—"

"I put my money on the counter first."

"So what? It wasn't enough, anyway."

"Yeah, well so what?"

"So nothing! I just want a little bite. You owe me."

"Do not!"

"Do too!"

Brenda fought the urge to get up and go in there and holler at the kids to shut up. Why couldn't they appreciate what she was going through and stop bickering for one night? *Just one night!*

She closed her eyes for a moment and tried to block them out.

Cheryl took another long sip of wine, draining the glass. They both glanced over at the entryway to the living room when the voices from the family room rose again, louder and angrier.

"If that's the way you're gonna be, then you can't have it either."

"Oh, yeah?"

"Yeah!"

There was a brief scuffle, then the sound of something hitting the floor followed by a dull thud that Brenda knew was someone—probably John—hitting someone else—no doubt his sister.

"You little creep! I'm telling your mother."

"Go ahead!"

"You're gonna be in more trouble than I am. You're the one who talked to her."

"So what?"

"So . . . you're not supposed to talk to strangers."

"You jerk! Look what you did. Now it's ruined."

"Serves you right."

Unable to pretend any longer that the quarrel wasn't going on, Brenda gave her friend an apologetic smile and stood up.

"Sounds just like me and my brother when we were kids," Cheryl offered with a light laugh.

"I don't think anyone can get as bad as they do."

Brenda knew this was Cheryl's way of telling her that overhearing a little fussing between the kids didn't really bother her, but she was divorced and had never had children of her own, so what did she know?

"Are you saying sibling rivalry's normal?" Brenda asked.

"Absolutely. There are even psychologists who say it's essential to normal social development."

Brenda smiled with disbelief and shook her head as she walked out of the living room.

"Then maybe I'm due for a little less *normal*," she muttered to herself as she stepped into the hall.

As soon as she was on her way, there was, of course, a brief lull in the squabbling in the family room, so she hesitated in the kitchen. Glancing at the wall clock, she saw that it was a little past eight o'clock. Matt still wasn't home. She wished he were here so he could deal with the children while she and Cheryl talked. She couldn't help but wonder again what was going on with him. He was usually so patient and understanding, but ever since the night her mother died, he'd been acting differently, a little strange, almost like he was hiding something from her. She sensed that it wasn't just her mother's death that was upsetting him. There was something more.

But what?

Before she could consider it too much, the argument started up again.

"I'm not buying you another one, either."

"The heck you aren't!"

"What are you two squabbling about in here?" Brenda shouted as she burst into the family room.

John was on one side of the room by the sliding glass doors that led out onto the deck. He was holding a candy bar protectively to his chest while Emily stood by the fireplace. Her arms were folded defiantly, her face was flushed, and she was breathing heavily.

"Nothing," Emily said quickly, looking at her guiltily.

At the same instant, John shouted, "She smooshed my Baby Ruth."

"Did not!"

"Did too!"

John peeled back the wrapper and presented it to his mother.

"See?"

Brenda stifled a laugh. The crushed chocolate and nuts looked like the huge, messy turd of someone who had just wolfed down a can of Planter's peanuts.

She stepped into the room so she was between the two kids.

"Look, you guys," she said, lowering her voice, "my friend and I are waiting for your father and Reverend Hayne to get here so we can plan Grammy Swanson's funeral. Is it too much to ask you to get along for just one hour?"

"I will if he will," Emily said.

"She started it," John said, pouting as he pointed angrily at Emily. He looked up at his mother with tears gathering in his eyes, but when Brenda looked over at Emily, she caught him sticking his tongue out at his sister.

"I did not!" Emily yelled, louder than necessary. "All I did was ask him for a bite—just one little bite—because I helped him pay for it."

"Did not!"

"Did too!"

Brenda struggled to curb her impatience. She knew John, as the little brother, was a master at manipulating situations so he came out looking like the innocent victim when, at least half the time, he wasn't.

"Oh, really," Brenda said, staring at long and hard at her son. "Did Emily pay for it?"

For an uncomfortable moment, John didn't say anything, and Brenda caught the quick glance that flashed between brother and sister as though they had a shared secret.

"Well . . . yeah. Kinda," he finally said, letting his gaze drop as his shoulders slumped. When he lowered his hand to his side, the chocolate smeared his pants leg.

"So why not cut it in half and share it with your sister?" Brenda said, keeping her voice low and reasonable-sounding.

"Half of it?" John asked, looking like she'd just asked him to cut off his right arm.

"Yes. Half," Brenda said firmly. "We all share in this family."

It was bad enough that Cheryl had to hear her children going at it like this, but she wanted it to stop before the minister showed up. She felt guilty that she and her family usually attended church only on Christmas and Easter, if then. It didn't seem right, now that she needed help, that she had called Reverend Hayne to do her mother's funeral. He had, of course, been completely understanding and willing to help, but she would be humiliated if he heard her kids fighting.

"I don't want *any* of it now," Emily said, her upper lip curling in disgust. "Not after you were such a big baby about it."

"It's *your* fault it got smooshed."

"Please! Stop now," Brenda shouted. "I've had enough. Both of you go up to your rooms and be quiet. Leave each other alone for once, will you? Please?"

Emily looked at Brenda like she had something more to say but didn't quite dare to. After another quick glance at John, she lowered her gaze and said softly, "All right," and darted out of the room. Her footsteps skittered up the stairs.

Once she was gone, Brenda placed her hand on John's shoulder and gently propelled him in the same direction. She pretended not to notice as he trudged upstairs, his feet scuffling on the carpeted steps. With a heavy sigh, Brenda walked back into the living room and sat down. The couch was still warm where she'd been sitting.

"So, do you think I'm crazy or what?" Brenda asked.

"What, you mean about thinking you saw your mother?"

Cheryl shrugged. "I wasn't there. I didn't see what you saw, so I can't know for sure, but . . . no, I don't think you're crazy."

Brenda still felt as though their conversation was unresolved, but she didn't want to burden her friend with her worries, so she decided simply to make small talk until the minister and her husband showed up.

MOONLIGHT glazed the backyard like a scrim of blue ice. Against the star-filled sky, the line of pine trees stood out like a row of jagged teeth. Emily sat in the darkness of her bedroom, the window beside her desk wide open as she stared out at the night. The railing of the back deck glowed like a silver bar in the moonlight. From the wetlands out back there came the steady song of spring peepers.

Usually she found the sound relaxing, but right now, she was too upset to let it soothe her.

Why does John always get his way?

Her fury rose all the higher whenever she thought about how selfish her little brother was.

He's such a spoiled little brat!

Clenching both hands into fists, she pounded on the windowsill hard enough to make the heels of her hands ache.

She didn't like feeling this angry, and she couldn't help but wonder why it was like this so much of the time. It hadn't always been like this. Things had been so much better before John was born, before her father married Brenda. She'd had her father all to herself.

That's just the way it goes, Emily thought, but she knew it wasn't just moving out to the country that was upsetting her. It was everything.

Forcing herself to take slow, even breaths, Emily stared out at the moon-bright vista of the backyard until it swelled in her vision with every heartbeat.

Maybe it is just the move, and I'm missing my friends in town, she told herself.

That made sense.

Up until a few weeks ago, she had lived in the same house in town since she was a baby, first with her dad, and then with

Brenda and—finally—John. Now she was stuck out here in the sticks with absolutely *no one* to hang out with in walking distance except Manda, and her house was more than half a mile away. Not that she didn't like Manda or anything, but getting a ride into town so she be with all of her old friends was more of a problem than she had expected. Brenda was so busy putting the finishing touches on the new house that Emily hardly ever dared ask her to help her out when her father was at work. And her father was so busy at the new law office that she felt as though she never saw him.

"Things'll get better. . . . Things have to get better," she whispered to herself, but the loneliness she felt made her think that things might not get better, that from now on, no matter what she wanted or said or did, things were going to get a lot worse.

She was so lost in her thoughts that she jumped when she realized she had seen something moving in the shadows of the trees. She whimpered softly and leaned forward, her nose pressed against the window screen as she tried to bring her eyes into focus. So far, all she could see was a faint black smudge against the darkness beneath the trees. She thought she might have imagined it, but after a long, tense moment, it moved again, and Emily realized someone was outside.

"Oh my God," she whispered as chills rushed through her.

Shifting slowly and quietly, she dropped down so her eyes were on level with the windowsill. There was no breeze, so none of the shadows cast by the trees could be moving. The black smudge under the trees was perfectly still now, but Emily was tensed and waiting for it to move again.

It's got to be that woman, she thought with a strong flush of panic. *Who else could it be? Does she realize I can see her?*

The longer Emily stared at the spot under the trees, the harder it was for her to see clearly. The rapid pounding of her pulse in her neck made her vision jump with every beat.

Why is she after me?

She wanted desperately to call out to her father, to let him know something was wrong, but she remembered that he wasn't home yet. Besides, she knew, as soon as she moved or made a noise, the person—*That woman!*—would run away.

The best thing, Emily decided, was to just sit here and

watch to see what the woman did. Of course, if she already
knew Emily was watching her, if she could see her silhouette
in the upstairs window, this would become a contest to see
who would move first.

If there even is anyone out there, Emily thought.

Maybe her eyes were playing tricks on her, and she was
staring at nothing but a moon shadow? She could sit here all
night waiting for the woman to move.

If she really was out there!

Emily couldn't help but think that, no matter how long she
waited, the instant she looked away, the figure would disappear.

And then what?

Emily's mind filled with all sorts of terrible thoughts.
None of them, she knew, could really happen.

Could they?

Maybe she was scaring herself. Maybe she had watched a
few too many scary shows on TV, like *Buffy*, or she had read
too many *Goosebumps* books when she was a little girl. She
was just letting her imagination get carried away.

Right?

After a long while, the blacker-than-night shape beneath
the trees suddenly did move. When it did, Emily had no doubt
that it really was a person. She whimpered softly, wishing she
had the strength or courage to cry out. If her daddy had been
home and heard her, he'd come and protect her like he always
did, but he wasn't. The only adults in the house were Brenda
and her friend Cheryl, and Emily didn't want or need either
one of them helping her. She'd rather deal with this alone.

Emily had been holding her breath so long her chest began
to ache, so she let it out slowly, listening to the high, whistling
hiss. A wave of dizziness swept over her. Afraid she was going to faint, she tightened her grip on the windowsill, digging
her fingernails into the freshly painted wood.

"Go away," she whispered as her pulse thundered in her
ears. "Please. Just go away and leave me alone."

Emily crouched, afraid to move. Even the slightest hint of
motion would give her away.

If she hasn't already seen me.

For what seemed like forever, she knelt on the floor by the
window and stared outside, not even daring to blink. Finally,

the shadowy figure moved again, withdrawing deeper into the woods. Emily jumped when she heard a twig snap underfoot. In the darkness, it sounded as loud as a gunshot. A moment later, she realized the person was leaving because a car was approaching. A bright wash of headlights swept across the backyard.

Even knowing she was safe now, Emily couldn't find the courage to move. She sensed that the person was still watching her. She was convinced she could feel cold, unblinking eyes focused on her. Trembling, Emily willed herself to stand up, but she couldn't. Her ribs throbbed from the pain of holding her breath too long. Her arms and legs felt rubbery and useless.

Straining to hear in the dark, Emily waited, listening as a car door opened and slammed shut. Then footsteps came up the walkway to the side door. Emily jumped when the doorbell rang, then relaxed, realizing it must be the minister her stepmother was waiting for.

Faintly, from downstairs, Emily heard Brenda go to the door and open it.

"Oh, good evening, Reverend Hayne." Brenda's voice was muffled with distance. "Thanks so much for coming by."

Emily snorted at the sound of Brenda's voice. The tone of fake hospitality irritated her. The minister said something unintelligible, and then their voices faded as they moved into the living room.

That left Emily alone with the shadowy figure somewhere out there in the darkness.

Can she see me? Is she still out there, watching me?

She wished she could find the courage to move away from the window, but she was frozen where she crouched.

What does she want? she wondered.

Still frightened, Emily stayed huddled against the wall as she watched and waited for her father to come home. Only then would she feel safe.

MATT got home just as Reverend Hayne was leaving. While they made small talk in the kitchen, he heated a pizza in the microwave. He was polite but distant with both Cheryl and the minister, responding mostly in monosyllables even when Brenda told him what they had decided on for the funeral service. His distance irked Brenda, but she didn't say anything until Cheryl and the minister had left.

"What's bugging you, hon?" Brenda asked, coming over to him and giving him a gentle hug once they were alone.

He looked at her, his eyes flat. His hands rested on the table beside his empty plate.

"Nothing," he replied. "Just work," but Brenda could tell it was more than that. Something was wrong.

Once he was finished eating, he put his dishes into the dishwasher, and they went upstairs to bed. Brenda was feeling exhausted and emotionally drained, and more than ready to try to get some sleep, but once she and Matt got into bed and turned out the lights, she surprised herself by rolling toward him. She started rubbing his chest with the flat of her hand.

Matt responded, as he always did, by sighing deeply and lying flat on his back while her hand explored the smooth curves of his body. Brenda was glad for that, and she nuzzled her face into the crook of his neck, deeply inhaling his rich, musky scent. Her hand started making wider circles across his skin, smoothing over the soft strip of fuzz that marked the centerline of his belly. Then her hand went lower and gently took hold of him, squeezing gently.

"Feel like getting lucky tonight?" she whispered. Her heated breath rebounded into her face off his neck.

Matt sighed but didn't say a word. He didn't even move as she clasped him more tightly and began stroking him up and down with a firm, steady pressure. He stiffened in her hand, and all the tension and sadness of the day seemed to disappear as she reveled in the firm hardness of his penis. Shifting over onto her side, she propped herself up on her elbow and nudged the covers aside so she could lower her head and kiss his chest. Her tongue darted out and playfully licked his nipples before gradually circling lower down his stomach.

Feeling her passion rising, Brenda moaned softly as she explored her husband's body. They had known each other for more than eight years now, and she was still amazed how new and exciting it felt whenever she touched him like this. She gloried in the waves of heat radiating off his body. As she moved her head lower, she inhaled deeply, enjoying the rich, warm smell of his body. Then, flicking her tongue across the tip of his penis, she shifted around so she was straddling his lower legs, pinning him down.

By now, Matt was fully erect and pressing against her, but she suddenly realized that he was curiously immobile. He barely moved when she took him full into her mouth and started running her tongue up and down the shaft of his penis. Frowning, she pulled her head back and sat up. In the diffuse light of their bedroom, she glared at him.

"Are you okay?" she asked, her voice husky with emotion and restrained anger.

Matt sighed deeply, making it clear that no, everything *wasn't* okay.

"What is it, baby?" she whispered, moving so his chin rested on the top of her head and her face pressed into his armpit. The lingering scent of his deodorant filled her nostrils. Her fingers continued to make tiny loops in his chest hairs, but the mood was already broken. Her excitement melted away.

"Nothing," Matt said at last. "Just . . . stuff."

"Stuff," Brenda echoed. "What do you mean, *stuff?*"

"I dunno. Just . . . stuff," Matt replied hollowly. He shrugged in the darkness, making the mattress shift with the motion.

"Is this *stuff* you want to talk about, or is it *stuff* you want to keep to yourself?"

She chastised herself for sounding sarcastic, but Matt had maintained his silence long enough for it to hurt her. She had always prided herself on the fact that they were open and honest with each other and talked things out no matter what was bothering them. Since they first started dating, they had been through a lot together, and they had always talked things out.

Why is he clamming up like this now?

It certainly seemed as though Matt had avoided being with her all day. He'd left her to handle the funeral home herself, he came home late from work, and just now—no matter what he might say—he had rejected her.

"Is this about the funeral?" she asked.

Matt's arm had been resting flat on the mattress. Now he raised it and gently rubbed her exposed shoulder as he took another, deeper breath. Brenda's head rose and fell as he breathed.

"No. Not really," he finally said.

"Okay, then. What?"

There was another long silence, broken only by the sound of spring peepers coming in through their open bedroom windows. Brenda's eyes were stinging with tears, but she told herself not to cry. She'd cried too much the past couple days already, but she couldn't deny the cold, empty feeling inside her.

"You going to talk about it, or are you going to bottle it all up inside?" Her voice was husky with emotion. "Remember how you said we wouldn't keep anything from each other?" She paused long enough to let her words sink in, then added, "So talk to me. Tell me what's going on?"

"It's just . . ." Matt sighed again, louder. "I don't know. A lot of things piling up, I guess."

Brenda sensed the distance in his voice and knew that he was wishing he could be far away from here right now.

"Is it anything I can help you with?"

"Not really," Matt said, sounding a touch exasperated.

Finally, Brenda rolled away from him and sagged back on the bed, yanking the sheets up over her shoulders. One part of her was telling her just to drop it, that Matt would tell her what was going on when he was ready to. But another part of her, a louder part, was telling her to draw it out of him now, even if it was as painful as extracting a rotten tooth.

"So . . . ?" she said, trying hard to keep the pain out of her voice; she felt as though she didn't succeed very well.

The mattress creaked loudly as Matt rolled over onto his side and looked at her in the darkness. His eyes glowed in the dim light as he raised his hand and placed it gently on her shoulder, then slid it around her back and pulled her close. He inhaled sharply as though in pain. Brenda waited, expecting that he might start crying, but he didn't.

"Is it about my mother?" she asked, her voice a trembling whisper that brushed against the darkness. "I mean, I know you and she didn't have the best relationship in the world, but are you feeling, like—you know, guilty that you didn't try harder to connect with her?"

"Of *course* that's part of it," Matt replied.

"Part of it?"

Without saying anything more, he pulled her even closer, but Brenda felt no passion in his embrace. After another lengthy silence, he said, "Let's just forget about it for now, okay?"

"No, Matt. It's not okay. I'm your wife. You can tell me anything . . . anything at all."

She eased out of his embrace and sat up in bed, staring at him in the darkness. For an instant, Matt's face seemed to shift, his features morphing into something else, a face she didn't recognize.

A quaking shiver shot up her spine.

This isn't happening! Am I dreaming again?

She sucked in a breath and held it as she waited for Matt to answer her. She tried to ignore the steadily rising fear that, when he spoke, it wouldn't be Matt's voice she heard.

"Just drop it for now, all right?" he said.

He sounded weary and strangely closed off from her, but Brenda felt at least a slight measure of relief hearing his voice, not someone else's. But there was a rift opening up between them, and she was suddenly afraid that it might be serious enough that they might not be able to close it.

"Please, honey. Talk to me," she pleaded.

But Matt had shut down. Closing his eyes, he rolled away from her, pulling the blankets with him. His body was rigid with tension.

Brenda lay motionless for a long time, listening to her pulse in her ears as she waited for him to say something . . . any-thing, but Matt remained stone silent. After a while, his breath-ing became shallow and rapid, but she knew he wasn't asleep. Finally, however, she gave up and settled down in the bed.

He'll talk to me when he's ready to, she decided as she shifted onto her side away from him and squeezed her eyes closed before she started crying again. She couldn't cry anymore tonight.

As she tried to drift off to asleep, a single thought kept echoing in her mind.

Am I losing him? Oh, dear God, am I losing him?

TEN

message

WHAT *a perfect day for a funeral,* Brenda thought.

She was sitting at the oval table in the breakfast nook, drinking coffee—her third this morning—and staring out at the lowering, gray clouds above the trees. Dense, tangled shreds of mist wove like scarves of smoke through the woods that bordered the backyard. The pine trees, their trunks looking moldy and black with dampness, dripped silver beads of water from every needled tip.

It was a little before noon. The funeral service at First Lutheran church wasn't until two o'clock, but Brenda had gotten ready well ahead of time. She was wearing a black dress with the silver cross pendant her mother had given her as a high school graduation present. For the last hour or more, she had been ready to leave, but everyone else was upstairs still getting ready. She could hear the back-and-forth tread of footsteps as Matt, Emily, and John shuffled from bathroom to bedroom. Every now and then one of the kids would start complaining. Usually it was John, insisting that he would rather go over to a friend's house instead of attending the funeral, even if it was for Grammy Swanson.

Brenda experienced a curious sense of detachment as she listened to the activity upstairs. Her thoughts were as bleak as the day, but the shock of her loss was receding, and the intensity of her sorrow had shrunken to little more than a steady, cold emptiness inside her. She was still concerned about Matt and why he hadn't been more open with her about what was bothering him, but for now, all she wanted to do was get through the funeral. She had already cried herself dry, but she was sure she'd probably break down all over again during the service.

She realized she probably shouldn't be drinking so much coffee. At the very least, she would have to go to the bathroom, probably in the middle of the service. At worst, it would jangle her already overwrought nerves, like now, when even the slightest commotion from upstairs made her grit her teeth and wish she didn't have to face what she had to face today.

"But you do," she whispered to herself, "and you'll get through it."

For what seemed like the thousandth time, she glanced at the kitchen clock. Time seemed to be frozen solid, like an insect trapped in amber.

Are the hands on the clock even moving?

The light in the kitchen steadily darkened as the clouds thickened and lowered. Rain was falling more heavily now, pattering on the roof and bouncing like fat silver bullets off the sundeck floor and railing. She considered turning on the overhead light but decided that sitting here in the gathering gloom suited her mood best.

It gave her time to think, time to remember her mother, time to begin to push aside her memories of the fights and disagreements they'd had over the years and make them better.

And it gave her time to think about the good times, such as they were. A twinge of guilt shot through her, and she reminded herself that of course there had been good times. Every family, even the most screwed-up family in the world, has to have some good times!

"It's just that I can't remember many of them," she said, and her eyes prickled with tears. The clearest memories were all tinged with sadness and hurt, and they left a bitter taste in the back of her mouth.

A single tear spilled from her eye and ran in a slippery, warm track down her cheek. She wiped it away, grasped her coffee cup, and steadied her hand as she took a tiny sip. The coffee had gone cold a long time ago, but she didn't care. All she cared about was getting through today.

"Then the next day . . . and the next," she whispered, repressing a deep shiver. After today, things would start getting better.

"But Dad-d-d. Mike's mother said I could!"

Upstairs, John's voice rose to an irritatingly high pitch, what Brenda called his "tippy-toe voice." She cringed and couldn't stop herself from thinking that someday in the future, John was going to have to handle her funeral.

How will he feel when he has to face losing his mother? Will he remember how much he was complaining today?

She hoped there wouldn't be nearly as much hurt and misunderstanding between her and her son as there had been between her and her mother.

"Well, I don't care what Mrs. Peterson says." Matt's voice boomed in the hallway. "You're not going over there. You're going to the funeral whether you want to or not, and that's final!"

"But it's stupid! The whole thing is *stupid!*"

Matt's voice dropped too low for Brenda to hear what he said next, and that was just as well. She couldn't stand to hear her son or Emily or anyone else complain about what they were doing today. She had the biggest burden to carry, so she didn't care if anyone else liked it or not. They were just going to have to hang in there for her.

Leaning back in her chair, she closed her eyes and started rubbing them so vigorously, bright splotches of light trailed across her sight. Hypnotized, she watched them for a while, letting the muted voices coming from upstairs fade into the distance as glowing globs of blue, red, and purple light twisted across the darkness of her closed eyes, keeping time with her pulse. At some point—she wasn't sure when—she realized that she wasn't breathing deeply enough, so she took a long, steady inhalation. The wash of cool air rushed into her lungs like water.

She moaned softly, wishing the pain and grief would go away if only for a little while.

As she stared into the pulsing darkness behind her closed

eyelids, she suddenly became aware that something around her had changed subtly. There was a peculiar energy or feeling in the air. She couldn't quite identify it, but she sensed it. Her body tensed, and she cringed, fighting an urge to open her eyes and look around; but she kept her eyes closed, knowing that, if she opened them now, she wouldn't be able to stop herself from crying out.

But why? What's the matter?

She took a shuddering breath and tried to focus on the weird feeling. After a few anxious seconds, it hit her: *Someone's watching me!*

The thought touched her like the teasing touch of unseen hands brushing lightly down the back of her neck. A prickling sensation washed through her, and she was suddenly terrified. Now she didn't dare open her eyes to look, yet she was afraid to keep them shut, too. The sounds from upstairs had faded away to nothing as panic surged up inside her. She stared into the swelling darkness of her closed eyes and experienced the peculiar feeling that somehow she could see through her eyelids and was staring at the impenetrable blackness that filled a cold, silent room.

Or a coffin!

That terrible thought filled her with dread.

The black emptiness she was staring at, no matter how thick, wasn't nearly as deep and dense as the darkness her mother was staring into—right now—and would stare into for the rest of eternity.

Fear spiked inside her with cold intensity. A faint, steady hissing sound filled her head, and it took her several heartbeats to realize that it was the falling rain. She wanted desperately to open her eyes and look around if only to convince herself that everything was normal, but she was more frightened by what she might see than she was of staring into the pulsating, sizzling darkness.

"Oh, dear God," she whispered, her voice almost lost beneath the sound of the falling rain.

She realized that, on some level, it didn't matter if her eyes were open or closed; this empty, scared feeling wasn't going to go away no matter what she did. With her eyes still closed and covered by her hands, she imagined that someone she couldn't see—*That old woman . . . that ghost I saw!*—was standing behind her and reaching out to take hold of her.

Somehow, she found the courage to lower her hands and open her eyes. Squinting in the dim light of day, she looked around the kitchen. Her view was distorted by a dense, watery blur that made everything look insubstantial.

And then she realized: *Someone really is watching me!*

The sense she'd had that someone was standing behind her was even stronger. The creepy, tingly feeling that someone was staring at her, and hands she couldn't see were reaching out for her became suddenly too intense to bear. With a muffled cry, she turned around quickly and looked at the kitchen doorway, hoping to see her husband or one of the kids standing there, but she was alone, absolutely alone, except for the sensation of an unseen presence watching her.

She took a shuddering breath, but the feeling didn't go away. With each passing second, it got stronger.

Is there someone outside in the backyard?

Brenda took another deep breath, ignoring the sharp pain that lanced between her ribs, and stared out at the rain-soaked woods. The clouds were lower now, drifting like billows of smoke above the pines. Underneath the trees, the shadows were dense and ink-black. No matter where she looked, everything seemed to be alive with menace. She could easily imagine that any one of those indistinct, dark shapes out there could be a person, crouching in the dampness and watching.

Watching me!

Shivering, she hugged herself and leaned back in the chair. Her eyes jerked back and forth as she scanned the backyard, but all she could see were wet rocks, trees, bushes, and mounds of damp pine needles and rotting logs. The steady hissing of rain lessened for a moment, and the sudden silence inside the house seemed dense and timeless.

Brenda wanted to get up and go upstairs so she could be with her husband, but she didn't dare move. She felt so lost and vulnerable, and she knew it had to be more than grief.

As she turned toward the kitchen doorway again, she glimpsed a reflection in the teakettle on the stove. It was fleeting, so quick it was gone before she realized it was there, but it was enough to send an electric jolt of fear through her.

Her own reflection was distorted in the rounded chrome of the teakettle, but behind her, she had seen something else: an indistinct figure, standing in the doorway. The figure's face was averted, so she couldn't see it clearly, but it was instantly familiar. She stopped breathing and, leaning forward, focused on the chrome teakettle, trying to see if the figure was still there. She hoped it was only an illusion, a trick of the eye, but after a heartbeat or two, the image resolved.

She's in the doorway, right behind me!

Shock immobilized Brenda.

It looked like an old woman, hunched over as though crippled with arthritis. Her long, gray hair hung in stringy clumps that framed her face.

And her face!

As Brenda watched, the woman raised her head slowly. Her eyes this time were deep, dark hollows, like smudges of soot within the pasty white wrinkles of her skin. One side of her face was marred by a long, tangled scar that ran from her scalp, down past her eye, to her chin. In the reflection, Brenda wasn't sure if it was the right side or the left.

Oh God!

Her fear was palpable. It filled the air in the kitchen with a weird, static charge that raised goose bumps on her arms. No matter how hard Brenda tried to convince herself that she had to be imagining this, it had to be an illusion, the terrible feeling of someone behind her wouldn't go away. Stunned, she watched with rising horror as the figure shifted closer behind her and leaned down as though about to whisper into her ear.

Somehow—she had no idea how—Brenda tore her gaze away from the reflection in the teakettle and started to turn around. For a dizzying instant, her panic crested, and the hard pounding of her pulse made it impossible for her to focus. A loud whooshing sound filled her ears, and she couldn't take a deep enough breath. Her lungs were screaming for air. She expected, before she could turn all the way around, to feel cold hands grasp her by the throat and start to squeeze until the air and life left her.

She realized she was making a low whimpering sound deep inside her chest. As much as she anticipated the cold touch of death before she could turn around, it didn't come. Her vision shifted into focus, and she gasped as she stared at the empty doorway behind her.

There was no one there.

Of course there isn't, she told herself. *How could there be?*

But Brenda felt no relief. The chills deep inside her hadn't subsided, and even though the hallway was empty, the feeling that someone was still watching her didn't go away. Somewhere, someone still lurked unseen behind her, shifting out of sight whenever she turned to look.

"God help me, am I losing my mind?" she whispered as she looked around the kitchen.

The sound of footsteps on the stairs drew her attention. Sucking in a shallow breath, she stared at the doorway until she saw her husband. Her body snapped with subtle electrical jolts that made it impossible for her to move. In stunned relief, she gazed with wide eyes at Matt. She opened her mouth as if about to say something, but she couldn't make a sound.

"Are you all right?" Matt asked, his face softening with concern as he moved closer to her.

Brenda twitched involuntarily as his arms encircled her and drew her close. The solid strength she felt, the warmth and comfort of his embrace, was almost too much for her. As she collapsed into his arms, hugging him desperately, she let out all of the grief, loneliness, and fear in a long, agonized moan.

ALL through her mother's funeral, Brenda was functioning on automatic at best. It was the only way she could cope with it. As she greeted friends, neighbors, and long-distant relatives, she knew her smile was plastered on her face like the overdone cosmetic job the mortician had done on her mother.

She suffered through John's and Emily's fidgeting during the service, and choked up and cried during the eulogy. While planning the service, Reverend Hayne had asked if she would like to say a few words, but she had declined. There was no way she could have stood up in front of all these people and said what was in her heart. She would have had to resort to platitudes.

During the drive out to the cemetery, Brenda began to feel marginally better. At least the worst was behind her. All she had to face now was the interment and then the little get-together they had planned at the house for family and close friends. Cheryl, Deb, Renee, and a few other friends had prepared sandwiches and refreshments. If they got back to the house by four o'clock, she figured everyone would be gone by six or seven at the latest.

Once the get-together was done, Brenda hoped things would get back to normal. The only difference was, her mother would no longer be a part of her life. Beyond the sadness of death, Brenda felt a sense of liberation after all the hoops they'd had to jump through with the nursing home, Social Security, and Medicaid.

The rain had let up while they were in the church, and during the drive out to the cemetery, the clouds started to break up, carried away by a strong, westerly breeze. When they arrived at the cemetery, the hearse parked close to the gravesite. Matt and the other pallbearers hefted the polished coffin out of the back of the hearse and carried it up to the freshly dug grave. People waited in their cars before solemnly walking up the slope to the gravesite.

The cemetery lawn was well trimmed. The grass was slick, and the ground was squishy underfoot from the recent rain. Brenda followed close behind the casket, all the while looking straight ahead and ignoring the people around her except for Matt, John, and Emily. Her breath caught in her throat whenever she glanced at her mother's coffin. Low staging and a heavy green cloth drape surrounded the grave so no one would actually have to look down into the cement-lined hole. The beige canvas awning the funeral director had erected in case of bad weather flapped like large bird wings in the gusty breeze.

With his hands folded and his head bowed, Reverend Hayne waited patiently by the side of the grave until the mourners were gathered. An eerie silence settled over the group, broken only by the steady hissing of the wind high in the trees. Brenda stood between Matt and John, clasping each of their hands tightly for fear that she might have another panic attack and faint. Emily positioned herself on the other side of her father, her right arm wrapped tightly around his waist, her face pressed against his side. People spoke in quiet murmurs until Reverend Hayne cleared his throat and began the burial service.

"We are gathered here today," he said, "to celebrate the life of Denise Swanson, not to mourn her death, because we come here secure in the knowledge that she is now reunited with her Lord and Savior, Jesus Christ."

As full and resonant as the minister's voice was, Brenda thought it sounded rather weak when measured against the vast, dreary expanse of the cemetery. All around her, polished gravestones glistened from the fresh rain. She couldn't help glancing at the mourners and wondering what they were thinking.

Are they thinking about my mother, remembering her life, or are they struggling with their own fears as they contemplate the cold, hard fact that someday, eventually, friends and relatives of theirs will gather like this for them?

Brenda cringed when she chanced a quick glance at Matt. His eyes were brimming with tears that he didn't bother to wipe away. When the minister asked everyone to pray, Brenda released her grip on Matt's and John's hands and, folding her hands, bowed her head. But as Reverend Hayne intoned the prayer for the burial service, she raised her eyes and looked up at the tatters of storm clouds as they rapidly receded. It filled her with a deep, unfathomable sadness and awe at the mystery of it all. It wasn't just acknowledging that someday she would die. Just as she had in the kitchen that morning, she was almost overwhelmed by a deep sense of loss, of acknowledging missed opportunities and ineffable sadness for things that could never be. Sadness stabbed deep into her mind and heart, but there was something more . . . something she couldn't identify.

What is it? What the hell am I feeling? Or am I too numb to feel?

As the service continued, the minister's words blended into a meaningless buzz. The air had a fresh ozone snap to it, and as the clouds blew away, sunlight lit the landscape with a strobelike flickering of light and shadow. No matter what she looked at, it seemed to take on a hallucinatory crispness. Brenda found herself squinting from the throbbing pain of a headache as she looked past the small scene of their mourning and focused on a stand of cypress trees across the road.

There was someone standing in the shade of the trees.

The person was stooped and indistinct. His or her face was shadowed by the trees, but the sight sent a chill through Brenda.

Who is that?

She gazed down at the person—a woman, she now realized.

The woman stood motionless, watching them and seeming to stare straight at—

Me!

Brenda felt uneasy and shifted her position. The woman's gaze bored into her like a laser beam.

As her panic rose, Brenda couldn't even hear what the minister was saying until a loud, rattling sound drew her attention. She turned to see that he was sprinkling a handful of dirt and gravel onto the dark, polished wood of the coffin while intoning the passage about "dust to dust." The dirt bounced off the brass rails and fell into the gaping hole into which the coffin would be lowered once everyone had left.

"Go in peace," Reverend Hayne said, turning to look at the mourners as he raised his arms and spread them wide for the blessing. "May the Lord strengthen and preserve you. May His face shine down upon you and give you peace. In the name of the Father, the Son, and the Holy Ghost. Amen."

As soon as the service was concluded, most of the mourners started silently down the slope to their cars after offering their condolences. Many of them would be dropping by the house later, and Brenda couldn't help but think that it had been just a few days ago when everyone was there to celebrate their housewarming.

And now, how things have changed!

Moving slowly, as if in a dream, still feeling the stranger's gaze fixed upon her, Brenda clasped Matt's hand and started with him down the slope to their car, averting her eyes. John and Emily followed silently beside them. As they got close to the car, Brenda looked again toward the cypress trees, ready to confront the person watching her.

The person was gone.

Brenda wasn't sure which would have been worse: seeing her still there, or realizing that she had left or—maybe—had never even been there.

Could it have been a ghost? What if it was my mother's spirit, watching her own funeral?

That thought unnerved Brenda so much she stumbled and would have fallen if Matt hadn't quickly tightened his grip on her arm and supported her.

Is that possible? Could that really have been my mother I saw in the kitchen this morning and then again out here?

But, when she considered it, Brenda had the impression that the figure under the cypress trees had looked different. The woman under the trees had appeared a bit taller and was not as slight as her mother. Also, in the quick glimpse she'd had of her, Brenda thought that the woman was leaning to one side as though favoring her left leg.

If she had really been there at all.

It was possible she might actually be having a breakdown. The thought coiled like a snake inside her. She leaned heavily against Matt, hoping to find strength in his closeness. Glancing at her, he smiled reassuringly, but Brenda recalled how distant he had been with her last night, and she wasn't sure she entirely trusted him. Even if she told him what she was going through, he probably wouldn't understand.

You must be going crazy when you start seeing things that aren't there.

A cloying, sour taste filled Brenda's mouth, and her stomach convulsed. She was suddenly sure she was going to vomit as a cold, clammy sensation gripped her stomach and a sheen of sweat broke out across her face.

"Matt, I . . ." Her voice trailed off as she drew to a halt and looked at him. She was filled with a desperate need to say or do something so this feeling would pass.

"What is it, hon?" Matt asked, looking at her with nothing but love and caring in his eyes. He put both hands on her shoulders and stared intently into her eyes. His lips moved as he said something else, but Brenda only heard a sludgy, dragging sound like a tape recording being played at slow speed.

"I—" she started to say, but that was all she got out.

The depth and confusion of what she was feeling and a sudden sense of absolute isolation crashed down on her. All the strength left her body as she started to black out. Blinking her eyes rapidly, she tried desperately to focus on her husband, hanging on to consciousness, but the pressure of a burden she could no longer carry crushed her down. Her knees buckled, and when she took another step, she staggered and started to fall. The world whirled around her like an insane merry-go-round as she let go of Matt's hand and spun away from him. She felt for an instant like she was flying and then, with a trailing groan, she crumpled onto the wet grass. She never felt the impact.

"Brenda!"

Matt's voice, sounding impossibly far away, echoed in her ears. A tiny part of her wanted to laugh at herself for fainting at a funeral, but the fleeting thought that she might be dying— might actually already be dead and not know it yet—sapped what strength remained as she spiraled down . . . down . . . down into the safe, warm arms of unconsciousness.

"GOD, I feel like such a jerk."

"You're not a jerk. You fainted. That's all."

"Yeah, but I . . ." Brenda shook her head. "I should have been able to hold it together better than that. I—"

With a heavy sigh, she covered her face with both hands. She still felt weak, but the embarrassment was much worse. She had regained consciousness seconds after collapsing onto the wet grass. She found herself looking up at Matt, who was leaning over her and gently patting her cheek. He had the most pathetic expression she had ever seen.

"I . . . Help me get up," she said as she shifted her legs underneath her and struggled to stand.

With Matt's help, she made it to her feet, but her legs still felt wobbly. She looked around the cemetery, surprised that the world seemed to have changed in the short time she had been unconscious.

Everything looked like it was back to normal.

The sun was shining through the last remnants of the rain

clouds. It felt warm and pleasant on her face. The grass and trees glistened with fresh rain, but they no longer had the brilliant, hallucinatory edge they'd had before. Most of the mourners hadn't even noticed what had happened and had already departed, but some of them, Reverend Hayne included, clustered around her, their faces marked with concern. Emily and John were standing off to one side, both of them, especially John, looking frightened and confused.

"You gonna be all right, Mom?" he asked, fighting a nervous quaver in his voice.

"Yes. Of course she is," Matt said without looking at him. "Take a few deep breaths, hon," he said to Brenda. "Clear your head before you try to walk."

He was holding her left arm tightly and, although Brenda was confident that she could stand without his assistance, the support felt good.

"Thanks," she said weakly as she turned to Matt and smiled at him.

On impulse, she leaned forward, wrapped her arms tightly around him, drew him close, and kissed him full on the lips. After a few seconds, she broke the kiss off. Matt pulled back and looked at her, surprise and confusion registering in his expression.

"Well," he said with an embarrassed laugh. "I guess you're feeling better."

Brenda moaned softly and kept hugging him close, reveling in his warmth. Tilting her head back, she brought her mouth close to his ear and whispered, "Thanks . . . for everything. I really do love you."

Matt pulled back and smiled at her, then reached out and traced a light touch across her cheek.

"I love you, too."

Brenda turned and bent down to give John a big hug. He trembled in her embrace, and she wished there was something she could say to help him get over his worry for her. It must have been terrifying for him to see her drop like that. Even Emily looked upset.

Side by side, with the children on either side of them, they walked down to the car and got in. The cemetery workers stayed behind to fill in the grave once everyone was gone. A few people didn't know how to get to the new house, so Matt started up the car and pulled away, making sure everyone was following him.

"**WHAT** the hell?"

Matt stepped down hard on the brakes as he pulled into the driveway. The car skidded to a stop at an odd angle in front of the garage doors.

Brenda started to chastise him for swearing in front of the kids, but when she looked up and saw what was wrong, she fell silent.

As they were rounding the last curve on Collette Road, Matt had pressed the garage door opener, so the heavy door was rattling up as they pulled into the driveway. What caught their attention was the side door of the house.

It was wide open.

A wide splash of mud and a smeared footprint marred the fresh white paint of the door.

"Someone broke in," Matt said with an edge of disbelief in his voice.

The latch plate was hanging down from a single, twisted screw. The edge of the doorframe was split all the way to the top of the jamb.

"No one's getting out of this car," Brenda said as she desperately fished in her purse for the cell phone. "Not until I call the police."

"What is it?" Emily asked from the backseat. Brenda noticed the frantic tone of her voice.

John said nothing as he shifted forward and, resting his arms on the back of the front seat, looked out the front window. His round, pale face was pinched with fear.

"Nothing serious, I hope," Matt replied grimly.

He glanced into the rearview mirror and saw the line of cars pulling to a stop at the top of the driveway and in front of the house. Ignoring Brenda's advice, he opened the driver's door and stepped out. Before he swung the car door shut, he leaned back inside and looked earnestly at the kids in the backseat.

"You guys stay right where you are, understand?" He inhaled sharply as he glanced over his shoulder at the house, then looked at Brenda. "It's probably nothing, but I want to check it out first."

"The hell you will!" Brenda shouted, glaring at him. "You're not going in there!" She had already dialed 911 and was holding the cell phone up to her ear, waiting for an answer. Her eyes were frantic. "You're not going *anywhere* until the police get here!"

"Don't be ridiculous," Matt said, scowling at her.

He knew she was right. It would be much smarter to wait, but he was pretty sure it was safe. The mud on the door had been there awhile. It was already drying dull yellow in the warmth of the sun following the rain.

"Whoever it was, they're long gone," he said, smiling tightly to reassure her. He knew it wouldn't do any good. After what they had just been through, he knew Brenda's nerves were fried. He didn't need anything else to upset her.

Straightening up, he turned and looked at Ed Lewis, who had parked at the top of the driveway and was waddling toward them.

"Something the matter?" he asked.

Matt indicated the broken side door. Ed froze, then glanced at Brenda and the children in the car.

"Let's check it out," Matt said.

"You got a gun?" Ed asked.

Matt almost laughed out loud. Under different circumstances, he would have, but he shook his head and said, "Of course not."

"How about in the house? Anything someone could use against you?"

"Not unless they brought it with them."

"That's why you're not going in there," Brenda said, cupping the cell phone in her hand. "They might still be in there, and they could have a gun."

Ed grimaced and shook his head. "I always say it's better to have a gun and not need it than need it and not have it."

Brenda opened the passenger's door and got out. As she walked around the car, her face was lined with worry but also was set with determination.

"The police are on their way," she said. "And you're not going in there until they get here."

"I agree," Ed said.

Matt regarded them both for a lengthening moment, then placed his hands on his hips and scowled. He had a pretty good idea what this was all about, but he didn't dare say anything to Brenda about it.

"This is *my* house, goddamnit, and some scumbag broke into it."

He felt an almost primal urge to protect and defend what was his. Now he wished he'd listened to Brenda when she had argued for having a security system installed along with the smoke detectors. Eventually this would turn into an "I told you so."

"Closing the barn door after the cow got out," Matt said to himself.

"What's that?" Brenda asked.

"Nothing," Matt replied, lowering his gaze.

He was seething with frustration, but he was certain any danger had passed. The intruder—and he had no doubt who it had been—wasn't in the house.

He could feel it.

The police would get here and make sure the house was safe before Brenda and the kids went inside. Then, at their leisure, they could take inventory to see if anything was missing.

"We'll have to cancel the get-together," Brenda said quietly, her brow creased with worry as she glanced up the slope at the cars parked in front of the house.

Matt considered for a moment, then nodded.

In the fifteen minutes it took for the police to get to the house, he and Brenda went from car to car and explained what had happened. Everyone said they understood, and many of their friends offered to wait with them, but Matt insisted that everything was fine, that the police would take care of the situation. Before she left, Cheryl made Brenda promise to call her as soon as the police were gone and things were settled.

When the two patrolmen drove up with their blue cruiser lights flashing, Matt took them aside and quickly explained what was going on. With their service revolvers drawn, the policemen entered the house while Matt, Brenda, and Ed waited outside with the kids. After a few minutes, one of them—Officer Stockwell, his badge said—came back outside, his expression dour.

"Would you come inside with me, Mr. Ireland?" he asked. His voice sounded tight, and Matt knew something was wrong. This cop seemed a little out of his depth.

"What's wrong?" Brenda snapped.

Officer Stockwell glanced at her and said, "If you don't mind, I'd like you and the children to stay in the car while I speak with your husband."

Brenda shot Matt a worried glance, but he shrugged and silently followed the policeman back into the house. His stomach was knotted with tension and anticipation.

"Whoever did this has already left the premises," Officer Stockwell said as they walked through the garage and into the family room. "And it doesn't appear as though anything's been taken, but there is this—"

When they entered the kitchen, the policeman didn't have to show Matt what was wrong. The intruder had spray-painted a message in huge, dripping red letters on the breakfast nook wall.

You kill me and I'll kill you!

"Any idea who might have done this?" the other officer, whose name was Murray, asked. He kept his voice flat, totally devoid of emotion as he fished a pen and notepad from the breast pocket of his shirt. He looked expectantly at Matt, ready to jot down any notes.

Matt's stomach tightened. His pulse whooshed in his ears, and his face was flushed.

"Yeah," Matt said after taking a moment to compose himself. His voice was dry and distant, and he couldn't stop staring at the words scrawled on the wall.

"Wanna tell me about it?" Officer Murray asked.

Matt licked his lips, feeling their dry roughness with his

tongue. He jumped and tore his gaze away from the wall when Brenda entered the kitchen and gasped when she saw what was written there.

"Yeah," Matt said, leaning close to Murray, "but not here. Let's go down to the station."

confessions

"MAYBE we should take a vacation or something. . . . I don't know. . . . Get away for a while. I mean—God, don't you think we deserve it?"

There was a distinct tremor in Brenda's voice, and she wondered if it was obvious to Matt or if he was too wiped out to notice.

Probably too wiped out, she thought, stifling a yawn behind her hand. She was feeling pretty wiped out herself. Overall, it had been one hell of a stressful day, the kind of day she hoped she would never have to experience again.

Standing at the foot of the bed by one of the open bedroom windows, she folded her arms across her chest and waited for him to respond. She was wearing what she usually wore to bed: one of Matt's extra-large T-shirts and her panties. Matt was already under the covers, lying on his side with his face turned toward the wall. A cool breeze blew through the windows, rustling the curtains and sending chills up her back.

"We can't take a vacation right now," Matt muttered, sounding absolutely exasperated. "The kids aren't done school yet, and besides, I have way too much work."

"Yeah, but—"

Brenda stopped herself, remembering how she was always telling the kids not to say "Yeah, but . . ."

Turning to the window, she pushed the curtains aside and leaned forward to look outside. The rain clouds had long since blown away, and a three-quarters moon shone in a clear sky. Moonlight trimmed everything in the backyard with a hard, silver edge, and the air had that distinctive ozone-tinged smell that always followed rain.

Shivering slightly and hugging herself, Brenda closed her eyes for a moment and inhaled deeply, relishing the smell of damp earth and growing things.

Life goes on, she told herself, trying to push aside some of the more morbid memories she had of the day. She wished the fresh air could penetrate every fiber of her being and relax her or, if not that, at least wash away the cloying smell of fresh paint that clung to the inside of her nose and throat.

It probably won't, though, she thought. *Not for a long time.*

After Detective Patoine and the Crime Investigation Division arrived, they took Polaroids of the spray-painted message and the muddy footprint on the door, and dusted for fingerprints on the inside doorknob. All they found were indistinct smudges that led them to speculate that the intruder must have been wearing gloves of some kind. They didn't find the discarded can of spray paint, so they had very little to go on.

With Matt present, they had briefly questioned Brenda and the kids, asking if any of them knew or suspected anyone who might have done something like this, or if they had noticed anyone hanging around the neighborhood recently. Both Emily and John said they hadn't seen anything, but Brenda had caught the funny little glance the kids exchanged.

When the patrolmen and detective left, Matt had followed them into town in his own car, saying he wanted to talk with his friend, Police Chief Keohane. Desperate to reclaim her home, Brenda had fetched a can of the kitchen wall paint from the cellar and painted over the message. Even after two coats with an hour in between to dry, though, faint red smears were still visible. She was satisfied that at least she no longer could read the message. After it dried overnight, another coat of paint in the morning should do the trick.

But although she couldn't see it, Brenda didn't like even

knowing that horrible message was underneath those coats of paint.

It's so creepy, she thought with a shiver. *Who would do such a terrible thing and—worse—did they really mean it? Is my family in any real danger?*

It annoyed her that the police hadn't done more, but then again, there wasn't much more they could do. They said they were going to canvass the neighbors to see if anyone had noticed anything suspicious, but their house was so isolated that she doubted it would do any good. She had visions of the police thrashing through the woods with packs of bloodhounds, tracking whoever had done this, but she knew that wasn't going to happen.

Although this might not be the right time to mention it to Matt, Brenda wanted him to promise that when he had time he'd cut out that section of sheetrock and replace it.

For now, three or four coats of beige paint and trusting that the local police were doing their jobs would have to suffice. Other than that, she and her family would just have to learn to live with it and pray to God that it had been a random stunt by some jerk.

Staring out into the darkness, she wished she could believe that, but she couldn't.

Something that concerned her even more was that, even after supper, Emily had seemed even more withdrawn than usual. Brenda sensed that something was bothering her, but she also knew there was no way Emily would talk to her about it. The distance between them was definitely getting worse as Emily got older, especially since the move to the new house, and Brenda had no idea what to do about it. She knew the best she could hope for was that Emily would eventually open up with her father about whatever was bugging her.

John, on the other hand, was dealing with everything as though it was no big deal. Maybe he was too young to grasp how threatening something like this was. He'd gotten swept up in the excitement of having policemen and a detective at his house, doing, as he put it, "all kinds of cool cop stuff." He said he couldn't wait to tell the kids about it at school.

As she stared out the bedroom window, once again Brenda had the feeling that someone was out there, out of sight.

Or maybe there was someone in the bedroom, lurking behind her? If that was the case, Brenda was sure that, no matter
how fast she turned around, she wouldn't see anyone. Still, the
feeling that someone was nearby, either behind her or outside
in the darkness, got stronger with each passing moment.

Or maybe, whatever it is, is inside me.

That thought sent a powerful shiver rippling through her,
and a low whimper escaped her. She started to say something
but stopped herself. Matt was either asleep or pretending not
to notice . . . or care.

Whatever it is, Brenda thought, *it's still here. . . . I know it
is. . . . I can feel it.*

She tried to focus on it, but no matter what she did, she
couldn't make the feeling go away or get it any clearer. It was
frustrating how elusive and indefinable it was, like the memory of a long-ago dream or an indistinct shadow that kept
shifting in and out of view in the corner of her eye.

*It's got to be some kind of free-floating anxiety or some-
thing,* she told herself, trying to calm down. *That's all it is.
It's just how I'm processing my grief.*

She wished she could believe that, but she simply couldn't.
On a deep level, she was worried that she might be having a
nervous breakdown. She knew she should talk to someone
about it . . . if not Matt, then Cheryl or Deb or maybe a doctor.

"Or *someone*," she whispered.

The problem was, she wasn't sure where or how to start.
She couldn't just sit her husband down and say: "Look, honey,
I think I'm cracking up."

No. That wouldn't work.

So how do I start?

The tension winding up inside her was so bad she thought
she might scream as soon as she opened her mouth. Kneeling
down and leaning both elbows on the windowsill, she pressed
her nose against the screen and inhaled the night air.

No, she thought as she clenched her teeth with resolve, *I'm
not cracking up. . . . I know I'm not. . . . It's just that I . . . just
that I . . .*

"Just that I *what?*"

She didn't realize she had spoken out loud until Matt

groaned and rolled over in bed. Propping himself up on one elbow, he looked at her.

"You say something?" he asked sleepily.

Brenda knew it wasn't fair of her to keep him awake. He'd been down at the police station for more than two hours, and when he'd come home, he was obviously wrung out from the ordeal. After eating the casserole Renee had brought over, and after a couple of hours of watching TV, he'd trudged upstairs, showered, and gone to bed without a word.

But like her, he seemed to be having trouble getting to sleep, and although she had practically begged him to tell her what had happened at the police station, he hadn't been very forthcoming.

Why won't he talk to me?

She didn't want to nag him. The day had been tough on all of them . . . maybe not as tough as it had been for her, but still tough. All she wanted was to be with her family and to find some kind of peace of mind, now that the funeral was over.

The kids had gone to bed at their usual time without too much complaining, and now, close to midnight, the house was quiet and dark. Maybe now she could talk to Matt about what was bothering her. It would help if she brought everything out into the open, but she had no idea where to begin.

She cleared her throat and turned her back to the window.

"Honey? I—uh, want to tell you something," she said. Her voice was halting and low, and with her back to the window, she didn't like feeling as though the unseen presence outside was watching her.

"What is it?" Matt asked, his voice slurring as he squinted at her.

Brenda thought he might be faking being so tired so he wouldn't have to talk to her about what was bothering him.

"I . . . I'm not quite sure how to put this," she said.

She stood up and started pacing back and forth at the foot of the bed, her head bowed and her shoulders hunched as she twisted her hands together like a little girl who was nervous about reciting something in front of her class.

"There's a . . . I've been . . . A couple of times, now, I think I've seen . . ."

She took a deep breath and let it out slowly before continuing.

"I think there's someone . . . lurking around the house."

Matt was silent for a long time. Finally, he let out a low groan. It sounded as though he was in pain. He rolled over so he was facing away from her.

A wild nervousness rose up inside Brenda, so strong she wanted to scream. She was close to tears, but she braced herself and choked back her emotions.

Don't cry now, she told herself.

Tears weren't an option if she was going to get through this. She had to tell him how she had been seeing what she was now convinced was the ghost of her dead mother. It was either that, or else she really was cracking up.

Moving so quickly it startled her, Matt flung the bed covers aside, swung his feet to the floor, and sat up on the edge of the bed. His shoulders were shaking as he hunched forward and groaned as he covered his face with both hands. His throat kept making a funny strangled noise that was halfway between a cry and a scream.

Brenda was suddenly afraid for him. She had never seen him like this.

"I know you have," he said before she could react. His raw voice broke the terrible silence of the room like a clap of thunder. "I've seen her too."

"What?" Brenda cried out.

Her body went numb, and a loud roaring sound filled her head. She staggered backward, her knees almost buckling, until her back was pressed against her bureau. The top edge jabbed like a mugger's knife into the small of her back.

"What—what are you talking about?" Panic squeezed her throat, tightening around it like steely fingers. She was afraid she was going to black out again, like she had at the cemetery today.

"That's not possible. . . . You couldn't have . . ."

She kept shaking her head in numbed denial and stared at her husband. Every shadow in the room seemed suddenly to be alive and seething with menace. The darkness behind her swelled as if it had a cold heartbeat of its own. She tried to swallow but couldn't. Her throat was twisted and dry.

"You . . . you don't understand," she said hoarsely. "I've been seeing . . . I saw—"

Her voice cut off, and she gasped with pain when she took a breath. A cold fist of ice hit her in the stomach. The rushing sound inside her head grew so loud she knew she couldn't take it much longer.

"Susan's back in town," Matt finally said.

His voice, muffled by his cupped hands, was so low Brenda wasn't sure she'd heard him correctly. Slowly, he lowered his hands and stared at her, desperation giving his eyes a dull flatness. He wasn't able to maintain eye contact for long, and he looked down at the floor.

"You mean your ex-wife?" Brenda said.

Still not looking at her, Matt nodded grimly. "Uh-huh."

"When did this all happen? What does she want?"

"What do you think she wants?" Matt asked, sounding tired. "That's why I went down to the police station." He took a shuddering breath. "I have no doubt she's the one who broke into the house and painted that message on the wall." He glanced at her and shivered. "I didn't want to tell the police about it in front of you and the kids."

"Good God, Matt, I . . . Why didn't you tell me?" Brenda struggled to keep her voice low so she wouldn't disturb the kids. She especially didn't want Emily to hear.

Matt kept staring down at the floor, but she could tell by the way his shoulders were shaking that he was crying.

"The other night," he said, his voice tightening, "when I left you at the hospital. She followed me to the house."

"No!"

"I didn't want to tell you. I was afraid you might—" He sighed again. "I don't know. Maybe I was afraid you'd freak out or something." He made a fist and punched the mattress in frustration. "I was hoping I could scare her off, that she'd just go away, but she seems determined to see Emily."

"Oh my God. She didn't see her, did she?"

"No. I made sure of that."

"What did you tell her? What are you going to do?"

Matt shook his head slowly from side to side and, straightening up, wiped his eyes with the heels of his hands.

"I'm not sure. I know I should have told you about it when

it happened, but she . . . you had enough to deal with as it was.
I was going to tell you after the funeral, but she must've
waited until she was sure we were out before breaking in."

"Why is she doing this? To scare us into letting her see her
daughter?"

Matt looked up at her, his eyes glazed and filled with tears.
Brenda didn't like seeing him looking so defeated, so frightened. After a moment, Matt's expression shifted, and she saw
a fire of resolve in his eyes.

"It's not going to happen." His voice didn't quaver now.
"There's no way in *hell* I'll let her see Emily. *Ever!*"

"But how can you—"

"Jesus, Bren. Give me some credit."

Brenda realized she was twisting her hands together. She
glanced over her shoulder, suddenly positive she could sense
an unseen presence behind her, moving closer, getting
stronger.

"How . . . how did she take it?" She shifted away from the
open window behind her. She didn't like the feeling of the
darkness, pressing against her back.

"How do you think she took it?" Matt said. "She was hurt
and pissed. She started in on how Emily was her daughter,
too, and now that she's got her act together, she should be able
to have a relationship with her."

"A relationship?" Brenda echoed hollowly.

Matt nodded, his mouth set in a hard line.

"It's not going to happen. I guarantee you that. Especially
not after what she did."

"The spray paint, you mean?" Brenda said.

Matt hesitated a moment, then nodded slowly and said,
"Yeah . . . that," but Brenda had the distinct impression he had
meant something else.

"She may have given birth to her," he said, his voice low
and controlled, "but that's all. I raised Emily alone for most of
the first eight years of her life, and then it's been you and me.
She's *our* daughter, certainly more than she's *Susan's.* I told
her that, and I told her that I'll do whatever I have to do to stop
her."

"Uh-huh," Brenda said, nodding numbly. This was too
much to take in. "But what if you can't stop her?"

She shivered and hugged herself tightly when she realized she could just as easily be talking about the ghost she'd been seeing in the house.

Matt waved his hand dismissively. "Don't worry about it. She doesn't have any money to fight me, and I know some people. I'll stop her dead in her tracks if she tries anything."

"She broke into our house and spray-painted the wall," Brenda said. Sucking in a deep breath, she let her gaze shift to the open window behind her. A shiver ran up her arms when she thought about how nervous she had been and how desperately she had wanted to tell Matt about the things she'd been seeing.

Imagining, she told herself. *It wasn't real. It couldn't be real.*

With this new threat from Matt's ex-wife, her concerns seemed silly and unimportant. Matt also shifted his gaze to the bedroom window, and she wondered if he had sensed that there was someone out there in the night . . . someone that was watching them.

"If she's dangerous . . . if she's a genuine threat to us . . . to Emily, then we have to do something about it."

"I know we do, and I will," Matt said, nodding.

Brenda moved closer to the bed and sat down next to him. She placed her hand on his leg and squeezed. He looked at her and smiled, but she didn't find as much reassurance in his smile as she had hoped. A terrible feeling of being alone and vulnerable swept over her. She looked back at Matt, frightened by how far away he looked.

"What if she doesn't take no for an answer?" she asked. A cold, empty pain filled her stomach. "What if she doesn't go away? Or what if she tries something else? Something worse?"

"We'll stop her before she can, I promise you," Matt said.

There was iron determination in his voice, but Brenda still didn't fully trust it. The threat to her and her family crackled like static electricity in the air, crawling across her skin and making the hairs on the back of her neck stir. She looked around the bedroom, expecting at any second to see the ghostly figure lurking in the corner, watching her.

There was no way she could talk to him now about what she'd been going through.

Forget about it, she told herself.

Maybe after a good night's sleep—if that were even possible—she'd see things more clearly in the morning. Once the kids were off to school, she and Matt could talk this through some more and figure out how they were going to make sure their family—especially Emily—was safe.

Maybe then she could tell him about the ghost she'd been seeing. If she told him now, she felt as though she would be violating some kind of trust or something.

Besides, she thought, *he's got enough to deal with as it is. He doesn't need to be worrying about me losing my sanity.*

"You coming to bed?" Matt asked as he flopped into the bed and pulled up the covers. He sighed as he settled his head into the pillow.

"Yeah," Brenda replied softly as she walked around to her side of the bed and slid in beside him. Her body was tingling, and when she turned out the light, a soft, fluttery sound filled her head.

"Don't you worry," Matt said, reaching behind himself to pat her on the leg. "Susan's not going to get away with this. Not after what happened last time."

Brenda jerked her head up and looked at him.

"What do you mean?"

Matt took a deep breath. When he let it out, Brenda heard the high shuddering sound he made.

"I don't want to talk about it, all right?" He paused, and she heard him swallow. "Not now, anyway. Just believe me. She's never . . . never going to get near Emily."

"I hope you're right," Brenda whispered, staring blankly up at the ceiling. "I hope to hell you're right."

"SOMETIMES you just can't talk to a man, you know? I mean, most of them just don't get it."

Sitting in Cheryl's kitchen, Brenda smiled as her best friend filled her cup with boiling water. The tea bag inflated and rose to the top, but Brenda sank it with her spoon and watched as dark brown threads of tea seeped into the water.

"Oh, Matt gets it, all right," Brenda said, addressing the teacup. "He's what you would call an evolved male."

"You mean he doesn't drag his knuckles on the floor when he walks?"

Brenda sniffed with laughter. "No, it's just that I'm—I was a little surprised, I guess, and hurt that he would keep something like that from me."

"You can't be serious, Brenda."

Cheryl couldn't help but smile as she poured hot water into her own cup and then placed the teakettle back on the stove. Brenda noticed that the enamel surface of the kettle was deep forest green. She felt a wave of relief that it wasn't chrome.

No ghostly figures will reflect in that!

"He'd have been a fool to tell you about it," Cheryl went on. "Seriously. Think about it. No man in the world is going to tell his wife that his ex is hanging around. No matter *what!* I guarantee it."

"Even if she's capable of doing what she did?" Brenda's throat was dry, and she wished the tea were cool enough so she could take a sip.

"How do you know what she's capable of doing?"

"I don't, but she threatened to kill us."

Cheryl nodded agreement on that point as she sat down at the table opposite Brenda. Morning sunlight was pouring in through the kitchen window, edging everything with a rich, golden glow. The day was warm, and the scent of lilacs from the backyard drifted through the open window.

"You have no idea how scary it was. 'You kill me and I'll kill you.' God, Cheryl, you just can't imagine."

"Oh, I bet I can," Cheryl replied, giving her a crooked half-smile. "I've dated my share of jerks and knuckle-draggers, believe me."

"Yeah, but none who broke into your house and left death threats, I'll bet."

"True . . . true," Cheryl said, nodding as she swirled her tea with her spoon. "But you said there was something else you wanted to talk to me about."

Brenda stiffened, and a short gasp escaped her. She wanted to look directly at her friend, but she couldn't quite do it. Instead, she folded her hands and, looking down at her lap, squeezed her fingers together so tightly her wedding and engagement rings bit into her flesh.

"You look kinda guilty. You're not having an affair or anything, are you?"

"Oh, God, no. It's nothing like that," Brenda said, but she still was unable to meet Cheryl's gaze. Now that she was so close to telling someone about what had been happening, she felt protective about it, as if—maybe—she was supposed to keep it all to herself. She wasn't afraid that Cheryl would think she was crazy or anything. Her friend had her own history of rather extreme exploits, many if not all of which she had discussed with Brenda.

But this felt different, somehow.

It's private, she thought, *and maybe talking about it will cheapen it.*

"So tell me," Cheryl said.

Or make it go away.

Brenda sighed and considered playing it off as nothing important, but she finally mustered up enough courage to look at her friend. Cheryl was leaning forward, her expression glowing with warmth and encouragement.

"It all seems so . . . so silly, now," Brenda began. Her voice was a faint whisper that barely left her mouth. Nervousness stirred inside her, making her squirm under her friend's intense gaze. "But . . . well, you see, remember I told you that I dreamed about my mother the night after she died? Well—it wasn't a dream. I think I actually saw her. More than once, since then."

Cheryl didn't react. She didn't say a word or do anything for a lengthening moment. As Brenda waited for some kind of reaction from her friend, she wanted to continue, but she couldn't find the words, so she simply watched Cheryl with an almost frantic desperation rising inside her.

"I asked you before—are you sure it was your mother?"

"Pretty sure," Brenda said, shaking her head and trying to make the image sharper in her memory. "But I . . . It looked a lot like her except there was a—" She traced a line down the left side of her face. "A terrible scar on the side of her face."

"A scar," Cheryl echoed, nodding.

"The first time I saw it . . . or her," Brenda continued haltingly, "was in the bedroom, the first night after she died. I saw her again the morning of her funeral, in the kitchen."

"That's absolutely amazing," Cheryl said without a trace of humor or irony in her voice. Brenda was upset with herself for thinking that Cheryl would react with anything other than understanding.

"You're sure you saw her? I mean, you looked right at her, and there she was?"

Biting on her lower lip, Brenda lowered her gaze and shook her head.

"Not really. I mean—it certainly wasn't like I'm looking at you now. The first time, I saw her in the bathroom mirror, but when I turned around, she was gone. Same thing in the kitchen. I saw her reflection in the teakettle. You know. My chrome teakettle."

"I love that teakettle."

"Well, I could feel that someone was standing behind me. You know that feeling?"

Cheryl nodded.

"I had it real intense, like there was this . . . this . . . I don't know how to describe it—this *presence,* like you know when you're being watched. Same thing happened in the kitchen, though. When I turned around, she wasn't there."

"But you're positive there was someone there," Cheryl said, leaning toward her across the table, her eyes alive and eager.

"I know I saw *someone.* And I think—I'm pretty sure it was my mother. I mean, who else could it be if it was a ghost? The only thing that didn't look like her was the scar. I . . . Let me think—"

Brenda narrowed her eyes with concentration as she tried to remember the figure exactly as she had seen it in the teakettle. Raising her hand, she touched the left side of her face and nodded.

"Yeah, it looked like it was on the right side, so that would be reversed. It was on the left side of her face. It was terrible. A big, ugly, white line that went from her hairline, down past her eye and nose, to the edge of her chin."

"Incredible," Cheryl said.

"Scary is what it is." Brenda shivered and hugged herself at the elusiveness of the memory. It was a struggle not to turn around quickly to see if there was anyone standing behind her now.

"Did she say anything? Did you try to talk to her?"

Brenda bit her lower lip and shook her head.

"Are you kidding? No way. I was scared out of my mind. I know or I think, anyway, there's no way she could have been there. Not really. I don't believe in ghosts. What I think it was—what I'm afraid it might mean is, I'm cracking up, that I might be losing my mind."

Cheryl reached across the table and patted Brenda on the shoulder. They maintained steady eye contact, and Brenda could see the genuine love and affection in her friend's face.

"Don't worry. You're not losing your mind," Cheryl said. "Trust me. I've known you a long time, and I'd know it if you were . . . you know—" She pointed her forefinger at her own head and made a quick, circular motion. "Cuckoo."

Brenda started to say something, but her breath caught like a dry pellet in her throat. Her hand was shaking slightly as she raised her cup and took a sip of tea, now that it was cool enough to drink. Without sugar or honey, the astringent taste made her throat feel constricted.

"You're grieving, Brenda. And you're under a lot of stress. But it doesn't matter if it was real or not. You know what I think?"

Brenda set the teacup down and raised her eyebrows in silent question.

"I think you should try to talk to her. Communicate with her. See what she has to say."

Brenda gave her friend a twisted smile and shook her head. "No. No way," she said as a chill coursed through her.

"Wait a second. Think about it," Cheryl said. "If this really is your mother's ghost . . . Why do ghosts come back?"

Brenda shrugged. "Well . . . in horror stories, anyway, it's usually because they weren't ready to die or because they have some unfinished business."

"Exactly," Cheryl said, snapping her fingers. "So which do you think it is? If this really is your mother, why would her soul still be hanging around? Do you think it's just that she wasn't ready to die?"

Brenda shook her head again, considering the question for a moment.

"Who's really ready to die?" she asked. "I mean—sure,

she'd been in the nursing home for a couple of years. She knew she wasn't going to get any better. She told me lots of times that she knew she'd probably never be able to go back home." Brenda took a breath and held it for a moment. "Besides, if it was something like that—if something like that was even possible—wouldn't she be stuck in the nursing home?"

"Probably, but not necessarily," Cheryl said. "But if it isn't that she can't let go, could there be something else? Some unfinished business? Something she didn't do while she was alive that needs to be taken care of now so she can—you know, pass on?"

"I don't think so," Brenda said. She stared past her friend at the view outside the window. The brilliant May morning looked impossibly far away, as if it were on a plane of existence that she could never reach.

"There's nothing I can think of," she said distantly, shaking her head. "We had her will and insurance and all that taken care of. Matt's a lawyer, so he got all the bases covered."

"There's nothing else—no family secrets or something that needs to be revealed before she can rest in peace?"

"No. Absolutely nothing, unless it's—"

She froze, the words almost out of her mouth as a thought struck her with near physical impact.

What if she's trying to tell me she's sorry, that she regrets not being closer to me? What if she misses having a more loving, more understanding relationship with me before she died?

Brenda looked down at the table, hoping she had hidden her reaction, but she knew Cheryl had caught it. Once again, she wished she hadn't even mentioned this to Cheryl. This was her problem to work out on her own.

"What if she knows something," Cheryl said, her voice dropping and sounding mysterious, "and what if she's trying to communicate it to you?"

"Then wouldn't she be haunting her own house instead of mine?" Brenda heard the tremor in her voice. "Look, I don't even believe in any of this stuff, all right? And to tell you the truth, that's why I'm worried, why I'm afraid I might be losing my grip. What I'm seeing isn't really my mother. It can't be." She tapped herself on the forehead. "It has to be all in my mind."

"So what's to lose if you try to talk to her and find out what she wants? Maybe she won't tell you unless you ask."

"So I should play guessing games with a ghost?" Brenda said. "Now *that's* what I'd call crazy."

Cheryl eased back in her chair, brushing her long blonde bangs away from her eyes while maintaining steady eye contact with Brenda. The look made Brenda feel nervous.

"No," Brenda finally said, her voice lowering to a whisper. "If I did something like *that*, then I think I really would be cuckoo."

"You really don't believe in any kind of afterlife?"

Brenda considered the question for a few seconds before answering. The icy tension inside her blossomed, and she had an unnerving feeling that it wasn't just Cheryl who was gazing at her. Somewhere, on some plane of reality she couldn't perceive, unseen eyes were watching her and listening.

"I don't know *what* I believe," she said at last, "but I'm not going to start talking to . . . to my hallucinations. Then Matt would have every right to lock me up and throw away the key."

"Bren. If you're really worried that you're—you know, that you may've slipped a few cogs—then get some therapy. I'm serious. You may need it, what with all the stress and grief you've got. But that's my point exactly. You *are* under a lot of stress, and maybe some part of you—some part of your mind—is open and trying to communicate something to you. Something important."

"Like what?" An oily shiver ran up Brenda's back.

Cheryl shrugged. "Ask."

"I only see her reflection. She disappears as soon as I turn around and look at her."

"Disappears," Cheryl said, one eyebrow cocking up.

"Well, she doesn't vanish out of sight, you know, like a slow fade. She isn't there. And I get this creepy feeling, like she's always behind me and then winks out of sight no matter how fast I try to turn around."

"Simple enough, then," Cheryl said with a carefree shrug. "Don't turn around. When you see her reflection, and you know she's there, just keep looking at whatever it is her reflection is in. But *talk* to her. Ask her what she wants. Find out what she wants to tell you."

"You make it sound so rational, but do you realize what you're saying? It seems . . . *insane!*"

Cheryl leaned back and took a sip of her tea, her lips widening into a smile as she did.

"So tell me," Brenda said after slowly sipping her tea. "Seriously. *Do* you think I'm crazy, imagining things like this, or do you think there really is a chance this is my mother?"

"There's only one way to find out," Cheryl said simply. "Do you really want to?"

Brenda let her breath out in a long, slow whooshing sigh as she leaned back in the chair, shook her head, and rubbed her eyes. Even for the short time her eyes were closed, she had the feeling that someone besides Cheryl was watching her. It intensified as long as she kept her eyes closed until she thought she was going to scream.

When she couldn't take it any longer, she opened her eyes and looked at Cheryl. To some degree, she regretted that she had even mentioned this to her friend, but she knew if she couldn't talk to Matt about it, she had to talk to someone!

This isn't like me, she thought bitterly. *I really am coming apart at the seams.*

"I . . . I have no idea what I want," she finally said in a trembling whisper. Her voice was so distant and dreamy it sounded almost like someone else was standing behind her back and whispering into her ear.

faces

"**WHY** am I even here? I haven't done anything wrong."

"I haven't said you have," the detective said, keeping his voice low and flat. Seated at his desk, he was leaning back in his chair and staring expressionlessly at Susan. He casually raised one hand as though to restrain her, even though she hadn't made any move toward him. She sat stiffly in the chair, her shoulders straight, her knees pressed together. A trickle of sweat ran down the inside of her blouse, tickling her, but she knew she couldn't let him see how nervous she was.

"I just want to ask you a few questions. That's all."

What the hell's his name again? Susan asked herself. She had never been any good at remembering names, and she had been so nervous when she got to the Three Rivers Police Station that his name had slipped out of her mind as soon as he said it.

Pat-something-or-other, she thought, irritated with herself. *Patten? Pation?*

She glanced at the laminated nameplate on his desk.

Patoine, that's it. Detective Phillip Patoine.

"I just want to verify where you were yesterday between noon and five o'clock."

"But you won't tell me why."

The detective shook his head and regarded her with a steely, unreadable gaze that was already getting on her nerves. She didn't like feeling as though he could see through her, like she was a pane of glass or something. She took a slow, deep breath to steady her nerves. She had to be careful and not do or say anything that would tip him off about what she had done and what she was planning to do.

But I haven't done anything . . . not yet, anyway.

She was suddenly convinced this detective could read her mind . . . was reading it right now! The way he looked at her, like she was a science experiment or something. It made her feel he knew things about her that even she didn't know.

"Well," she said, "if you *must* know, I was at a meeting."

"A meeting?"

The detective's expression never cracked as he waited patiently for her to continue, but Susan wasn't fooled. He was far from patient. He was just waiting for her to mess up and admit that she had done whatever it was he suspected she had done. After a long silence, when she didn't respond, he asked, "Exactly what kind of meeting might that have been?"

Susan winced and wrung her hands together. They were slick with sweat, but she knew if he saw her sweat, no matter how innocent she was, he would assume the worst and be convinced of her guilt, whatever it was.

Unless this is about what happened long ago, how can he know what I want to do?

She wished she could be cool and calculating, but she knew she looked guilty, and she had plenty to feel guilty about.

"An AA meeting," she said. Her voice was full of surrender, and she cringed inwardly, convinced that Detective Patoine would now write her off as a drunk and thus, unreliable and possibly dangerous and guilty of . . . whatever it was he was investigating.

This must have something to do with Matt and Emily, Susan thought with a cold gnawing in her stomach, *but what?*

Unable to meet the detective's eyes, she stared at her hands in her lap and wished she had never agreed to come down to the station to talk to him.

Isn't that like admitting guilt? Or does coming down here willingly and cooperating prove that I don't have anything to hide? And I don't have anything to hide!

Not yet, whispered a faint voice inside her head, and she closed her eyes for a moment, willing that voice to go away. Once the voices started, she got confused, and if she got confused, this detective would trip her up.

She had no idea what to think, but she knew that the longer this interrogation went on—*And that's exactly what it is, no matter how much he pretends otherwise*—the more nervous she was going to get.

And if she got nervous, then maybe she would let spill what she was planning to do. She wished she hadn't stopped taking her medication, because she could feel herself gradually unraveling.

"I—ah, I've been in AA for several years, now," she said. She wished she didn't hear that note of apology in her voice. "I go to regular meetings every week."

"Even when you're so far from home?" Detective Patoine asked.

"Even then," Susan said, nodding. "Especially then."

"So why did you come to Maine in the first place?"

One of the voices in her head was constantly reminding her to say as little as possible because no matter what she said, no matter how innocent she might try to make it sound, this guy was a trained professional; first chance he got, he would take it and twist it around and use it against her.

"Family issues," she said softly. "I . . . I'm trying to iron out some family issues."

"Uh-huh," Patoine said, nodding. His expression was flat and unchanging. "Well, yesterday afternoon between noon and five o'clock . . . That was one of those times?"

"One of what times?"

"When you were at a meeting."

Susan didn't like the way he made it sound as if he didn't believe a single word she was saying.

Is this how he's gonna wear me down? If it is, it's working. Just shut up! Don't say a word! Just like the last time, he can't make you talk!

She clasped her hands tightly together, feeling how clammy

they were. She started to reach to wipe the sweat from her upper lip but checked herself, not daring to let any nervousness show. Any second, now, she feared she would melt down in front of him.

Would that make you happy, you goddamned son of a bitch? Will you feel like you've done your job for the day if you make me fall apart? Is that what you want, to see me cry and admit it's wrong of me to want to see my daughter? Well, it isn't wrong!

"Care to tell me where that meeting was? Was there anyone there who could confirm your presence?"

"You mean give me an alibi, right?" Susan said sharply. She raised her eyes and stared straight at him, trying to match his icy stare. A hard lump formed in her throat, making it almost impossible for her to swallow or take a breath. She was trembling inside.

Detective Patoine didn't say a word. He didn't even blink as he looked at her, just waiting for her to crack. Susan licked the sweat on her upper lip, tasting the salt.

"It's called Alcoholics *Anonymous* for a reason," she finally managed to say. "We're supposed to remain anonymous. Even for the police, I would imagine."

"Oh, I have a pretty good idea of some of the folks who might have been there."

"Maybe, but I can't give you their names. Besides, I'm not from around here. I don't know anybody there except for a handful of people by their first name."

"Care to tell me where this meeting was?" Patoine asked. "That way, I could at least confirm there was one."

"First Baptist Church on River Road."

Detective Patoine nodded as he took a small notepad from his desk and jotted something down.

He's just pretending to take notes. . . . He already knows what I'm planning to do, and he's going to try to stop me.

"What time was this?"

"Two o'clock," Susan said. "Look, if you think I've done anything wrong, if I'm under suspicion for some crime, shouldn't I get a lawyer?"

"Do you think you need a lawyer?"

"No, but—"

"You're free to call whomever you'd like," Patoine said, his glassy-eyed stare never leaving her.

"Of course I don't need one! I haven't done anything wrong!" Susan shouted, surprised how her anger and fear burst out of her. Sudden rage constricted her throat, making her voice twist up unnaturally high. Clenching her hands into fists, she pounded the arms of her chair.

"I never accused you of doing anything wrong," Detective Patoine said placidly. "I'm simply asking you to cooperate with me in relation to an ongoing investigation."

Susan hated how he was able to remain so calm and collected, but she wasn't a fool. She could see exactly what his game was.

Don't let him break you! a voice in her head screamed.

"But you won't tell me what it is," Susan said. She desperately wanted to say more, to find out what this had to do with Emily. Not knowing was driving her crazy.

Is she in trouble? Has something happened to her? Has she been hurt or has she disappeared or . . . or worse? What if she's dead? . . . Like the last time . . . Maybe she's been killed.

These thoughts ripped through her like iron spikes, but she knew she couldn't let her worries show. She could see that the detective was just waiting for her to crack and admit what she was planning to do so Matt could get her out of his and Emily's life for good.

I know that's his game. But I'm not going to let it show! I can't! Not if I ever want to see her again!

Detective Patoine didn't say a word. He had already made it clear that he wasn't going to tell her anything that he absolutely didn't have to. If something had happened to Emily, maybe he wanted to sweat it out of her so they could pin it on her.

"I . . . I haven't done anything to Emily," she said, her voice a breathy whisper that grated on her ears. "Honest."

For the first time since she entered his office, Detective Patoine's expression shifted. For just an instant, the left corner of his mouth twitched into a tight grin, but it was gone in a moment.

"Emily?" he said, leaning forward and staring at Susan like a bird of prey about to strike.

"Yes. . . . My daughter," Susan said, sighing with resignation as she shifted her gaze and looked him straight in the eyes. "I'm not stupid, you know. I know what you're trying to do here."

"I'm not trying to do anything except establish where you were yesterday afternoon."

Blinking her eyes rapidly to keep herself from crying, Susan tilted her head back, grinning as she stared up at the ceiling. It blurred in a watery smear of white that shifted with subtle, iridescent tones. A bone-deep shudder ran through her, shaking her shoulders and clenching her gut. She was angry at herself for not shutting up, but now it was too late.

He did it. He broke me.

"I know this is all because of my ex-husband, Matt Ireland. Isn't it?"

She gasped for breath as her vision began to distort, and vague figures formed in the swirls of the ceiling. Faint voices whispered in her ears.

"He won't allow me to see my daughter, and I know he's doing everything he can to keep me from her. He told you to talk to me to . . . to . . . I don't know. Do what? Scare me off or something?"

Detective Patoine didn't say a word. His expression remained fixed. He didn't even blink as he studied her with a level, laser-beam gaze.

"All I want is to see my daughter," Susan said. She knew she sounded desperate and didn't care if he knew it. Taking a tissue from her purse, she blotted her eyes. Detective Patoine slid a box of Kleenex across his desk so it was within reach. Susan nodded her thanks as she took a handful and, hunching forward, wiped her eyes.

"That's all I want," she whispered.

"You weren't at the Ireland home yesterday afternoon?"

Susan's shoulders were shaking uncontrollably as she rested her elbows on her knees and viciously wiped the tears from her eyes. The voices chattering in her head were getting louder, but she couldn't distinguish anything any of them were saying.

"No. . . . No, I wasn't. . . . I already told you . . . I was at my meeting."

Susan kept wiping her eyes, smearing her tears into oily streaks across her cheeks. She looked up at the detective, not caring how pathetic or broken she looked.

"You have to tell me," she said, her voice hitching with emotion. "Has something happened to Emily? I have to know if she's all right."

Detective Patoine steepled his fingers under his chin and didn't answer for a few seconds. Then he slowly nodded.

"Your daughter's fine," he said. His eyes were still flat and unreadable, but for the first time since she got here, Susan detected just a hint of caring in his expression. "We're investigating something entirely unrelated and wanted to know your whereabouts. That's all."

He rose quickly from his desk, indicating that their conversation was over.

"Thank you for cooperating."

He extended his hand for her to shake. Susan knew that her own handshake must feel clammy and weak in his grasp, but she didn't care. She despised herself for breaking down so easily. It had taken him less than fifteen minutes to get her to admit that she wanted to see Emily.

Is that what Matt wants—an official witness so he can get a restraining order or whatever he needs to keep me away from her?

Her knees sagged and almost folded as she stood up and started for the door. Moving quickly, Detective Patoine walked to the door and opened it for her, stepping aside to let her out.

"Thanks again, Mrs. Ireland," he said, and once again she heard a trace . . . just a trace of sympathy in his voice.

As she started down the corridor to the front door, Susan squared her shoulders. She didn't care what he thought of her. Matt had probably told him she was a pathetic mess wallowing in self-pity and depression. He may have even told him about how she had been committed to the psych ward. But that was years ago, and she was much better. So what if he thought she was a messed-up woman whose recovery wasn't working and who very well might prove to be dangerous both to herself and to her daughter and ex-husband.

Well, Matt may be a lawyer and know how to play hard-ball, but that doesn't make him right. Does it?

As she opened the station door and stepped out onto the front steps, the sudden burst of sunlight burned her eyes, making her squint. Every muscle and nerve in her body was screaming in agony, but she didn't care that he had seen her break down.

It's not a crime to want to see your daughter.

Her limp was more pronounced as she walked over to her car, seething with self-loathing.

But it is a crime if you do what you're thinking of doing, she told herself.

Her hands were shaking so badly, she had trouble unlocking the car door.

"But I *have* to do it," she whispered. Tears blurred her vision as she swung the door open and sat down. "And I don't have a choice. Matt hasn't left me any other choice."

She clenched her fist and slammed the steering wheel hard enough to hurt.

"And I am going to see my daughter!"

GARDENING *always helps,* Brenda thought as she knelt down and dug her gloved fingers into the dark, loose topsoil.

This is good. . . . This is what I need.

She inhaled the rich, earthy smell so deeply it made her head spin. Last weekend, before the housewarming, she and Matt had borrowed a Rototiller from a neighbor and broken ground for a vegetable garden in the sunny area beside the house at the end of the driveway. Because there were so many other things they had to do to the new house, Matt had suggested waiting until next spring before they started a garden, but Brenda wouldn't hear of it.

She had to garden because of the peace of mind it always brought her, but she also had to get it done today. The tomato and pepper starter plants she had bought at Woodbury's Farm Stand almost three weeks ago were so root-bound they were starting to wilt. She hoped it wasn't already too late for them.

Most of all, she had to keep busy.

She had tried to take a nap, but she hadn't dozed off, and she still felt much too wound up about everything that had happened. The caffeine in the tea she'd had at Cheryl's this morning wasn't helping, either. Whatever was bugging her, though, it was a gorgeous day and, since the kids wouldn't be home from school for another hour or so, she wanted to accomplish something.

Her talk with Cheryl had helped quite a bit, but Brenda knew it hadn't really solved anything. For all she knew, she might be having a nervous breakdown and not even realize it. And nothing Cheryl had said could erase the simple fact that she had seen . . . *something.*

"But what?" she whispered, huffing her breath to blow back the strand of hair that had fallen across her eyes. "Or who?"

She shivered and glanced behind herself, still feeling as though someone was watching her. But the more she thought about it, the more convinced she became that it had to have been her dead mother.

Who else could it be?

And maybe Cheryl was right. Maybe the next time she saw her mother's ghost—*If there is a next time*—she should talk to it, try to communicate with it.

What harm would there be?

She was already seeing someone who wasn't there, so it wasn't all that big a step to start talking to it.

"It," she said softly.

She couldn't quite bring herself to think of the apparition as *her.* And what unnerved her most was wondering what she would do, how she would react if the ghost actually responded.

Then what?

"Bullshit! This is total, absolute, complete *bullshit!*"

Gritting her teeth, she shook her head as she scooped out a shallow hole in the dirt for the first tomato plant. Sweat beaded on her forehead and tickled as it dripped down the sides of her face. When it ran into her eyes, the salty sting felt like tears, and Brenda couldn't say for sure if she was crying and didn't know it or wouldn't admit it.

She grieved her mother's death. No matter what problems and unresolved issues they had, the woman who had given birth to her had died. Of course there was deep sadness and regret. No matter what she did or didn't do, there would always be more she could have done; but something else was wrong. She felt an indefinable darkness was pulling inside her, and it made her fearful and worried and depressed and so sad she wanted to cry, even now when she was gardening, one of her favorite things in the world to do.

"Damn, woman! Pull yourself together," she whispered to herself, wiping away the sweat—*or tears*—on the back of her work glove.

She wanted to believe that it was all over, that telling Cheryl everything had given her a measure of control over her feelings. Maybe now things would start getting better between her and Matt, and her and the kids, especially between her and Emily.

"Please," she whispered. "Let everything be better."

If she were done with her grieving, then—hopefully—she would stop seeing her mother's ghost or anything else that frightened her. Unfinished business or not, she didn't want to deal with anything she couldn't explain.

Using an old table knife, she broke apart the tomato plants in the flat, took one, and placed it into the fist-sized depression she had dug in the soil. Cupping both hands around the stalk, she pressed the clump of roots down firmly, then scooped dirt into a small mound around the pale green stem. Taking a plastic cup, she cut the bottom off and collared the plant to keep cutworms away. Satisfied that she was making progress, she sat back on her heels, looked up at the blue arc of the sky, and took a deep breath.

"This is good," she whispered, squinting against the glare and nodding. "This is really good."

After savoring the moment, reveling in the warmth of the sun on her back, the sweat on her skin, and the dirt on her hands, she dug another hole for the next tomato. Working systematically and without really being aware of it, an hour quickly passed in quiet, meditative silence. She was so involved in her work that she didn't notice the car when it pulled to a stop at the top of the driveway. Only when the engine shut off, and the cylinders knocked loudly a few times, did she look up.

Brenda didn't recognize the dark blue car. Feeling a slight stirring of apprehension, she watched as the driver, a thin, middle-aged woman, got out and walked around the back of the car. She had a noticeable limp, and she slid her hand along the car's trunk as though she needed it for extra support. She hesitated as she looked down the driveway toward the house.

"Good afternoon," Brenda called out, raising a hand in greeting as she stood up and brushed her gloved hands on her pants, leaving long, dark smears of loam on her thighs.

"Oh . . . hello," the woman replied.

She seemed surprised to see Brenda, and for an instant, she looked as though she wanted to jump back into the car and drive off. Then, with shoulders hunched, she faced Brenda.

"Can I help you with something?" Brenda asked as she started toward her.

The woman didn't move. She just stood there, looking pale and drawn in the bright daylight, as if she'd just awakened and was confused as to where she was. She looked so frightened Brenda couldn't help but feel sorry for her.

As she approached, Brenda took a moment to evaluate her. She was wearing a brightly colored blouse and blue jeans that hung loosely on her thin frame. She was attractive in a natural sort of way, but Brenda had the distinct impression that this woman hadn't been sleeping very well. Either that, or else she didn't spend much time outside. Her skin had an odd, almost translucent paleness, and her eyes—a chilling, icy blue—were nervous and twitchy. Her thin lips were almost colorless, and she wore her dark hair cut short.

"Hello. My name is—ah, Laurie Porter," the woman said.

She held out her hand as Brenda came close to her. Brenda slipped off her gardening gloves before shaking hands. She was surprised how, even on such a warm day, the woman's touch was cold and damp. Either she drove with the air conditioner on full blast, or she was really nervous.

"You looking for someone?" Brenda asked.

She wasn't sure why, but she suddenly felt another strong wave of pity for this woman. She looked so nervous she seemed like she was going to start crying or screaming. Her eyes twitched as she stared at Brenda for a few seconds. She seemed to be at a total loss for words.

"I was . . . No. That is . . . I'm not looking for anyone in particular. You see, I—uh, I recently moved to this area, and . . . I thought . . . I was told that your house was up for sale. This is your house, right?"

"Yes it is," Brenda said, nodding, "but it's definitely not for sale. We just moved in a couple of weeks ago."

"I see," the woman said, nodding thoughtfully but still looking like she was mentally scrambling for what to say next. "I—uh, I must've gotten the wrong directions or something." She shrugged, but the motion seemed tight and unnatural. "So this isn't—uh, Firestone Road?"

Brenda shook her head.

"'Fraid not," she said. "I've never heard of a Firestone Road around here. Are you sure you're in the right neighborhood?"

"I thought so," the woman said, glancing up and down the road. Her poorly concealed nervousness was putting Brenda on edge, and it was obvious that she was lying.

"Yeah. Firestone Road," the woman said, her voice faint and halting as she nodded. "I'm sure that's the name the real estate agent in town gave me."

"Which real estate agent was that?" Brenda asked. "I've lived here awhile, so I know just about everyone in town."

"Oh, I—umm, I don't remember the name. It was . . . No, no one in town. Someone I spoke to at a real estate agency in Augusta." She patted her jeans pockets. "I—I thought I had his card. I guess I left it in the car."

Whoever she is and whatever she wants, Brenda thought, *she's not a good actress. Something's really bothering her.*

And then in a flash it hit her.

This must be Susan!

A bolt of panic shot through Brenda, and she took a couple of involuntary steps backward. Her fists clenched, and her arms stiffened as she prepared to defend herself if she had to.

"It was this house he described, I'm pretty sure," the woman said as her gaze shifted past Brenda and focused on the front of the house. "It sure looks like the one he showed me in the brochure."

Brenda turned and glanced back at the house, and what she saw sent an icy jolt through her. In John's bedroom window upstairs, a hint of dark motion behind the glass caught her attention. It wasn't much, just a suggestion of a shadow behind the glass; but in an instant, it transformed into a face.

Someone is upstairs, watching!

Before Brenda could look away, the face shifted closer to the glass, resolving more clearly. She immediately recognized the old woman she had seen twice before. The same pale skin . . . the same wisps of gray hair . . . the same vacant, staring eyes.

Brenda froze where she stood, unable to look away from the unblinking stare of the apparition. It held her as though she were hypnotized. A second later, she saw something moving in one of the other upstairs windows. When she shifted her gaze from John's bedroom window to another window, she realized the face was there, too.

The same face!

An exact duplicate of the old woman's face was looking out at her. Even with direct sunlight hitting the side of the house, the shadowed features of the woman's face were poorly illuminated. The dark smudges of the old woman's eyes were oddly indistinct. Brenda wanted to believe they were nothing more than shadows and folds in the curtains, but undeniably, they assumed the shape of a human face.

This can't be happening, Brenda thought desperately. *It's an illusion! I'm seeing things!*

She blinked and tried to refocus, trying to see how the two identical faces could be a trick of the sky and clouds reflected in the glass. She nearly screamed when she shifted her gaze to the other windows on the front of the house and saw the same face reproduced in every one. The multiple figures stared back at her with flat, dark, empty eyes.

"No," Brenda whispered, struggling hard to maintain control. Her voice sounded flat and far away, like she was speaking from the bottom of a deep well. "They can't be there."

Her visitor made a comment, but Brenda didn't hear or understand it.

Can she see it too? she wondered vaguely, but she was so riveted by her own fear that she could hardly breathe. She wanted to look away from the house and deal with Susan, if that's who this really was, but the old woman's face in every

window transfixed her. She watched as the multiple appari-
tions slowly became more clear.

Brenda became aware of a low, steady thumping sound. It
took her a moment to realize it was the rapid hammering of
her pulse in her ears. Her throat closed off, and no amount of
swallowing could make the tightness go away.

As she watched, nearly suffocated by fear, she realized that
the apparition in every window was shaking its head. The lips
were moving as though each one was speaking.

She's trying to talk to me! Brenda thought as fear surged
inside her like an onrushing tide. She strained to hear what the
apparition was saying, but the glassy barrier between them
blocked any sound. Brenda was too terrified to move or try to
speak because she knew, if she did, she would scream.

"I . . . ah, I guess I'd better go then," Brenda's visitor said
haltingly.

Without turning around, Brenda listened to the loud crunch
of gravel behind her as the woman walked back to her car.
Somehow, at last, Brenda managed to tear her gaze away from
the house and look at her. In the shade of the pine trees, the
woman—*It has to be Susan!*—looked ethereal, almost transparent. No more real than the faces in the windows. Brenda
couldn't help but wonder which was more real. Her vision got
watery and unfocused, and the muffled beating in her ears got
steadily louder. She was suddenly fearful that she might be
having a heart attack or a stroke.

*Is that what's happening? I'm going to blow a blood vessel
in my brain and just drop dead?*

There might be some relief in that, she thought, but as she
stared blankly straight ahead, she realized she could hear
voices in the distance. For a frozen instant, she assumed it had
to be the old woman in the windows, but then she distinctly
heard two voices, a boy's and a girl's.

Shifting her gaze up the road, she saw Emily and John
making their way home from the bus stop. In the heat haze re-
bounding from the asphalt, they also looked like mirages, illu-
sions. They were arguing about something, but their voices
were muffled by the heavy air.

Brenda sensed that the woman was looking up the road,
too, and she turned to see Susan staring at the children.

They're my children! Brenda wanted to shout. *Emily may be your daughter, but she's mine now!*

The woman started to say something, and Brenda distinctly heard a whispering voice.

"Emily . . ."

Brenda wasn't sure if the woman had spoken or someone else, or if she had thought her stepdaughter's name or said it out loud. Trembling with fear, she watched as Susan hurried back to her car, flung the door open, and got inside. She started up the car, loudly grinding the starter before it caught. Then she took off down the road with an ear-piercing squeal of tires and left behind a blue cloud of exhaust.

Still quaking with fear and barely able to breathe, Brenda looked at the kids again, and then—somehow—found the courage to glance over her shoulder at the house.

The numbed shock she felt when she saw that the faces in the windows were gone was almost worse than if they had still been there. She darted her eyes back and forth from window to window, but all she saw was glass that mirrored the blue sky overhead.

Nothing else. No faces. Not even the hint of one in any of them.

"What the hell is going on?" Brenda murmured as she rubbed her eyes. The damp smell of earth on her hands filled her nostrils as she forced herself to breathe evenly.

"Hi-yah, Mom," John called out as he started running toward her. His cheerful voice was so loud and real it was like a ray of pure sunlight piercing the darkness that filled her. She forced herself to smile as John and Emily got closer, but she noticed that Emily had a curious expression on her face as she stared down the road. She looked confused or frightened about something.

John gave his mother a quick hug, and she kissed the top of his head. His hair smelled like chalk dust.

"Who was that who just left?" he asked.

Brenda inhaled sharply and shook her head as she stared down the road and shrugged. The car had disappeared from sight, leaving her with the peculiar feeling that it might never have really been there.

"Huh? Oh, no one," she said, trying her best to dismiss the question. "Someone had the wrong address."

As she told this lie, she looked closely at Emily and saw how confused and worried she looked.

She's afraid of something, Brenda thought.

Emily was unconsciously gnawing her lower lip as she stared down the road. She looked like she desperately wanted to say something but didn't quite dare to.

"Everything all right?" Brenda asked her, pushing aside her own panic. She had directed her question at Emily, but it was John who answered.

"Yeah," he said. "I did all my homework in study hall, so can I go over to Sean's? He's got a new PlayStation game."

Brenda barely registered what he'd said, but now that Susan was gone—*I know it was her!*—everything was back the way it belonged. It amazed her to think how, only moments ago, she had been in such a weird place, and now her world had snapped back to normal.

Did I really see those faces in the windows?

Tension gripped her back as she sucked in a breath and turned slowly toward the house. All of the faces had vanished. She felt a little foolish for imagining them in the first place.

"So can I go?"

"Uh . . . yeah. Sure," she replied distantly. "I—ah, I'll give you a ride. Wanna come with us, Em?"

Emily, still looking really worried about something, seemed to consider the request, but then she frowned and shook her head quickly.

"No. Thanks," she said as she walked toward the house. "I've got homework and stuff to do."

"**OF** *course* it was her! It *had* to be!"

"You're sure."

"Yes, I'm sure!"

"Describe her. What did she look like?"

Speaking into the cell phone, Brenda gave Matt a detailed description of her visitor, as much as she could remember. She had just dropped John off at Sean's house and was driving back home. She resisted the urge to drive into town to be with her husband because she felt more needed at home. She couldn't quite admit to herself that Emily might really be in any danger from her mother, but it would be best to take precautions. She wished Emily had come with them so she wouldn't be worried that Susan would return, now that Brenda wasn't home. And Brenda couldn't forget that someone had broken into their house and spray-painted that threatening message.

Matt was silent on the other end of the line for a moment; then he grunted and sighed.

"Sure sounds like her, all right."

"So what are you—what are we going to do?"

"I'm not sure there's anything we can do. I've already filed a report with the police. They say they don't really have enough cause, not to mention man power, to stake out the house."

Brenda sighed and shook her head wearily.

"So . . . what? We have to wait until she actually threatens us?"

"I don't think stopping by the house in broad daylight is exactly threatening," Matt said mildly. "If anything, I'll bet she was hoping to catch a glimpse of Em. From what you said, it sounded like she was just as surprised to see you as you were to see her."

"Yeah," Brenda said, shivering with the memory of the faces she had seen in the windows. She certainly didn't want to mention that. Not now, anyway.

"It's just that . . . I don't know." She exhaled noisily, but that didn't relieve the tension inside her. "I don't like feeling like she's . . . you know, watching us or stalking us."

"Emily's the only one I'm worried about," Matt said.

She could hear the frustration in his voice.

"I know someone who does private detective work. Maybe I could ask him to look into things. I suppose I should start the paperwork to get a restraining order on her, too."

"You think that's really necessary?"

"You don't?"

"I just am not convinced they're that effective. I mean, if she wants to see Emily, she'll find a way." She realized she was gripping the cell phone too tightly and had to consciously ease her grip.

"I just wish none of this was happening."

"Me too, babe. Believe me," Matt said. "Look, I still have a ton of work to do here before I can leave. If you're really worried, call the police and ask them to drive by the house a few times. They said they'd do that."

"Okay," Brenda said, but even as she said it, she knew that wasn't what was really bothering her. What was really bothering her was that she had seen those faces in the windows.

"Try to take it easy. Relax. Don't let her ruin your day, for God's sake. She's done enough damage already."

"Yeah, okay," Brenda said, shaking her head impatiently.

"Seriously. Try to forget all about it. Finish planting your tomatoes. You'll feel better. I'll take care of everything else."

"Uh-huh."

"See you for supper around six?"

"Sounds good."

"I'll call if I'll be any later than that. Love you, hon. Bye-bye."

"Love you, too," Brenda said.

She clicked off the phone just as she was taking the turn onto Collette Road. Over the crest of the hill ahead, she could see the roof of her house, and as she got closer, she was relieved to see that Susan's car wasn't anywhere in sight. Brenda wished she had thought to write down the make and model or the license plate number, but she'd been too upset to think clearly. Besides, if the police were doing their job like they were supposed to, they would know what kind of car Susan was driving.

No, something else was bothering her . . . something she was having a lot of trouble facing. It was knowing that she hadn't dared to ask her husband how he thought she was supposed to relax when she was convinced that the ghost of her dead mother was haunting her and that she might have something important to communicate to her.

THIRTEEN

pursuit

SOOT-GRAY clouds scudded low across the sky, driven by a northerly wind that hissed through the tops of the pines. The rain, which had started late in the morning, was still coming down hard in the afternoon. It bounced off the road in a silvery mist that made the surface look almost electrified. An eighteen-wheeler roared by, its huge tires spewing spray from under the mud flaps as the driver worked through the gears on the down slope. Other than that, there wasn't much traffic on the road, and that suited Susan just fine.

Just in case I actually get what I want, she thought with a strange, twisted glee that made her almost giddy.

Her insides were quivering, and she was nervous that she'd hyperventilate as she waited where she'd pulled over to the side of the road. She was about twenty or thirty feet behind the school bus, which had just stopped. Leaning forward, she squinted with anticipation and watched as only three kids got off the bus into the downpour. Two of them crossed the road and headed in the opposite direction, down Burnt Mill Road, running as fast as they could. No one was waiting for them.

Good, Susan thought. *No eyewitnesses.*

Another dizzying wave swept over her when she saw Emily, her shoulders hunched against the rain, start up the road alone. The rivulets of rain that streaked the windshield distorted her figure, but Susan knew it was her.

"Even better," she whispered when she realized that Emily's brother wasn't with her. It didn't matter where he was—if he had a doctor's appointment or had stayed home sick or was over at a friend's house.

As long as Emily is here . . . as long as I can talk to her . . . that's all I want, she thought, but as soon as she thought it, another voice deep inside her head whispered, *You know that's not all you want!*

She struggled to be honest with herself, to admit the truth. It was difficult, but she couldn't kid herself. She knew exactly what she had done and why Brenda wasn't here to give Emily a ride home.

Susan also knew that she had to hurry.

Her anxiety spiked when the school bus started to pull away in a billowing cloud of exhaust. An instant later, Emily was alone on the road. Susan shifted into gear and pulled ahead, stopping only a few feet behind Emily.

When she heard the car behind her, Emily stopped and turned. Her face was tight with apprehension as Susan opened the car door, stuck her head out into the downpour, and waved wildly to her.

"Come on! Hurry up!"

Susan was barely able to hear her own voice above the beating of rain on the car. Glancing up the road, she saw the school bus disappear over the crest of the hill.

Emily just stood there with her mouth hanging open, looking terrified as she stared back at Susan. Rain matted the strands of hair that stuck out from under the hood of her purple raincoat, plastering them in dark ringlets against her pale forehead. Her eyes were wide with fear and suspicion.

"Who are you?" Emily asked, her voice trembling. "Why are you following me around?"

"It's okay, Emily. Really." Susan impatiently waved her on. "Your mom asked me to pick you up and give you a ride home. She's getting her hair done and is running a little late, is all."

Emily didn't move. She looked like she wanted to run, but Susan knew there was no safe place nearby. The dismal day gave Emily's face a ghastly cast, and Susan's heart nearly broke when she considered how cold and miserable her daughter looked.

If only she knew. But she has to know! She's going to know!

"Hurry up," Susan shouted. "You're getting soaked. You don't want to catch a cold, do you?"

After casting an anxious glance up and down the road, Emily came closer to the car, moving as though hypnotized. She avoided the puddles, which were filling with tea-colored water from the muddy roadside.

"Where's your brother?" Susan shouted when Emily was about halfway to the open car door. "I was supposed to pick him up, too."

Emily drew to a sudden stop, and fresh apprehension filled Susan. She could practically read her daughter's mind.

Why doesn't she know where John is? If Brenda sent her to pick me up, she would know where my brother is, wouldn't she?

Susan tried desperately to think of something to say to allay Emily's fears, but nothing came to mind. The voices inside her head rose in a terrible cacophony. The only clear thought she had was that, if she scared Emily away now, she wouldn't get a second chance. If she screwed this up, it was because—once again—she had tried to do something without thinking through every contingency.

"Well," she said, as mildly as she could. "Don't just stand there. Come on. Get in."

"How do you know my . . . mother?" Emily asked in a quavering voice. Susan caught the slight hesitation before she said the word *mother.*

"We're friends," Susan replied simply, cringing inwardly at the lie.

They stared at each other in silence for several tense seconds, Susan frantically trying to calculate what might happen next and what she would do about it.

If she starts running, will I go after her?

It was about a mile to Emily's house from here, and Susan could guess that the prospect of walking—or running—there in this downpour didn't appeal to her daughter. Then again, she was positive that, like any child these days, Emily had been warned about accepting rides from strangers.

But I'm not a stranger! I'm her mother!

Susan knew she had to lure Emily into the car and get out of here quickly before anyone passing by saw them. If Brenda had been planning to pick her up, it probably wouldn't take her very long to repair the tire Susan had let the air out of earlier this morning.

"You didn't answer me. Why've you been following me around?"

All Susan wanted to do was get out of the car, run to her, and hug her . . . hold her close . . . and let her know that she was safe.

"I haven't been following you around," Susan replied, shaking her head in adamant denial, and once again she almost choked on the lie.

"Yes you have," Emily said with more control in her voice. "You followed the school bus. And then in the store the other night."

So she has seen me. . . . I knew I blew it!

Susan cast a worried glance up the road to see if Brenda or anyone else was in the vicinity.

How could she not have noticed you?

Goddamn, I should have been more careful. . . . I should have thought this through better!

You always screw things up. Always! Remember what happened fourteen years ago?

"I haven't been following you. Honestly, I—"

Susan cut herself off. The time for lying was long since past. Now—finally, after fourteen years—it was time to start telling her daughter the truth.

"Emily. I . . . I'm not sure how to say this." Susan winced, hearing her voice break on almost every word. "I have to talk to you about something. Something really important."

Emily didn't budge. She stood with her arms tensed at her side as though she was ready to fight or run if she had to.

A car sped toward them, heading toward town. Its headlights shone like yellow beacons in the rainy mist as it approached. Susan tracked it with her eyes, her body winding with tension until she was sure it wasn't either Brenda or Matt. She saw Emily shift her eyes also, watching the car with a look of near desperation and panic as it zipped past them in a spray of mist. Susan was expecting her daughter to turn and run and try to wave the car down as she called out for help.

If she does that, if she makes a run for it, it will be all over. Not if you do what you have to do!

Susan didn't want to give up. She couldn't. How could she come so far and go through so much to let Emily slip away from her?

You'll never get her if you don't do it now.

Susan wouldn't have the heart to chase after her, and the last thing she wanted to do was terrorize her daughter. All she wanted was to talk to her and love her and be with her.

That's all. What's so wrong about that?

"You were at our house yesterday afternoon, too. I recognize your car. You were talking to Brenda."

Good, Susan thought, allowing herself a tight smile. *At least she didn't call her Mother!*

"Like I told you . . . your mother and I are friends."

"She said she didn't know you, that you stopped by and were lost, looking for someone else."

"Yes. Well, the truth is, it's you I wanted to see," Susan said.

Emily stiffened, and her face drained of color.

"So how come you took off as soon as I showed up? Why didn't you stay and talk to me then, with Brenda there?"

"Because I—"

Susan sucked in a breath of damp air, not knowing how to finish the sentence. Chills were working their way deep into her bones. The rain splashing off the car roof splattered her face, but she could also feel warm tears building up in her eyes.

"Stay away from me, or I'll tell my father," Emily said, and she started moving back, away from the car.

No, don't run! Don't run!

See? I knew you'd fuck it up again!

"I'm not a stranger, Emily. Honest, I'm not. If you'd just let me—"

"How do you know my name? I don't know you!"

Emily's face twisted with mixed emotions as she tossed between fear and what Susan hoped was a subconscious desire to trust her.

She knows who I am. On some level, she knows I'm her mother.

"I've known you ever since you were born, Emily . . . even *before* you were born."

Susan's voice broke on the last word, and she could no longer hold back her own tears as she stared earnestly at her daughter, willing her to get into the car.

"How . . . how could you—" Emily asked, but then she stopped short, her shoulders drooping as a look of utter confusion passed over her.

"Emily . . . please. Get into the car. Just let me talk to you for a few minutes. I have to tell you something very important."

"You can tell me here."

"No, please. I promise I won't hurt you. I would never hurt you."

Susan's pulse accelerated when Emily, after hesitating a few seconds, took another couple of steps closer to the car. She slung her backpack, dripping with water, off her shoulders and held it in front of her chest like protective padding.

She's going to do it! Good God Almighty! She's going to do it!

Don't worry. You'll do or say something to screw it up.

A wave of dizzying elation swept over Susan as Emily came even closer to the car. Once she was convinced that she wasn't going to turn around and bolt, Susan eased back in the car seat, twisted around, and leaned over to open the passenger's door for her. When the door swung open, a cold, wet gust of wind blew in, making her shiver so hard her teeth chattered. She waved Emily on before closing her own door.

"Please let this work out. Please, please, please," she whispered, clenching her hands and closing her eyes for a moment in urgent prayer.

What you're doing is wrong. You know that, I hope.

She's mine! She's my daughter!

Emily approached the open passenger's door, then bent down and looked into the car, but she didn't get in right away. With one hand resting on the top of the door, the other clutching her backpack, she stared in at Susan. Her eyes had a frightened glow, and her lower lip was pale and trembling. Silver strings of rainwater dripped from her nose and chin.

"Why should I believe you?" she asked, her voice twisting to a high pitch.

"It's okay. Really, it is. I promise I'm not going to hurt you."

Emily ran her teeth over her lower lip, sawing them back and forth several times. Susan remembered that Matt used to do the same thing whenever he was nervous.

"So what is it? What do you want to tell me?" Emily asked, shivering in the cold rain.

She didn't make a move to get into the car, but she was leaning down so the roof protected her face from the direct rain. The bill of her raincoat hood fell over her eyes, so she flipped it back.

"Please, Emily. Just get into the car. I'll explain it all to you on the way home. I promise."

Unconvinced, Emily shook her head from side to side and leaned back. Rain trickled down the sides of her face like sweat. Her purple raincoat was as shiny as sealskin.

"Come on. You're getting the inside of the car all wet," Susan said a little edgily, and then, before she even thought about it and before Emily could react, she lunged across the seat and grabbed her. Her fingers snagged the pocket of Emily's raincoat, almost tearing it off as she pulled her daughter into the car.

Emily let out an ear-piercing scream as she tried to scramble away, but her feet kept slipping on the slick roadside. She almost went down, and in the struggle, she let go of her backpack. It landed with a splash in a puddle.

As she struggled with Emily, Susan inadvertently stepped down on the accelerator, and the engine revved loudly. A gray plume of exhaust billowed like fog behind the car. The squeal of the loose fan belt drilled Susan's nerves and she almost started screaming, too. Emily didn't let up as she pulled back, trying to break Susan's hold on her. She almost succeeded, but then Susan lunged forward and grabbed her under the left armpit. Grunting loudly, she hauled her like a heavy sack into the car. Leaning over her and crushing her against the seat, Susan hauled the girl's legs in and then slammed the passenger's door shut and punched the lock down. She was sweating and panting heavily from the sudden exertion. Bright white spots of light weaved in front of her eyes, making it difficult for her to see.

"I'm not going to hurt you!" she shouted as she quickly shifted the car into gear and stepped on the gas. The car took off with a squeal of tires. Realizing how frightened Emily was, Susan made a conscious effort to lower her voice. "Really, Emily. I'm not going to hurt you."

Emily's voice broke, and she stopped screaming, but tears and rainwater were streaming down her face as she stared wide-eyed at Susan. A drop of blood glistened on her lower lip where she had bitten it.

Or did I do that? Did I hurt her?

Of course you did. You wanted to hurt her all along, didn't you?

Susan was filled with burning guilt, but she told herself that she had only done what any mother would do.

"Look," she said, panting heavily and holding a trembling hand out to touch Emily gently on the mouth. "You bit your lip."

Without taking her eyes off the road, Susan fished a tissue from her purse and held it out to Emily, who jerked away from her so fast she banged her head against the side window. She was hyperventilating, her chest hitching as she struggled to catch her breath and fight back tears.

"What do you want?" Emily rasped, sniffing loudly and wiping her eyes with the flats of her hands.

Susan realized she was speeding down the road, but she glanced at her daughter to make sure she was all right.

"Stop crying," she said, leaning forward and peering through the rain-smeared windshield at the road ahead. It was a struggle not to shout. "Just be quiet. I'm not going to hurt you."

Still looking absolutely terrified, Emily stopped crying, but she couldn't stop her wrenching sobs. Fat tears rolled from her eyes, streaking her face. She gave the door latch a sudden savage jerk, and when it didn't open, she started fumbling with the lock.

"Don't do that," Susan snapped, looking back and forth between her daughter and the road. "We're going too fast. If you fell out now, you'd get really hurt."

Gritting her teeth, Susan pressed down even harder on the accelerator. The car sped down the road, leaving a gray spray in its wake. The windshield wipers slapped steadily back and forth, and the tires made a loud tearing noise on the wet pavement. The only sounds in the car were Emily's hitching sobs and Susan's labored breathing. After a tense moment, the girl slumped forward and covered her face with her hands, apparently resigning herself to whatever was going to happen. She turned away and pressed her cheek against the side window, her face a twisted mask of misery.

"Don't cry, Emily. . . . Please, don't cry," Susan whispered mildly, but she realized that she was crying, too.

How can I not cry?

You're going to scare the hell out of her!

Yeah, but this is it. . . . I got her. . . . She's where she belongs . . . with me.

This was everything Susan had thought about and wished and dreamed and prayed for. After not seeing her daughter for fourteen long years, as incredible as it seemed, Susan had no doubt that, in spite of the chorus of voices that sometimes filled her head, from now on, things were going to be much, much better.

KYLE Hanson arrived at the school bus stop a few seconds too late. He was just in time to see the woman he had been hired to follow grab his client's daughter, pull her into her car, and take off down the road.

"Christ almighty," he muttered as he dropped his hand to his cell phone and hit the speed dial button for the police station. The dispatcher answered the call on the second ring.

"Three Rivers Police. How may I help you?"

"This is Kyle Hanson. I'm a private investigator who has been hired by Matt Ireland to keep tabs on his ex-wife. She's abducted his daughter. I just witnessed it."

"Where are you?" the dispatcher, a woman, asked.

"Route 202, just past the turn onto Burnt Mill Road. She's driving a late model Toyota, dark blue or black, and is headed west on 202 toward Newbury. She grabbed her when she got off the school bus. I want a cruiser out here right away."

"There's an officer patrolling the area," the dispatcher said. "I'll notify him immediately. You should come down to the police station to file a report."

"Yeah, I'll do that," Hanson said as he stepped on the accelerator and sped down the road in pursuit. Over the phone, he listened as the dispatcher communicated by radio with the patrolman in the area. Because of the noise in the car from the rain and the wipers, he couldn't make out everything she said, but he heard his own name mentioned twice.

"Did you happen to notice the license plate number of the vehicle?" the dispatcher asked when she came back on the phone.

Hanson knew the number from his conversation with Matt yesterday. "I'm positive this is the person I was hired to watch. She has Iowa plates. The tag's one-five-five P C. That's Iowa, one-five-five P, as in Peter, C as in Charlie. Got it?"

"Yes. There's a patrolman on his way," the dispatcher said.

"I'll keep her in sight until he catches up."

"I would advise you not to pursue the suspect," the dispatcher said. "Let the police handle it from here."

"What's that you said? I didn't quite hear what you said. Maybe my cell phone's not working right."

After a short hesitation and a conversation on the radio with the patrolman again, the dispatcher came back on.

"The patrolman is on his way up Route 202 toward Newbury. Please stop your pursuit. It will only make it more difficult for the officer to do his job."

"Radio ahead to the next town and get someone to head her off. Set up a roadblock if you have to."

"Mr. Hanson," the dispatcher said, her voice now icy with command. "If you proceed to follow the car, you could be charged with obstruction of—"

"I know what I'm doing, okay?" Hanson said, lowering his voice and trying hard not to shout at the dispatcher. It didn't pay to get the police angry. Besides, he shouldn't be angry with this woman just because he had screwed up. If he hadn't stopped for a cup of coffee and a donut, Susan wouldn't have gotten away so easily. At least she didn't have many options as to where to go.

"Mr. Hanson. May I remind you that—"

"What's your name?" Hanson asked.

"My name?"

"Yeah, your name. Do you know who I am?" Before the dispatcher could reply, he continued. "I was a cop for better than twenty years. Probably before you were born. So don't tell me what I should and shouldn't do. I'll stop following this suspect as soon as I see a Three Rivers police cruiser pull her over. Got that?"

With that, he thumbed off the cell phone and dropped it onto the seat beside him. He winced when he took a sip of coffee. It was already stone cold.

Hanson had no difficulty keeping Susan's car in sight. Without much traffic on the road, she wasn't going more than five to ten miles per hour over the speed limit. He figured she didn't even realize yet that she was being followed.

"You're not gonna get very far," he said out loud, chuckling to himself.

After driving through Newbury, heading toward Livermore Falls, a police cruiser with flashing emergency lights appeared in Hanson's rearview mirror. The patrolman gave him a quick blast of his siren as he pulled out around Hanson to pass. Hanson snapped on his turn signal and eased over into the breakdown lane to let the cop zip by. The cruiser's tires raised a fine mist in its wake.

Up ahead, Hanson saw Susan's Toyota round a corner and disappear from sight. Either she hadn't seen the cop behind her, or else she was hoping to outrun him. Hanson listened to the distant wail of the cruiser's siren and knew he had to follow. He wanted to be there when the cop pulled her over so he could make sure the police had the right person and report to Matt that everything was settled. He needed to earn his fee.

THE instant the flashing lights of the police cruiser appeared in her rearview, Susan tromped down on the accelerator. Emily immediately sensed that something was wrong. She straightened up in the seat and looked over her shoulder as the warbling wail of the siren sounded behind them. The cruiser quickly closed the gap between them.

"I wasn't doing anything wrong," Susan muttered as she gripped the steering wheel and kept driving.

What the hell are you talking about? whispered a voice in her head.

"Don't you have to pull over and let him by?" Emily asked.

Susan didn't like the tension she heard in her daughter's voice. She knew Emily wasn't comfortable with her . . . not yet, anyway, but that was understandable.

She will with time.

What are you thinking? You're scaring her half to death!

All I want is a chance to explain, but this isn't good.

Susan had convinced herself that things would change once Emily knew who she was, but she didn't want to tell her this way. They needed time to let things happen slowly, naturally, so Emily would be able to accept the truth.

Will she even believe me?

A cold churning of apprehension filled her belly.

What do you think?

Clenching her teeth, she glanced at Emily.

"I—" she started to say but then stopped herself.

No, not like this. Why does it have to be like this?

You made it happen like this. It's all your fault . . . again!

She was sure the cop was after her, but she was confused by how he could have found out so quickly. There hadn't been anyone at the bus stop who might have seen and reported her. She was sure of that.

This isn't right! she thought bitterly.

And who told you life was fair?

The steady slapping of the windshield wipers was maddening, working her nerves like a metronome and making her all too aware that her time was running out.

You blew it! I knew you would!

The wailing siren and flashing blue lights drew closer. The strobe effect in her rearview mirror hurt her eyes.

"It's all Matt's fault," she whispered. Her hands gripped the steering wheel, and she realized she was grinding her teeth. "He had me followed."

"My dad, you mean?" Emily said, looking at her with eyebrows raised.

Susan started to say something but then caught herself.

Where do I start? What do I say?

There's nothing you can say. You've failed . . . again!

"Look, uh . . . Emily, I—"

She jumped as the piercing wail of the siren stripped her nerves.

"I can't pull over. I'm not going to. They're after me—"

"Because you kidnapped me."

A surge of powerful emotion raged inside Susan. She choked back her tears as she tried to reply, but she was having trouble focusing on the road ahead. She glanced quickly at Emily.

"You have to know something."

Emily was staring at her, her eyes wide with fear and confusion, her face drained of color.

"There's no easy way to tell you this, Emily, but I—" She sucked in a breath that made her ribs ache. "I'm your mother."

"No you're not," Emily said, her voice a broken whisper. "You can't be. . . . My real mother's dead."

Before Susan could say anything more, she saw the Dangerous Curve sign with flashing yellow warning lights up ahead. Her gaze shifted back and forth from the cruiser in the rearview mirror to the road ahead and then to her daughter. Tears blinded her as she gazed at Emily.

"Put on your seat belt, sweetie. Just in case," she said.

Without hesitation, Emily stretched the seat belt across her chest and clipped it with a reassuring click. Susan didn't have her own seat belt on, but she knew it was already too late. The curve was just ahead. She gripped the steering wheel tightly with both hands, her knuckles white as she got ready. The car's tires hissed on the wet pavement, and before she was through the turn, she lost control. The car went into a slow, gliding skid.

The police cruiser was almost on her rear bumper. The flashing blue lights in the rearview mirror confused her, and the wailing siren pierced her ears like an ice pick.

"Leave me alone!" she screamed.

Her car was going well over fifty miles an hour. For a second, Susan thought she was going to regain control, but then she saw a pickup truck on her left as it started pulling out onto the main road, cutting in front of her. She let out a terrified shriek that was lost beneath the wailing of the siren. Her foot came down hard on the brake, and she tried to swing out around the truck, but the tires lost traction on the rain-slick pavement. The back end of the car started fishtailing around in a stomach-lifting spin.

No. . . . God, please! . . . No-o-o-o!

Susan tried to keep control of her car by steering into the skid, but her brakes locked up, and the momentum carried her car around in a slow, gliding spiral. She heard a loud thump on the bottom of the car as it hit the shoulder of the road. As the car careened across the weed-choked roadside ditch, the rear end dropped down heavily. The momentum was enough to make it shoot up into the air.

A green screen of trees and brush rushed toward the windshield. Susan heard another shriek but didn't know if it was her or her daughter. The engine raced, and then a loud thump was followed by the sound of breaking glass and crunching metal. Susan was thrown forward. Her head slammed so hard against the steering wheel her vision filled with bright light. The pain of impact was lost as she felt herself lifted up and over the dashboard.

For a terrifying, timeless instant, she was weightless, suspended in midair. Below her she saw a smear of gray sky that looked curiously out of place. The trees, the ground, and sky all dissolved into a crazy swirl of green, brown, and gray. Something thumped inside the car, sounding like a clap of thunder, but Susan was barely aware of it as she was propelled forward.

She never felt the pain as her head smashed through the windshield, and her body catapulted over the steering wheel and onto the ground beneath the overturned car.

PATROLMAN Haringa hit his brakes and skidded to a stop just before he rounded the corner. He watched in stunned amazement as the car he'd been pursuing flipped over and came to rest on its roof. Broken glass exploded from the windows and scattered like diamonds across the wet grass. Billowing steam rose from the exposed underside of the car. The wheels were still spinning, spewing out fans of mud from their treads. Haringa slammed the cruiser into Park and was out of the car in an instant, but even as he leaped across the gully and ran toward the wreck, he was expecting the worst.

I shouldn't have chased her, he thought. *Goddamn it! I should have done something different!*

Then again, he hadn't thought the suspect would try to outrun him. He had expected her to pull over as soon as she saw his flashing lights in her rearview.

Wet branches slapped his legs, arms, and face. Within seconds, his pants and jacket were soaked through as he plowed through the underbrush toward the wreck. His only concern was to get the passenger or passengers away from the car before any leaking gasoline ignited; but as he approached the wreck and bent down to look inside, he realized that he probably didn't have to worry about the driver.

Her crumpled body was stuck halfway through the shattered windshield. Wide swatches of blood smeared the dashboard and roof of the overturned car. The gentle rainfall quickly washed them away in thin, pink streaks, and a widening pool of blood spread across the dark ground. The woman's features were lost behind the mask of dark blood. Her eyes were closed, and if she wasn't already dead, Haringa knew she wasn't going to last long.

"God have mercy," he muttered, trying to absorb the fact that he had caused this.

This wouldn't have happened if I had just kept her in sight and waited for the units up ahead to set up a roadblock.

Haringa was young and relatively new on the police force. He hadn't seen many car accidents, much less fatalities, but it sure looked like this woman was dead. When he touched her wrist, her skin was cold, but he wasn't sure if he could feel a pulse.

Feeling hollow inside, he looked inside the car through the shattered driver's side window. His heart skipped a few beats when he saw a small figure on the passenger's side. After a paralyzed moment, Haringa realized it was a young girl. Her purple rain slicker was smeared with blood that rolled off in large red droplets that plopped onto the roof of the upended car.

Slipping on the wet ground, Haringa ran around to the other side of the wreck and, steeling himself, got down on his hands and knees and reached into the car to undo the seat belt. It wasn't easy with the girl's weight pulling the strap taut. He jumped, startled, when a voice called out behind him, "Hold on. I'll help you with her."

"You got a cell phone?" Haringa shouted, not bothering to look to see who it was. He guessed it was the driver of the pickup truck that had pulled into the road and caused all of this. "Call for a goddamned ambulance!"

"Already did that," the person said.

Unmindful of the wet and cold, Haringa wedged himself into the crushed interior of the car. After a bit of a struggle, he got the seat belt to release. Cradling the girl in his arms, he gently lowered her to the ground and then started easing her out of the car. The rain was falling around them as he looked down at her blood-streaked face.

The person who had stopped to help was standing a short distance behind him. "She alive?" he asked.

Turning slowly, his shoulders knotted with tension, Haringa glared at him, numb with shock. It took him a moment to recognize Kyle Hanson, a town cop who had retired several years ago.

Haringa nodded. "Yeah. I think so," he said as he reached under her hood and held his fingertips against her neck. "Not much of a pulse."

"Christ, you're not even doing that right," Hanson said with a snarl as he knelt beside them and yanked the hood of the girl's raincoat down. He felt for her jugular vein, pressed his fingers against her neck, and waited a moment, silently counting, then nodded and smiled.

"She'll be okay."

Leaning close, he wiped the blood off the girl's face. "Got a helluva cut on her head, but scalp wounds bleed like a bastard." He sniffed. "Lucky for her she was wearing her seat belt. The driver, though . . ."

They both looked over at the motionless figure on the ground in front of the car. After a frozen minute, Haringa sat back on his heels and looked up at the shifting storm clouds. They were darkening with every passing second. A cold breeze hissed through the undergrowth, shaking the leaves.

The rain fell in a steady, prickling downpour that washed over his face, chilling him. He cringed when he heard the distant wail of an approaching siren.

"Damn it," Haringa whispered as a deep shudder shook his shoulders. "It's all my fault." He looked at Hanson. "If she's . . . if either one of these people is dead, it's *my* fault." He let out a sob and covered his face with both hands. "I never should've gone after her like that."

"Get used to it," Hanson said without a trace of sympathy in his voice as he walked over and knelt down beside the dead or unconscious woman. "You didn't know she'd try to run." He shrugged. "Them's just the breaks."

seeking help

"IF you think you might need something . . . you know, maybe something to take the edge off, I could prescribe a mild sedative."

Brenda pursed her lips as she considered the offer; then she sighed and slowly shook her head.

"I don't know if I need it," she said softly.

So is this what it's come to. . . . I need medication?

"Maybe I could try a sedative. You don't think I need an antidepressant, do you?" She chuckled. "I mean, most everyone I know is on Prozac . . . or should be. But . . . I don't know. At this point, I'm not sure *what* to think."

Dr. Gregory Joyce smiled reassuringly as he laid his hand gently on Brenda's shoulder. He had been her doctor ever since he set up his practice in Three Rivers more than ten years ago. He had coached her through her pregnancy with John, and he had treated all of his and Emily's childhood diseases. Brenda had always trusted him implicitly, so she couldn't understand why she cringed at his touch. Beneath her clothes, her skin felt oily and cold.

"That's why you visit a doctor," Dr. Joyce said, a half-smile twitching a corner of his mouth. "Because we modern medical practitioners know absolutely *everything* there is to know about the human body and mind." He paused, then added, "Except how to cure the common cold, of course."

His attempted joke didn't do much to raise Brenda's spirits. Usually, she looked forward to her visits with him, but today she felt an indefinable tightness inside her, and it wouldn't go away. She looked at him with raised eyebrows and a tremor in her voice.

"What is it, then? What's wrong with me?"

"You're under a great deal of stress, Brenda," Dr. Joyce said, suddenly serious. "If you're experiencing mental states that you don't normally experience, it's entirely understandable. Grief can do some strange things to people."

"Even make them hallucinate?"

Biting down on her lower lip and shaking her head, Brenda stared at him, wishing she didn't feel so desperate, so vulnerable.

"I—I've been seeing things, Greg." She struggled to push back the sense of desperation that was rising up inside her. "I mean honest-to-God hallucinations." She paused for a moment and licked her upper lip, tasting the salt. "I know it sounds crazy, but at times I'm actually convinced . . . I even accept that there's a ghost in my house."

"Your mother's ghost," Dr. Joyce said.

"Maybe. I'm not sure."

Brenda closed her eyes and covered them with both hands as she tried to bring the mental image of what she had seen into focus. Each time, the face of the old woman had been distorted, either warped in reflection in the mirror or the teakettle or, in the case of the multiple faces in the windows, obscured by the reflections in the glass.

"Yes . . . yes," she whispered dreamily. Her eyes were still closed, and the image sharpened in her mind, sending teasing tingles up and down her spine. Against the swirling black background of her closed eyes, a blurry visage arose: an old woman's face that certainly *could* be her mother, but the features were indistinct, like a smeared watercolor; the lips were thin and cracked, gray and bloodless.

But it was the scar that burned the clearest in her memory.

A twisted white gash ran from the woman's forehead, down between her left eye and ear, and over her cheekbone to her chin. The old scar tissue was gray and knotted. Although Brenda realized she might be inventing some of the details instead of remembering them exactly, she was convinced of this one detail. The scar was distinct, and she had noticed it all three times.

She was confused because her mother hadn't suffered any facial injuries in the fall that had killed her.

So why was she appearing to her with this horrible disfigurement?

"It certainly *looks* like my mother," she said dreamily.

When she opened her eyes, she was surprised by the sudden brightness of the room as she looked at her doctor. His blue eyes looked cold, and his mouth was unsmiling and set.

"It has to be her," Brenda said, "but you have to understand. This isn't, like, some memory. When I see her, it feels . . . real. Like she's really there. I can *feel* her behind me. Her presence is palpable."

"You said you don't see her directly, though? Only in reflection?"

Brenda nodded as the rush of cold sliding up her back intensified. A sour taste filled her mouth. When she turned her head, the room distorted with an odd telescoping effect. She was suddenly afraid that she was going to pass out.

Her gaze shifted to the window, and she looked out at the overcast sky. The trees in the distance waved with hallucinatory slowness, and rain hissed like tiny voices against the windowpane. Water droplets distorted her view, but she cringed when she saw her own reflection in the glass.

An intense feeling of déjà vu gripped her, making her shake wildly. It was only a flash, but she had the distinct impression that what was happening had already happened before, and she was merely remembering this visit to her doctor.

Something's really wrong with me, she thought. *Terribly wrong!*

A faint whimper escaped her as she turned and looked at her doctor. She wanted desperately to say something, to keep the conversation going as though everything was perfectly normal, but a nameless anxiety gripped her. She already knew what she was going to say and what he would say in response.

Her pulse surged with a rapid, muffled thundering deep inside her head. The antiseptic air of the office seemed cloying, possibly poisonous to breathe. The room tilted, seeming to slip away under her feet like a glaze of ice.

"If you think it would help," Dr. Joyce said, "I could refer you to a therapist. Maybe you need someone to talk to about this."

Fighting to keep her balance, Brenda nodded stiffly. Somehow, she had already known he was going to say those exact words. She struggled to stay connected to what was going on. She felt as though she was drifting away, trapped in the shifting unreality of a dream. When her cell phone beeped, it sounded so far away it took her several heartbeats to recognize it. Shaking her head as though dazed, she forced a smile as she reached into her purse, took out the phone, and snapped it open.

"Yes," she said, amazed by the remote quality of her own voice even though it was so close to her ear.

"Yeah, Brenda. It's me. Where are you?"

She barely recognized Matt's voice while, at the same time, she realized she had known it was him before she answered the phone or even before it rang.

"I'm at the doctor—"

"There's been an accident," Matt said before she could finish. "Emily was in a car accident."

"What?"

The single word exploded out of her, and the weird thoughts and feelings she'd been having instantly dissolved. Sensing that something was wrong, Dr. Joyce stepped closer to her. Brenda barely noticed him as the walls of the examination room seemed to collapse inward on her.

"I'm not sure exactly what happened, but Susan picked her up, and she drove off the road when the cops chased her."

"Oh my God! Where is she?"

Brenda's grip on the phone tightened so hard a jolt of pain shot up her arm.

"She's in an ambulance. They're taking her to the hospital in Augusta. I'm heading over there now."

"Is she—? Oh, my God! Is she all right?"

"I'm not sure. I just got the call." Matt's voice was strained and laced with panic. "A . . . someone I know saw it happen.

He says he's pretty sure she's going to be all right, but we don't know for sure."

"I'll be right there. Have you heard from John?"

In the brief silence before he answered, Brenda imagined several worst-case scenarios. Perspiration broke out on her forehead, and tickling streams ran down the inside of her blouse.

"Didn't you say he was going over to Mike's after school?" Matt asked.

"That was the plan. I'll call Mrs. Peterson and make sure he's there, and I'll see you at the hospital within half an hour." Before she hung up, she paused to take a sip of a breath. "Don't worry. She's going to be all right, Matt."

"I hope you're right."

"No, I know she is."

And somehow, as if it were already a memory, Brenda knew she was right.

"Be careful," Brenda said, but Matt had already broken the connection. Feeling dazed, she looked at Dr. Joyce and shook her head.

"I have to go. Emily's been taken to the hospital."

She slid off the examination table and fumbled to straighten out her clothes. Dr. Joyce's face was set in a grim expression.

"If there's anything I can do to help . . ."

"I know," Brenda said with a nod.

"I'll have that prescription for you at the desk whenever you can pick it up."

As she started for the door, her legs felt stiff, as though she were walking on stilts. She still felt echoes of that weird sense of unreality that had gripped her. It clung to her like the faint smell of cigarette smoke on clothes.

"Yeah . . . okay . . . thanks," she said distantly, but as she stepped out of the exam room and closed the door behind her, she knew there was no way her doctor was going to be able to help her.

No matter what was happening to her, antidepressants, sedatives, and therapy weren't even going to begin to touch it. And now, if after the death of her mother, she and Matt were going to have to deal with this . . .

"No. Don't think like that," she told herself as she dashed

across the parking lot to her car. She wouldn't allow herself to think that the worst had happened. As she got into her car and started it up, she kept repeating to herself, "Everything's gonna be all right. . . . Everything's gonna be all right. . . ."

"CAN you at least tell me where they are?"

Brenda was trying not to shout into the cell phone, but she was frantic to find out where John was before she got to the hospital. She didn't really care for Edna Peterson. The woman was much too *laissez-faire* when it came to her own son, much less other people's children.

"How should I know where they are?" Mrs. Peterson snapped. "Mike didn't leave a note or nothing. I just got home from work and was about to take a nap. Mike usually don't show up until suppertime, if then."

If she wasn't so worried about Emily, Brenda would have told Mrs. Peterson off then and there and hung up.

"This is a family emergency, Mrs. Peterson," she said, struggling to keep her voice low and measured. "I'd appreciate it if you'd have John call me as soon you see him. He knows my cell number."

"I can't make any guarantees," Mrs. Peterson said. "I'll probably be asleep."

"It's really important that I speak with him," Brenda said, and before Mrs. Peterson could reply—if she were inclined— Brenda broke the connection.

There was a determined set to her jaw as she gripped the steering wheel and drove down River Road to Central Maine Medical. She couldn't stop worrying about Emily, but she knew it was irrational to be afraid that just because something had happened to her, something was also wrong with John.

She regretted that she hadn't gotten John his own cell phone when he'd asked for one last Christmas. Right this minute, she desperately needed to hear his voice or see him to reassure herself that he was fine.

Her mind filled with frightening scenarios, and she found it difficult to stay under the speed limit. The last thing she needed was to have an accident or get a ticket.

Calm down. She's all right. You know she's all right.

The rain was letting up by the time she pulled into the parking lot by the emergency room entrance. She jumped out of the car and dashed inside, slipping and almost falling on the wet linoleum. She found Matt in the waiting room, looking pale and drawn as he paced back and forth. He broke down and started to cry as soon as he saw her coming toward him. Without a word, she hugged him. His body trembled against her, and he hung onto her like a drowning man clinging to a life raft.

"Any word yet?" she asked, pulling back and looking him straight in the eyes.

Biting his lower lip, Matt shook his head. He looked lost and bewildered. His warm breath blew across her face.

"Nothing yet." His voice caught with an audible click. The panic in the depths of his eyes froze her. "She's in the exam room now, but they haven't told me what her injuries are. They won't even let me see her."

"Don't worry," Brenda whispered. "She's going to be just fine."

And although she had nothing concrete on which to base it, she knew it was true. She didn't know how she knew. It was almost as if a faint voice was whispering into her ear, telling her that Emily was going to survive.

Gripping both of her husband's arms just above the elbows, she leaned close to him and stared directly into his eyes, which glistened with tears. When she saw herself reflected in the glassy surface of his eyes, a sudden surge of panic rose up inside her.

"What if she—" He left the thought unfinished as if merely saying the words would make it so.

I was in a hospital just a few days ago, Brenda thought as the sadness opened up inside her, *and I lost someone close to me, but it's not going to happen this time . . . not so soon . . . not now . . . not here. . . .*

Before she could say anything more to reassure Matt, the double doors of the emergency room swung open. A doctor wearing green scrubs caught their attention and started toward them. Brenda thought he looked too young to be a doctor, but she immediately noticed that his expression was calm and relaxed.

"Mr. Ireland?" he said, shaking hands first with Matt, then

with Brenda. "I'm Dr. Finch. Would you come with me, please?" He clamped a translucent green clipboard between his arm and chest as he held the door open for them with his shoulder.

For a moment, Matt couldn't move. He gaped at Dr. Finch, then finally shook himself and nodded his understanding. Desperation was evident on his face, but he was too anxious to speak.

Brenda and Matt exchanged nervous glances before following the doctor a short distance down the corridor to an opened office door. With a wave of his hand, Dr. Finch indicated for them to enter.

Brenda could feel Matt's panic rising, and she realized that she was going to have to be the strong one now.

Still, she couldn't ignore the panicky rushes she was feeling as they sat down in the two chairs that had been drawn up beside the desk.

"Your daughter is fine," Dr. Finch said without preamble as he took a seat behind the desk. He placed the clipboard on the desk in front of him and folded his hands on top of it.

As soon as the words were out of his mouth, Matt heaved a shuddering sigh of relief and groaned as he collapsed back in the chair and covered his face with both hands. He took a deep, noisy breath.

"Oh, Jesus. Thank God. . . . Thank God," he whispered as he lowered his hands and glanced at Brenda. He reached out and took her hand, giving it a squeeze. His cheeks were flushed bright red, and tears were streaming from his eyes.

"She sustained some minor abrasions and a particularly nasty scalp wound, but there's absolutely no indication of any serious internal injury."

Dr. Finch paused, then smiled tightly.

"She's lucky she was wearing her seat belt. I'd like to keep her overnight for observation, but I don't see why she wouldn't be able to go home tomorrow." He cleared his throat and shifted uneasily in the chair.

"Unfortunately . . ."

He swallowed hard and broke eye contact with Matt for an instant as he glanced down at his folded hands.

"I'm afraid your wife, Susan, is in critical condition."

Matt gasped but said nothing and kept staring straight ahead, his mouth hanging open, his lips absolutely bloodless. Concerned for Matt, Brenda decided not to correct the doctor.

"She suffered severe head trauma and is in surgery right now, but I must be candid with you, Mr. Ireland. I wouldn't hold out too much hope."

Dr. Finch's words knocked the wind out of Brenda. She made an involuntary sound in her throat, and her body stiffened as if she had received a mild electrical shock.

"My . . . wife?" Matt said.

He was staring blankly ahead as if, in his relief, he hadn't quite understood what the doctor had said. He gave Brenda's hand another squeeze that was almost painful this time.

"I'm terribly sorry," Dr. Finch said, his voice lowered with sympathy.

"No, no. You don't understand," Matt finally said, still trembling with relief. "She isn't my wife. Susan and I are divorced."

"I see," Dr. Finch replied with a quick nod.

A brief silence followed, but Matt broke it by asking, "When can we see my daughter?"

"Right now. Come with me," Dr. Finch said. He stood up and walked over to the door, apparently glad to be doing something to get past the awkwardness of his faux pas. "She's in an exam room right down the hall."

He held the door open for them and walked with them down the corridor past the curtained enclosures to the last cubicle on the left. The metal rings scraped loudly as Dr. Finch slid the curtain open, and there was Emily, sitting on a paper-covered table, wearing a thin cotton hospital Johnny. A medical assistant, a good-looking young man with long, sandy hair and oval glasses, was tending to the numerous cuts on her right hand. A thick pad of white bandage was taped to the side of her head at the hairline above her left eye.

Is that going to leave a scar? Brenda wondered, realizing that, if the cut had been any more serious, Emily might have ended up with a scar similar to the one the ghostly old woman had.

"Daddy!" Emily squealed as soon as Matt entered the

room. She almost jumped off the examination table to run to him, but the attending MA gently held her back with one hand.

"Easy, there, little lady," he said with a slight Southern drawl. "I'm not quite done with you."

Emily sighed with exaggerated frustration as she settled back down on the exam table so he could continue his work. Unable to restrain himself, Matt walked over to his daughter and placed his hand on her shoulders. He kept staring at her as though he still didn't quite believe she was really here and was really all right. He kept patting her on the back as if to reassure himself that she was alive.

"You'll have to tell me what happened," Matt said as tears filled his eyes.

"I know, I—*owwww!*"

Emily winced and jerked her hand away from the MA, who was dabbing antiseptic onto one of her cuts. He glanced up at her and shrugged apologetically.

"You can tell me about it later," Matt said, "once we're through here."

"It was really scary, Daddy," Emily said. Her face twisted into a pained expression, but Brenda wasn't sure if it was from the memory of what had happened or from the pain of having her wounds cleaned.

"It must have been," Matt replied softly, still rubbing her shoulder. His face was pale and marked with utter disbelief.

"Do you know who she was?" Emily asked, her voice rising an octave at the end of her question. She turned again to look at her father, but the MA restrained her.

Matt's mouth dropped open, and a short gasp escaped him before he stiffened his shoulders and said softly, "No, honey. I have no idea who she was. I—uh, I'll have to talk to the police about her and find out what I can."

Suddenly flushed with embarrassment, Brenda looked down at the floor, hoping Emily didn't catch her reaction.

"Is she okay?" Emily asked. "Did she get hurt? I—I don't remember much. We were driving and all, but then it all kinda goes blank." She squinted and shook her head as though straining to remember.

Brenda thought Emily seemed genuinely concerned for Susan. Her face was ashen, and there was a terrified look deep within her eyes that made Brenda feel a powerful surge of pity for both her and Susan.

Emily winced and jerked her head back when the MA dabbed another cut with antiseptic.

"She was driving real fast," Emily said through clenched teeth, "and she wasn't wearing her seat belt. She told me to put mine on, and I did."

"I'm glad you did," Matt said.

Brenda narrowed her eyes, wondering why Matt had lied to his daughter. Then again, he had known Susan was back in town for . . . how long before he told her?

"There was a policeman chasing us, but after that it . . . it's . . . a complete blank. I guess I passed out. It's weird. We had an accident, right?"

"You sure did," Matt said. "You went right off the road into the woods. You're one lucky girl to be alive."

"Did the lady live?"

"I don't know. . . . I'll have to find out," Matt said as he cast a guilty glance at Brenda. His body was tensed, making it clear—to Brenda, at least—how much it bothered him to be lying like this to his daughter.

"Look, honey-pie. We can talk all about this later, okay? What you have to do right now is sit still so the doctor can get those cuts bandaged. They want you to stay in the hospital overnight just to make sure you haven't got a concussion or anything."

"Aww, do I have to? I want to go home. I'm fine. Really."

Matt glanced at the MA, who said, "I'm afraid you don't have a choice." Then he turned to Matt and asked, "Once we're done here, Dr. Finch wants to get a few X rays, especially of her right shoulder. It's pretty badly bruised. He wants to make sure she didn't chip a bone." As he was talking, he lifted the collar of Emily's Johnny and exposed a wide, purple mark across her shoulder. "It's probably just from the seat belt, but we have to make sure. Plus, she's going to have quite a bit of joint and muscle pain for a few days. We want to monitor her pain medications, at least at first, to make sure she doesn't have a reaction to them."

"You have to do what the doctor says," Matt said, turning to Emily with a shrug.

Emily didn't look like she relished the thought at all, but she let her shoulders droop and settled down to let the MA work. Throughout all of this, Brenda couldn't help but notice that not even once did Emily look at her or even acknowledge that she was in the room.

What am I, the invisible woman or something? she thought. *Maybe I'm the ghost.*

She pushed aside any bitterness she was feeling, thankful that Emily was all right, but she knew this wasn't going to change anything between them. She had to accept that their relationship would probably never be very strong, no matter what she did, and it saddened her that, the older Emily got, the worse it seemed to be.

Brenda was about to say something to Emily when her cell phone beeped. She fumbled it from her purse as she ducked out into the corridor so she could talk.

"Hello?" she said into the mouthpiece, her breath catching in her throat.

"Hi yah, Mom."

Brenda let out a gasp of relief the instant she heard her son's voice.

"Good God, John. Where have you been? I've been calling all over for you."

"Me and Mike were at Sean's."

"Well, you should have checked with me first. You know better than to just take off."

"Sorry," John said, his voice dropping a register. He knew not to argue.

"Are you at Sean's now?"

"No, we're back at Mike's. That's how I knew to call you. His mother was asleep on the couch, but she woke up and told me to call you."

"Oh . . . okay." Brenda said, thinking she might have to upgrade her opinion of Mrs. Peterson, at least a little. "We're at the hospital in Augusta. Emily was in a car accident. She's not hurt badly, but I'm leaving for home now. I'll pick you up at Mike's in half an hour."

"Do you have to?"

"Yes. I do. Just wait for me there. Got it?"

"Yeah, okay," John said sullenly.

Brenda noticed with some annoyance that he hadn't asked how Emily was doing or how serious her accident had been. He would never think to ask how she was feeling.

Is he really that insensitive, or is he just preoccupied, doing his own thing? Or is he just being a seven-year-old?

"Okay," Brenda said. "See you soon. Love yah."

Her ears started ringing in the brief silence as she waited for her son to tell her he loved her, too, but he didn't. He just hung up. Sniffing and wiping away the tears that had formed in her eyes, she closed the cell phone and slipped it into her purse. With a heavy sigh, she leaned back against the wall and glanced up and down the hospital corridor. Faint voices and a clanking of equipment echoed from the far end of the corridor.

She pursed her lips and shook her head sadly. She didn't like feeling vulnerable like this. John wasn't rejecting her. She knew he loved her. He might have been embarrassed to say anything if Mike or his mother could overhear. This was her problem more than his, she knew, and after everything that had happened over the last few days, she knew she was in a particularly vulnerable state of mind.

But the least he could do is tell me he loves me, she thought.

case closed

"I'D like to stay with you guys, but I told John I'd pick him up shortly," Brenda said.

Of course she was concerned for Emily, but she felt almost desperate to get out of the hospital. She couldn't stop thinking about how, less than a week ago, she had been in another hospital, watching as her mother died.

Matt smiled at Emily and said, "I'll be right back. I'm just going to walk Brenda out to the car."

Tight-lipped, Emily gave him a quick nod.

Brenda's hands were sweaty, and she could barely keep them from trembling as she and Matt left the cubicle and, hand in hand, walked down the corridor to the exit. The twin automatic doors swung open with a loud whoosh, and a blast of cool, moist air hit them in the face as they walked out onto the wide sidewalk. Although the rain had stopped, the day was still dreary and gray. Driven by the wind, low-hanging clouds streaked through the sky like dirty smoke.

As she glanced at her husband, a shiver ran through Brenda. She wanted him to understand why she was so anxious to pick up John, but she wasn't sure what to say without sounding as though she was more worried about John than Emily.

"I guess that's it, then, huh?" she said, her voice low, just above a whisper. "It's all over. Susan won't trouble us anymore."

Matt paused on the curb, his lips pursed as he stared down at the pavement. He looked absolutely drained.

"No, I . . . I guess not," he said distantly, shifting his eyes from side to side. He seemed to be having trouble focusing on anything for very long. With a sigh, he shook his head. "I just . . . It seems so surreal. I feel like I have to slap myself to make sure I'm not dreaming." He inhaled noisily and rubbed his face with both hands.

"I know what you mean," Brenda said, remembering the weird feelings she'd been having earlier.

She wasn't sure what—if anything—she could say or do to feel more connected with her husband. His ex-wife's return certainly had frightened her, and after what she had tried to do— *she actually tried to kidnap Emily!*—the stark sense of danger narrowly escaped left her feeling weak and empty. She tried not to imagine all the terrible things that could have happened.

It just as easily could have been Emily who's in a coma and not expected to live. . . .

Or John.

"God," she whispered, fighting back a wave of panic. "I remember how, back when we first started seeing each other, Susan would call you all the time and get on your case about . . . whatever, especially when she'd been drinking, and how after you hung up, you'd mumble something about how you wished she'd fall off the face of the earth—"

"I didn't mean it. Not like this!" Matt said tiredly.

"I know," Brenda said. "I suppose we should feel sorry for her."

Her voice trailed away. She could see that Matt needed time to process everything that had happened. The full impact still hadn't hit him. All they could do now, Brenda knew, was be there for each other.

The good thing, though, she thought, *the important thing is, Emily's alive and safe. . . . And so is John. It could have been so much worse.*

"But still . . ." she said after an awkward moment of silence.

"Yeah," Matt said, shaking his head slowly, as though dazed, "she *did* try to kidnap our daughter."

Brenda wasn't sure if by "our" he meant him and Susan or

him and her, but the twist of fear in his voice was palpable, and her heart went out to him.

"Yes she did," Brenda said as she tightened her grip on his hand, "and it won't happen again." Reaching up, she touched his face lightly, forcing him to turn and look at her. "It's all over, Matt. We can get on with our lives now."

"I guess so," he said, his voice as soft as an echo.

They didn't speak any more as they walked across the parking lot to Brenda's car. She wished she could make him understand that she wouldn't really feel as though John was safe until he was in her arms, but she remained silent. On some level, she knew he understood. Emily was out of danger, but the aftershocks were still rolling over him.

"She really was going to take her, wasn't she?" Matt said in a voice tinged with utter disbelief. "I mean, she really would have done it. . . . She was trying to take her from us. And she almost killed her in the process." He shivered.

"And she's probably going to end up paying for it with her life."

When they reached Brenda's car, she let go of his hand to get her car keys from her purse. As she did, she glanced at him, trying to understand the depths of his fear.

"I'm sure it will all work out for the best," she said. "You know I would never wish harm on anyone, but . . . God, Matt . . . When you think about what *could* have happened."

Matt pursed his lips and whistled as he shook his head. "I don't want to go there. That's what's going to keep me awake for a lot of nights to come, I'm afraid."

"Just remember, she didn't get away with it," Brenda said, feeling her own spark of apprehension in spite of the strength in her voice. "And she probably isn't going to survive. And if she does . . . well . . ."

Even as she said it, she realized that running through this list of might-have-beens was going to hurt them more than help.

"She'll be looking at jail time if I decide to press charges," Matt said. Suddenly tensing, he clenched his fists and regarded her with fire in his eyes. "Hell, I'll make goddamned *sure* of it."

Brenda pressed the remote keyless entry button on her key

ring. The horn beeped, and the headlights flashed once quickly.

"Let's just count our blessings," she said, resting her hand gently on his arm just above the elbow. "Think how lucky we are for simple things: that Emily had the sense to put on her seat belt, that she was barely hurt at all in what easily could have been a terrible accident. You have to count your blessings, honey."

"I do," Matt said huskily. "Every day."

Leaning close, he kissed her on the mouth. The kiss took on a passionate intensity as he pressed his lips against hers. His tongue darted out and slid across her teeth, sending a tingle through her body. Clutching her purse in one hand and her car keys in the other, Brenda encircled his waist with both arms and held him tightly against her, reveling in his warmth and the soft, musky smell in the crook of his neck.

"I love you, darling," she whispered, feeling the heated wash of her breath rebound against her face.

"I love you, too, Bren," he said, squeezing her so hard he trembled. "God, I love you!"

As she held him, his body slumped and began to shake as he leaned forward and cried onto her shoulder. Closing her eyes, Brenda held onto him, whispering softly in his ear so he knew it was all right. He dissolved into her embrace.

We're all alive, she thought. *It's all over, and we're all alive, and we're all still a family.*

And in the back of her mind, a tiny voice whispered, asking her how long she thought that would last.

"**O**KAY, you win," Brenda said as John slid onto the car seat beside her and pulled the door shut. "I'll get both you and Emily your own cell phones. From now on, I want to know exactly where you are and what you're doing."

"Mike is such a jerk," John said as if he wasn't even listening to her. His hand went up to the light bruise on his left cheek. Brenda jumped when she saw it.

"Did you get into another fight?"

"I was playing Vice City—"

"I told you I didn't want you to play that game. Did Mike's mother know you were playing it?"

John shrugged and went on, "Well he turned it off right when I was going to beat the drug lord."

"Then don't hang out with him," Brenda said. "This happens every time you go over there."

"Yeah, but he's the only friend I have within walking distance."

"I don't want to hear it," Brenda snapped with a sudden flush of anger. "You sound just like your—" She caught herself before she finished the thought and took a deep breath. "Do you know where I've been for the last two hours? Do you have any idea how worried I've been about you?"

John looked at her but didn't say a word. He just sat with his arms folded across his chest, pouting as he turned and stared out the side window at the passing scenery.

During the short drive home, Brenda filled him in on the accident, but thinking it might confuse and upset him if she told him everything, she decided to wait until they were all home together before she mentioned that someone had tried to kidnap Emily.

It didn't seem to matter. John was far from being confused or upset. He stared out the side window, tuning his mother out. It bothered her that John seemed so unaffected by what had happened. Maybe, at his age, he simply couldn't grasp the seriousness of the situation. Maybe he was conditioned by video games and movies to think that all you had to do was hit the Reset button if you got into trouble or were hurt.

"She's going to be all right," she concluded as she took the turn into the driveway and pulled to a stop in the turnaround. The pine trees at the end of the driveway were still dripping with the rain. The asphalt held a black, seal-like gleam that reflected the trees.

"Okay . . . cool," John said as he unclipped his seat belt and scrambled out of the car. He walked quickly to the side door and unlocked it, then disappeared inside, leaving it halfway open for his mother.

Alone in the car, Brenda finally allowed herself to feel some of what she'd been holding back ever since she had gotten that phone call at her doctor's office. With a shuddering sigh, she sank into the car seat and closed her eyes, fighting back an almost overwhelming sense of defeat.

"Damn it," she whispered as her vision stung with gathering tears.

Suddenly fearful that someone she couldn't see was watching her, she sat up and looked around. After the rain, the white siding of the garage glistened with moisture. She sat there staring at it and for the first time noticed details in the woodwork that she had never noticed before. Fading daylight cast a surrealistic pale-gold glow over everything.

From where she sat, she couldn't see the front of the house, but she couldn't help but wonder if the old woman's face was still in all of the windows. She felt certain that, on some level, it didn't matter whether or not she could see them. The ghostly figure would always be there like a photographic negative burned into the glass. That old woman would always be staring out through the thin, reflective barrier that separated her from the world.

But it's all over now, she told herself, even as a bone-deep tremor ran through her.

Emily would be coming home tomorrow or the next day at the latest, and then they could all get on with their lives.

But something has changed, she told herself. *Something fundamental.*

She had no idea what it was, but the thought filled her with deep, unfathomable sadness.

We'll never be the same again. I'll never be the same again.

A wave of self-pity swept through her.

What about how I feel? Does anyone care about what I'm going through? Does Matt or John or anyone care?

Trying to be objective, she acknowledged that what she was feeling was perfectly understandable. She was still grieving for her mother. Family, friends, and doctors were all telling her that this was normal, but she couldn't help wondering if it was really only stress and grief, like Dr. Joyce said, or something else.

Am I having a mental breakdown?

The cold trembling in her stomach told her that it might be more serious than anyone was admitting. She wanted to believe that their problems were over and that, given time, the damage they had all suffered would be repaired. Even her relationship with Emily, which had gotten worse since they moved into the new house, could get better with time.

"As long as I don't keep seeing things," Brenda whispered to herself, trying to ignore the tremor in her voice, "I'll be just fine. Besides . . . who says I can't allow myself a little pity party now and again?"

Lost in thought as she was, it took her a moment to realize that John had been standing in the doorway for some time. Brenda jumped when she saw him, thinking for an instant that he was another apparition in the darkened garage. Straightening up in the car seat, she stared at him curiously when she saw his stunned expression. His face had gone pale, and his eyes were wide and staring. His mouth gaped open as though he was trying to say something, but no sound came out.

"John?" she called out as she fumbled to open the car door. Her knees buckled as she got out of the car, slammed the door shut behind her, and started toward him.

"What is it, honey?"

Her heart was racing. Cold sweat bathed her skin when she reached him and, kneeling down, gripped him by the shoulders and looked at him.

"What's the matter?"

He shook his head slowly, still unable to say anything, but he was trembling so badly his teeth chattered as he raised one hand and pointed back into the house. A low, moaning sound escaped from him.

A jolt of fear shot through Brenda when she looked over his shoulder, into the garage. The side door leading into the family room was halfway open. The darkness inside the house swelled with danger.

Is she in there? Did he see her, too?

"They . . . they did it again," John finally managed to say.

Fighting for control, Brenda straightened up and started into the garage. Her eyes jerked nervously back and forth as she looked for something—anything—to use as a weapon if she needed one. The dirt-crusted hoe was leaning against the garage wall where she had left it after gardening the other day. She picked it up and hefted it, gripping it with both hands like a baseball bat.

John kept close to her side, his fingers hooked through her belt loops. She wanted to tell him to get back into the car and lock the doors and wait for her, but she didn't. They would face this together.

"Is someone there?" she whispered to him. "Did you see someone?"

John shook his head quickly and whispered, "No, but they did it again."

"Did what?" Brenda asked, but just as she said it, she leaned forward and peered into the family room. Spray-painted in bright red letters on the wall above the TV was the same message they had found after her mother's funeral:

You kill me and I'll kill you!

Brenda let out a scream that tore her throat. She stumbled backward, bumping into John, who let out his own sharp yelp. Crouching defensively, Brenda leaned forward and looked into the kitchen and the doorway leading into the dining room. She was ready to fight if she had to. Easing her grip on the hoe, she slipped her purse off her shoulder and opened it. Her throat was dry, and she licked her lips to little effect as she opened her cell phone and dialed 911.

"Yes. Hello," she said, keeping her voice low when the dispatcher answered. "This is Brenda Ireland, out on 21 Collette Road. There's been another break-in at our house. I want a patrol car out here right away. I'm home alone with my son."

THE view from the third-floor hospital window was as bleak as Matt's thoughts. Less than thirty feet across the alley was a solid brick wall. Down in the alley, piles of litter surrounded a row of industrial trash Dumpsters. Plastic bags, old paper coffee cups, and dead leaves had been flattened by the rain. Leaning forward until his nose pressed against the glass, Matt looked across the parking lot to the woods beyond. The gray sky cast a cold, depressing light into the room, which the fluorescent lights barely cut.

Still wearing a hospital Johnny, Emily was lying on the bed closest to the window. The white curtain that divided the room in half had been pulled around to give her roommate—an older girl who had just had knee surgery that morning—some privacy.

"I'm sure it'll just be overnight," Matt said. "Dr. Finch said the X rays look good. No broken bones. You're lucky."

Biting her lower lip, Emily lowered her gaze and nodded.

"I know, but I want to go home now. It's just my neck and shoulder that are a little sore."

"But they want to make sure you don't have a reaction to the pain medication."

"This sucks," Emily muttered, her lower lip sticking out petulantly.

Honestly, Matt didn't think she looked ready to go home. Her face was sallow, almost yellow, and her eyes were puffy and red-rimmed. A prune-colored bruise ringed her left eye up to the bandage that covered her forehead. The worst thing, though, was the frightened, mistrustful look he saw deep within her eyes.

"So you're still not going to tell me?" Emily said.

Matt gnawed on his lower lip, unable to turn and face his daughter. He studied her pale reflection in the window.

"Tell you what?" he asked.

Emily rolled her eyes in exasperation.

"Who she was. She told me she was my mother."

Matt swallowed hard, but the dry lump in his throat wouldn't go away.

"Is she?" Emily's voice edged higher. "I know Brenda's not my real mom, so is she? You always told me my mother was dead."

"Brenda is your mother as much—more than anyone else," Matt said. He wished there was some way to avoid this conversation, but he knew his daughter all too well. She wouldn't give up. He dreaded telling her the whole truth now, after maintaining a lie for so many years. Eventually, he knew he would have to, but not now, not tonight.

"But Brenda's not my *real* mom," Emily said, "and that lady said she was."

"Well she isn't!" Matt snapped, spinning around and staring her down. After a moment, he took a deep breath and held it long enough for his pulse to slow its steady pounding in his head. "She lied to you. Your mother died when you were a baby."

"Then why would she say something like that?"

"She was trying to trick you, to gain your trust."

"And why would she try to kidnap me?"

"I have no idea," Matt replied, staring her straight in the eyes and feeling the lie inside him bubble up like poison in his system. "She was a nut case, and she lied to get you to come with her."

"I still don't understand *why.*"

Matt shrugged. "Maybe she was going to try to get money from me—you know, hold you for ransom. I don't know who she is, but you can be *damned* sure I'm going to find out."

Emily stared back at him but didn't say anything. Her steady gaze probed deeply into him, and he couldn't help but feel that she had exposed him for the liar he was.

Tell her the truth, a voice whispered in his head. *This is your chance to come clean. Christ, you owe her at least that much.*

But another, stronger voice warned him not to say anything until he had thought it all through and talked it over with Brenda. They had to come up with a consistent story, and he wasn't sure he wanted his daughter to know the complete truth about her real mother, not now and maybe not ever.

"Look," he finally said, walking over to her bedside and resting his hand lightly on her shoulder. "The only thing you have to think about is getting better. You'll be home tomorrow. I'll bet you'll even be feeling well enough to go back to school in a couple of days."

"Oh, yippee," Emily said, rolling her head away from him. "You mean I don't even get a couple of days off?"

It took Matt a second or two to realize she was joking. He chuckled and reached out to stroke her hair but then quickly withdrew his hand.

"We'll see about that," he said softly. "I'm just glad you didn't—"

He didn't finish the thought out loud, but a voice inside his head shouted the word: *Die!*

He checked himself and said, "I'm glad to see you haven't lost your sense of humor."

Just then, his cell phone beeped. He answered it quickly, automatically turning away from Emily so he could have some privacy.

"Hello."

"They did it again."

"What? Brenda? What are you talking about?"

Matt glanced at Emily on the bed. She seemed not to be paying any attention to his call. She had rolled over onto her side and was staring out the window at the gorgeous view of brick wall and gray sky.

"Someone broke into the house again and spray-painted the same message. In the family room this time."

A cold twist of fear uncoiled inside him. His hand holding the cell phone got slippery with sweat, and his pulse started ticking like a drum in his head.

"You okay?"

"Yes. The cops are on their way."

"You're sure no one's in the house?"

"We checked everywhere," Brenda said. "They're long gone, the bastards."

"You should have waited for the police before you went in. You shouldn't take risks like that."

"It was safe," Brenda said with a measure of control in her voice. "I . . . just knew."

"I'm on my way. Emily's all set for the night. Shouldn't be more than twenty minutes."

"Okay," Brenda said. "See you then."

And then she clicked off, leaving Matt with a dead phone in his hand as he stared unfocused at his daughter, who was already asleep in the bed.

MARCUS Card was cold and wet and tired, and he didn't like skulking around in the woods on a damp day like this, but he was also feeling a peculiar exhilaration. His blood was roaring through his veins like lava, and although his face and hands were plastered with mud and wet pine needles and bark, and his clothes clung to his body like clammy hands, a rich, damp earth smell filled his nostrils, making him almost dizzy with excitement.

But he knew he shouldn't still be out here.

He should have left as soon as he'd done what he came to do, but he was curious to see what happened next.

Crouching behind the moss-covered trunk of a fallen tree, he shifted the damp fern fronds away from his face and focused on the back of the house.

Why am I even doing this? he wondered. *It doesn't make any sense.*

He didn't even know these people. He had never seen them before in his life, but somehow he had found his way here—twice, now—and done something he knew was both dangerous and stupid. And cruel.

He didn't have anything against these people. He certainly wouldn't have recognized them if they passed on the street, so why was he doing this? Why was he threatening them?

At times, it almost seemed as though someone else was making these decisions for him. Faint voices whispered inside his head, especially late at night when he couldn't sleep, and they told him what to do, forced him against his will to do these things.

Still, he couldn't deny a certain joy in it. There was an element of fun, and he thought of it as a game, trying to get away with something while imagining the genuine fear he was causing the family who lived here.

And on some level, he was sure they *deserved* it.

His knees had pressed shallow divots into the damp topsoil. His pants were saturated from the knees down. From his hiding place, he could watch the back of the house and the driveway. He cringed when the first police cruiser pulled in, and two cops got out. He snickered as the woman dashed outside and talked to them, gesticulating wildly at the house. Although she was too far away for him to make out what she was saying, it was obvious by her terrified expression that she was absolutely freaking out.

And that's a good thing. . . . That's a really good thing.

That was exactly what he wanted to have happen, even though he couldn't say exactly *why* he wanted it.

It just felt right, knowing that he'd done something to

make this particular woman feel unsafe in her own home. That's what he wanted. He wanted her and her whole family to feel as though they were in serious danger.

"Because they are!" he hissed, his breath coming out as thin steam in the cool air. "Oh, yeah, you all are!"

He sniffed with laughter because this was just the beginning. He meant those words he had spray-painted on their walls. He wasn't clear about what he was going to do next. He wasn't even absolutely clear what those words meant, but he would figure it out, even if it meant he really did want to kill them.

He inhaled deeply, the damp smell of rot filling his head and making him dizzy. His hooked fingers clawed at the rotting log, tearing away wet, black bark and exposing a myriad of scurrying insects, which he casually brushed away.

I may really want to kill them, he thought with a deep, dark glee, *but why did I say I want them to kill me? I don't mean that. I want to live. But them . . . all of them not only need to die, they are going to die, and I'm going to do it.*

He didn't have a plan yet. He hadn't even tried to figure out any of the particulars, but he was confident that it would all work out. It would come to him when that voice inside his head that didn't sound like his own voice whispered to him late at night. That's when it was loudest and clearest, when he was trying to go to sleep and was drifting somewhere between sleeping and wakefulness.

Although on some level it disturbed him to think that these were real, flesh-and-blood people he was tormenting, and that this family meant absolutely nothing to him personally, he was confident that in the end—like everything else—he would figure out *why* he was doing this as well as the *when* and the *how.*

Narrowing his eyes, Marcus watched the woman as she talked to the police. He froze for an instant when she gestured with her hand and seemed to point right to where he was hiding, but then he realized that she was indicating the back of the house.

Go ahead. Talk all you want, he thought as his anger boiled up inside him. *It's not gonna save you.*

Maybe this was a good time to head back to the motel, he

thought. He could get cleaned up, then go out and find a place to eat. Moving slowly, he crawled backward, withdrawing deeper into the woods before daring to stand up and walk away.

I'll be back, he thought as a malicious grin spread across his face.

The saturated ground squished underfoot as he went back the way he had come, following a narrow trail through the damp underbrush. Wet branches swished his face, and twigs snapped underfoot as he made his way back to his car, where he'd parked it on a dirt road just past a small corner store.

It doesn't matter what you do or say. . . . You're not safe. . . . None of you are safe anymore.

SIXTEEN

suspicions

"**YOU** really think she could have done something like that? Is she the type?"

It was late at night, and Brenda and Matt were sitting in the living room. The windows throughout the house were open to get the smell of fresh paint out. A cool breeze rustled the lacy curtains back and forth, carrying with it the steady song of the spring peepers from the pond behind the house.

Brenda was sitting on the couch with her legs folded up underneath her while Matt sat in the easy chair on the opposite side of the room. He didn't look the least bit comfortable. The reading lamp beside his chair cast a cone of yellow light around him, silhouetting his figure as he leaned forward. His hands were clasped together so tightly his knuckles had turned into pale knobs.

Brenda wished he could read her mind and know how much she wanted him to come over and sit with her. She needed him to comfort her and reassure her. But after getting home from the hospital and talking with the police, he seemed more distant than ever.

She was leery of telling him how she really felt.

Eventually, she knew, they would bring everything out into

the open, no matter how painful, but they weren't going to get very far with Matt being so agitated.

"I have no idea what she might be capable of doing," he said a little snappily. "The only thing that matters now is that it's over. She's comatose, and when and if she ever gets out of it, she'll never have a chance to do something like that again, so forget about it. It's over. Done. *Kaput. Fini.*"

"You don't know that for sure."

Matt bristled and glared at her.

"The hell I don't!"

"We can't even say for sure she's the one who did it—the spray-painting, I mean."

"Who else could it be?"

Matt sighed and shook his head in resignation, his gaze shifting to the billowing white curtains. Brenda could feel him shutting down, pulling away from her even more.

It struck her as so sad. Here they were, just moved into their brand-new home that they had designed and built, and they were more apart than they had ever been. They should be feeling happy and secure and loving, but pretty much from day one, their lives and affection for each other had been steadily ripping apart.

"I was home until a little after one o'clock," Brenda said, her voice low and measured. "In fact, I was running late for my doctor's appointment because of that flat tire."

"That's right," Matt said. "You ought to bring that over to Roger's and have him take a look at that. Probably a slow leak, or maybe there's something wrong with the valve stem."

"Fine. I'll do it on Monday," Brenda said. She suspected he was focusing on a trivial matter so he could avoid the real issue. It was hard to keep her rising anger in check. "But that's not my point."

"Ohh?" Matt glared at her. "And just what *is* your point?"

"Well . . . my point is that I don't think Susan had enough time to break into the house and do that and still have time to kidnap Emily when she got off the bus at two-fifteen. She couldn't have had more than fifteen or twenty minutes."

"Yeah? So how long do you think it would take?"

"I have no idea, but wouldn't you think she'd have to be careful and check everything out to make sure no one was home?"

Brenda was feeling really angry now, but she struggled to keep her voice down. John had gone up to his bedroom, and she didn't want him to hear them arguing.

"There was no sign of forced entry," she said. "So how did she get in so easily? I know I locked the door when I left. I double-checked it. And neither of the kids was home yet, so she would have had to jimmy the lock. Don't you think it would take some time to jimmy a door lock?"

Matt shrugged. "I've never tried, but I don't think it'd take long if you knew what you're doing."

"And your ex-wife does?" Brenda waved her hands in frustration. "What, did she have a career doing B and Es before you met? Is that how you met? You were her defense lawyer for some robberies she committed?"

"Cut it out, Bren. Listen to yourself. You sound ridiculous."

"*I* sound ridiculous? I'm scared, Matt. That's what I am. I'm not totally convinced Susan did this. Why would she draw attention to herself if what she really wanted to do was kidnap Emily? You'd think she'd be sneaking around, not breaking in and leaving threatening messages. Wouldn't you?"

Matt didn't have an answer for that. Huffing angrily, he stood up and began pacing back and forth, all the while twisting his hands together like he was washing them. He looked tired and worn down with worry, and Brenda felt sorry for him, but she was frightened. Whenever she gazed at the windows or into the corners of the room or through a darkened doorway, she could feel herself tense up as if she was expecting someone to leap out at her.

"Well I'll tell you what's really bugging me," Matt finally said, lowering his voice. "It's what the Christ do I tell Emily?" He paused and took a deep breath, then let it out with a slow hiss. "She's got to be traumatized by all of this."

Brenda shot him a harsh look as she slowly shook her head from side to side, telling herself to let go of her hostility and fear.

"You have to tell her the truth," she finally said. "Just like

I'm going to tell John the truth when I go upstairs to tuck him in."

She took a deep breath, measuring what she was going to say next before she said it. "They have to know the truth. It's a dangerous world, and there are crazy people out there who will hurt you for no reason whatsoever. And I'm not just talking about religious cultists or paranoid schizophrenics or whatever. Remember that little girl out in California a few years back who was—"

"Yes, yes. I remember. But—come on, Bren. You and I both know that most kidnappers are family members, usually estranged fathers or mothers who want custody. Like Susan. But now that she's—"

He didn't finish. He didn't have to.

An awkward silence settled between them, broken only by the steady sound of the peepers outside and the gentle wind, whistling through the window screens. Brenda looked from her husband to the window, remembering the woman's face she had seen—or imagined—in the gauzy folds of the curtains. A shiver ran up her back, and she hugged herself. Matt didn't seem to notice.

"We can't hide any more of this from them or from each other," she said, leaning forward and gazing at him intently. "We have to be honest with each other."

"I know, I know," Matt said, nodding.

He looked at her and forced a weak smile, but it looked false. Brenda wasn't used to seeing him hostile like this, and it bothered her deeply. Shifting her feet to the floor, she stood up, feeling the stiffness in her joints. Her heart was hammering hard in her chest as she walked over to him and slid her arms around his waist. Sighing, she pulled him close.

"I have to tuck John in," she said. Her voice was muffled against his chest, her breath warm and moist on her face. The hug felt good, but somehow it didn't feel complete.

"And I'm going to start by telling him everything. You can be there with me if you want."

Matt pulled away from her, a frosty look in his eyes. The barriers were back up in an instant.

"No. We have to do it, honey," she whispered urgently. "We have to be honest about everything."

Even as she said it, a cold tingling sensation filled her chest because she knew that she was as much to blame as he was. Over the last several days, she had tried a number of times to tell him what she was experiencing, but she hadn't been able to. She wasn't sure why she was withholding from him, but she felt almost as if she couldn't trust him.

Now, she suddenly realized that she wasn't even going to try; she knew she had to keep what was happening to her private.

If she couldn't or wouldn't talk to her husband about it, and if she didn't hear what she needed to hear from him or Cheryl or her doctor, then her only option was to keep it to herself.

"I'd appreciate it if you didn't," Matt said. "Not yet, anyway. I have to talk it over with Emily first. I don't—it's not right that John would know before she does."

Brenda inhaled sharply and considered for a moment, then slowly nodded.

"Okay, then. But when are you going to tell her?"

Matt was silent for a long time as he stared past her at the open window. Brenda couldn't stop thinking that somewhere out there in the darkness, a ghostly figure was watching her. At last, Matt cleared his throat and, focusing on her, slowly nodded.

"I'm not sure, but I'll do it. I promise. I'll tell her . . . when the time is right."

"Sounds like a cop-out to me."

"No. I'll tell her."

"And how will you know when the time is right?"

Matt didn't answer her. He just stared blankly at her while shaking his head slowly from side to side.

Brenda had to turn away because she knew, if Matt looked at her too closely, he would see in her eyes that she was doing to him exactly what she was insisting he not to do to Emily.

But there's a difference between not telling him what's going on with me and him outright lying to his daughter, she thought.

Talk to him. . . . Tell him about it now, an urgent voice whispered inside her head, but she was so wrung out from the day's events that she knew she didn't have the stamina, much less courage, right now.

"Some way or another," she said tiredly. "We'll work it out." She sighed as she collapsed into his embrace, and Matt hugged her tightly. For some reason, though, his embrace—as tight and good as it felt—didn't seem to be anywhere near enough to hold back the gnawing doubts and worries that were building up inside her.

THE door was partway open, so Matt rapped once lightly on the doorjamb before walking into Detective Patoine's office.

"You said you'd have a patrolman out my way," Matt said. It took effort to keep his anger in check. "Was anyone out there last night or early this morning?"

Detective Patoine, who was sitting at his paper-strewn desk, slid his reading glasses down to the tip of his nose and looked up at him. Matt was holding a rolled-up newspaper in one hand, gripping it like a hammer.

"Yeah," Patoine said, wincing as he took a sip of coffee from a Styrofoam cup. "We increased the patrols in your neighborhood like we said we would, but—please, Matt. You think we have the budget to park someone out in front of your house twenty-four seven?"

"That may be what we need. Look at this."

Matt opened up the newspaper. Folded inside it, between the local news and the sports sections, was a single sheet of white paper. Its edges were curled from being rolled up, so he flattened it down on the detective's desk with the heels of his hands and turned it so Patoine could read the childish scrawl in the center of the sheet of paper.

You kill me and I'll kill you!

"That's the same thing that was spray-painted in my house. Twice." Matt trembled with barely repressed fury.

"I know," Patoine replied. "I was out there again yesterday afternoon."

"Well *this* was inside the newspaper on my doorstep this morning."

He paused dramatically, waiting for some kind of reaction from Patoine as he picked up the sheet of paper and inspected it carefully for a few seconds without saying a word.

"We've got the wrong suspect. There's no way my ex-wife could have done this. She's been in a coma in the hospital since yesterday afternoon. I think we can safely assume that today's newspaper hadn't been printed before her accident."

Patoine looked at him over the top of his glasses.

"This is the newspaper it came in?" he asked.

Matt nodded as he handed it to him over the desk.

"Too bad the printing plants use those new smudge-proof inks," Patoine said. "Couple a years ago, we could have lifted fingerprints off it, no sweat."

"It was on my doorstep this morning, before I got up," Matt said. "There weren't any fingerprints at the house both times you guys checked. You really think whoever's doing this wouldn't wear rubber gloves?"

"Probably right." Patoine nodded as he leaned forward and shifted his gaze to the note again. "I'd like to have the lab take a look at 'em, though."

"Well *I'd* like to have you and your department *do* something!" Matt shouted. "My family is being terrorized by someone. We don't know who or why, but you'd better do something to stop it."

"Calm down, Matt. We're doing everything we can," Patoine said patiently. He got up from his desk, walked over to a file cabinet, and took a large, clear plastic bag from the bottom drawer. After slipping on blue rubber gloves, he placed the newspaper and note into the evidence bag and zipped it shut.

"I'll get it down to the lab right away," he said. "Maybe they can find something. In the meantime, we have to come up with a list of possible suspects besides your ex."

Patoine moved a chair away from the wall over to his desk and indicated for Matt to sit down.

"Want a cup of coffee? I'm due for a heat-up myself."

Matt shook his head sharply, no.

"Be right back."

Still trembling with rage, Matt walked over and sat down in the chair as Patoine left the office. The detective returned a few minutes later with two Styrofoam cups of coffee and a handful of sugar packets and powdered creamer. In that time, Matt had calmed down a little.

"Figured you'd want one anyway," Patoine said, handing a cup to Matt. "Didn't know how you took it."

"Cream and sugar," Matt said. He placed the cup on the edge of the desk, then tore open two packs of sugar, dumped them in, then stirred in a packet of Coffee-mate.

"Okay, then," Patoine said as he settled back down at his desk. "First question. Who have you dealt with in your legal practice who might have a reason to threaten you like this?"

After placing his coffee on the desk—it was too hot to gulp—Matt sat back, folded his hands across his stomach, and considered for a moment. His mind drew a complete blank. He had no idea where to start.

"Anything at all," Patoine prodded. "You have a trial recently or was there a court decision or something that might've pissed someone off enough to do something like this?"

Gnawing his lower lip, Matt shook his head.

"Nothing. Honest to Christ, I can't think of anyone."

Patoine frowned, deep in thought. "This doesn't strike me as something someone's doing rashly, out of anger. It seems very calculated."

"They certainly know when no one's home," Matt said as he picked up his coffee and took a tentative sip. It was still too hot. "I've got dozens of cases I'm working on, but there's nothing—" He clapped his hands together and rubbed them. "There's no one I can think of."

"You summons anyone recently or is there a family member who might be pissed off about a particular case, someone you got convicted?"

"Nothing springs to mind." Matt blew across the top of his coffee before taking another sip. The coffee had been on the burner too long and was burned and bitter. "The biggest case I ever handled was Jeromy Bowker, but that was years ago and he died in prison last week anyway."

"He have family? Wife? Lover? Someone who might take

it personally that you put him behind bars and that he died there?"

"Bowker didn't just die there. He committed suicide," Matt said. He stopped as a shiver ran through him as he remembered what Bowker had done to his girlfriend and her daughter. A mental image of the crime scene photos formed in his mind. "Far as I know, he was a loner. A psychopath. No family or friends other than his girlfriend and her kid."

"The ones he torched."

Matt nodded. "Any friends or relatives of his girlfriend would be ecstatic that he was dead," he said.

"You didn't get too personally involved in this case, did you?" Patoine asked with an ironic edge in his voice.

"You see the pictures of what he did?"

Patoine narrowed his eyes and shook his head, then winced as he sipped from his own coffee. "No," he said, looking earnestly at Matt. "No need to, but I followed the case close enough to know what happened. Frankly, a piece of shit like Bowker got what he deserved. One reason I wish we'd bring back the death penalty to this state is to get scum like that off the planet. One less pimple on the ass of the world, far as I'm concerned. I just hope he suffered before he died, just in case there's no hell. You did society a favor putting him away for life. But if it ain't Bowker and it's not your ex-wife, then who the fuck is it?"

"That's your job to find out," Matt said. "I'd gotten plenty of convictions and put my fair share of people away over the years, either in Warren or Windham, but I'm just doing family law now. No one's going to go to this extreme."

"You'd be surprised. First thing I want you to do is go over all of your case files, no matter how old, and see if anyone stands out as someone who might be mad enough to threaten your life."

"How do we know it's me they're threatening?"

In spite of the coffee, coldness filled his belly. His hand was shaking as he raised the cup to his mouth and took another sip.

"What if they're after my wife . . . or one of my kids?"

Patoine frowned as he considered this and then shook his head.

"Not likely," he said. "This isn't your typical death threat. Maybe if it happened once, I'd pass it off, and after a while we'd forget all about it and get on with our lives. But whoever's doing this is obviously disturbed, and they're being surprisingly persistent and methodical. They're good, too, not leaving anything we can go on. Usually someone who does something like this is unbalanced enough to leave a clue or two behind if only to taunt us."

"Well if they're trying to frighten us, it's working. My wife is scared out of her mind." Matt hit the edge of the desk with the flat of his hand hard enough to make his cup of coffee jump. "If it's directed at me—then fine. I can handle it. I've been threatened before by scumbags, believe me. What I want to know is, what is the police department doing to stop it?"

"Like I said—" Patoine shrugged. "We don't have the personnel or the resources to have someone out to your house around the clock. You want to hire private security, that's your business. Maybe a burglar alarm wouldn't be a bad idea, although that'd probably take a couple of weeks to get lined up."

"Brenda's mentioned staying in a motel for a few days or weeks, but I won't do that. I'm not going to disrupt my family that much. And I'm not going to run from my own house."

Patoine nodded. "No, I don't see any need for that. You have a gun or a dog?"

"No," Matt said, shaking his head.

"Probably just as well," Patoine said. "About the gun, I mean. For starters then, why don't you make a list of everyone connected with any cases you've had who might be holding a grudge and want to get back at you?"

"You think that's all they want to do, get back at me? Or do you think they really mean to kill me?"

"No way of knowing," Patoine said.

The detective's attitude irritated Matt. It bothered him that Patoine didn't seem to be taking this all that seriously. As Patoine took another slurping sip of coffee, all Matt could think was, *I'll bet he wouldn't be so goddamned casual if he was being threatened.*

"Could be serious," Patoine said. "Could be they're just trying to shake you up a bit. Throw you off balance. Let's start with a list of everything you've worked on in the last three years."

Patoine lowered his head and stared at Matt over the rim of his glasses. "And don't give me any of that lawyer-client confidentiality bullshit," he said. "You come in here squawking about how we gotta do our job, then give me something to go on. Between you and me—fuck client confidentiality. Someone's threatening you and your family? Then we do what we gotta do. Until we figure out who it is and how serious they are, you probably want to cooperate with me."

Matt considered for a moment, then slowly nodded.

"Okay," he said. "I have to pick my daughter up at the hospital today, but later this afternoon, I'll get you a list of everyone who's still in the area. It has to be someone local, because they've done this over a period of days."

"True, but I'll have someone check the local motels and bed-'n-breakfasts, see if there's been anyone hanging around for the last couple of days who looks like he might be up to no good."

Patoine stood up and held his hand out for Matt to shake.

"The important thing is," he said, "don't worry. We'll beef up the patrols in your neighborhood, but you may want to consider hiring someone to watch your house. Just in case."

"I'll consider it," Matt said as he let go of the detective's hand. "I'll give you a call later today, once I'm back from the hospital."

"Talk to you then."

As he walked out of the police station and across the parking lot to his car, Matt had to admit that he didn't feel any better after his conversation with Patoine. But maybe by going through his files he'd come up with something they could go on. He didn't hold out much hope, but what else did he have?

He was sure of one thing, though. This person wasn't finished. He or she was going to do something else to threaten him, and like Patoine had said, he was going to have to do everything he could to protect his family and himself.

Before heading over to the hospital, he stopped by Harding's Sporting Goods on Main Street and bought a handgun. He considered getting something with a big caliber but settled on a .22 pistol. He also bought a trigger lock and a box of bullets.

Even then, though, he didn't feel any safer. Maybe he

might contact Kyle Hansen again. He'd have to think about that.

Around nine o'clock that evening, the whole family was home. John was playing PlayStation 2 in the family room; Brenda was in the living room reading; and Emily was upstairs, having gone to bed early, complaining that her neck and shoulder still hurt in spite of the support collar she was wearing and the pain medication she had taken.

Right after supper, Matt had tucked her into bed but, contrary to what he had promised Brenda, he didn't tell Emily the truth about what had happened.

"You talk to her?" Brenda asked, already knowing the answer as she looked up from her book when he came downstairs. She closed the book on her forefinger, marking her place.

Matt shook his head, avoiding looking directly at her.

"Why not?" Brenda pressed. "You think it's going to be any easier later?"

Matt licked his lips but didn't say a thing.

"It's only going to get worse, you know. As it is, she's going to end up not trusting you once she finds out that you lied to her about her mother."

"Keep your voice down, and I didn't lie to her," Matt said tightly. "I just . . . didn't tell her everything."

Brenda shook her head and scowled. "No, Matt. You told her that you didn't know who Susan was. I heard you. You lied. There's no other word for it."

Matt shuddered as he exhaled.

"I want to hold off . . . for now. I have to figure out who this lunatic is who's threatening us. That's the most important thing right now."

Brenda started to reply but stopped herself. She stared at him in silence until he turned and walked away. He went to his study, closing the door behind him, and sat down at his desk. Surrounded by bookcases and with the curtains drawn, he felt like he was holed up in a bunker, awaiting an attack.

But an attack from who? And what are they going to do next?

For the next fifteen minutes or so, he just sat there, staring blankly at the bookcase on the wall opposite his desk. Finally, he turned on his laptop and started going through his case summaries. As he worked, he jotted down a few names, but no one leaped out at him. This would at least give Patoine someplace to start, he thought, but he wasn't convinced that anyone on his list was angry or deranged enough to do something as overt as threaten him.

Scrolling through file after file, he quickly concluded that this was a dead end. The cops weren't going to figure out who it was or why they were doing it this way. It was going to come down to that they would simply have to have to wait and see if the idiot tried anything else. Hopefully, if he did, he would slip up and get caught.

But Matt didn't like sitting around waiting, either. His nerves already felt shredded. More than once during the evening, he had gone to the front door and looked out one of the narrow windows to see if a police cruiser was in sight. Around eight o'clock, he was surprised to see a cruiser parked in front of the house. He could just barely make out the silhouette of the cop behind the wheel. Matt felt at least marginally safer.

The gun he'd bought that morning was another matter.

Without even taking it from its packaging, he'd locked it in the bottom drawer of his desk. He put the box of bullets in the file cabinet on the other side of the room and locked it.

So what good is that going to do me? If someone breaks in, I'll have to unlock two different drawers on opposite sides of the room just to get what I need.

"Some protection," he muttered, shaking his head with bewilderment.

But with kids in the house who might snoop around in his office, Matt wasn't about to leave a gun where either of them might find it.

There were other things bothering him as well, like how withdrawn Brenda had been with him lately. He recognized that there was some distance between them, but he didn't have any idea how to bridge it.

If she'd just get off my ass about telling Emily about her mother, he thought bitterly.

Couldn't she see how upset he was about what was happening? It wasn't only that his first marriage had failed. Divorces happen all the time. It would be bad enough if it was

just that he had a drunk for an ex-wife. That was a social embarrassment that he didn't want to have to deal with, not with
his job and position in the community. And it wasn't something he was eager to tell Emily.

But it was more than that.

Years ago, just before they got divorced, Susan had been
diagnosed as a borderline personality. That made her a legiti-
mate danger, especially after the terrible thing that had happened when Emily was less than two years old. There was no
way Matt would *ever* trust his ex-wife with his daughter, so
deep down inside, as horrible as it was, he was glad that Susan
might not survive. He knew he would never really be able to
relax until he was sure Susan was no longer a danger to him or
to Emily.

Now there was something about Brenda that was bothering
him, too. There was no question that she had been withdrawing from him lately. Although he wasn't sure if it was her grief
over her mother's death or something to do with the kids,
maybe Emily in particular, or something he'd said or done or
not said or done, there was *something* she wasn't telling him.
Of course she was just as frazzled about what was going on as
he was. He could see that it was getting to her, but there was
something else . . . something he couldn't identify.

On top of all that, there were death threats against him and
his family, but were they genuine, or was someone just messing with him?

How can you know? he asked himself. *And who's going to
risk not doing something about it?*

Matt muttered to himself, barely focusing on the computer
screen as he scrolled down through a list of folders and hardly
registering the names as they flashed by. So many of the cases
seemed like something that had happened to him in another
lifetime. He was so lost in his own thoughts that he jumped
and let out a shout when the telephone on his desk rang.

He was reaching for the receiver before it could ring a
second time when Brenda yelled from the living room, "I've
got it."

Without another thought, he let his hand drop and focused
on his files, but a few seconds later, Brenda called out that it
was for him.

Matt hit the Save key on the computer out of habit, then picked up the phone.

"Hello," he said.

In the instant between when he had spoken and when the caller spoke, he tensed, wondering if this might be the person who had been threatening his family.

"Yes, Mr. Ireland. This is Dr. Finch at Central Maine Medical."

"Yes, Dr. Finch."

"I'm afraid I have some bad news for you." The doctor paused for a moment, then continued, "Susan Ireland passed away earlier this evening."

A cold, clammy feeling clenched like a fist in Matt's stomach.

"Oh Jesus," he whispered, his voice sounding fragile over the receiver.

"Your daughter Emily is listed as next of kin in her personal effects. I wanted to notify you to see how you want to handle the situation."

Matt started to speak, but before he could, he caught a shifting of motion across the room. Looking up, he saw Brenda standing in the doorway. Her eyebrows were raised in silent question. Cupping his hand over the phone, Matt lowered his head and whispered, "Susan died."

Brenda's face paled. She covered her mouth with her hand and moved over beside him and slid her arm around his neck.

"I guess I . . . I'd like you to send her over to Chadbourne's Funeral Home," Matt finally said. "I—yes. I want them to handle the arrangements."

"I'll take care of everything," Doctor Finch said, his voice deepening with sympathy. "I—I'm sorry for your loss."

"Yes. Thank you. Thank you for calling."

Without waiting to hear if the doctor had anything else to say, Matt lowered the receiver and, turning in his chair, encircled Brenda's waist with his arms. Dry sobs racked him as he pulled her close, crushing his face against her side and flattening his nose so he breathed funny.

"Well then," he said brokenly. "That's that. She's gone."

He was surprised when tears filled his eyes. For so long, he had felt such distance from Susan that his relationship felt as though it had happened to someone else, in another lifetime. All he could feel now was a deep, cold hollowness inside him.

"There's nothing you could have done, baby," Brenda said, holding him tightly. "Nothing at all."

"I know. I know," he said in a torn whisper. "It's just that . . . that . . ." He inhaled noisily and looked up at her. "I wouldn't wish what happened to her on anyone, you know?"

"I know, baby. . . . I know . . . but it's all over now."

SOMEONE'S *out there! In the woods!*

Emily sucked her breath in and held it as her gaze snapped to the bedroom window. Her lights were out, and her bedroom was dark. Moonlight cast a faint, blue sheen across the windowsill, and the curtains shifted, rippling slightly in the gentle breeze. She had been listening to a Beatles CD her father had given her for Christmas last year but had turned it off after the first song.

Now she knew why. It was so she could hear better if there really was someone outside the house. She didn't want whoever it was to be able to sneak up on her.

In spite of the pills she'd taken, burning pain shot through her neck and shoulders as she shifted on her bed, tensed to re-act to the slightest sound. The neck support she had to wear was uncomfortable, even with several pillows to support her head. A roaring rush of blood filled her ears, making it diffi-cult for her to hear anything else. She was suddenly more afraid of what she couldn't hear than what she could.

She was convinced someone was hiding in the woods be-hind the house, and she had no doubt who it was.

It's that lady who tried to kidnap me! She's come back for me! She's out there . . . waiting for me . . . waiting to take me away!

One small, rational corner of her mind told her that was impossible. Although her father hadn't told her everything, he had said that the woman had been seriously injured in the ac-cident and was in the hospital, in intensive care.

There's no way she can be out there!

Wild shivers sent splinters of pain through her neck. She was trying desperately to convince herself that everything was fine, that she had just imagined hearing something—*someone*—moving around in the woods.

And even if she had heard something, it couldn't really be the woman. It was an animal: a raccoon or some deer prowling around in the dark. Her father had told her that, contrary to what most people think, deer aren't at all graceful and silent in the woods. They thrashed through the underbrush, sounding like a herd of elephants.

But in her heart, Emily knew it wasn't an animal. It was a person. Her sense of danger cut through the gauzy haze of her pain medication and reached for her in the darkness, like invisible hands, groping, touching, brushing against her skin in the dark and raising goose bumps all over her body.

"Daddy?" she called out. Her voice, faint and twisted, sounded pathetic in the darkness.

No reply.

Is he still downstairs in his office? He never has time for me anymore. But where's Brenda? What's she doing?

Fear tingled like electricity inside her, filling her with cold, vibrating pressure. When she moved her head, sparks of pain flashed through her neck and back. As far as she could tell, the pain meds weren't doing anything except making her feel groggy and out of it. The tension winding up inside her was getting steadily worse.

"Daddy? . . . Can you come here?"

She wished she didn't sound so afraid, but she couldn't stop wondering if the person outside could hear her through the open window.

Then they'll know how scared I am.

She glanced at her alarm clock and saw that it was a little past eleven o'clock. On a typical night, even if she had school the next day, she'd be downstairs, watching *The Daily Show* before getting ready for bed. She didn't like the show all that much, but she thought Jon Stewart was kind of cute. Silly, but cute.

She wanted to believe that she was being silly now. She was fifteen years old, for God's sake, not some stupid little four-year-old who was afraid of the dark.

Still, right now, anyway, she didn't want to think about the darkness and the darker shadows that might be lurking inside it. Her breath kept catching in her throat, and she didn't dare look around her bedroom too carefully because of what she might see in the shadows. Her heartbeat skipped several beats every time she glanced over at the window.

"Daddy!"

She sighed with relief when she heard footsteps on the stairs and recognized her father's heavy tread. Wincing with pain, she turned to face the door as he swung it open and entered the room.

"Hey, Em? Everything okay?"

Behind him, silhouetted against the brightly lit hallway, she could see Brenda. Emily's heart sank. She had wanted to talk to her father alone, not with *her* here.

"Yeah . . . I'm okay," Emily said, forcing herself to sound a lot braver than she really felt. "I was just—"

She focused past her father on Brenda, wishing she weren't there so she could tell her father what was really bothering her.

"You want the light on?" her father asked.

"No," she said quickly, thinking, *With the light on, whoever's outside will be able to see me better.*

"Do you need another pill?"

"Maybe." It took effort not to whine. "It doesn't seem to be doing much. I'm still really sore."

"Believe me," Brenda said, taking a single step into the room, "you'd notice it if you didn't have it."

Her father turned to leave, but then Brenda said, "Stay here. I'll get it," and she went down the hall as her father walked over to the bed and sat down on the edge. The mattress sagged and creaked beneath his weight. He reached out in the darkness until he found her shoulder and patted her gently.

"Having trouble falling asleep?" he asked.

"Kinda," she said with a fake yawn.

His voice was so soothing Emily wished she could feel like she did right now when he wasn't here, and she couldn't help but remember how their life had been before he married Brenda. Feeling safe now, she allowed herself to glance at the rectangle of the window again. When she did, she thought she heard a faint voice whisper her name.

"Em-i-ly . . ."

She stiffened and moaned softly.

"Where's it hurt?" her father asked.

"Just my neck a little."

She wondered if he could tell that she was lying, if he knew she was afraid of something she didn't even dare mention. He was only an indistinct blob in the darkness, and she had a sudden rush of fear that this wasn't her father in the room with her. Her throat tightened, and every nerve in her body tingled as she waited to hear her name being called again.

"It'll be a while before you feel back to normal," he said.

Emily let out a short sigh of relief, hearing his voice, not someone else's.

"I still can't believe how lucky you were. It's a miracle you weren't more seriously hurt. You must've been pretty scared."

Emily had no idea how to respond, but she didn't have to think about it long because just then Brenda returned with a glass of water and two Tylenol 3s.

"Here yah go," Brenda said, her voice tinged with that fake friendliness she always used with her as she walked over to the bed and handed the pills to Emily. Although she didn't mean to, Emily jumped when their hands inadvertently touched. She quickly slipped both pills into her mouth and emptied the glass with a couple of noisy gulps.

"There. Better already," she said, although it hurt like hell when she tilted her head back to swallow. She shifted down onto the bed, positioning her head carefully on the pillow. Although the night was warm, her father tucked her in with the blankets under her chin, then leaned forward and kissed her on the top of the head.

"Try to get some rest, honey," he whispered, "but if you need anything, don't be afraid to call."

"I won't, Daddy," she said as she snuggled her head into the well of the pillow. The support on the back of her neck felt marginally better. "Thanks."

"No problem," her father said as he stood up and started out the door.

"Could you leave the door open? Just a little?" she asked. "I like the light."

"As you wish," he replied, using the line from *The Princess Bride* that always made her smile. "G'night."

"G'night."

He and Brenda left, their footsteps fading down the hall, leaving Emily alone in the semidarkness. Eventually, she drifted off to sleep, but the night breeze stirred the curtains, and from far off, a faint voice in the night seemed to be whispering her name.

SEVENTEEN

floating

BRENDA couldn't sleep.

No matter how long she lay there in the darkness, trying to drop off, she simply couldn't make it happen. She was all wound up inside like she'd had too many cups of coffee, and for the past two hours, she'd been staring up at the dark ceiling, unable even to close her eyes.

Matt was sleeping soundly beside her, his breathing deep and regular. She didn't blame him. It had been one heck of a day. She'd noticed that he'd had two or three drinks throughout the evening, which was unusual for him. Maybe that's why he was sleeping so soundly.

Sometime around two o'clock, she heard Emily call out. Before Matt stirred, she tossed the bedcovers aside and hurried down to her stepdaughter's bedroom.

"You okay?" she whispered at the door, which was open a crack.

The hallway light behind her cast her shadow over the doorframe and into the room.

Absolute silence.

Brenda craned her head forward, trying to determine if Emily was awake. She waited with bated breath until she heard the rhythmic sound of her stepdaughter's breathing.

There's nothing to worry about. She's fine. We're all going to be fine.

She knew on some level that it was true, but she simply couldn't believe it. The thought rang false, and her body was alive with the sense of lurking danger. Something serious was still going to happen; she just didn't know what . . . or when.

As she stared at the shadowed form of her stepdaughter, Brenda struggled to push aside these doubts and fears she'd been having. Her gaze snapped over to the partially open window by the bed when she heard . . . something.

It was fleeting, gone before she realized it was even there, so she couldn't identify it, but it had sounded almost like a soft, feathery sigh, as if someone outside the open window had whispered something. Then, holding her breath, she heard it again, and this time she recognized her own name.

"Brenda . . ."

Her heartbeat accelerated as perspiration broke out across her face. The numbing cold slithered up the back of her neck, making her scalp crawl.

I didn't hear that! I didn't really hear that!

Leaning into the room, her hand braced on the doorframe, she strained to hear the sound again, all the while trying to convince herself that all it had been was a gust of wind, hissing in the trees outside or her stepdaughter's low breathing as she slept.

Brenda wished she had the courage to walk over to the window and look outside, but she was frozen where she stood. Her pulse skipped a beat when she caught sight of her reflection in the bedroom window, a dark silhouette outlined by the dim glow of light behind her.

That's not me! was her first, improbable thought.

Fear gripped her heart, squeezing it to stillness as she stared straight ahead.

The figure in the window appeared to be stooped over and much smaller than she knew she was. Even if it was a shadow cast by the curtain or a distortion in the glass, Brenda couldn't shake the distinct impression that she was looking at someone else.

My mother's ghost!

A sudden electric shock burned along her nerves. Her hands began to tingle, and she was suddenly convinced that, if she shifted her gaze down, she would see thin, blue tendrils of electricity encircling her hands and wrists.

She was desperate to see if the figure changed position when she did, but she didn't dare to move. She hardly dared even to take a breath.

Please let it not be there!

Every nerve in her body was vibrating in time with the night. The darkness wrapped around her like a second skin. When she finally dared to take a breath, she had the clear impression that the bedroom walls swelled and contracted as she inhaled and then exhaled.

I must be dreaming this!

The darkness outside the bedroom windows draped across the windowsill and spilled onto the floor like ink. The stooped figure reflected in the glass shifted and took on shape as the features of a face—*That's not my face!*—slowly resolved.

And Brenda saw a haggard old woman staring back at her. Although with the light behind her it was almost impossible for her to see clearly, she saw the thick, ropy white scar that ran the length of her left cheek. She gaped at the reflection, wanting to say or do something to break the spell, but she couldn't move. Then, very faintly, she heard a voice rasping like grinding metal in the dark.

"Who's outside?"

A lancet of pain shot down her throat, making her gasp. The darkness was squeezing in on her, throbbing and keeping time with her rapidly hammering pulse.

"Is it her?"

Somehow, Brenda pushed aside her rising panic long enough to realize that it was Emily who had spoken. Brenda took a deep breath, but her chest felt constricted, as if someone was pinning her from behind and squeezing the life out of her. Trailing white lines jiggled across her vision, and although the words were unintelligible, she heard another, fainter voice coming through the open window.

"Brenda . . ."

"She's out there, isn't she?" Emily whispered. Her voice cracked with fear. "She's coming back to get me."

"No, she isn't," Brenda gasped. Her throat made a raw, tearing sound as she inhaled. She pulled her gaze away from the figure reflected in the window and started to move closer to Emily's bed. She couldn't help but notice that the figure in the window remained outlined in the doorway, bottomless black framed by the yellow glow of light behind her.

"She isn't," Brenda said again. "There—there's no one out there, Em. I promise you that."

"I heard her," Emily replied. "She was calling my name."

Terror tightened Emily's voice to a tiny squeak, and Brenda wished to God she could reassure her stepdaughter, but her own fear was bordering on panic now.

She wasn't calling you, she thought. *She was calling to me!*

Brenda couldn't believe that she hadn't fainted from fear. A high-pitched ringing in her ears was blocking out every other sound in the room except for the faint hint of a voice calling to her from the darkness outside the window.

"Brenda . . ."

"Nobody's out there," she repeated, struggling with all her strength to find reassurance in her own voice. "That woman, your—" She cut herself off before she finished the sentence. "It *can't* be her."

"Yes it is. She's come back to get me," Emily whispered in a strangled voice.

How much can I tell her? Brenda wondered desperately. *How much does she already know or guess?*

"Did your father tell you everything about what happened?" she asked.

Amazingly, she found the nerve to take a few more steps into the room. When she looked at the window again, she saw that the dark, motionless figure was still in the doorway. It hadn't moved or shifted position when she did.

There has to be some rational explanation for this, Brenda thought. She wanted to believe it was a trick of the light from the hallway or the shadow cast by the curtains or an imperfection in the window or the shadow of a tree on the window or something . . . anything but what it looked like. But she knew in her soul that it wasn't any of those things.

She struggled to focus her mind, telling herself that she had to calm Emily down first. The rest—whatever it was— could wait. She'd deal with it later.

"He . . . my dad told me that she was still in the hospital," Emily said, her voice trembling and breaking with almost every word.

"She is," Brenda said softly, "but did he tell you that he got a call from the hospital late tonight?"

Emily shook her head but didn't say a word.

"He did," Brenda continued, "and they told him the lady died from her injuries."

Emily let out a deep groan of despair, and Brenda couldn't help but jump.

Even if she doesn't know who Susan really is, she must feel sad for her, despite what happened.

"So, you see, you don't have anything to worry about," Brenda said. "You're perfectly safe. She can't hurt you."

She was standing by the side of the bed, and she reached out in the darkness to give Emily a reassuring touch. When her hand brushed Emily's shoulder, she felt the girl flinch beneath her touch. A deep, unnamable sadness filled her when she realized that she couldn't hold Emily and comfort her like she wanted to. They were too far apart, and the gulf between them seemed unbridgeable.

What's wrong with us? she wondered as tears filled her eyes, blurring her vision.

"She was out there. She called my name."

"No, she didn't. You must have been dreaming or something."

Even as she said it, Brenda didn't believe it herself. She, too, had heard something, but she'd had the impression the voice had been whispering *her* name.

"She can't hurt you. Nobody can hurt you. Your father and I won't allow it."

Emily was silent for so long that, for an instant, Brenda thought the girl had fallen asleep and that she was standing here in the darkness, talking to herself.

"Let me tuck you in," she said, "and don't you worry about anything, okay?"

"Okay," Emily said, not sounding the least bit convinced.

Brenda pulled the blankets up tightly around Emily's neck, but when she glanced at the window again, she still saw the silhouette of someone standing in the half-open doorway. The lacy curtains made it impossible for her to see the figure more clearly, but she didn't have to see it to know who it was. She could feel the ghost's presence in the bedroom even when she looked directly at the doorway and saw no one standing there.

She remembered Cheryl's advice that she should talk to the apparition if she ever saw it again, but she wasn't about to do that now. She didn't want to frighten Emily any more than she already was.

"I'll leave the door all the way open," she said as she stood up from the bed. "If you need anything, just call, okay?

For a moment or two, Emily didn't say anything. Then she took a deep breath and sighed. "Okay," she said.

"Good night, dear."

As Brenda backed slowly away from the bed, her body started to tingle. Her knees almost buckled as she approached the door, and as she passed out into the hall, a heavy pressure made it impossible for her to breathe. She was almost overwhelmed by a disorienting sense of unreality, and she wondered if she was the invisible person in the room. Stifling a scream, she looked down at her hand—*Yes, that's me. That's my real hand!*—and touched the painted wood of the door and pushed it all the way open.

"Is this too much light?" she asked, wondering if Emily could hear the tremor in her voice.

"No. That's good," Emily said.

Brenda looked back at her and saw her stepdaughter's fear-filled eyes staring at her. It nearly broke her heart to realize how frightened the girl was, and it was even worse, knowing that she couldn't reach her and might never reach her.

"Good night, then," Brenda whispered, hearing her voice rasp like a cold wind in the dark.

"G'night."

As she walked down the hallway back to her bedroom, Brenda was almost overwhelmed by the cold, winding tension inside her. The raw, primal instinct of knowing that someone was watching her made her scalp tighten and her flesh go cold. Even worse was knowing, if she turned around and looked, she wouldn't see anyone.

"I know you're there," she whispered.

She hesitated at her bedroom door, frozen as she raised her hand to open the door. She shivered and fought against the feeling that unseen eyes were staring at her, boring into her. A palpable tension filled the air like a static charge, and she had the feeling that she needed to say or do something very important, but she couldn't remember what.

Frozen outside her bedroom door, Brenda wished she dared to turn around and confront what she knew was lurking, unseen, behind her.

Who do you think it is? she asked herself, but she already sensed she knew the answer. That's what she was so afraid of.

"You . . ."

The word brushed like a feather against the back of her neck, raising goose bumps all along her arms. She clamped her jaw shut to keep from crying out. A small part of her mind told her that this was impossible. No one had whispered anything to her, but the word *you* had sounded as clearly as if she had spoken it herself.

She raised her hand to the freshly painted wood of her bedroom door, surprised that she couldn't see through it as she began to push it open. She was so close to the door she could see her distorted reflection in the glossy, white paint. And beyond that, lurking behind her, she saw a thick, dark smear that seemed to assume a vague human form.

Whimpering deep in her throat, Brenda shouldered the door completely open and ducked into the dark bedroom, then slammed the door shut behind her. Panting heavily, she leaned against the door, waiting for a terrible moment to feel a heavy thump against the wood.

Don't be so foolish! she chastised herself. *Whatever it is, it's not going to be stopped by a simple door.*

Shaking with tension, she waited to feel the pressure of the entity leaning against the other side of the door or to hear and see the doorknob slowly turn.

"Go away. . . . Please go away," she whispered heatedly, the words burning in her throat.

"You say something?"

The suddenness of Matt's voice startled her and made her cry out.

"How come you're not in bed, honey?" he asked.

The sheets rustled as he tossed them aside and sat up.

"Want a light?"

Brenda tried to answer him, but the only sound she could make was a choking gasp. She heard a faint click, and the bedroom was suddenly filled by a harsh, white glare that made her wince. Covering her eyes with one hand, she waved for Matt to turn the light off.

"What are you doing?" he asked.

Brenda peeled her hand away from her eyes and squinted at him, but he was lost in a bright, watery blur.

"Emily," she said, short of breath. "She woke up. You didn't hear her, so I went to see what she wanted."

"She okay?"

"Yeah. She's fine now."

"Come on. Get back to bed." Matt's arm was nothing but a dark smear as he waved her over to him.

Brenda moved slowly to the bed. She was shivering as she slipped under the covers and turned so she could hug her husband. He reached behind him and rested his hand on her side, running it up and down the rounded contour of her hip.

"Let's get some sleep, huh?" he asked.

Before Brenda could say anything, he snapped the light off, and the room was plunged into darkness. Brenda realized she was holding her breath. She wasn't sure which was worse: lying here in the dark and feeling alone, no matter how tightly she held her husband, or leaving the light on so she could see the thing that might be lurking in the room.

"Good night," she said softly.

Brenda took his hand and squeezed it tightly. Closing her eyes, she let her breath out in a long, slow sigh.

"You seem kinda wound up," Matt said. His voice was already dragging as sleep overtook him.

"I'll be all right," Brenda replied, but she could taste the sourness of the lie on her tongue.

She didn't know if she would be all right, and she wanted

reassurance from Matt, but no matter how much her grip on
his hand tightened, she couldn't get rid of the vague feeling of
insubstantiality. He seemed so distant he might as well not
even be there. She wanted to believe that this was all a dream,
a terrible nightmare, and maybe, hopefully, she would wake
up in the morning, and everything would be back to normal.

But what's normal? she wondered as she rolled onto her
back and settled her head on her pillow. She consciously
slowed her breathing, willing herself to fade off to sleep.

When finally she did, it was a shallow, disturbed sleep that
was filled with anxious dreams that, fortunately, she couldn't
remember once she awoke in the morning.

SUNDAY morning never really dawned. Overnight, more
rain clouds blew in from the west, and it was raining hard by
the time Brenda and Matt roused themselves around nine
o'clock. John was up early and, as usual, was taking advan-
tage of his parents' slugabed habits to plant himself in front of
the TV and play a video game. Before showering, Matt
checked in on Emily and found her still fast asleep, so he decided to let her be. Rest was what she needed most.

He showered quickly, got dressed, and went downstairs, so
Brenda would have all the time she needed to get ready.

"You end up getting any sleep?" he asked her, looking up
from the morning newspaper when she wandered into the
kitchen half an hour later.

Brenda grunted and nodded. "A little, I guess," she said as
she rubbed her face with the flats of her hands, then poured
herself a cup of coffee. Before she took a sip, she regarded
him for several seconds in silence, then shifted her gaze outside. Slate-gray rain clouds were moving heavily across the
sky. The rain looked like silver needles against the dark backdrop of the pine trees. She stifled a yawn behind her hand,
hearing her jaw click a few times as she worked it from side to
side.

"Too bad it's such a crappy day," she said. "Maybe we
should go to the movies or something. Get our minds off
everything."

Before Matt could reply, the answering machine clicked on, and their greeting played.

"You have the ringer turned off?" she asked.

"And the volume on the machine is as far down as it will go," Matt said, looking back at his newspaper.

Brenda moved toward the breakfast table, casually glancing at the newspaper over his shoulder. It took her a moment or two to realize that he was reading—or rereading—an article about what had happened to Emily.

"The phone started ringing off the hook while you were in the shower. Everyone's calling to see how we're doing. A couple of reporters have called, wanting to ask questions, too." He huffed and shook his head with disgust. "I finally couldn't take it, so I went around the house and turned off all the phones."

As he was speaking, he got up from the table and went over to the answering machine. Leaning forward with both elbows on the counter, he waited to hear the message being left. He scowled and pressed Delete before the caller was finished.

"Goddamned reporters," he said. He sat back down at the table and picked up the newspaper.

"Cheryl or Deb call?"

Matt looked like he wasn't even listening, but he nodded and said, "Yeah. Both of 'em. I saved their messages if you want to call them back."

His eyes never left the newspaper.

"So what're they saying?" Brenda asked with a slight tremor in her voice as she indicated the newspaper.

"Pretty much sticks to the facts," he said. "Got a picture of the wreck." He turned the paper so she could see it. When they made eye contact, she saw a trace of worry in his eyes. "Want to read it?"

"Not really," Brenda said with a quick shake of her head. Cupping her coffee mug with both hands, she sat back and stared outside. The trunks of the pine trees were slick and black with rain. Puddles the color of melted chocolate had collected in depressions in the lawn and on the deck. Rain had beaten down the tomato starts she'd planted the other day.

"I don't know about a movie," Matt said after taking a sip of coffee. "They're always so crowded on rainy days. Plus, I still have a lot of files to go through for Patoine."

"As if that will do any good."

Matt lowered the newspaper and looked at her for an uncomfortable length of time.

" 'Sides, there's nothing I really want to see," he said.

How about just doing it to do something with the family? she wanted to say, but she held back.

Matt put the paper down onto the table and shifted it to one side. Leaning back in his chair, he smiled weakly.

"I guess it's May showers bring June flowers this year," he said distantly.

Brenda sighed and shook her head, not knowing what to say.

After a long silence, Matt whistled and said, "That car wreck. I still can't get over how lucky we are that she wasn't killed."

"I know, Brenda said. She slid her hand across the table, took hold of his, and squeezed it with quiet desperation.

They sat in silence for a long time just holding hands as the rain splattered against the window. The faint sounds of sirens and whistles of John's video game drifted from the family room, and for once, Brenda found the sound actually soothing, reassuring her that things actually might be getting back to normal.

Although she still needed sleep, she thought that, with John occupied and Emily still in bed, this might be a good time to tell Matt about what was happening to her.

Maybe he'll listen now. . . . Then again, maybe not, she thought bitterly.

Tears started to fill her eyes, but she wiped them away with the back of her hand. She knew if Matt noticed them at all, he would think she was crying for Emily. Suddenly fearful, she looked at her husband and wished she didn't feel so distant from him.

What is it? What the hell is happening to me? Or is it something wrong with both of us?

She knew it could be fatal to their relationship if she allowed what was happening to drive a wedge between them. Then *they*—whoever the hell *they* were—would win.

A couple of times Brenda took a shallow breath and tried to get up the courage to say what was on her mind, but she wasn't sure where or how to begin.

Would he even understand? Is how I'm feeling because of my grief and overworked nerves, or is it symptomatic of something else, something far more serious? What if I really am having a nervous breakdown? And what if I'm so far gone I don't even realize how bad off I am?

These thoughts made her feel so empty and alone, so choked up, as she stared out at the rain. A powerful urge to get up and run out of the room gripped her. She needed to be alone so she could try to figure what the hell was going on. Covering her mouth with her hand, she stifled the scream that was threatening to burst out of her. Leaving her coffee cup on the kitchen table, she got up and went over to the kitchen sink. The chrome of the faucet glowed dully in the dim daylight. It hurt her eyes, so she looked away and focused instead on the view outside the window over the sink.

The familiar feeling that she was being watched swept over her again with renewed intensity.

A low whimper escaped her when she noticed how dark the corners up near the ceiling looked. Without a word, she switched on the overhead light, but the bright light only made her feel all the more visible and vulnerable.

Am I getting paranoid?

Of course she was. What else did she expect? Someone was stalking her family. The sense of danger wasn't imagined. It was immediate and real.

It's right here . . . right now . . . watching me . . . waiting for me. . . . I just can't see it . . . not yet, anyway.

Her gaze came to rest on the wall phone beside the refrigerator. She was filled with a sudden urge to call someone, but who?

Cheryl? Deb? Dr. Joyce? Maybe Reverend Hayne?

Why are you thinking like this? Talk to Matt. He's your husband, for God's sake. You can't avoid him like this.

She knew, if she couldn't confide in her husband, then their marriage was in serious trouble. But Matt seemed so preoccupied with his own thoughts and feelings he could care less how she felt.

"I—umm, I'm still kinda tired," she said, yawning behind her hand. The truth was, she was so wound up she felt close to collapse. "I think I'm gonna go lie down for a bit."

Matt hardly glanced at her. "Good idea," he said. "Kinda hard to get motivated on a day like this."

"Uh-huh," Brenda managed to say. Her legs felt rubbery, almost too weak to keep holding her up as she moved down the hall to the living room. As she lowered herself onto the couch, she let out an aching sob and leaned her head back. Sliding the afghan off the back of the couch over her shoulder didn't come close to dispelling the sudden chill that had gripped her.

"Come on, come on," she whispered to herself. "Pull it together. You're coming apart at the seams."

Her eyes kept darting back and forth, trying to take in the expanse of the living room and the soot-gray shadows that seemed to fill the room. Getting up off the couch slowly, she moved to the window and, kneeling down, looked outside. The rain splattering against the glass distorted her view of the front yard and the road beyond.

With a jolt, she realized that she was looking out one of the windows where she had seen the old woman's face.

If someone was out in the front yard right now, she thought with a shiver, *I'd be the face, staring out through the thin barrier of glass.*

"Mom?" she said in a breathy whisper that fogged the glass for a moment. "Is it you? Are you really here?"

She tensed, listening for a reply, but all she heard was the steady tapping of rain against the house and the far-off sounds of John's video game.

She took a deep breath and held it long enough so she got dizzy. She was trying to adjust her senses, tune them to the same level of feeling she'd had last night when she had seen the figure in the doorway of Emily's bedroom.

"I know you're here," she whispered. Her breath came in hitching sips, and the cool air sent chills up her back. "If you have something to say to me . . . if you want to tell me something . . . anything . . . I'm ready to listen."

The room was filled with dense silence. The air was so

heavy it made everything look like it was underwater. A subtle whooshing sound filled Brenda's head, and her eyelids grew heavy as she turned and looked over her shoulder at the living room. As soon as her back was to the window, she felt uncomfortable, so she darted back to the couch and closed her eyes as she lay down. Within seconds, she could feel herself sliding into sleep but, oddly, she also felt wide awake at the same time.

This is really weird, she thought as the feeling intensified. She knew she was hovering in that state of mind between sleep and wakefulness, and she found it both unnerving and oddly comforting. She had no sense that she was breathing, and her body felt so light she thought, with a minimum of effort, she would be able to float right up off the couch if she wanted to.

I am floating.

The thought sent a subtle thrill racing through her as she rose off the couch, her body lighter than smoke. Pushing back a wave of doubt and fear, she looked around the too-quiet living room, surprised that it was suffused with a subtle, iridescent purple glow. It reminded her of the western sky at sunset in winter and seemed to be coming through all of the windows, pouring in on her from every possible direction.

But the light was also inside the room. It seemed to radiate out of the furniture, casting dusky shadows that intersected at odd angles on the floor and walls.

After the initial rush of disorientation, she experienced no real fear or resistance to the weightless feeling.

Just go with it, she told herself, but then another thought intruded. *What if I'm dying?*

A ripple of fear shot through her, but it quickly lost its power and was replaced by rapt amazement as she rose higher above the couch until she seemed to be hovering up near the ceiling, looking down at herself on the couch.

I look so old . . . so worn out, she thought with a deep sense of sadness.

A peculiar muffled silence filled the room, like the hush before a storm. The vertigo of weightlessness lifted her up, making her feel like a dandelion puff being tossed by way-

ward winds. She accepted that she had no control over what
was happening to her. Like morning mist being driven away
by a warm, gentle wind, she let herself go with it, floating
lazily on the unseen currents of air.

Somehow—she wasn't aware of an abrupt transition—she
realized that she was outside, hovering like smoke in the rain-
soaked woods behind the house. The popping sound of raindrops hitting the undergrowth was deafening, and the bracing
smell of fresh earth and rotting vegetation filled her nose.

She raised her left hand in front of her face and studied it,
noticing with an amused detachment that her skin wasn't getting wet, even though the rain was coming down in torrents.
When she moved her hands, faint smears of light burned in af-
terimage on her retina.

What is going on? Am I dreaming?

She didn't think so. It certainly didn't feel like any dream
she had ever had before. Everything around her—the woods,
the sky, the house—seemed somehow more real than she had
ever experienced them. A subtle current of apprehension ran
thorough her when she felt herself shifting deeper into the
woods where the shadows were thick and black, but she let
herself go with the feeling. All around her, things that she had
never noticed before suddenly appeared with hallucinatory
clarity. The rough texture of the tree bark was as black and
wrinkled as ancient, rotting flesh. Twisted roots poked
through the ground like thickly muscled arms that moved subtly, like twining snakes. Raindrops shimmered in the air,
falling in slow motion and gleaming as they ran along the in-
terlaced branches and leaves before falling to the ground and
soaking into the rich, aromatic topsoil.

Brenda couldn't help but enjoy this odd sensation of flying
through the woods, unhindered by the dense undergrowth that
would have tripped her up if she had actually been walking.
Glancing down at her feet, she saw that they were moving
slowly as if she were in fact walking, but she appeared to be
hovering several feet off the ground. The walking motion she
was making didn't correspond with the terrain over which she
was moving.

I'm flying!

A sense of dark foreboding was growing progressively

stronger inside her, but it wasn't because of the disembodied
sensation. She was aware that there was something else—a
dangerous presence—lurking in the deeper woods.

Is this what's threatening us?

Sudden fear arced like electricity inside her as she looked
all around, trying to find the source of the danger. She turned
her head back and forth so quickly waves of vertigo rolled
over her, threatening to pull her down.

He's out here!

Brenda didn't know if it was a thought or if she or someone had spoken the words out loud, but she tingled with unnamable dread as she moved deeper and deeper into the
woods. Wet branches slid across her face and bare arms, chilling her but, curiously, leaving her skin dry. She could hear
faint footsteps in the undergrowth, but she wasn't sure if they
were hers or someone else's.

Who's out here?

Again, she didn't know if she had thought the words or
said them, but she froze when a hint of motion off to her right
drew her attention.

Who are you?

The damp forest muffled her voice, stuffing it back inside
her, but the words echoed in her head with an odd reverberation that seemed to come at her from several directions at
once. Somewhere deep in the woods, a tree branch snapped
with a thick, dull pop that sounded like a distant gunshot.

Brenda jumped.

Turning quickly, she looked all around her, trying to determine the direction of the sound. It was impossible. The floating sensation swept her up with dizzying vertigo. She was
completely disoriented.

Who are you? What do you want from us?

The words rang inside her head and echoed like a throaty
bell through the woods. Looking up, she caught a glimpse of
the sky through the intertwining branches. The lowering rain
clouds, looking as heavy as stones, were stained with a thick,
bruised purple that bled into swirls of black. Brenda wondered
how rain could be falling from clouds as solid as rock. She
gasped as burning pressure bore down on her back and shoulders. Her chest was squeezed inward, crushing her lungs.

Something was drawing her forward, bringing her deeper and
deeper into the damp shadows of the forest. Whimpering softly,
she beat back the foliage with her bare hands, trying to stop or
slow down her flight, but she moved inexorably forward.

As helpless as a feather, she was tossed back and forth by
powerful winds, and all the while she was moving deeper into
the forest to where the trees were as thick and black as the bars
of a jail cell. A terrifying feeling of being trapped gripped her.

And then she saw him.

In a flash, just by his shape and posture, she knew it was a
man. He was crouching in the wet woods, his face shielded
from the rain, his body drawn up and coiled like a snake about
to strike. As she moved closer to him, Brenda tried to get a
good look at his face, but he appeared oddly flat, like a two-
dimensional cutout, black against the trees and as featureless
as the center of night.

No . . . no!

As the words left her mouth, the man cocked his head. He
moved with unnatural slowness as he looked around. He
seemed to look straight at her, his eyes black and hollow.
Everything around him shimmered and distorted, like he was
sucking all of the light from the air into the center of his being. Strands of purple light danced and waved around him like
static electricity.

Brenda tried to scream, but no sound would come out as
she stared back at the dimensionless emptiness where the
man's face should be.

What the hell are you? What do you want?

The man stared at her with deep, unseeing eyes until a
snapping branch behind him drew his attention. He turned
slowly toward the sound. Then, with a sudden rush of sound,
he shifted away, rippling like black water as he dissolved into
the rain-soaked foliage.

Go away! Leave us alone!

Without conscious thought, Brenda floated through the
trees, ducking her head to avoid the rain-laden branches. An
uncanny sense of unreality filled her when, up ahead, she saw
her house. The white siding glowed as if the sun were shining
full on it. It stood out like wet ivory against the dark backdrop

of the raging storm clouds. And in the downstairs window, in what Brenda knew was the living room, she saw a figure behind the curtains.

Fear tightened around her heart, and she gasped for breath as she drew closer to the house, her gaze transfixed by the face in the downstairs window.

It's her!

The glaring reflection of the sky in the windows made it almost impossible for her to see clearly, but Brenda knew who it was. The old woman's eyes glowed as she stared out at Brenda.

Behind her, Brenda sensed motion and, turning, saw the shadow-man moving through the rain-soaked brush that bordered the lawn. A low, steady buzz filled the air, and she knew that the old woman was saying something. Her lips moved, but Brenda couldn't hear her through the barrier of glass.

The shadow-man crouched low as if to avoid being seen by the old woman in the window, but he moved closer to the house, sliding like thick oil across the rain-soaked ground.

Go away! Leave us alone!

Panic flared inside Brenda. She was absolutely helpless to stop the shadow-man from getting nearer to the house, but he stopped at the edge of the lawn. Somehow, she realized it was the old woman's steady, watchful stare that was holding him back.

Brenda turned to look at the face in the window. Even through the glass, she discerned the thick scar that ran the length of the woman's face, distorting her features.

The shadow-man remained perfectly motionless for so long Brenda thought he might be an illusion, a trick of the shadows cast by the trees and undergrowth. She wanted to believe that, but the winding sense of impending doom was as thick and palpable as the damp earth smell that filled her nostrils.

He's out there, waiting! He hasn't gone away!

With a sudden roaring intake of breath, Brenda sat bolt upright on the couch, her eyes wide open and staring. She clasped the sides of her head and groaned as a stab of pain shot through her.

When she lurched off the couch, her feet got tangled in the afghan, and she almost fell, but she kicked free of the blanket and lunged over to the window.

"He's out there!" she screamed, the words tearing from her throat as she looked outside. "Matt! Come here! Quick! He's outside!"

out there

"**HE'S** out there!"

Matt leaped up from the kitchen table the instant he heard his wife cry out. He banged his hip hard enough against the table to splash coffee all over the newspaper and place mat.

"What is it?" he shouted as he dashed down the hallway to the living room. He saw Brenda crouching by one of the windows, looking outside. Her shoulders were hunched up, and she was trembling violently as she leaned forward, her face close to the glass. A dim reflection stared back at him, wide-eyed and crazed looking. The rain on the window distorted it.

"I saw someone out there! He just ran off into the woods!"

With a few quick strides, Matt was beside her, but when he looked outside, he didn't see anything except the dreary day. The grass was silvered with rain, and the woods beyond were thick and dark. The tops of the trees stood out sharply against the soot-gray sky. Close to the ground, the hanging boughs and black trunks were lost in low-lying, cottony clots of mist.

"Over there. See the footprints in the grass?" Brenda pointed, the tip of her finger touching the window and leaving behind a foggy oval.

Matt's eyes didn't focus for a second or two, but then he

saw what she meant. A weaving trail cut across the wet grass
and angled off into the woods.

"Son of a bitch," he muttered.

Without another word, he sprinted out into the kitchen,
threw open the sliding glass door, and charged out onto the
deck. The rain stung as it pelted his face, and he was already
breathing heavily as he leaped down the steps to the ground.
He twisted his ankle when he landed, but the pain wasn't
enough to stop him. Scrambling for balance on the slippery
ground, he started around the side of the house.

It wasn't difficult to pick up the trail. He could see an obvious dark line where the grass had been trampled. Heedless of
the rain and cold, Matt plunged into the underbrush, beating it
aside with his hands.

"Stop right there, you son of a bitch!" he shouted. As
Brenda watched, he disappeared into the damp woods. Nearly
thirty minutes later, panting and dripping, he burst into the
breakfast nook. Brenda was standing at the kitchen sink. She
had a cup of coffee in her hands, halfway to her mouth.

"Matt?" she said, her eyes widening with shock. "Where
have you been? I've been frantic with worry."

He staggered forward and pulled out the nearest chair so he
could sit down. His body was shaking wildly, and he struggled
to catch his breath as he grabbed a handful of napkins and
wiped his face. He felt numb as he looked at the smears of dirt
and blood on his hands. Brenda stared at him incredulously.

"He's not here?" Matt gasped, the air scorching his lungs
and throat.

"I called the cops as soon as you left. They're on their
way."

"You didn't see him? He didn't come back?"

"Who, the prowler? No. I didn't see anyone."

Biting her lower lip, her face pale, Brenda shook her head
as she placed her coffee cup carefully on the counter and
walked over to him. Her expression was one of absolute pity.
She picked up a dish towel from the counter and wiped his
face.

"You look absolutely terrible," she said.

Matt swallowed and tried to slow his breathing, but he
couldn't draw nearly enough air into his lungs to make them

stop aching. The dizziness that had swept over him in the forest was even stronger now, and it threatened to pull him under.

"Yeah, I . . . got lost and . . . and fell," he said.

He wished his hands would stop shaking as he took the dish towel from her and wiped his face and neck. The grit scraped his skin and got into the cuts he had. The pain made him wince.

"I thought he . . . might be . . . leading me on a . . . on a wild-goose chase so he could . . . could get back here and . . . and—"

He didn't finish. He couldn't. The mental images he had created of his family's murder were still too strong in his mind. He jerked around in his chair and looked at the wall behind him to reassure himself that the threat hadn't been spray-painted there again while he was gone.

Just then the doorbell gonged. John's voice rang out from upstairs.

"Someone's at the front door."

Matt and Brenda exchanged glances, then Matt heaved himself out of the chair and started down the hallway. His legs ached so badly he thought they might give out on him. The muscles in his thighs were vibrating like plucked guitar strings. His hand had so little strength he could barely grip the doorknob as he turned it and swung the door open. A policeman Matt didn't recognize was standing on the doorstep.

"Morning," the cop said, raising his hand to tip his hat. Silver beads of water dripped off the clear plastic protective covering. "I was just—"

"Terrific response time," Matt said, unable to hold back his sarcasm. "My wife called you guys—what? Almost half an hour ago."

The cop narrowed his eyes as he took in Matt's disheveled appearance.

"Is everything all right here?" the cop asked.

"No. Everything is *not* all right," Matt said, trying not to shout. "Did you see him? There was a prowler out here just now."

The cop was young, practically a kid. Matt had seen him around town but didn't know his name.

"I chased him into the woods, but I lost him." He took a

breath that hurt his ribs. "Can you get some people out here to scour the area? He can't be very far."

For a moment, the young policeman looked indecisive, but then he nodded as though not quite believing Matt.

"Come with me," Matt said, shouldering past him onto the doorstep. "I'll show you where he went." He led the cop out to the backyard.

The rain had stopped, and for the next ten or fifteen minutes, Matt and the policeman—his name was Mark Cornell—walked around looking for any indication of the prowler. They found Matt's tracks easily enough, but they were unable to find anything that clearly looked like anyone else's footprints.

"Maybe the rain washed them away," Matt suggested, but he couldn't help feeling like he was covering up for his own inability to catch the man.

The more they searched, the more frustrated Matt became until he was half-convinced he might have imagined the whole thing.

"Look," Patrolman Cornell said mildly, once they left the fringe of woods and were heading back to the house. "I'll call this in, but I—" He shook his head and scratched behind his ear. "I don't think there's a whole lot to go on here. If there really was someone out here—"

"No *if* about it."

Matt was trembling inside from the effort to control his anger and apprehension. The taste of fear for the safety of his family still lingered on his tongue, like the sharp taste of tarnished metal.

"I saw him. I know it was the same guy."

"I appreciate your concern," Cornell said, "but we have nothing to go on, Mr. Ireland. I'll call it in and write up a complaint. There's supposed to be another cruiser in the area, but I don't see what we can do. Maybe one of your neighbors reported seeing someone."

"Thanks," Matt said, still fuming. "Let me ask you a favor. Would you please stay close to the house for the rest of the day? My family's pretty upset by all of this."

"I understand," Cornell said with a curt nod.

He shook hands with Matt before walking up the driveway to his cruiser. Watching him go, Matt couldn't stop thinking that he didn't feel the least bit safer with an inexperienced kid like this patrolling the neighborhood. True, he was a kid with a revolver, a can of mace, a nightstick, and all the latest technological toys the town's budget could afford, but did he know how to use any of them? Even if he did, Matt had a troubling suspicion that no amount of weaponry was going to be effective against this prowler. Not if he could disappear into the woods without leaving behind any footprints.

"I know you have something to tell me."

Not quite believing that she dared to do this, Brenda leaned forward and held her breath as a prickly cold sensation gripped her throat.

"That's why you came back, isn't it? You want to tell me something."

She paused and exhaled, then took a slow, shallow breath. The aftershock of hearing her voice in the darkened silence of the kitchen was like waiting to hear the flutter of a moth's wings in the dark. She questioned if she had spoken aloud or simply thought the words.

"If you want to talk to me . . . if you have anything to say . . . I'm ready to listen."

The kitchen was hushed with expectancy. It was almost midnight. There was only a single light on, the small one over the stove. She was sitting alone at the table in the breakfast nook. The semidarkness wrapped around her like a thin blanket that couldn't fend off the chilly night air. She was facing the sliding glass door, her back to the doorway that led into the hall. Reflected in the glass, she could see the black rectangle of the doorway behind her. It loomed like an open mouth. She shivered, her breath catching in her throat when a hint of motion flickered across the glass, a dark blur against the deeper black of the unlit hallway behind her.

"Please," she whispered desperately. "Talk to me. I want to hear what you have to say."

Her elbows were propped on the table, and her hands were folded in front of her as if she were praying. The warm moisture of her breath bathed her hands, and she couldn't help but think, *My breath is warm. . . . I'm alive.*

The hushed silence in the house was total, almost unnatural, as though the air could no longer transmit sound. She couldn't even hear the faint tick-tick of the kitchen clock on the wall. A wave of lightheadedness swept over her. As she stared at her reflection in the sliding glass door, she experienced an odd feeling of dissociation, as though she were somehow outside her body, looking down at . . .

Someone else. That's not me. How can that be me?

The feeling of not being herself was deeply unsettling. The coldness inside her intensified as it spread down her back like a thin coating of oil. She shivered wildly and tried to stop the tears that were gathering in her eyes, but she couldn't. Her vision blurred.

"I . . . I know we didn't always agree on everything, Mom, but you have to know that I loved you. I loved and trusted you, so whatever you have to say, you can trust me. Tell me what it is. I know it's important."

The silence thickened as though heavy curtains were closing silently around her, smothering her, making it almost impossible to breathe. Her view of herself in reflection blurred like an old watercolor, but the transparent figure looked somehow more real than she felt.

And then, in an instant, she saw a figure standing in the doorway behind her. The figure didn't suddenly pop into view, but it didn't resolve gradually, either. Brenda had the distinct impression that it was a trick of the shadows or of her eyesight where something that had always been there just finally came into focus.

Or maybe it's a trick of the mind, she thought. She couldn't shake the feeling that she had been looking at the figure all along and had only just now realized it.

"Mom—" she whispered before her throat closed off and she couldn't continue.

Her eyes widened with rising fear as warm tears trickled from her eyes. When she raised her hand to wipe them away, she jumped. The left side of her face was so deeply in shadow it looked as though the remnants of an old scar ran across her cheek.

She focused intently on the figure behind her.

Is that Matt or Emily or John? Maybe one of them has come downstairs to see why I'm still awake.

The desire to turn and look directly at the figure almost overwhelmed her, but she was sure that, if she did turn around, the figure wouldn't be there. It was only in reflection—in a looking glass—that she could see her.

Why am I so sure it's my mother? Brenda wondered.

The figure wavered as though made of mist, but Brenda could see the old woman's slouched shoulders and bowed head. Her features blended into shadow, but inside the charcoal smudges of her hollow eyes, there burned a dull, blue glow, like ice under a full moon.

Brenda shivered, struggling not to cry out.

"Talk to me . . . please," she begged, tensing her shoulders and leaning forward, forcing herself to remain looking at the glass door and not behind her. The figure appeared to be trapped inside the thick pane of glass.

"Talk to me . . . please. . . ."

The words echoed close to her ear as if someone was leaning close to her, whispering in her ear, but the voice was her own. Brenda had no doubt some kind of entity was in the room with her. The presence was palpable. She could feel a cool breeze blowing across the back of her neck, and a deep, almost overwhelming sense of sadness, of loss filled her.

"What do you want to tell me?" she whispered, and then held her breath, waiting.

"He's still out there. . . ."

The words hit with a jolt, but once again they were so close she had to wonder if she had spoken out loud or had heard or thought them. Tension coiled inside her as she focused past the reflective glass of the sliding door and stared at the solid wall of night beyond. The darkness outside was like a velvet curtain. Only dimly could Brenda discern the jagged line of trees against the star-dusted night sky. It was all too easy to imagine that the two-dimensional shadow-man she had seen or dreamed earlier was still out there, lurking in the woods, pulling the surrounding darkness of the night into himself. She could feel his flat, dimensionless black eyes boring into her as his darkest thoughts reached out to her: *You kill me, and I'll kill you.*

"Who—who is he?" Brenda asked, her voice modulating wildly. She found it difficult to focus on the figure behind her because it wavered as though it were underwater.

"You don't know him. . . . Not yet . . ."

"Is he dangerous? Is he going to hurt us?"

The figure shifted, and for a terrifying instant, Brenda couldn't tell if it was behind her or hovering outside in the night. It was almost as if a piece of the night had somehow detached itself and taken on a human form. She felt trapped between the figure that appeared to be both in front of her and behind her.

He wants to hurt me. . . . He's going to try . . .

"What did you say?"

Brenda leaned forward, her neck as stiff as iron as she started to turn around but stopped herself just in time and froze. She didn't dare to shift her gaze away from the window, but the feeling of a presence behind her grew stronger, swelling ever larger as it drew closer, its arms raised as if to grab her. Chills danced like pinpricks up and down her neck. Steadily building pressure tightened her muscles, making her nauseous.

"What did you say?"

Brenda was unable to distinguish between what she said and what she thought the ghostly figure behind her was whispering into her ear.

"Who is he?" she asked, desperate with fear. "Why does he want to hurt me?"

"It's not you he's after."

"Who, then? Who does he want to hurt? Is it Emily or Matt or John? *Who?*"

Brenda struggled not to cry out and turn to look directly at the apparition. She could see it, leaning close behind her, almost brushing its cold, dead fingers across the back of her neck. Her skin crawled at the thought.

"Is there—" Her voice cut off and she gulped before continuing. "Is there anything I can do to stop him?"

"Yes. . . . There's something you can do . . . to save yourself . . . to save your family."

Brenda's eyes widened as the figure behind her raised its

hands above its head. She brought her wrists together and spread her hands backward like someone making a shadow figure of a flying bird. Slowly, without a sound, the figure spread its hands farther outward until its palms were raised almost flat toward the ceiling.

"You can stop him . . . but it will cost you. . . . It will cost you terribly."

"I'll do it. Whatever it is. Just tell me. Tell me what to do," Brenda whispered all the while staring at the figure's upraised hands and wondering what the motion signified. The old woman looked like she was asking for a blessing or trying to shield herself from something that was about to fall onto her. As it drew closer, growing larger and blocking out the doorway to the hallway, Brenda could no longer resist the urge to confront it. She still couldn't see the apparition's face clearly in the glass door, but if this really was her mother, she wanted to look at her directly and listen to what she had to say.

"Mom, I—"

Her throat closed off as she turned, but she wasn't the least bit surprised to see no one there.

"Tell me what to do," she whispered desperately, but she knew it was already too late.

She was talking to empty air.

Then faintly, just at the edge of hearing, the echo of a voice said, *"You'll know when the time comes."*

Brenda realized she was crying. Her vision was swimming, and even the dull light from the stove stung her eyes. When she tried to take a breath, her ribs felt as though they would crack from the effort. Her nerves were like burned-out electrical wires, and every muscle and bone in her body felt as brittle as eggshell.

Pushing her chair back with her legs, she stood up slowly and turned to face the doorway squarely. Trembling inside, she took a few steps forward. The empty space where the figure had been seemed several degrees colder than the rest of the room. When she exhaled, she saw the faint, bluish mist of her breath dissolve into the darkness. She wanted to call out to Matt, but her voice was locked inside her chest.

"Come back," she whispered with tears streaming down her face. "Please. Come back."

The harsh edge in her voice made her cringe. She was surprised how foreign she sounded to herself.

"Come back and tell me what to do."

A desperate sense of helplessness gripped her, and her shoulders jerked with heavy, painful sobs. But she also experienced a slight measure of relief and reassurance because, even though she had no idea what she was supposed to do, the figure—*my mother*—had told her that she would know when the time came.

Moving mechanically, Brenda walked to the front door and looked out one of the sidelights at the front yard. She was surprised to see a town police cruiser still parked on the side of the road in front of the house. It had been there all evening. She could just barely make out the form of the patrolman behind the steering wheel. She couldn't tell if he was drinking coffee, sleeping, or watching the house, but she felt marginally better.

Without consciously thinking about it, Brenda brought her hands together until the insides of her wrists touched. Then she spread her palms open, holding them as flat as they would go. She could have rested her chin in the cup she formed. Making this gesture gave her a peculiar sense of comfort as she stared out at the dark night and thought to herself, *He's still out there!*

NINETEEN

visitor

"**AMBIVALENT.**"

Marcus Card said the word out loud and watched the small, gray puff of mist his breath made in the cool night air. The breeze quickly whisked it away, dissolving it into the crosshatched pattern of shadows beneath the trees. Rain was falling steadily, but underneath the trees, he was sheltered from the direct downpour.

"Am-*fucking*-bivalent."

Marcus had only recently started paying attention to words and the power they held. During his five years in prison, he had read more books than he had read in his entire life before. Not that he was grateful for the forced isolation, but while he was in prison, he had started to think about things in many new and deeper ways.

And one thing he had learned was the value of words.

He had learned that people often misused the word *ambivalent* to mean that they just didn't care about something when, in fact, Marcus knew it actually meant to be equally and powerfully drawn in opposite directions simultaneously. He figured it must be related to the word *ambidextrous,* which meant being equally competent left-handed or right-handed. If he had his dictionary with him right now, he would have looked it up just to make sure. That was how he educated himself, by checking things out when they occurred to him, but a dictionary was one thing he hadn't thought to bring with him.

Not tonight.

And no matter what, he sure as hell was feeling *ambivalent* about being out here in the woods behind Matt Ireland's house. He most definitely was being equally and powerfully drawn between wanting to get out of the cold and the darkness and wanting to finish off what he had started and felt compelled to do.

Compelled? he thought. *Good word, and goddamned right I'm feeling compelled!*

Something he couldn't identify, something inside him, was driving him on, forcing him to do this. The best thing he could imagine right now was a nice hot shower back at the motel, then knocking back a few or more than a few stiff drinks, and going to sleep, nice and dry and warm.

But if the last several nights were any indication, sleep wasn't going to be an option. It hadn't been, actually, ever since he was released from prison. And no matter what he might want right now, the impulse to do more than lurk out here in the woods and watch the scumbag lawyer's house was impossible to ignore. That dark and dangerous thing inside him was pushing him, forcing him to want to do more than just break into the house and spray-paint stupid little messages on the walls.

Problem was, he wasn't sure exactly what he would do. Not yet, anyway. But maybe, before long, he'd figure it out. He was certain he would. Maybe he had to get things started, and it would come to him.

"Yeah . . . just get started," he whispered to himself. "Then improvise."

He felt the darkness inside, a cold presence that seemed almost alive. A soft, strangled whimper escaped from him, and he clenched his fists hard enough to make a dull ache throb painfully in his wrists.

His blood was like fire in his veins. His pulse throbbed.

"Jesus Christ," he whispered, grinding his fists hard against his eyes until spiraling explosions of light swept across his vision.

He was confident that he had everything he might need
with him although, when he thought about it, he had no idea
how he could know what he was going to need when he still
hadn't decided—or been told—what he was going to do. He
was waiting for the voice inside his head, the voice that wasn't
his own thoughts, to tell him what to do. Ever since his release
from prison, the new voice had become not necessarily
stronger, but clearer. Usually it wasn't much more than a
whisper at the edge of his awareness, but sometimes—like
now—it was so loud he could almost convince himself someone else was standing behind him, shouting into his ear.

*Get going, man! Get your thumb out of your ass and take
care of things! Do it!*

"Yeah," Marcus whispered, as though he was speaking to
someone who was standing unseen close by. "I'll do it now!"

The floodlights behind the house suddenly came on, illuminating the backyard with the brightness of a flare. Marcus
grunted and dropped to the ground, digging his hands into the
soggy humus of the forest floor. The smell of wet loam and
rotting vegetation filled his nostrils, intoxicating him and
making his head spin. The rain shone like silver needles inside
the cones of light. The machine-gun pattering of water on the
leaves and branches overhead set his teeth on edge.

"Guess I'm gonna have to do it now, regardless," he whispered. He couldn't help but think how *regardless* was another
one of those misused words. He remembered how surprised
he was to learn that *irregardless* wasn't even a real word. He
had used it all the time before he went to jail.

Marcus chuckled to himself, wondering if he thought
about shit like this to try to silence the voice. But the truth
was, he had to make up his mind pretty quickly if he was going to do something tonight or wait for another, better time.

*When the fuck would be a better time, you dumb-ass piece
of shit?*

The voice snarled at him like a chain saw. Every muscle in
his body tensed as he squinted and stared up at the brightly lit
back porch. When the outside lights winked off, he sighed and
relaxed as the backyard and forest plunged back into darkness. Marcus waited as his eyes adjusted to the darkness, his
mind all the while churning over what he was going to do

next. He knew he had to follow through tonight, because of what he'd done to the cop who was parked in front of the house.

"Damn fool never should have left his window open," Marcus whispered, and when he laughed out loud, he was left with the distinct impression that someone standing behind him in the darkness was laughing too. Reaching out blindly, he picked up the vinyl gym bag he had brought with him. His fingers brushed lovingly across the faux leather handles.

I've got everything I need. Now all I have to do is get in there and do what I have to do.

So even if he didn't have a clear plan in mind, he was confident that, once things started happening, he'd know exactly what to do.

Or else the voice will tell me.

THE sudden creak of floorboards upstairs set Brenda's teeth on edge, but she was surprised that she didn't jump at the sound. Even with the heavy padding of the carpet, the new flooring underneath made loud snaps that sounded like gunshots. She guessed Matt had gotten up to go to the bathroom. Moving quietly, she stepped away from the front-door window and looked up the darkened stairwell. She hunched her shoulders as the shuffling steps grew louder.

When the upstairs light winked on, she cried out, "Ahh. That's too bright." Shielding her eyes with one hand, she waited until her eyesight adjusted before looking up the stairs.

"Bren?"

"Yeah. I'm down here," she replied, her voice only a breathy whisper. She found it curious that her voice sounded completely normal to her. It was as if the air in the hallway had a different density than the air in the kitchen moments ago.

Matt appeared at the head of the stairs wearing his baggy boxer shorts and faded college T-shirt. His hair was rumpled from sleep, and there was a shadowed crease on the side of his face from the pillow.

"What are you doing up so late?" he asked as he squinted down at her while reaching behind himself to scratch the small of his back.

"Couldn't sleep," she replied. She chuckled to herself when she realized how that didn't even come close to describing why she was still awake.

"You have any idea what time it is?" Matt asked.

"Not really," she said, shaking her head.

While she'd been in the kitchen watching the apparition in the sliding glass door, time seemed to have lost all meaning.

"Almost three o'clock. You coming up soon?"

Brenda was about to say that of course she was coming up soon, but she caught herself. She shook her head from side to side, struggling to find the right words to say, but she was drawing a complete blank.

"You okay?" Matt asked. His eyes seemed to be focusing better, and he looked down at her with an odd expression of deep concern.

"Yeah. Sure. I'm fine," she said, wondering if he could detect the lie. Over the last few—*How long has it been?*—Days? . . . Weeks? . . . Months?

It didn't matter how long. She had to acknowledge that for some time now, although she hadn't been outright lying to her husband, she hadn't been entirely truthful with him, either.

What are you hiding from? What are you afraid of? Are you worried about what he'll think if you tell him the truth? Maybe now's the time to start.

"You—ah, are you awake enough to talk?" she asked. Her voice twisted up a register.

Matt rubbed his face and considered a moment as though taking inventory, then nodded.

"Yeah . . . I guess so." He shook like he'd just splashed himself with cold water. "What's up?"

"How 'bout a cup of tea?"

"Okay," he said as he started down the stairs.

His right hand slid along the banister for support as he descended. She couldn't help but notice the Band-Aids covering the cuts he'd gotten in the woods earlier. When he reached the bottom of the stairs, Brenda slid her arms around his waist and pulled him close. Leaning toward him and tilting her head back, she kissed him full on the mouth. Standing on tiptoes, she pressed her face into the crook of his neck and inhaled his warm, sleepy scent.

"What's up?" Matt asked sleepily as they walked side by side into the kitchen.

Brenda had left the light on over the stove, and that was enough for her to see by. When Matt drew a chair away from the table, the footpads chattered as they scraped across the linoleum. He sat down heavily, sighing as he leaned forward with his elbows on the table and stared blankly at his cut and bruised hands.

Brenda cast a nervous glance at his thin reflection in the glass of the sliding door. She wouldn't have been at all surprised to see another transparent figure lurking behind him, but she only saw him and the darkened hallway behind. Still, she couldn't shake the feeling that the ghost she had seen earlier was still close by in the darkness, watching her every move.

"Looks like Patoine got the message," she said, trying to sound chipper. "There's been a cop parked out front all night."

She took the teakettle from the stove, poured out the water still in it, then filled it with fresh water from the faucet. The hissing of the aerator sounded like escaping steam and set her nerves all the more on edge.

"You feel any better, knowing they're out there?" Matt asked.

"No. Not really."

Matt looked like he would much rather be back in bed, and Brenda was grateful that he decided to join her. Seeing the concern in his expression gave her the courage she needed to try to tell him what had been bothering her.

After filling the kettle, she set it on the burner and turned the dial. Within seconds, the metal coil went from gray to a glowing red spiral. Drops of water on the outside of the kettle hissed and crackled as they dripped onto the burner and evaporated.

"Maybe a little better, I guess," she said with a shrug as she came and sat down next to him. Her right knee brushed against his leg underneath the table. Reaching out, she took both of his hands into hers and clasped them tightly. Their eyes met, and Brenda saw the love in his eyes, but she was filled with conflicting thoughts.

I know he loves me, and I trust him, but how much can I tell him? Will he even believe me, or will he just think that I'm crazy?

She cleared her throat, trying to think of where to begin, but just as she opened her mouth to say something, she caught a glimpse of—something—in the corner of her eye. It was only a flicker of motion outside on the deck, but Brenda jumped from her chair, making a funny little noise in her throat as she turned to look.

"Did you see that?" she asked, trying hard not to yell.

"Huh? See what?"

"Outside . . . just now. . . . There was a—"

Releasing her husband's hands, she stood up and went to the door to make sure it was locked. Standing close to the glass, she peered outside into the darkness, afraid of what she might see.

A high raft of clouds hid the moon, so the backyard was in deep shadow. It was still raining. She could hear the steady pattering on the deck. Her warm breath fogged the water-streaked glass, leaving small, gray ovals that quickly disappeared when she inhaled.

Without consciously thinking about it, she reached over to the light switch and flipped it on. The sudden brightness of the outside floodlights illuminated a large area of the yard. Beneath the trees, the shadows were as crisp as black stencils.

"You're way too jumpy, Bren," Matt said. "You gotta calm down."

"I know I do," Brenda said without turning to look at him. She could see her own and Matt's reflections in the glass. Her heart started racing when she thought how insubstantial they both looked. She was suddenly swept by the frightening impression that both of them were almost perfectly transparent. Staring into her own eyes, she tried to anchor herself, but a strange feeling of vertigo swept through her, and she could feel herself slipping away.

The teakettle gurgled as the water inside it heated up. When she shifted her gaze over to it, she noticed the rounded reflection of her husband in the chrome surface, but for a panicky instant she didn't see herself. Only when she shifted her focus did she see her image in the curved, polished metal.

"Yeah. . . . Maybe I am a little stressed out," she said in a husky whisper. She took a shuddering breath and, turning, looked directly at Matt before adding, "Can you blame me?"

Matt gave her a tight smile and shook his head as though he were helpless.

"I'm doing everything I can," he said, sounding a little defensive.

"I know you are."

The kettle hadn't reached a boil yet, so Brenda came over and stood behind him, sliding her hands down his chest and stomach and hugging him. The position was awkward, so she broke it off after a few seconds and went to get cups and tea bags.

"Sugar or honey?" she asked.

"Honey, if we have any."

Brenda opened a cupboard door and pulled out the small, plastic honey bear, which was half-full. The honey looked a little sugary, but it would dissolve in the hot liquid. She busied herself, trying to find comfort in such an ordinary activity as making tea, but she still was angry and frustrated that she felt so distant from her husband.

Why can't I talk to him?

She tried not to grind her teeth as she stirred the brewing tea, watching the threads of brown liquid swirl and dissolve in the water.

Just tell him straight out what's on your mind!

But it wasn't that easy. She didn't know where or how to begin.

Once the tea was steeping, and the water had turned a rich, nut brown, she brought the cups over to the table and sat down. Matt smiled at her, nodding his thanks as he took the spoon and honey bear she offered and squirted some honey into his tea. The clinking of the spoon on the cup as he stirred seemed unnaturally loud.

"You're absolutely right," Brenda said after clearing her throat. She found it difficult to look him in the eye, so she stared down at her own cup of tea.

"'Bout what?" Matt asked, a bit distracted.

"About me . . . being too nervous."

She took a shallow breath, and when she swallowed, her throat made a loud gulping sound. Matt looked up at her and then leaned forward, touching her lightly on the forearm.

"I'm afraid sometimes," Brenda said, "that I might be— you know, having some kind of breakdown or something." Before he could respond, she added, "I've been seeing things."

"Seeing things?" Matt asked, looking genuinely concerned.

Brenda tipped her head to one side and gave him a tight smile.

"You know . . . things . . . like . . . like ghosts."

"Ghosts," Matt said, looking at her like he was going to laugh out loud, but then he caught himself. "What do you mean?" he asked with a deepening frown.

As Brenda stared at him, a blur of motion in the doorway behind him startled her, drawing her attention. Matt saw her reaction and stiffened, then turned and looked over his shoulder. Icy rushes were shooting through Brenda as she stared past him into the hallway. After a breathless moment, she realized that she had seen something move on the front doorstep, through the sidelights by the door.

Matt shoved his chair back and stood up quickly, turning with his fists clenched at his sides. He looked back and forth between Brenda and the front door.

"I think there's someone on the front steps," she whispered.

"It's probably the cop. Maybe he needs to take a leak or something." Matt was trying to sound casual, but Brenda caught the tension in his voice. Without hesitating, he walked down the hallway to the front door with Brenda only a step or two behind him. The clutching sensation in her chest was so intense she was afraid she might not be able to stop herself from screaming as Matt reached for the doorknob. She grabbed his hand.

"No," she whispered. "Look first."

Matt shifted closer to the sidelights, bending over as he pulled the sheer curtain aside. Watching over his shoulder, Brenda looked out at the night, tensed and waiting for something to suddenly explode through the glass.

She could hear Matt's steady breathing as he looked outside. The light from the kitchen cast a thin shadow across his face. As far as she could see, the front steps and yard were lost in darkness.

"Can't see a thing," Matt said. "Turn on the outside light, will you?"

Brenda almost refused, but then she nodded. Her hand was shaking uncontrollably as she reached for the wall switch. She jumped when she heard the loud click as Matt unbolted the lock and started turning the doorknob.

No! she wanted to cry out. *Don't do it!* But the words were lodged in her chest. She suddenly was convinced that what she had been so afraid was lurking in the woods behind the house was out there on their front doorstep. A shiver tightened the skin on the back of her neck, and she realized that it was already too late. She could have changed what was going to happen if she had spoken, if Matt had listened to her and not unlocked the door. Numb with terror and holding her breath, she watched as Matt started to pull the door open just as she flicked the light switch.

The sudden, glaring brightness outside burned her eyes, but there was something there. A large, black shape shifted as fast as a moon-cast shadow up the front steps. While Matt was still pulling the door open, the shape rose up like a column of smoke, blocking her view of the front yard and the street beyond.

"No!" she screamed.

In that instant, the black shape filled the doorway, taking on terrible substance as it slammed like a freight train into the door. The heavy thud resounded throughout the house like a sudden clap of thunder.

"Son of a bitch," Matt cried out, but that was all he said before the door slammed into him, knocking him backward. Brenda heard a loud crack as his head banged against the wall, leaving a dent in the wallboard to the right of the hall closet door.

Matt looked stunned as his knees buckled, and he slid down, slumped against the wall. Frozen in time, Brenda stared at him, waiting for him to get up, but he didn't move. His head was cocked at a frightening angle, and his eyes were closed. Before Brenda could react, the black figure burst into the house and lunged at her with both arms outstretched.

She let out a single, piercing scream as she spun away from the intruder. With the outside light behind him, she couldn't make out his face. In that first frightening flash, all she saw was a tall, slender man who let loose a low, rumbling laugh as he stormed into the house. Snorting like an animal, he shifted around, cocked back his foot, and kicked Matt hard in the stomach. Matt grunted as the air was expelled from his lungs, and he flopped onto the floor on his side, his head bouncing a couple of times on the carpet.

"No!" Brenda cried out, but it was already too late. She knew her husband couldn't hear her and was unconscious if not already dead.

Run! Run for your life! a voice screamed inside her head, but she was rooted where she stood, cowering as the intruder slammed the door shut behind him. The deadbolt lock made a loud click when he snapped it.

"You fuckin' people," he said, clicking his tongue as he shook his head with disgust. "Living way out in the country like this, and you just open your door like that in the middle of the night. Don't you know there are dangerous people out there?"

Numb with shock and fear, Brenda couldn't think straight. She wanted to shout at the man, ask him what he wanted and why he was doing this to them, but her voice was caught like a fishbone in her throat. A loud, hammering sound filled her ears as she stared in dumb amazement at the hole in the wall where Matt's head had hit.

"We've got some business to take care of," the man said, turning to her. He was keeping his voice low, but there was a brittle edge to it that made Brenda think he was a little frightened at what was happening.

Maybe he's strung out on drugs, Brenda thought, *and he can't maintain.*

"Mom?"

John's voice sounded faintly from upstairs, making Brenda jump. She could tell by the sound that he was still in his bedroom and that the door was closed. Almost blind with fear, she turned and looked up the stairwell.

"What are you guys doing down there?" John called out.

There was a faint click, and she knew he had opened his bedroom door and had stepped out into the hall.

Brenda started to say something, but her mind drew a complete blank. She couldn't believe this was really happening. It all had the surreal cast of a dream, but she was filled with a sudden real terror about what might happen to her son if he were to come downstairs.

God, what do I do? Tell him to run? Tell him to call the cops? He and Emily have to get away from here and hide!

Brenda flinched when, through the chaos of her thoughts, she heard a second faint click. Turning back to the intruder, she saw that he had a gun and was aiming it at her. She could feel a cold spot in the center of her chest and she cringed, waiting to hear the gun go off and feel a sudden burning in her chest as the bullet tore through her.

"You say one word," the intruder said in a rasping whisper. "One lousy, fucking word, and it'll be your last."

Brenda's eyes widened with shock, and her mouth moved soundlessly as she nodded her head up and down.

"Why?" she whispered, surprised that her voice didn't choke off. "What do you want? Why are you doing this? Money? Drugs? We don't have any prescription drugs."

From the upstairs hallway, she heard footsteps in the hallway, dragging on the plush carpet.

"Mom?"

"You tell him you're just fine," the intruder snarled, "or I swear to Christ, I'll kill you where you stand . . . and then him." He flicked the gun toward the stairwell. Terrible coldness squeezed her chest.

"I . . . I'm fine, honey," she called out, her voice almost out of control. "I just . . . I dropped something. That's all."

"It's almost morning, isn't it?" John asked.

"Go on back to bed, honey. I'll be right up."

"You sound funny," John said.

Brenda looked up the stairwell. John still hadn't appeared at the head of the stairs, but she dreaded that he would and that he would see the absolute terror on her face. The intruder moved closer to her, gripping her arm tightly with one hand and pinning her from behind. His heated breath blew across

her neck as he cocked her arm up behind her back so her wrist
was between her shoulder blades. The lance of pain was like a
streak of white light inside her head. She winced but didn't
cry out. The cold circle of the pistol pressed into her temple.

"Go back to bed, honey," she called out, struggling to keep
her voice steady and not cry out.

A sooty shadow shifted across the wall upstairs. Brenda
was frantic with fear for her son. She wished she had the
strength and courage to wheel around on the intruder and rip
open his throat with her bare hands, but fear paralyzed her.
She wanted to believe that John and Emily would be all right
if she just cooperated with this man and gave him what he
wanted, but she knew that wasn't going to happen.

You kill me and I'll kill you.

But maybe if she cooperated, he would go away without
hurting anyone else. Matt still hadn't moved and she feared
he was dead. The man released her and shoved her closer to
the bottom of the stairs. She was surprised that she didn't
stumble.

"I'll let you watch him die if you want," the intruder said,
his voice rasping in her ear. "Is that what you want?"

"No. . . . Please," Brenda whimpered, shaking her head violently back and forth and staring at the man. Tears blurred
her vision, and in the dim glow of light from upstairs, she
couldn't see his face clearly. It looked like a dark well that
was sucking in all the light around him.

I have to protect my children, no matter what, Brenda
thought wildly even as she was swept up by a feeling of total
helplessness.

This can't be happening! But it is. . . . God held me . . . it is!

Brenda gazed at the intruder, torn between wanting to
strike back and fearful that it would mean certain death for her
and everyone else. Tightening his grip, he pinned her arm to
her side. Panic burned along her nerves, and she struggled
wildly, kicking at his shins with her bare heels. In desperation,
she thrashed and turned, baring her teeth as she lunged forward, trying to bite him.

Quickly sidestepping, the intruder glared at her, his face
contorted with surprise and rage as he swung his arm around

in a wide arc and slammed the butt of the pistol against the side of her head.

Shattering pain and a single bright flash of white light filled her head and then quickly winked out with a faint hissing sound, like firebrands being extinguished in water. Darkness swelled around her like the ocean as it rose up and then dragged her down . . . down . . . down into deep and total silence.

TWENTY

looking glass

CONSCIOUSNESS returned slowly and painfully.

Long before she was able to—or dared to—open her eyes, Brenda was aware of sounds that drew her gently up from the deep well of unconsciousness. For a long time, she was aware that she was floating dreamily, suspended in an odd in-between state where she knew she was unconscious. Then there came a sudden tearing, rushing sound like an unseen train passing in the night.

As she struggled closer to consciousness, she realized dimly that she was propped up unsteadily in what had to be a chair. Hard wood was pressing uncomfortably into her shoulders and at several points along her spine. She was as limp as a sack of grain, but something was holding her up, keeping her from slipping to the floor.

I'm in one of the dining room chairs.

She struggled to break through the dark bubble that enclosed her mind.

How did I get here? What's holding me up? What's going on?

Before she could answer any of these questions, rough hands grabbed her by the shoulders and pressed her against the chair back. The sudden motion sent a bright lance of pain through her. It was echoed by a dull ache on the side of her head. She tried to raise her hand to touch where she'd been hurt, but she couldn't move her arm.

Yes. . . . That man . . . the one who broke into the house . . . He hit me.

Oh my God! Where are the kids?

Choking panic filled Brenda, making her skin feel cold and dead. She cried out when the intruder jerked her arms roughly behind her back, and then something—*A rope? . . . A wire?*—encircled her wrists, digging into her flesh with a terrible burn.

"Ahh, I see you're awake now."

The voice came from far away, but it sounded frighteningly familiar. It reverberated like a roll of distant thunder in her ears, sending even colder rushes across her back and scalp. The intruder—*Who is he, and why is he doing this?*—jerked her hands behind her back so hard her shoulders cracked. Then he crossed them at the wrist.

In the grayness of her semiconsciousness, an image suddenly popped into Brenda's mind. She saw the reflection of an old woman—the ghost that was haunting her house—standing with her hands raised and held together, touching at the wrists. Her fingers were splayed open like a fan. Without conscious thought, Brenda imitated the position and held her hands the same way, keeping her forearms as close together as she could but spreading her hands as far apart as she could while the man bound her wrists.

The intruder grunted, his breath hot and moist on her neck as he looped the rope or wire around a few more times before tying it off. Flashes of pain sparked like electrical shocks up and down Brenda's shoulders and neck. She cried out again but kept her wrists tensed and her fingers spread open as wide as possible.

"Oh, I'm so sorry. Is that too tight?" the man said, cooing with mock sentiment. His breath was a stinking gush of warmth in her face. Then he laughed, a deep rumble of laughter that sounded almost as if it came from someone else who was in the room.

Is someone helping him?

The fog was slowly lifting from her mind, and even though

she hadn't opened her eyes, Brenda was sure that she was propped up in one of the dining room chairs. The pain in her arms and shoulders was bringing her steadily closer and closer to full awareness, even though she was strongly tempted to give up and stay where she was, drifting in the soft, charcoal shadows of oblivion.

After a few heartbeats, she chanced to open her eyes, but the splinters of light made her wince and cry out. It was almost impossible to see where she was because light exploded across her vision in a blinding, dazzling display. A huge blob of a shadow shifted silently in front of her, and she knew the intruder was standing there. The heat of his body carried with it a sick, sour stench that made her stomach churn. Underneath it, she could also smell something sharp, medicinal almost.

"Nice and snug now, are we?" the man asked.

There was an odd, twisted edge in his voice that sounded strange to Brenda. She had only heard him speak briefly before he knocked her unconscious—*He hit me with his gun.*—but once again, she had the clear impression that someone else had spoken, not the man in front of her.

She groaned as she exhaled loudly, allowing her body to slump forward until the pull of the rope or wire that was binding her got painfully tight. Again, the memory of the ghostly woman holding her hands together at the wrists filled her mind. Knowing the man was standing in front of her, Brenda sighed and dropped her head as though utterly defeated. Behind her, she relaxed her hands and realized, to her amazement, that there was a small amount of slack. A flicker of hope leapt inside her, but she struggled not to show any reaction as she shifted the binding a fraction of an inch up and down her wrist.

Is that what she was trying to show me?

Brenda wriggled her fingers to restore the circulation that had been cut off. A warm, prickling rush of pins and needles ran through the palms of her hands. It felt as if she had dipped her hands into a fire, but the rope loosened around her wrists. She knew, given time, she might be able to work her hands free.

And then what? How much time do I have?

She was filled with a rush of panic. *And what's happened to Matt . . . and the kids?*

Her vision was still a blurry smear of light when she opened her eyes a little wider. The brightness was nearly unbearable. As she looked around, she saw a pale blue wash surrounding her and realized she must be in the living room. Narrowing her eyes and wincing with pain, she struggled to see more clearly. She had to make sure that's where she was before she tried to think of what to do to save herself and her family.

But the more her mind cleared, the sharper her fear rose until it reached an almost unbearable level. After a long, horrible moment, she saw some shapes off to her right. Dark, motionless lumps were sprawled on the couch. After a heart-stopping second, she realized what they were.

Oh my God, no!

She wanted to cry out, but her voice was stuffed down into her chest.

It's Emily and John!

They looked like they were sleeping, curled up on the sofa, but as Brenda's vision shifted into focus, she realized they were trussed up like she was with their arms and legs bound.

"You son of a—" she started to say, but before she could finish, the intruder smacked her across the face with the flat of his hand. The stinging impact rattled her teeth and snapped her head back. A sheet of white light shot across her vision, and a high-pitched ringing sound sang in her ears.

"Don't talk like that to me," the man said. *"Ever!"*

His voice was low and calm, but beneath it, Brenda could hear an odd strain, like he was struggling hard against—

What? Is he afraid of something? Is he worried he'll get caught? Or is it something else?

"Don't you *dare* hurt my children," Brenda said in spite of the stinging pain. She cringed, expecting him to hit her again, but he leaned closer to her and chuckled softly.

"Hurt them?" he said, casting a quick glance over his shoulder at the two bound children. Once again, his voice sounded unnaturally strained. As groggy as she was, she was convinced she had heard two distinct voices. She shook her head to clear it, wanting desperately to know how many people there were in the house. She had to know exactly what she was up against before she tried anything.

"Hell, I'm not going to hurt them," the man said. "I'm only going to kill them."

He laughed softly, a short, huffing laugh.

"Problem is, before I can do that, I have to wait for your useless sack of shit husband to come to."

He looked toward the entryway, and Brenda followed his gaze over to the dark figure that was lying on the floor beside the closet.

"I must have hit him harder than I thought," the intruder said, "but I think he'll come around soon. I really want him to watch with you. And then—"

He paused and took a long, watery breath. When he spoke again, his voice was subtly altered, and for the first time he sounded a bit frightened and indecisive.

"Then . . . I don't know. I—I haven't decided yet. I might let him watch me fuck you before you die." The man hesitated a moment, stroking his chin, then suddenly let out a belly-deep grunt, bent over, and clutched his hands to his stomach. His face contorted in pain, the tendons in his neck standing out like cords under his skin. After a terrifying moment, his features gradually softened and returned to normal, and he finished in a strangled voice, "But then again, I like you, so maybe I'll kill you last."

Brenda sucked in a quick breath. Needles of pain prickled between her ribs, and a cold, greasy feeling slid beneath her skin. Her ears filled with a loud rushing sound, and she was afraid she was going to pass out again. No matter how hard she tried, she couldn't pull enough oxygen into her lungs.

"I am kinda worried, though," the intruder continued, and Brenda had the distinct impression he was explaining, almost apologizing to someone else, not her. "I think I may have hit him a little too hard. He's been out for quite a while." He stretched his arm out and glanced at his wristwatch. "Going on almost half an hour."

"Why?" Brenda asked, her voice nothing more than a croak.

The word was out of her before she could stop it. Cringing, she tilted her head to one side, anticipating another slap, but the man simply regarded her with a steady, glimmering stare.

The look in his eyes was crazy as he stood up straight, looming above her, and folded his arms across his chest. With the light behind him, his body was dark and featureless. Brenda shuddered, remembering the shadow-man she had dreamed was outside in the woods.

Maybe it wasn't a dream after all.

"What? What do you mean, *why?*" he said in a short, harsh whisper.

"Why are you doing this?" Brenda said, her voice breaking as tears filled her eyes. "I . . . We never . . . never did anything to you. I don't even know you."

The intruder tilted his head back, took another sharp, shuddering breath, and held it for a few seconds as he glared at her. Once again, his face twisted through a series of odd expressions, and in that brief moment before he exhaled, Brenda imagined all kinds of terrible thoughts raging in his head.

Kill me now! she wanted to shriek at him. *Kill us all now and get it over with if that's what you're going to do! Please don't torture us! Just do it and get it over with quickly!*

But in her heart, she knew that killing them quickly was the last thing this man intended to do.

"You don't know who I am?" the man finally said, his voice fluctuating so wildly it created an odd auditory effect that made Brenda think two people were speaking simultaneously. He bent down, bringing his face so close to hers she could smell his sweat and his unwashed, soiled clothes. "Do you want to know?"

His face flushed bright scarlet, and his eyes looked like pits of blackness.

"My name is Marcus Card. And you're right. You don't know me. And your piece of shit lawyer husband doesn't know me, either, but he'll know soon enough who I . . . who I—"

The man's voice cut off with a strangled gag and, turning to one side, he gripped his head and leaned forward until his elbows rested on his knees. He closed his eyes, and a thick, foamy string of saliva dripped from his mouth to the floor. Whimpering like a wounded animal, he took several quick, snorting breaths that rattled in his chest, and he groaned loudly, as though he were fighting back wave after wave of intense pain.

"He knows who Jeromy Bowker is, though, doesn't he?" the man said, his voice twisting up higher and higher until it broke. He grabbed Brenda by the chin and shook her head so hard her teeth rattled. "Oh, yeah! Jeromy Bowker! That name mean anything to you?"

Riveted by fear, Brenda couldn't react. She just sat there, trembling. Of course she knew who Jeromy Bowker was. How could she ever forget the man her husband had sent to jail for burning his girlfriend and her one-year-old daughter to death with a blowtorch?

"Yeah? Does that name ring a bell, dingy-dingy?" Card shrieked. His eyes widened as he forced Brenda's head back until her neck felt like it was going to snap. He brought his face so close to hers that for a moment she thought he was going to kiss her. Her breath caught in her throat, and her stomach churned with sour acid.

"Oh, yeah. You know who I'm talking about. And your useless piece of shit husband does, too. He knows all about it. All of it. He was the son of a bitch who sent Bowker away."

Mucus had collected in the corners of the man's mouth, and it made a disgusting, smacking sound as he spoke. Flecks of it flew into Brenda's face, but she fought back the urge to retch.

"It's his fault, what happened to me . . . to him . . . to Bowker! Don't you see? He put me—*us* there, and now he—he's inside me." The man clenched his fists and pounded the sides of his head. "He's inside me forever because of what he did to me, so you . . . you and your whole goddamned family have to die . . . to pay for what he did to me!"

The man's face twisted and contorted with rage. His eyes rolled back in his head so all Brenda could see were the sickly white undersides lined with red threads of veins. His face turned a plum purple, and the vein in the center of his forehead bulged dangerously. His jaw muscles clenched and unclenched furiously as he gnashed his teeth. His lower lip was trembling, and his body was shaking so badly Brenda thought he was having a seizure of some kind.

"He died! He died, but he's inside me! Understand? I can't . . . I can't do *anything* he doesn't want me to do. Even if I don't want to. No matter how much I try to stop him, he can make me do anything!"

Groaning in pain, he clawed at his own face, his fingernails raking down his cheeks, leaving long, wavering red welts that beaded with blood. Flecks of spittle stained pink with blood flew from his lips.

Horrified and amazed, Brenda recoiled from the man, but as frightened as she was, her vision had cleared, and she could see that Marcus Card—*If that's his name*—wasn't nearly as big or imposing as she had first imagined. In fact, he was slightly built, but the raw, violent energy that writhed inside him seemed to blur the outlines of his body. Brenda had the distinct impression that his body was like a tuning fork, vibrating at a very high frequency. She silently prayed that he would have a stroke and die right then and there before he could carry out his threats and harm her family.

"Look," Card said, his voice lowering and sounding a bit more calm and rational. "I don't have time for this shit, all right? I don't want to do this. I really don't. But he . . . he's *making* me do it. I don't want to—Oh, God!" He gasped and gripped his head as his eyes rolled back, eyelids fluttering. "He inside me! He's inside me, and I can't get him out! I have to do what he wants!"

Card wailed incoherently as he rocked back and forth, all the while punching the sides of his head. His shoulders shook violently, but after a long, terrible moment, he seemed to gain a measure of control over himself. He sighed loudly and, wiping his face with the flats of his hands, looked around the living room as though dazed and unsure of where he was. Then he took a deep breath and smiled wickedly as he focused on Brenda. Kneeling down, he unzipped a vinyl gym bag on the floor near his feet that Brenda hadn't noticed before. A sick grin twisted the corners of his mouth as he pulled out a roll of duct tape, picked at the edge with his thumbnail until he got it, and then tore off a strip several inches long.

"I'm sorry, but I've got to do this," Card said, speaking softly now, his voice deep and resonant. He sounded to Brenda like another person entirely, and she realized that's why she had thought there were two people in the house.

"But don't worry. It will all be over soon." He approached her, holding the strip of tape out with both hands and positioning it so he could cover her mouth. "I won't block your nose so you can't breathe. I wouldn't want you to suffocate or any-thing. That'd be too easy, don't you think? I want you to see it all. I want you to see what I do to your brats and that sack-of-shit husband of yours."

He snorted with laughter and wiped his mouth with the back of his hand, looking startled when he saw the streak of bloody mucus. Then he wiped his hand on his pants leg.

"I want him to see what I'm gonna do to you to make you all suffer. To make him suffer for what he did."

Before Brenda could scream, Card slapped the duct tape hard across her mouth, cutting off her breath. The stinging im-pact brought more tears to her eyes, but she couldn't stop star-ing at him, her eyes wide with fear. Deep, twisting shadows moved across Card's face, shifting as though the light source in the room was moving from side to side.

"Shut your fucking mouth," he said softly, almost lovingly, and then, leaning close, he whispered, "You kill me, and I'll kill you."

His words buzzed like hornets in Brenda's ears. They echoed in her brain and stabbed like a dagger into her heart. She had been looking right at him, and she knew that his lips hadn't moved when she heard him as clearly as if someone standing behind her had spoken directly into her ear.

Without another word, his expression suddenly went slack, Card turned and left the living room. Stunned and wrung out with fear and hopelessness, Brenda slouched in the chair.

You kill me, and I'll kill you!

Brenda couldn't move. She could barely breathe.

As if the sounds were coming from far away, she listened as Card struggled with . . . something. After a moment, she re-alized with a dull shock that he was dragging the dead weight of her unconscious husband into the living room. Dazed, she stared at the darkened doorway of the entryway, only mildly surprised when she caught a glimpse of the ghostly woman looming out of the darkness. Before Brenda could focus on her, the woman's face dissolved like smoke. Only then did she remember her hands.

Keeping her body as still as possible, she started to twist her hands back and forth. The cord burned her wrists as she tried to free herself. Her only hope was that Card was so busy with Matt that he wouldn't notice what she was doing.

Brenda watched with steadily rising terror as the man lifted her unconscious husband and propped him into another one of the dining room chairs. Matt's body was limp and kept sliding from the seat, but Card threw a few loops of clothesline—*So that's what he's using!*—around him to keep him in the chair.

"Poor bastard," Card muttered as he tightened the rope around Matt's chest, yanking it tight. Matt's head lolled loosely to one side, but Card grabbed a fistful of hair and held him in an upright position. Leaning close to Matt's face, he stared intently at his closed eyes.

"Come on. Wake up. Time to have some fun."

All the while, Brenda worked to get free. She feared Card would notice what she was doing, so she kept her efforts to a minimum, twisting her hands back and forth. The rope easily slid up her wrists but caught on her wrist bone. She couldn't get it over the heels of her thumbs. Filled with silent frustration, she took a deep breath and, in spite of her burning wrists, pulled the rope, hoping to stretch it.

"Man, he's out like a light," Card said, shaking his head and casting a quick glance at her over his shoulder.

Brenda froze but didn't miss the expression of what appeared to be genuine regret on his face. For an instant, Card's eyes were suffused with a compassionate glow. He looked confused, as though he didn't quite grasp what he was doing. With the living room light illuminating the side of his face, he looked like someone who had come to help, not hurt them.

"Maybe some ice will bring him around. You think?"

Dumbfounded that he would even consider that she might offer a helpful suggestion, Brenda lowered her gaze, letting her chin sag to her chest. She wanted him to think she had given up all hope and was simply waiting for death. The last thing she wanted was for him to check the rope.

"There any ice in the freezer?"

Card's knees popped when he stood up. Brenda caught the sudden wince of pain that shot across his face. Amazed how quickly his expressions changed, she thought he looked for a moment like a hurt little boy. He hesitated, waiting for her to nod. When she didn't, he hawked deep in his throat and then spat at her. Globs of spit landed in her hair and dripped down the back of her scalp. They felt like spiders crawling in her hair.

Without another word, Card stomped out of the living room. The instant he was around the corner, Brenda started working furiously to loosen her hands. The soft cotton rope chafed her terribly, peeling off skin, but she worked the loops down to the base of her thumbs and, closing her eyes and grimacing with pain, pulled until her hands slipped free.

I can't believe it.

Relief filled her as the rope fell away, but before it hit the floor, she gripped it and squeezed tightly, knowing if Card saw it on the floor, he'd bind her up again tighter.

Once again, a mental image of the ghost with her hands held together filled Brenda's mind.

Is that what you were doing? You were trying to show me how to get away. How did you know that? How did you know this was going to happen?

Right now, Brenda decided, it didn't matter. She had to save her family. Card had a gun. Although she hadn't seen it since she regained consciousness, she remembered he had knocked her out with it.

So what do I do now?

She couldn't get to the phone and call 911, not without Card catching her. And she knew she wouldn't stand a chance if she attacked him. Card wasn't a large man, but he could certainly overpower her, even if she surprised him. Besides, he had a gun, and she knew he wasn't afraid to use it.

You've got to think of something!

In a flash, she remembered that the cops were parked outside. Obviously they hadn't seen anything unusual that needed to be checked out, so as far as they were concerned, everyone in the house was fine.

Brenda knew her best—maybe her only chance—was to get outside and get to the cruiser before Card could stop her. All she had to do was alert the cop out front, and then he would take care of Card.

If she could get out fast enough, without making too much noise, the cops could be in the house before Card got back from the kitchen.

Her body hummed with tension as she listened to Card rummage around in the kitchen. She heard a cupboard door open and slam shut, then the whining, crunching sound of the icemaker as he depressed the lever and filled a container with chunks of ice.

Brenda knew she had to act now, but she was paralyzed with fear.

What if I don't make it out in time? What if he kills Matt and the kids before he comes after me? I can't just leave them all here. Can I?

No.

She had to make sure Card was either down for the count or that he came after her before he had a chance to do anything else. She had to draw him out and get him to chase her so her family would be safe. That was her only concern, even if he hurt or killed her.

She would do it. She had to do it.

Without hesitation, she would sacrifice herself for her family. There was no question about it.

And as far as she could see, the only way to do that was to wait.

Wait until Card came back into the living room, and then surprise him. Jump him. If she caught him off guard, even if she didn't knock him out or kill him, if she could just hurt him enough so she could get out of the house, then he would come for her and leave Matt and the kids alone.

A lot of ifs and maybes, she thought, but she didn't see any alternative.

Every muscle in her body was so coiled and tensed she ached. She listened as Card came down the hallway from the kitchen. The back of her head where he'd hit her with his gun was numb. A roaring sound like gushing water filled her ears. She struggled to keep her legs from trembling as she squeezed her hands as tightly as she could to steady them as he came closer . . . closer . . .

His dark silhouette filled the living room door. For an instant, Brenda thought it wasn't Card but someone else standing there. He looked huge in the doorway. Even with the living room light shining directly onto his face, Card's features were cast in shadows that shifted subtly.

Winding the rope behind her back into a knotted clump, Brenda squeezed with her right hand until the blood throbbed in her fingernails.

You're not going to get away with this, you bastard.

Her anger surged, and she prayed that she would find the strength and courage to act. All of their lives depended on it.

Card was carrying a plastic bowl with ice cubes mounded up so high a couple of them fell onto the floor as he knelt down beside Matt. Again, as he bent down, Card's knees popped loudly. Brenda wasn't sure if she thought it or said it out loud, or if someone she couldn't see actually whispered the words, but she distinctly heard a voice say,

Go for the knees.

"There, there," Card cooed, sounding like a concerned father caring for a sick child as he took a handful of ice cubes and gingerly dabbed them across Matt's brow. Matt didn't react, and Brenda wondered again with a stab in her heart if he was already dead.

"You have to run."

Faint, barely audible, like the touch of a feather in the dark, the voice whispered in Brenda's ear. A wave of cold air washed across the back of her neck, raising goose bumps on her arms.

Card suddenly turned and glared at her, his face contorting into a mask of rage. His eyes narrowed, and once again Brenda thought his features were so altered he looked like someone else.

"I mean it. Shut up!" Card snapped, raising a clenched fist at her. "One more word out of you, and I swear to Christ I'll kill you."

With the tape across her mouth, Brenda knew she hadn't made a sound. A tremor of fear shook her. Card was disintegrating rapidly, and she was running out of time. Perspiration broke out like dew on her forehead. Chilling trickles of sweat ran down inside her nightgown along her sides. Circling spots of light danced like wandering dust motes in front of her eyes.

"You have to run!"

The voice rose louder, now, insistent. It sounded like a woman's voice, filling the room with a heavy sigh like a cool night breeze wafting through an open window.

"You have no choice! You have to run."

"I said keep your fucking mouth *shut!*" Card snarled. His back was to Brenda as he slapped Matt's face, trying to bring him around, but he turned and glared at her, his eyes gleaming, his lower lip trembling with barely repressed fury.

"I'll deal with you once I'm done with them."

On the far wall, above the stereo system, was a large mirror. Brenda had hung it there to add space and light to the living room. As she looked at it now, her reflection caught her attention, and she shifted her gaze to stare at herself. In the foreground, she could see Card leaning over her unconscious husband. But the longer she stared at the reflection, the more she realized something wasn't quite right. The reflection seemed off somehow, as if it didn't match what was happening in the living room.

A powerful feeling of dissociation swept through her. She whimpered faintly when she saw something dark moving behind her.

She couldn't see what it was. The light was behind her, and the object wasn't anything more than an indistinct gray blur. It shifted like smoke. After a tense moment, it seemed to take on a vaguely human form.

It's her!

Forgetting all about Card, Brenda stared at the reflection in the mirror, her eyes watering as she struggled to see what was behind her.

Icy prickling sensations ran up her back. She saw Matt, reflected in the mirror, start to move. A flash of hope filled her, but when she looked directly at her bound husband, she saw that he was still unconscious, motionless in the chair except when Card rolled his head from side to side.

Fear and confusion flooded Brenda when she looked at the mirror again and saw the dark, misty shape looming behind her. Things were happening in the mirror that didn't match what was happening in the living room. A sense of utter unreality gripped her, freezing her into inaction. In the living room, Card was leaning over Matt, trying to bring him around, but in the mirror, their positions were different. Brenda was convinced it wasn't just because of the different angle of the mirror.

Her fear spiked, and the flow of blood roared like the tide in her ears. She couldn't look away. Unable to say or do anything, she watched the reflection in the mirror as Matt began to move. His arms and legs stiffened. Moving in slow motion, he raised his arms. Brenda knew that this wasn't really happening.

It's all an illusion . . . a dream. . . .

Tucking his clenched fist close to his body, Matt swung his elbow around so it caught Card under the jaw. Card was knocked off balance. In the reflection of the mirror, Brenda saw a fan of blood spray from his mouth and nose as his head snapped violently back. Something white—probably a tooth—shot out of his mouth.

The air in the living room seemed to be suddenly dead. There was absolutely no sound. Everything happened in excruciating slow motion, as though the two men were struggling underwater, their movements heavy and dragging.

Card keeled over backward. His arms flailed helplessly behind him to break his fall, but his head slammed soundlessly against the floor, bouncing once. She imagined but didn't hear the resounding thump.

Her gaze fixed on the mirror, Brenda watched Matt scramble to his feet, thrashing wildly to shake off the ropes that bound his hands and feet.

Card's lips moved as he shouted a curse, but no sound issued from his mouth. Instead, a sheet of blood poured down his chin. When he raised his hands to his face and covered his mouth, blood seeped like scarlet ribbons between his fingers and flowed down his wrists and forearms, staining his shirt.

"Run."

The voice—the only sound in the dead air of the room—filled Brenda's head as if it were her own thought. It screamed inside her skull, reverberating with a high-pitched, warbling crescendo.

"Run. . . . Run. . . ."

But Brenda was frozen, gripped by fear and confusion.

Is this what's going to happen if I don't do something? Or is this what's going to happen no matter what I do?

She couldn't pull her gaze away from the mirror and the eerie tableau being enacted in reflection but not in the reality of the living room. In mute horror, she watched as her husband scrambled to his feet, struggling to keep his balance as the ropes around his feet tripped him up. Card had collapsed in a heap on the floor, but he rolled away, clawing for purchase on the carpet. His bloody fingers left long red streaks on the plush pile. Tucking his arms close to his body, he rolled over again. Brenda realized with a shock what he was doing. He wasn't trying to get away from her enraged husband. He was reaching for the vinyl gym bag on the floor just inside the living room doorway.

In the reflection, Matt staggered, trying to intercept him, but Card got to the gym bag first. Shoving his hand inside it, he came up with a pistol that Brenda immediately recognized was the same one he'd used to knock her unconscious. The room was lit with an eerie, vibrating glow, giving it an unreal cast as if it was part of a dream or a memory from a long time ago.

Still lying on the floor and pivoting around, Card raised the gun in a slow, sludgy arc. Brenda stopped breathing when three times, bright flashes of light issued from the gun barrel. There was no sound, but she couldn't help but cringe when Matt's body jerked spastically backward.

Card shifted around, cocking a leg under himself, getting up on one knee. He steadied himself with one hand on the floor and seemed to have all the time he needed as he aimed at the center of Matt's chest and pulled the trigger again.

Once.

Twice.

Three times.

The silent shots exploded Matt's chest, sending blood and fragments of bone and lung tissue flying in a wide, spraying arc. Brenda's scream was trapped inside her chest. She cowered in the chair, watching mutely as her husband was knocked backward by the impact. His arms windmilled wildly in the air until he landed on his back, hitting the floor hard and then not moving. Eyes closed, he lay still as blood as thick and dark as ink in reflection pooled on the carpet beneath him. His face paled to a ghastly white and collapsed in on itself, the skin shrinking and melting away to reveal the skull beneath.

When Brenda shifted her gaze and looked at herself in the mirror, she saw herself staring back. A terrified gleam lit her eyes. As she watched, her own face began to change subtly, gradually blending until it transformed into the face of an old woman.

A frightening sense of dissociation took hold of her. Her body seemed less substantial than drifting mist, and for a dizzying instant, she had the impression that she could see right through herself, as if she herself had become the ghost.

No! This isn't real. It's not really happening!

She wanted to close her eyes, thinking if she could force herself to look away, the terror would disappear.

It can't be real! I won't let it happen!

"Run. . . . Run. . . ."

The voice seemed to come from somewhere behind her, and Brenda wondered if it was her reflection that was speaking, shouting to her.

"Run."

But she couldn't move.

The muscles in her arms and legs were locked. She could hardly breathe. The cold pressure building up inside her chest was getting intolerable.

"Run. . . . Run. . . . Run!" the voice shrieked from behind her, higher and higher until it became a hysterical wail inside her head.

"Run . . . now!"

blown away

TEARS blurred Brenda's vision, and she experienced a near physical pain as she tore her gaze away from the mirror and stared at Card's back. There was an odd sense of disorientation as she tried to process the terrible events she had seen.

That hadn't happened. . . . Not yet, anyway.

She took several quick, shallow breaths, struggling to comprehend that she was still in her living room and that Card wasn't bluffing or playing some sick, twisted game. He had every intention of killing her and her family.

I'm here . . . now. This is really me.

Moving slowly, she wouldn't let her rage or her panic and confusion rise any higher inside her. She willed it to galvanize her into action. She caught a glimpse of herself in the mirror and once again had a curiously dissociated sensation, but she pushed it aside as she stood up on weak, trembling legs. After tearing the duct tape from her mouth, she squeezed the knotted rope tightly in her fist and, without thinking, lunged at Card.

He had sensed her moving behind him and was just starting to turn around when she swung the hand holding the rope, connecting solidly against the side of his head. The impact made his jaw clack and was hard enough to throw him backward. His foot kicked over the bowl, spilling ice across the floor. He let out a horrible sound—a strange combination of a grunt and a bellow—as he collapsed backward, hitting his head on the fireplace.

Filled with confusion and elation, Brenda stood for a heartbeat on wobbly legs, staring at him in disbelief. Swept up in her fury, she wished she had hit him hard enough to kill him or at least knock him unconscious, but she saw the rage flame in his eyes as he tried to scramble to his feet. His shoes kept slipping on the spilled ice, but she knew he wasn't going to stay down.

Fear as clean and bright as chrome cut through Brenda. Mouthing unintelligible words, she started backing up until her legs bumped against the chair she'd been sitting in.

Card sagged back on the floor for a moment, shaking his head and gathering his energy before trying to stand up again. Moving with a speed that shocked her, Brenda wheeled around, grabbed the heavy dining room chair by the back, and swung at him with all her strength, hitting him just above the knees. She smiled when she heard a loud crack that had to have been breaking bone.

"You can't do this to us!" she screeched. "You're not going to get away with it!"

Card's face was a frightening mixture of pain and rage as he rolled over onto his side, shielding his head with both hands.

But Brenda had no intention of hitting him again with the chair or anything else. Her only clear thought was to get out of the house, to the police cruiser, before he recovered. Clenching her fists and doubling over to make a smaller target if Card got to his gun in time, she ran to the front door, spurred on by the dark, angry presence that was swelling like a storm cloud behind her.

"All right! That's it!" Card bellowed. "You're gonna be the first to die!"

Good, Brenda thought, cringing inwardly, expecting any second to feel a bullet slam into her as she fumbled to open the front door. Her fingers kept slipping on the metal doorknob, but finally the latch clicked, and she threw the door open. The sudden blast of night air hit her, reviving her as she looked up the slope at the police cruiser, parked on the street.

"Help! . . . Please! . . . Help us!" she cried out as she ran barefoot up the brick walkway. Her feet jolted with pain as they slapped on the wet bricks, and she screamed when a sudden explosion from behind her thumped the night, and one of the sidelights beside the front door shattered. The high-pitched whine of a bullet buzzed past her ear like an angry wasp, making her cringe. Hot pressure squeezed her bladder, and she almost fell, but she kept her balance and sped across the lawn to the street and the parked cruiser.

"Help! Help me!"

As she got closer to the vehicle, she could clearly see the silhouette of the patrolman behind the steering wheel. Even through her panic, she realized that he wasn't moving, and she wondered why. He hadn't turned to look toward the house, even after the gunshot. For an instant, Brenda had the unnerving sensation that she was insubstantial, that she wasn't even real, and nothing she could say or do would get the patrolman's attention.

"He's in the house!" she wailed, her voice shrill in the night. "He's going to kill us!"

The lights from the house didn't reflect off the driver's window, so she knew it was down. He *had* to have heard her, but still he hadn't moved. The weird sense of unreality heightened, and Brenda's eyes were burning, making it almost impossible for her to see clearly. Then a terrifying realization suddenly dawned on her. It was confirmed the instant she crossed the street at a run and slammed into the side of the cruiser. She let out a horrible shriek as she looked inside.

The patrolman was slumped back in the front seat, his head tilted back, resting at an awkward angle against the wire mesh cage that separated the front seat from the back. His eyes were wide open, staring up at the ceiling of the cruiser. His mouth hung open like he'd been frozen in midscream. Brenda winced as the strong stench of urine filled her nose. The polished wooden handle of a knife protruded from the center of the cop's chest. His uniform and jacket were saturated with dark, coagulating blood.

Numb with shock and disbelief, her heart thundering in her ears so loudly it blocked out every other sound, Brenda stared at the dead cop for several seconds.

"I'm sure he'd help you if he could," Card shouted from the front steps, his voice breaking into insane laughter as he watched her, all the while idly playing with the revolver in his hands.

On reflex, Brenda dropped to a crouch and scurried around to the other side of the car as another shot rang out in the night. The bullet smacked into the side panel of the cruiser with a dull thud that made her jump and squeal. Her breath came in short, hitching gulps as she cowered behind the cruiser and looked all around.

Where do I go? What do I do?

Rain-soaked darkness filled the woods behind her, and she thought she might find safety there, but only for a while. She didn't doubt that Card would find her. Besides, she didn't want to get away. She had to save her family.

In the cruiser! she thought with a flash of sudden hope. *There have to be weapons—guns and mace and nightsticks— in there,* but when she grabbed the latch to open the passenger's door, she found it locked, and the window was rolled up all the way.

"Damn!" she muttered, punching the car so hard it hurt her fist.

After a tense moment, cringing and waiting for another shot to hit the cruiser—or her—she eased up so she could see the house. Through the window, past the dead patrolman, she saw that Card was still standing in the doorway, framed by the light behind him, looking up to where she was.

She was suddenly convinced that, like a cat, Card could see as well in the darkness as he could in daylight. With the light behind him, his silhouette looked oddly flat, like a two-dimensional cutout in the night. Brenda assured herself that it wasn't possible, but she was convinced she could see his eyes, blazing with a furious red glow as he watched and waited for her to make her move. She struggled not to think about the terrifying figure she had seen in her dream.

Was it really a dream, or had it really happened? Have I seen him before? How did I know he was out there and that he was coming for us?

Dizzying waves of terror tugged at her like an irresistible undertow, threatening to pull her under. Numbing cold filled her stomach as she dropped to the ground. She was panting hard, and sweat and tears stung her eyes. She cautioned herself not to hyperventilate. She had to control her fear, but she couldn't help but think that Card was still watching her, his eyes able to penetrate the solid body of the cruiser. She was certain that he knew exactly where she was, and she fought against the despairing thought that he knew what she would do next.

I'm not going to give up, she thought, even though she had no idea where to go or what to do.

If she made a run for it into the woods, he would see her easily, calmly take aim, and shoot her in the back before she'd taken ten steps.

Besides, there was nowhere to run.

The nearest house was too far down the road. Even if he didn't shoot her, Card could run her down long before she made it there to raise the alarm. If no one had heard the first two gunshots, all the shouting and screaming in the world wasn't going to help.

But if she stayed where she was, trembling with fear, it would just be a matter of time before Card strode over and executed her on the spot . . . unless he brought her back to the house to witness what he was going to do to her family, first.

"Come on! Think! *Think!*" she whispered harshly as she clenched her fists in frustration.

"I know where you are," Card called out in an airy, singsong voice that echoed in the night with an odd reverberation. "You can't get away from me, so don't even try. You *really* think you have a chance?"

A wave of taunting laughter rolled through the night, crashing against Brenda's eardrums. She jumped when she sensed a presence somewhere nearby, hovering unseen in the darkness behind or beside her. The fringes of her vision were breaking up into wavering spots of flashing light, and her breath burned like acid in her throat. A dizzying sensation of light-headedness swept over her, and she had to lean forward and press her hands flat on the roadside gravel to steady herself.

"I can see in the dark, you know," Card called. "I *belong* to the night. And so will you. Soon you'll be swallowed by the darkness. Forever. But I'm willing to make a deal with you. . . ."

Brenda sucked in a breath of air, feeling razor-sharp slices of pain between her ribs. The gravel on the roadside dug into her hands and knees, the pain the only real thing about all of this.

"Do you wanna make a deal?"

Brenda resisted the impulse to shout back and remained absolutely silent and motionless. The darkness squeezed her with unrelenting pressure.

Maybe he's bluffing? she thought, grasping desperately at any ray of hope. *Maybe he doesn't really know where I am, and he's trying to lure me out?*

She glanced over her shoulder at the dark woods again. For all she knew, Card might think she was already deep into the forest, running and trying to hide. He obviously wasn't in any hurry to come after her. If he was going to finish what he'd started, he needed to stay close to the house.

But what if he doesn't come after me?

The thought lanced her heart like a cold spike.

What if he kills Matt and the kids first?

"You might as well give up now. No one's gonna save you."

A rush of anger combined with absolute desperation and a powerful need to save her family coursed through Brenda, filling her with renewed strength. Trembling so badly she thought she would collapse, she eased herself up slowly until she could see him again. His voice sounded closer, as if he had been moving nearer to her, and she was shocked to see that he was still in the lighted doorway.

As soon as her face cleared the edge of the car door, Card raised his right arm. Simultaneously, there was a flash of light and the window on the passenger's side of the cruiser exploded outward in a shower of glass. A split second later, the ear-shattering explosion punched a hole in the night. Fiery, stinging pain engulfed the left side of Brenda's face as shards of glass sliced into her.

She cried out and was thrown backward by the impact. On one level, the pain was ferocious beyond belief, unlike anything she had ever experienced before. It was as though thousands of wasps were swarming across her face, tearing into her flesh with their poisonous stingers.

On another level, though, Brenda experienced a curious detachment similar to what she had felt when she had watched herself in the living room mirror. It was as if she had somehow risen above or floated beyond all pain; it was as if the pain belonged to someone else, and she was observing it, or it was nothing more than the dulled memory of a pain she had experienced long, long ago.

I'm dying, she thought, trying to push back the icy onrush of panic and disorientation that threatened to overwhelm her. But then a curious, floating sensation lifted her up as if unseen hands were supporting her, suspending her in the air.

The night was no longer as dark as it had been just moments before. A strange, iridescent glow shimmered all around her like waves of heat lightning. Everything was suffused with a rippling blue white light that cast razor-sharp shadows across the roadside and beneath the trees behind her.

The gunshot was still echoing in her head, gathering in volume rather than fading away until it gradually blended into another sound: a loud rushing of wind, high overhead. Every other sound in the night—the wind sighing in the pines above her, the distant chorus of spring peepers, the snap and swish of branches overhead—everything had a crystal clarity that filled her with a heartbreaking sense of loneliness for the beauty and terrible mystery of it all.

Oh my God, I must be dead!

With that thought came another icy rush that raced through her like a bitter winter wind. Without any physical effort, she felt herself rising up into the air as though hovering on powerful, unseen wings.

I'm a bubble. . . . I'm nothing, she thought, but the thought held no fear for her—not until she looked down the sloping yard to the house and saw Card standing in the doorway. He appeared to be frozen in place, a motionless, black husk that Brenda somehow knew wasn't really human. Above and behind him, all around him, darkness spread out into the night in thick, twisting tendrils. The hallway light haloed behind him, bending in a long arc as it was swallowed by the darkness. Long, dark shadows reached out across the yard like grasping hands, clawing at the night.

Brenda watched with a sense of security, convinced that Card couldn't hurt her now.

But he can still hurt my family!

That thought pulled her up short, and the airy feeling of detachment instantly evaporated. The figure in the doorway remained motionless, sucking the light and strands of the surrounding night into itself. Darkness writhed around Card in thick, ropy clots that gradually blended and re-formed until they took on the shape of another person—a person who dwarfed Card and obscured her view of him.

Is that what's inside him?

"*You'll never get away from me.*"

Although the voice was familiar, Brenda knew it wasn't Card's. It vibrated like the deafening crash of cymbals. Fear gripped her, and she was convinced that, although she might be safe from Card, this other presence, this entity that seemed to be issuing from him, posed a serious danger to her.

"You *all* have to pay! You killed me, now I'll kill you!"

The words rolled like thunder in the night, sweeping Brenda away with a terrifying feeling of vertigo. She looked behind her for a path of escape but knew there was none.

The woods aren't safe. Nothing . . . nowhere is safe!

Somehow she knew that this entity, whatever it was, had been inside Card all along, directing him, forcing him to do the things he'd done, but now it was released, and it would easily find and destroy her. Even if she were dead, she wouldn't be safe from it.

Through her panic, Brenda noticed a distant sound. It took her a long time to realize that it was her, screaming. But the sound of her voice was lost beneath another howling that pierced the darkness all around her, rising and falling in a long, terrifying shriek.

"*Your soul is mine now.*"

Immobilized by her fear, Brenda had no idea what to do or where to turn, but her eyes were drawn inside the cruiser where a dull, white light bathed the interior with a shimmering glow. It didn't cast any shadows, even under the car seat and dashboard. Splinters of light danced and wavered around the face of the dead cop, and Brenda whimpered when she

saw his eyes open and roll up before meeting hers. The dead
expression on the cop's face pleaded with her before his gaze
shifted down to something on the car floor.

Brenda followed his glance and saw the shotgun in the
bracket on the dashboard. Still feeling as though she was
floating out of her body, she reached through the shattered
window for the gun. In the strange white light, her hands
looked as thin and translucent as fog pierced by morning
light. She was surprised when her hand clasped the solid
wooden stock of the gun, and she felt the weight of it.

TRICKLES of ice water ran down the sides of his face,
gradually bringing Matt back to consciousness. He dimly realized that he was lying on his side, but for the longest time,
he couldn't figure out what had happened or what had gone
wrong. Moaning softly, he tried to roll over onto his back, but
something was holding him where he was. Opening his eyes
to slits, he saw that his arms were tied to his sides, and he was
lashed in one of the dining room chairs. Pain burned in his
shoulders, and when he twisted his head to one side, something made a loud *crack* behind his ears. His head throbbed in
time with his racing pulse.

"Jesus," he whispered, feeling the heat of his breath rebound from the floor. When he focused on the off-white carpet, he realized that he was lying on the living room floor.

How did I get here? What the hell's going on?

He struggled to clear his mind of the dense fog that embraced it. Vague images flashed through his mind, but nothing
clear or coherent. He remembered having tea with Brenda and
then going to the front door, but then everything became a
blur.

Nothing . . . a total blank.

He took a shuddering breath and ended up coughing. The
pain in his neck and back got worse, and he felt a painful
throb on the side of his head. He wished he could sink back
down into oblivion where things didn't hurt so much, but he
knew something was wrong. His family was in danger.

Then the image of the man standing on the doorstep flashed
into his memory. His heartbeat started pounding in his neck,

and the back of his head throbbed as twinges of pain flashed behind his eyes. It was almost impossible to focus. He could see that the room was well lit, but the buttery light washed everything with an indistinct, gauzy glow. Close to his head, he could see another one of the dining room chairs. It was tipped over onto its side, and one of its legs was broken.

Matt gasped and jumped involuntarily when a sudden explosion ripped the air. His first thought was that a car on the street had backfired, but he realized it had to have been a firecracker or a gunshot.

Is John screwing around with fireworks? he wondered.

Matt twisted his head as far around as he could while struggling to free himself of the rope that bound him to the chair. His face flushed with the effort, the muscles and blood vessels in his neck and arms straining terribly, but no amount of effort seemed to loosen the bounds.

"Help! Please help us. He's in the house. He's going to kill us!"

He jumped and grunted when he heard Brenda's voice. It sounded like she was outside.

What's she doing? Is there someone in the house? What the fuck is going on?

There was a loud commotion in the hallway, and something banged against the floor or wall. Then he heard the sound of running feet outside the house. He tried to see what was going on, but his vision was still hazy. All he could make out was a dark silhouette, standing in the doorway with its back to him. The only thing he was sure of was that it wasn't Brenda; it was a man. As he thrashed about trying to free himself, Matt gradually skittered the chair around and saw two small figures slumped on the couch.

"Oh, Jesus," he muttered, realizing in an instant that it was Emily and John. They weren't moving, and he feared they both might be dead. Their arms and legs were tied with the same cotton rope that held him, and swatches of duct tape covered their mouths. Their eyes were closed, and if it weren't for the rope and duct tape, he might have thought they had both fallen asleep on the couch while watching TV.

"John . . . Emily," he whispered, his voice a gravelly moan that grated his ears.

Nothing. No movement. No sign of life. Are they even breathing?

More shouting from outside the house drew his attention. The man was calling to Brenda, taunting her and telling her that it was useless for her to run, that he would find her and kill her first. Grunting and swearing under his breath, Matt struggled with every ounce of strength he could muster to free himself from the rope. It cut into his wrists, cutting off his circulation and making his hands and arms go numb. Something sticky and wet was running down his fingers. He realized it was blood. Sweat drenched his face, and he was sure his head was going to explode as he strained against his bonds.

All I need is a little slack . . . just a little slack.

He hoped the person who had tied him up had used new rope that might stretch just enough for him to wiggle his hands free. It wasn't long, though, before his efforts exhausted him, and he slumped back down, panting heavily. The man in the doorway must have heard him because he turned and glared at Matt before looking back outside.

"You ain't getting away from me, asshole," the man said. His voice echoed oddly in the night. "You all have to pay! . . . You killed me, now I'll kill you!"

Matt groaned. How could he ever forget those words? His throat was raw, and the muscles in his shoulders bunched in painful knots as he renewed his struggle to loosen the rope. His body strained and vibrated with the effort, but he jumped when another blast of a gun thundered in the night. Something thumped into the side of the house like a giant's fist.

That same instant, the man in the doorway let out a piercing wail as he spun in a crazy pirouette and collapsed onto the floor. He covered his face with his hands, but Matt could see blood splattered on the man's shoulders and chest.

"Mother of Christ!" the intruder wailed as he lurched forward and started to crawl on his hands and knees into the living room. The gun in his hand thumped on the floor, and Matt was suddenly fearful for his children's lives.

If they're still alive.

He tried to focus on what he could do to save his family,

but he lost all hope when he found himself staring into the face of a man he didn't recognize. The man leered at him. The side of his head was bleeding profusely, and pointed splinters of wood stuck out of his skin like a porcupine's quills. Blood bubbled from his mouth as he gasped in pain and heaved himself into a sitting position against the wall where the mirror hung. Blood stained his teeth pink when he smiled wickedly at Matt.

"So who's gonna die first? Huh?" he asked. His voice sounded shattered and filled with fear, and the moist gleam in his eyes made him look positively insane.

I'm a dead man, Matt thought as he opened his mouth to say something, to beg for his and his children's lives, but the connection between his mind and mouth just wasn't there. All he could think was, any second now, that man was going to raise the gun, aim it at him, and pull the trigger. There would be a flash and a blast that he wouldn't even hear because the lights would go out. Forever.

Trussed and helpless, Matt cringed and tried to turn away, bracing himself for the end, but then a hint of motion in the doorway behind the man caught his attention. It took him a heartbeat or two before he realized that Brenda was standing in the doorway. He hardly recognized her beneath the bloody mess that was her face. Her hair hung down in dark, wet tangles that dripped blood. All that remained of the left side of her face from the eye down to the jaw was shredded chunks of pink flesh. Along her cheek and jaw, glistening pieces of shattered bone and tooth poked through the mangled flesh and muscle. Blood ran in a thick wash down the side of her neck, saturating the front of her nightgown.

But it was her eyes that held Matt.

They were as wild and crazy-looking as their assailant's, and she was holding a shotgun.

Jesus! Where did she get a shotgun?

He remembered the .22 pistol he had bought a few days ago and thought about how useless it was, locked away in his desk drawer. Brenda was panting, her breath making watery, bubbly sounds as she leaned against the doorjamb, steadying herself as she leveled the shotgun at the man on the floor. Her

body was trembling as though she were racked by fever, and
the barrel of the shotgun kept weaving back and forth.

"You," she said, her voice slurred from the blood that
clogged her throat. She snorted and spat a glob of blood onto
the living room floor, looking like she was about to drop
where she stood and obviously fighting to maintain control.

"You're going to be the *first* and *only* one to die."

HOW *in the name of God is this even happening?* Brenda
wondered as she rose up and reached into the police cruiser.

She felt as though she were watching a movie, and confusion filled her as she saw her hands—*Are those really my
hands? They don't look at all like flesh and bone*—take the
shotgun from the dashboard bracket. She had never handled a
gun before in her life, but she watched with frightened detachment as she pumped the slide and heard the shell click into the
chamber.

Locked and loaded, she thought grimly as she straightened
up and started moving around the side of the cruiser. The figure in the doorway, darker than the surrounding night, swelled
even larger, taking on immense proportions. Strands of darkness seeped like twisting, negative energy from out of Card's
body. Huge, dark arms with grasping hands reached out for
her and just as quickly dissolved into the night.

*There's something inside him . . . something horrible and
evil.*

She didn't know where that idea came from, but she was
convinced that Card was nothing more than a shell, a container for . . .

For what? For this . . . thing, whatever it is.

She raised one hand to the left side of her face as though
to wipe away a tear and felt the sticky wetness trickling down
her cheek. She was surprised to see that her hand was
smeared with blood and shreds of something pink, like raw
hamburger.

There's no way you can hurt me now, she thought, and she
almost laughed out loud as a wave of giddiness swept through
her. The night crackled with energy, and the eerie, sourceless
light that cast no shadows glowed all the brighter around her,

illuminating the dreadful shape on the doorstep. She could see every detail of the road and the car and the woods and lawn with excruciating, hallucinatory clarity.

Moving silently and effortlessly, she shifted around the side of the cruiser and started across the road toward the house. She had no sensation of walking; she was floating, gliding, her feet barely skimming the ground.

The only solid reality was the shotgun in her hands. It had heft, and her left hand, the one smeared with her own blood, felt slippery on the barrel. She had to grip it tightly so as not to drop it.

"You can't touch me now," she called out, her voice sounding close and clear, as though someone was shouting into her ear.

The man in the doorway froze as the dark shape issuing out of him wavered. The light from the house bent in a buttery smear with twisting threads of darker brown swirling inside it that looked like sulfurous smoke, rising into the night and flowing into the dark shape. Brenda inhaled and caught the strong whiff of rotten eggs.

Everything—the night, the house, the man who wasn't a man in the doorway—looked so far away she had the sensation she was watching it all through a foot-thick pane of glass that deadened all sound and distorted her vision. She watched in stunned amazement as her hands—*Are those really my hands?*—raised the shotgun, and then, without hesitation, her right index finger squeezed the trigger.

The report of the shotgun was little more than a hollow thump. A spike of light bloomed from the muzzle, and she heard the shotgun pellets whistle through the night. Time slowed to a sludgy crawl and seemed almost to stop. Brenda imagined that she could actually see the shotgun pellets flying in a dark cluster toward the open front door. She imagined that she could outrun them and get to the door first if she wanted to.

Then, from a great distance, came a ragged, splintering sound. She watched as the man in the doorway doubled over and spun around before falling to the floor. Another sound—a faint, trailing howl of pain—echoed through the night, filling Brenda with an eerie sense of loss and loneliness.

I know that sound. . . . I've heard it before, she thought, but she couldn't quite place where or when.

Her bloody left hand almost lost its grip on the shotgun when she pumped the action again and started moving toward the house. The sensation of flying grew even stronger, and she realized that she was moving much faster than she ordinarily could have to close the distance. Marcus Card was sprawled on the hallway floor, twisting and writhing with excruciating slowness. She heard another shotgun shell snap into the chamber. Then she raised the shotgun to fire a second time as the man scrambled out of sight into the living room.

Brenda found herself standing in the entryway, not sure how she had gotten there. She had a vague memory of having passed unhindered through the wall of the house, but now she was looking into the living room. The glaring light stung her eyes, and a high-pitched buzzing sound filled her head. For a moment she thought that the shotgun pellets had turned into insects that were swarming inside the house.

The man was slumped on the floor. Brenda saw that he was holding a pistol and was trying to raise it and bring it around so he could shoot.

"Who's gonna be first to die, huh?" she heard him say, his voice breaking with the effort.

All around her, Brenda saw deepening black shadows swirl and twist, twining like grasping fingers. The man's face was contorted with pain and fear. Brenda could feel it as much as see it and smell it and taste it, oozing out of him like poison.

"You . . ." she said shaking her head and forcing herself to focus even as the darkness at the edges of her vision drew in like a surging tide. She saw not one, but two men writhing on the floor in front of her. For a horrifying instant, she wasn't sure who they were.

Is one of them Matt?

A loud, roaring rush filled her head, rising in hissing gusts that tore at her and threatened to blow her away.

"You're going to be the *first* and the *only* one to die."

And then the darkness collapsed around her with a sudden, crushing weight. From somewhere far away, she heard a heavy thump and felt a powerful punch to the gut. Numbing cold gripped her, and a horrible metallic taste flooded her mouth and throat, making her gasp. She had the sensation of falling backward, of tumbling head over heels over . . . and over . . . and over until—finally—the overwhelming darkness embraced her completely, and she no longer existed.

TWENTY-TWO

return

BRENDA was gliding in a slow spiral, circling like a hawk riding a hot summer thermal high above the fields and forests. Warm air caressed her face. She was aware of the darkness and the absolute silence that embraced her, but she didn't feel any apprehension. It was like being enveloped by cushions that protected her from . . . from . . .

What?

She knew she had to do something, but she couldn't remember what.

Do I have to go back? Is there some unfinished business?

An unspecified danger was lurking nearby. She knew that much. Its presence was palpable. Still, she wasn't afraid. Fear, like everything else, had melted away and was no more than a distant memory. She was beyond it all.

When she noticed the muted brown glow that infused the darkness, she shifted her eyes back and forth, wanting to see clearly what it was and where it was coming from. Once she acknowledged the intrusion of the light, she realized she couldn't remember when she had first noticed it. It was as if it had always been here, and only now had she become aware of it.

The light was warm and had a comfortable, chocolate glow but at some point smeared twists of dull gold and lemony yellow mixed with it, drawing her closer and closer to consciousness.

Was I asleep, and now I'm waking up?

The thought gave her a feeling of urgency but still, she was emotionally detached, positive that she wasn't in any real danger. She was beyond danger and pain and everything else.

Am I dead? Is that why I'm not afraid?

Even this thought held no real terror for her. She felt insulated from strong emotional reactions, as though there were an invisible divider between her and . . . what?

Life? . . . Death? . . . Why aren't you afraid? she asked herself.

The caramel light grew steadily brighter, warming her until it actually began to hurt her eyes. She winced and tried to turn away, to shield herself from it, but it emanated from all directions. With a mild jolt of surprise and amusement, she noticed that she was able to react physically.

If I can wince . . . if I can turn my head . . . if my eyes can hurt . . . then maybe I'm not dead.

So where am I?

As soothing as the light was, a sense of urgency grew within her. Hot, throbbing pressure pounded inside her head like ocean waves, rising and swelling.

She couldn't tell when the sensation had started, but now she was aware of motion and the dragging weight of her body, pressing down onto something soft and cushiony.

All right, she thought. *If I'm not dead, and I'm not alive, where am I? What's happening to me?*

The brown light intensified, turning into a curtain of rich, shimmering radiance. Her eyelids fluttered, and she realized she was seeing light through her closed eyelids. After a brief struggle, she opened her eyes and found herself lying on her back, looking up at—

What?

Hovering above her were two large, glowing white spheres. She winced, and her vision kept shifting. She was unable to focus. At first the objects looked far away, but then they were too close for her to focus on. Groaning softly, she shook her head—*Did I really just move or did I imagine it?*—thinking she must be seeing double as the luminous orbs—

Are there two of them, or am I seeing double?—hovered inches above her face. They threw off splinters of light that shifted randomly through subtle changes of rainbow colors. Brenda willed herself closer and closer to consciousness, pushing against the gentle force that was tugging her down with an almost irresistible, backward falling pressure.

No, she thought, still not afraid but not wanting to go back down into the darkness. *I'm not dead, and I'm not going to die!*

A strangled groan filled her ears, the sound coming from deep within her chest where spikes of pain shot along her nerves, stinging like glowing embers, falling onto her skin. Her vision gradually cleared, and the two bright spheres above her grew smaller and more defined. Something dark floated in the middle of each, making them look like—

Eyes.

This time the shock of fear was immediate and real. It snapped through her like a whip.

Someone's here! Someone's watching me!

Her fingers clutched involuntarily. Her arms and legs stiffened. She was amazed that she could distinguish individual body parts because she had been feeling totally disembodied for—

How long?

Time didn't mean anything in the place she had been, but now, suddenly, it did. It struck her as peculiar to be so aware of her body once again, like returning to an old friend. The glowing orbs loomed above her, swelling and flashing. Waves of warm, moist air caressed her face, reassuring her and, at the same time, filling her with fear.

She tried to move or call out but she was immobilized.

Go away! she screamed inside her mind. *Leave me alone! I can't take any more!*

But she couldn't move, and after a while, she began to make out the face that belonged to those steady, staring eyes. Dark hair and pale, smooth cheeks and a thin mouth gradually resolved above her. Her fear spiked when she realized that she was staring up at herself as if she were holding a mirror inches from her face. As her vision cleared, she saw the expression on her face. It was placid, absolutely neutral, at rest. She had expected to see fear etched in every line. If it hadn't been for her open eyes, she would have thought she was looking at the face of someone sleeping.

Or dead, she thought, unable to summon the strength to cry out.

Her own face floated above her, and the eyes—*My eyes!*—drilled into her.

She looked young, the way she remembered herself from so long ago, but a swatch of burning pain etched the left side of her face. She caught a hint of motion off to one side and shifted to see what it was.

A hand, pale and withered—*Is that my hand?*—was reaching out to touch the face that hovered above her. The parchment-white skin on the hand was wrinkled and pale. Her fingertips made contact with her face. Beneath her touch, the skin felt as cold and hard as polished marble. She watched dreamily as her other hand rose and brushed lightly along the cheek of the face above her.

Your face is perfect.

She wasn't sure if she said these words out loud or merely thought them, but it didn't matter. The person leaning over her smiled and nodded with deep understanding.

Yours is perfect, and mine is . . .

Before she could finish the thought, a wave of sadness crashed over her. Her eyes filled with tears that trickled in warm tracks down the sides of her face. Someone gently wiped them away. Her hands were still reaching upward, caressing the image of the face that floated above her.

My face has been destroyed, hasn't it?

The eyes gazing down at her filled with deep sympathy, and Brenda was swept up by that now-familiar sensation of floating as she looked down at herself, lying in bed. She saw an old woman without bandages, and couldn't help but stare at the long, twisted scar that ran from above her ear down the side of her face to the bottom edge of her jaw. It was thin and silvery, almost lost in the mass of deep wrinkles. She was convinced she was gazing into a mirror, and with that thought came sudden confusion and fear.

I didn't die, did I?

The expression on the face watching her mellowed as she narrowed her eyes and nodded slowly.

Brenda took a deep breath and closed her eyes for a moment, but the darkness behind her eyelids pulled her down, frightening her even more, so she opened them again and looked up. The light in the room had softened to a rich, beige glow. Trying to calm her racing pulse, she took another breath, surprised by the deep ache that stabbed her chest. The light shattered into thousands of fiery fragments. As she shifted her gaze to one side, she saw a single window. Dazzling light poured into the room, and there was a dark silhouette by the window. The person's features were lost in the glare.

And then in a rush, it all came back to her.

All of it.

"Oh my God, I shot him!"

The words ripped out of her in a ragged cry. Her body snapped upright, and she found herself sitting in a bed, her eyes wide open and staring. She still couldn't make out who it was by the window, but she screamed when he moved toward her.

Is that him? . . . He's come to finish the job!

She whimpered and raised her arms in a feeble attempt to defend herself. The tubes and needles stuck into her arm held her back.

I'm trapped!

"Whoa, take it easy there," the man said.

Swept up in her panic, she at first didn't recognize the voice. All she knew was that she was in danger, her whole family was in danger.

And I have to save them.

Hands reached out for her, but these hands weren't like the withered ones she had seen moments before. They were someone else's hands. She squealed in terror as they grasped her by the shoulders and gently held her so she couldn't move. She didn't have the strength to resist as they eased her back onto the bed.

"God. You scared the crap out of me," the man said.

Panting and trembling from the sudden exertion, Brenda still resisted, her body wire-tight and ready to fight or try to get away. As the mist across her vision gradually receded, she finally recognized Matt leaning over her, a look of love and

concern warming his eyes. Recognition broke through her
panic, and she started to calm down by taking a deep breath
and listening to the rapid thumping of her pulse in her ears.

"Where . . . where am I? What's happened?"

"You were in pretty bad shape," Matt said, smiling at her.
"What you need is rest. I'll tell you all about it later."

"No. I have to know *now,*" she said.

Already, the impression she'd had of being outside her
body, of being two people at once, was fading like a dream.
She felt compelled to talk about it now, to tell him about it so
she wouldn't forget how weird it felt, but the dream was slipping away, like water running through her fingers.

"I was there, Matt," she said dreamily after licking her lips.
"I watched it all like I . . . like I was flying."

When Matt nodded, she detected the tightness in his expression that told her something was wrong.

"Oh my God! The kids! Are John and Emily all right?"

Matt sighed and patted her gently on the forearm.

"Don't worry," he said softly. "They're both fine. Other
than a few bumps and bruises that have healed, they weren't
hurt at all. Card knocked them out with chloroform. It wore
off without any side effects."

"Where are ?"

"At school, but they'll be in this afternoon like always to
sit with you. They'll be so happy to—"

"Like always?" Brenda said, blinking her eyes and shaking
her head, trying to process what he had just said. Something
was wrong. It wasn't just his tone of voice. He wasn't lying to
her. She knew the kids were fine because she had a feeling, as
true as a real memory, that they both had already grown up
and become adults, happy and well-adjusted, in their own
ways.

It wasn't that, but something was wrong, and then it hit her.

"How long?" she asked, her voice a deep, dry rasp. "How
long have I—? I'm in the hospital, right? How long have I
been here?"

Matt started to say something, then seemed to think better
of it and averted his eyes. Finally, he gave her hand a gentle
squeeze and, gazing deeply into her eyes, said, "You've been
in pretty bad shape ever since that night."

"How long?" The note of urgency in her voice whined like a dentist's drill in her ears. "Please, tell me, Matt!" There was no strength in her hand, but she squeezed his hand as hard as she could. "How long have I been here?"

Matt shifted his gaze to the window where the closed venetian blinds filtered the daylight to a soft, brown glow.

"A little over a month," he finally said.

Brenda gasped so loudly it hurt her chest as she let her head sink back into the warm well of the pillow.

"You were in a coma for quite a while—a couple of weeks, but once you came out of it, you've been drifting in and out of consciousness for another couple of weeks."

An audible rush filled her ears as she tried to absorb what Matt was saying.

"How long . . . exactly?" she finally managed to croak.

"Five weeks, three days, and—" He stretched out his arm and glanced at his wristwatch. "And twelve and a half hours."

His hand slid up her arm to her shoulder and gripped her gently but reassuringly.

"So it's—"

"The first week of July. Monday, the third," he finished for her.

"I—I can't believe it," she whispered.

Her gaze shifted away from Matt, and she let her vision go out of focus as she stared at the ceiling. The roaring sound in her ears muffled everything else as she tried to process this information. She couldn't imagine how she had lost all that time. It was like she had been—

"Dead."

She whispered the word so softly Matt leaned closer to her and said, "What?"

"I feel like . . . I was dead."

Tears filled her eyes and ran down the sides of her face. She noticed that one side of her face—*the left side*—was numb, but she paid little attention to it. Matt's hand slid down the length of her arm, and he entwined his fingers with hers. Moving close, his face loomed above her, but Brenda knew this wasn't the face she had been looking at when she first came to.

It was me. . . . I was looking at myself.

The thought was simultaneously reassuring and terrifying. She whimpered and let go of Matt's hand. When she raised her hands to wipe away her tears, her fingertips brushed the thick pad that covered the left side of her face. The instant she acknowledged it was there, stinging pain swept across her face.

"I . . . was . . . hurt," she whispered.

Matt nodded but said nothing.

"That night, the man . . . What was his name?"

Matt cleared his throat and, once again, shifted his gaze away from her for a moment.

"His name was Marcus Card."

"Yes . . . Marcus Card."

She let the name drift out of her as she slowly rolled her head from side to side. Tears were streaming down her face, but she didn't care. She was alive—really *alive,* now—and she was grateful for that.

"Did you know him?" she asked.

Matt bit down on his lower lip and shook his head thoughtfully, but Brenda could read him easily. He was hiding something from her.

"Who was he?" she said, her voice sharp enough to make Matt jump. "Why did he do that to us? Why did he want to hurt us?"

"I'm not sure." Matt looked down at the floor. "The only thing is—"

He hesitated and, still looking at the floor, shook his head again.

"Tell me. What is it?" Brenda said. She shifted in the bed, ignoring the pain.

Matt drew close to her again and placed his hand on her shoulder. She could read the worry and misery in his eyes, but it was nothing compared to the rush of panic that gripped her.

"What's the only thing?" she asked, keeping her voice level only with great effort.

Matt took a long, shuddering breath, held it, then let it out slowly. He made eye contact with her, but only for a moment. When he tried to look away again, she snagged him by the arm and said softly, "Matt. Tell me now."

"It's nothing, honey. Really, nothing important."

"I killed him, didn't I?" Brenda said. "Tell me the truth. Come on, Matt."

Matt nodded, but the look of worry in his eyes changed to one of almost stark fear.

"Yes, you did," he said. His shoulders hunched up, and he shivered. "You took the cop's shotgun, and you . . . you used it."

"I had to, though. He was going to kill us."

The memory of that night was still a riot of confusion in her mind, but judging by Matt's expression, that was probably a good thing for her, for now.

"Card was in Warren. At the same time as—" Matt sucked in a deep breath and exhaled before finishing. "Jeromy Bowker."

The mention of Bowker's name brought a sharp mental image of Card to Brenda.

"I know. He said something about it before he—" Her voice broke, and a horrible taste filled her mouth as if she were about to vomit.

"Well," Matt continued, "the night before Card was to be released, the guards put him in a cell with Bowker—Jesus! You don't need to hear this now. You have to get your strength back. There'll be plenty of time later to—"

"Tell me," Brenda said, her voice broken and barely audible. Matt looked at her, his features softening.

"He raped Card once lights were out," Matt said, licking his lips as he spoke. "And while he was doing it, he slit his own throat with a knife."

"Oh my God."

"Bowker died while he was still on top of Card, who was screaming like crazy because he was pinned to the bed. One of the guards who was on duty that night told me that Card couldn't stop screaming about how Bowker had gotten inside him."

Brenda took a shallow breath and let her vision go unfocused as she stared up at ceiling. The memory of Marcus Card in their front doorway with the hall light behind him was etched in acid in her mind.

"I . . . I saw what was inside him," she said distantly. "When I shot him, it . . . it came out of him." The image grew clearer in her mind, but it was too terrifying to contemplate, and she pushed it away, not wanting to revisit any of the horrors of that night.

"I really don't think he wanted to do it," she said, still looking up at the ceiling and only half aware that she was speaking out loud. "Card, I mean. That evil inside. I saw it, and it was making him do what he was doing to us—what he was going to do to us. It's because you were the one who put him away. You sent him to jail."

"And I would have pressed for the death penalty if we had it in Maine," Matt said, "but no." He shook his head. "I can't believe that. That's . . . It's impossible that he, that Bowker, a dead man, could use someone to try to get even with me."

"He did. I saw," Brenda said. "So it's a good thing I did what I did. It's a good thing I killed him."

"When you shot him, while he was dying on the living room floor—" Matt shivered and hugged himself, his eyes widening with fear. "Card was making these sounds that—" He exhaled with a shudder. "—that I never thought a human being could make."

Brenda's eyes were closed, but she could still hear her husband's voice, gradually fading away as waves of exhaustion dragged her down, and darkness swelled across her vision. She raised her hands and gently touched the bandage on the side of her face. When she did, the image of the ghost of the old woman she had seen filled her mind.

"This is going to leave a really bad scar, isn't it?" she said.

Matt clasped her hand and gently guided it away from the damaged side of her face. He swallowed hard; his throat made a loud gulping sound.

"The doctors think they can fix it eventually with plastic surgery and skin grafts, but it's going to take a lot of time. First thing, though, is you have to rest and regain your strength. It's—I can't believe how good it is to . . . to talk to you. I've been so worried. We all have."

"No," Brenda said. The face of the old woman loomed up in her memory as clearly as if Brenda were looking at herself in a mirror. The old woman's eyes were clouded with age. Thin, gray wisps of hair haloed her face. Brenda knew it was all in her mind, but she was convinced that she could have reached out and traced with her finger the knotted, jagged gray line of scar tissue that zigzagged from her scalp to her chin.

"I'm not . . ."

She sighed and wiped away the tears that had formed in her eyes as the old woman's face gradually receded into darkness, blending into the warm, brown light behind her closed eyes.

Not much of what had happened made any sense, at least in the everyday world, but on a deep level, Brenda was suddenly convinced that the ghostly figure haunting her new house was—somehow—herself, years from now, long after she had grown old and died and the children had gone off to create lives of their own.

Somehow, she had been trying to communicate with herself across the abyss of time, trying to show herself how she could save herself and her family by so simple a thing as holding her hands together at the wrists so Card couldn't tie them tightly.

Her rational mind told her that something like that was impossible. A ghost—even her *own* ghost—couldn't come from the future and warn her by showing her things in reflection that *could* have happened, that *would* have happened if she hadn't done what she had done. If she had just sat there, and Matt had regained consciousness before she attacked Card, they might all be dead now. Matt would have been shot and killed, like she had seen in the mirror.

And maybe on some level of reality that's exactly what *did* happen, but the ghost had shown her what to do to prevent it from happening to her. The barrier between alternate realities, between what did happen and what could have happened, was so thin, so tenuous, and somehow it had opened up, and she had saved herself and her family.

Brenda sighed, and as she began to drift off to sleep, once again she raised her hand to the bandage on her face and laughed softly.

A disfiguring scar seemed like an awfully small price to pay when balanced against the lives of her husband, her children, and herself.

"We—uh, we'll just have to see how it heals, I guess," she said dreamily as sleep swept over her, tugging her down into unconsciousness, down to a place where all of these things did make sense . . . a place where she could accept what had happened as real and try to forget about what might have happened.

She listened to herself speaking, but her voice sounded far away, as if someone else was talking to her from another room . . . or another world and another time.

"Let's . . . just. . . let nature . . . take its course," she said, drifting farther and farther away. "Because I want to . . . I'll have to be able to . . . to recognize myself . . . when the time comes. . . ."

TWENTY-THREE

soul deep

IT'S *changed me. . . . I'm different in so many ways. . . . I can't say how . . . but I know it. . . . I can feel it.*

It was mid-September, and Brenda had been home from the hospital for a little over a month. She was slowly regaining her health and strength, but her face was still bandaged from the repeated attempts to graft skin over her facial wounds. She was facing many more. Often, the skin beneath the bandages itched and burned furiously, but sometimes it had a cold, dead feeling, almost as if it belonged to someone else. Dr. Erickson, the specialist in Portland who was handling her case, told her that these sensations were normal because her skin and nerves were growing and connecting with the new grafts, but he admitted that he couldn't understand why the grafts weren't taking better than they were. In some areas, especially around her left eye, the skin had healed perfectly; but along her cheek and jaw, it was still almost as fresh and raw as the night she'd gotten injured. Time and again, Dr. Erickson reassured her that eventually the grafts would take, and most if not all of the damage would not be visible, but Brenda knew differently.

She wasn't sure how she knew, but she had no doubt that her face was never going to heal properly. For the rest of her life, she would have a disfiguring scar on the side of her face. She could accept that and, in some ways, she was happy for it.

She knew this the same way she knew other things.

Like, for instance, she knew that a severe thunderstorm was going to sweep through the area later that night, probably between ten o'clock and midnight. There would be significant storm damage, including some power outages and downed trees and utility poles, but—thankfully—no loss of life, at least not as a direct result of the storm.

She glanced at her wristwatch. It was almost ten o'clock now. Both Emily and John were in their bedrooms, and she and Matt were upstairs, getting ready for bed. She hadn't heard the severe storm warnings on the TV or radio, but she had known since early morning that the thunderstorm—and something else—was coming. She hadn't mentioned it to Matt. She didn't see any point bothering him if there wasn't any serious danger.

Still, a feeling deep inside told her something was brewing; it wasn't just the storm. *Something* was going to happen . . . something she should be concerned about. She wished she could clear her mind and get a better picture of what it was.

She tried to dismiss her discomfort as only the feeling the approaching storm was giving her. It could be simply that; since her injury, she was more sensitive, more keenly attuned to atmospheric variations and fluctuations. Maybe even through the bandages, her damaged skin responded more readily than normal skin to subtle electrostatic charges in the air.

All she knew for certain was, something bad was on its way. She knew it with the same clarity that she knew things that had already happened. It was almost like what was going to happen was already a memory for her and as real as the static charge that filled the night air and snaked across her body like unseen fingers.

As the storm drew closer, Brenda tried to put aside her growing worry. If she thought about things too much, she might start getting scared, and fear would make it all the more difficult for her to see and "remember" clearly. Then there would be no way she could try to make things better.

Sitting on the edge of the bed, she stared blankly ahead at the open door to the bathroom. Matt was already in bed, lying on his side facing away from her. The bedroom light was off,

but the bathroom light was still on. It cast a soft white wedge
of light into the bedroom. Brenda was slowly brushing her
hair, listening to the faint static crackling sounds the brush
made as she stroked it down. Glancing up, she caught her reflection in the mirror and stiffened. She stared at herself wide-
eyed for a long time, remembering that night not so long
ago—*It feels like a lifetime ago*—when she had been standing
by the bathroom sink, and for the first time had seen the old
woman sitting, reflected in the mirror. She had been where she
was sitting right now, on the edge of the bed, staring back at
her.

Was that really me?

Is this *really me?*

A frightening sense of duality swept over her. For a giddy
instant, she was unable to distinguish which was the real her
and which was the reflection. Coldness gripped her, and she
shivered, but things like this had been happening so often
since that horrible night that she was almost getting used to
them.

Almost.

At times like this, when the past, present, and future
seemed to blend together, she knew—or remembered—other
things that she knew were real, even though they hadn't happened yet. Just a few minutes ago, for instance, when she had
looked over at Matt, she had caught a glimpse of what had
happened—or would happen—to him. In that brief flash, she
had seen her husband much older than he was now. He was lying in this same bed, in the same room, on his back with his
head propped up with pillows, but he was wasting away. In
that instant of insight or memory, she had known—again she
had no idea how she had known this, but she didn't question
it—that Matt was dying of leukemia.

She was filled with profound sadness. Her hand holding
the hairbrush dropped to her lap. Her shoulders slumped as
the sadness swept over her. She struggled to push it back, but
a subtle panic was also rising inside her. She reminded herself
that it might not happen. It didn't have to be that way. Like
those things she had seen in the living room mirror that night,
it might just be something that could happen.

Maybe we can avoid it.

A silent flicker of lightning pulsed like a strobe in the darkness, bathing the bedroom for an instant with a soft, blue glow. Sharp shadows leaped out and then vanished. The static charge in the air grew stronger, stirring the hairs on Brenda's arms and on the back of her neck. A stinging whiff of ozone swept into the bedroom through the open window as the breeze picked up.

What's wrong? she wondered. *What's going to happen?*

"Storm coming," she said softly.

Her grip on the hairbrush handle tightened so hard her knuckles turned white. She took a quick sip of air through her mouth, hearing it hiss between her teeth.

Matt grunted in his sleep and stirred. Brenda looked at him again, her heart aching for what she knew—or thought she knew—was going to happen to him eventually.

That's the key word, she told herself. *Eventually. And anyway, it won't happen for a long time, and there's no guarantee it will even happen. Maybe we can do things—like I did that night—to change what's supposed to happen.*

Maybe everything is fated; maybe nothing is absolutely fated. Maybe we always have a choice.

The problem, she knew, was being able to tell the difference between those things that could be changed or prevented and those that couldn't. As unnerving and uncanny as this new feeling was, she knew she had to learn to trust it.

"With time," she whispered as, from far off, a low rumble of thunder rolled through the night. The breeze suddenly gusted, rustling the trees outside the window and billowing the curtains inward with a soft, rasping sound. The temperature in the room dropped noticeably, and the burning itch on the left side of her face intensified. Like so many times before, she wanted to rip the bandages off and scratch the itch, but she knew it wouldn't do any good.

The itch was inside her brain.

Something's coming. . . . Something bad is going to happen.

"But what? What is it?" she whispered as she hugged herself and shivered in the darkness. "What's coming?"

Once again, she glanced into the bathroom and saw her reflection in the mirror. She looked so old, so tired . . . like an old woman.

If this is the price I have to pay for having stopped what was going to happen, then I accept it, gladly. And I'd do it again, a thousand times, to save my family.

Rising slowly from the bed so as not to disturb Matt, she tiptoed into the bathroom and carefully placed her hairbrush on the sink. Her body was charged with subtle energy as though she drew power from the approaching storm. Another lightning flash lit the dark bedroom behind her, brighter, and the thunder that followed was closer. The storm was drawing rapidly nearer.

"Just wait," she whispered to her reflection. "Just wait and see."

Bracing her hands on either side of the sink, she leaned forward and stared into the mirror, watching her lips form the words. She knew—bone deep, soul deep—that whatever it was, it might be unavoidable. She trusted that she would know what to do when it came, and do what she could do to help.

Maybe it's already happened, she thought as the chills racking her body grew stronger.

Another flicker of lightning lit up the room like a flashbulb, leaving afterimages in her vision. The clap of thunder that followed seconds later was loud enough to make her jump and step quickly back from the sink. She could feel the low, rumbling roll of thunder that followed all the way to the roots of her teeth. The sudden hiss of rain as it began to fall was like a whisper in the night. Brenda checked the windows to make sure rain wasn't blowing in.

Something's wrong, but it's not too late to fix it. Not yet.

"But what *is* it?"

Clenching her fists and squeezing her eyes tightly shut, she banged the sides of her head as if that would help her focus.

It has something to do with . . . with . . .

"The kids . . . Oh my God!"

The thought entered her head with an audible rush. It was only a fraction of a second, like a flash of lightning, but she had a clear mental image of both children—Emily and John—outside in the pouring rain as lightning flashed above and thunder boomed all around them.

And in that flash, Brenda knew exactly where they were.

"Emily and John," she cried out as she rushed back into the bedroom, leaped onto the bed, and shook Matt's shoulder. He awoke with a start, his eyes glistening in the sudden brilliant flash of lightning.

"Huh—wha—?"

"The kids," Brenda said breathlessly. "They're in trouble."

"What are you talking about? They're both in . . . What time is it?" Matt shook his head and, rolling over, glanced at the clock on his bedstand. Then he turned to Brenda. She could read what he was thinking by his expression.

"Trust me," she said, although it was a struggle to keep her voice low and even. "I'm not crazy."

As rain pelted against the house like marbles, she jumped off the bed, suddenly sure that she knew what had been bothering her all along. Rather than argue the point, she dashed out of the bedroom and down the hall.

John's room was the first door on the right. She swung the door open, snapped on the wall switch, and looked. The sudden blast of light hurt her eyes, but she saw that John's bed was empty. It hadn't been slept in since she'd made it that morning.

Behind her, she heard Matt scuffling down the hall in her wake, but she was already down the hall to Emily's bedroom, knowing what she would find.

"See?" she cried as she swung Emily's door open and turned on the light. She stepped aside so Matt could see that his daughter's bed, while rumpled, was unoccupied.

"Jesus Christ," he muttered "Where did they—? How did you—?"

Brenda didn't say a word as she raced back to their bedroom and quickly dressed, tugging on the jeans and blouse she had worn that day. Matt stood in the doorway, looking absolutely dumbfounded. He shook his head from side to side as though unable to comprehend what was happening.

"You coming or not?" Brenda said as she pulled a sweatshirt on over her head.

"Yeah. Where?"

"Just get dressed," she said as she sat down on the edge of the bed and pulled on her socks and sneakers. Moving mechanically, as though he were in a dream and still not quite comprehending what he was doing, Matt got dressed while Brenda waited impatiently. Then the two of them raced downstairs.

"They didn't—" Matt started to say but then stopped himself.

Brenda saw the helpless, frightened look in his eyes, and it worried her, but she didn't say anything more as she grabbed his slicker from the front hall closet and handed it to him. The rubber made an irritating squeaky sound as he pulled it on. After sliding on her raincoat, Brenda walked briskly through the kitchen, grabbing her purse and car keys from the counter, and out the door into the garage.

The rattling of the garage door as it opened set her teeth on edge, but she got in on the driver's side and started the car while Matt scrambled to get in on the passenger's side.

"Where are we going, Bren?" he asked as he clipped on his seat belt. "How do you know—"

She turned and looked at him, and without a word backed the car out into the driveway. The rain was coming down so hard it looked more like snow than water in the harsh glare of the headlights. The windshield wipers had trouble keeping up with the downpour as Brenda did a quick three-point turn in the driveway and started up to the road. Again, Matt started to say something but ended up sighing instead as he sagged back into the seat and folded his arms across his chest.

Brenda could see that he doubted her sanity at the moment, but—more importantly—he was worried for his children. She wanted to assure him that everything would be all right, but she wasn't entirely sure it would be. Sometimes it was difficult to find words to express what she knew.

But I know.

They crossed Route 25 and drove in silence down Old County Road. The steady slapping of the windshield wipers swept the rain away, but the night wrapped around the car like a shroud.

"Jesus, Brenda!" Matt finally said when she turned onto Brook Street. She guessed he'd realized where she was heading, and after a few minutes, she pulled to a stop at the entrance to the Oak Grove Cemetery. The cemetery gates were closed, and a chain had been pulled through the bars and locked in place. A flash of lightning turned the metal bars white against the night sky.

Without a word, Brenda slammed the car into Park and opened her door. She left the car running with the defroster blasting at high. The headlights shone at an angle across the cemetery gate. The massive trunks of the oak tres that lined either side of the entrance were black and dripping, their wide leaves beaten down by the falling rain.

Brenda pulled the hood of her raincoat up. Clutching it to her throat, she stepped out into the downpour, slamming the door behind her, not bothering to look back to see if Matt was following. Raindrops drummed loudly on the car roof and hood. Wide puddles dotted the uneven gravel of the entrance, and powerful little streams gushed down to the gully along the side of the road.

Brenda moved quickly up the slight incline to the cemetery gate, then paused, tilting her head back to look up at the sky for a moment. Cold pinpricks of rain splashed against her face, and she knew she would have to replace the sodden bandage when she got home. She jumped when a flash of lightning illuminated the roiling clouds overhead, but in the sudden flash, she caught a glimpse in the corner of her eye of a figure, huddled behind one of the oaks at the gate.

"John?" she called out, not really sure it was him.

A cold, tingling rush ran up her back as she strained to hear a response above the downpour and the deafening claps of thunder that seemed to shake the earth.

"We shouldn't be out here," Matt hollered above the falling rain. Brenda hadn't heard him come up behind her. She had forgotten all about him, and his voice startled her. She wheeled around and glared at him, then started walking toward the oak tree. Another flash of lightning revealed John, squatting on the soggy ground, his shoulders hunched, his knees pulled up against his chest. He was shivering. His face was luminous in the dark—ghastly white and terrified.

"Oh, baby," Brenda whispered as she rushed to him, knelt down on the soggy grass, and wrapped her arms around him. He resisted her embrace, but only for a moment. Whimpering, he pressed himself against her, trembling in her arms.

"Oh, baby . . . baby," Brenda cooed as she hugged him close. He was wearing his light spring jacket, and it was soaked through. The smell of his wet hair filled her nostrils.

"I'm sorry I came," he said, his voice threatening to break on every syllable, "but I had to see what she was doing."

When he pulled back and looked up at her, his eyes were wide and glowing. For a dizzying instant, Brenda feared that he wasn't real, that he was just an illusion, a ghost as lost as she was in the stormy night.

But then she touched his face and felt the cold slickness of his skin. A plume of mist issued from his nostrils and mouth as he exhaled.

"Don't worry. Everything's gonna be all right. I know where she is," Brenda said. "But how did she get inside?" She indicated the locked cemetery gate with a nod of her head.

For a moment, John was silent as he shivered in her arms. Brenda was only vaguely aware that Matt was standing behind them. She had the distinct impression that her husband was still confused by all that was going on. She also sensed something else about him. There was a palpable nervousness radiating off him like a frigid draft of a winter wind.

"She's in the cemetery," Brenda said, her voice low and controlled. "I think you know where."

When she looked closely at Matt, she was shocked to see the expression of worry and genuine fear on his face. Brenda let go of her son and stood up slowly. Rain was streaming down her face and neck and running inside the collar of her sweatshirt, chilling her. The bandage on her face was saturated and drooped heavily. After a lengthening moment, she glanced at John, who was struggling to stand up. He moved stiffly from the cold and damp.

"The chain is loose," John said. "You can probably squeeze through like she did." He took a step forward, then hesitated, looking fearfully at his parents. "She's gonna be mad that I followed her. You aren't gonna tell her, are you?"

Before Matt said anything, Brenda smiled and rested her hand on his shoulder. She was still trembling, but she knew now that it was more from the cold and damp than from fear.

"We're just glad you're safe," she said. "Let's get your sister and go home."

Brenda started for the cemetery gate, but Matt caught her by the shoulder. She looked at him, feeling a rush of determination inside her.

"How did you know they were out here?" he asked, his voice quavering.

For a moment or two, she considered telling him the truth, but that would take too long. Besides, he probably wouldn't believe her. She shrugged free of his grasp and started walking through the puddles toward the cemetery gate. The black wrought-iron bars were like ice when she gripped them. A stirring of apprehension ran though her as she watched the wisps of ground fog that rose in the damp air and twisted like sheets in the wind. In the darkness, the tombstones looked insubstantial, and Brenda had the clear impression that, were she to approach any one of them and touch it, her hand would pass through the solid rock like it was mist.

It's not over yet.

A cold, sinking feeling filled her gut.

We're not out of this yet.

"Wait for us in the car, hon," she said to John over her shoulder. "The heater's running. You'll warm up in no time."

Without a word, John did as he was told. Brenda tightened her grip around the metal bars and pulled. The heavy gate creaked horribly as a narrow gap opened up, just enough for her to squeeze through if she slid in sideways. The sound of grinding metal set her teeth on edge, but she was thankful for that because the sharp sense of unreality about what she was doing made her feel as though she truly might be the ghost out here. She wiggled between the metal bars and then started up the road without looking back.

Her feet made loud sucking sounds in the mud. Her breath came in short, painful gulps. Waves of dizziness swept over her, and the frightening sense of unreality that swept through her was almost unbearable.

Maybe I am dead. . . . Maybe I'm just a ghost, haunting this cemetery.

But the cold rain on her face and the bone-deep chill was a harsh dose of reality that convinced her that this was all too real.

Although she would not have been able to articulate how

she knew where she was going, she walked up the road until it forked and, without hesitation, turned to the right and walked another hundred yards or so until she cut across the grass, wending her way between the tombstones and ankle-deep puddles.

She could hear Matt, breathing hard as he followed behind her, but she had no sense of exertion or of moving fast. That familiar feeling of being a disembodied spirit came over her as she drifted through the darkness, broken now and then by flashes of lightning. She could almost imagine that her feet were hovering several inches above the ground. It wasn't until she saw the tiny, pale figure up ahead that she slowed down. Matt drew to a stop beside her, and they both stared up the sloping hill to where Emily knelt in front of two small, white marble tombstones.

"There she is," Brenda said, raising her arm and pointing to her.

"She—" Matt said, but then his voice choked off. His eyes were wide as he looked at Brenda. "How did you know?"

Brenda unconsciously raised her hand to the bandage on her face and shook her head from side to side.

"I have no idea," she said.

Matt swallowed hard, rain streaming from his hair. His eyes shifted back and forth as though he were too nervous to focus on anything for long. Cupping his hands to his mouth, he called out, "Hey, Em."

For a moment or two, the girl didn't move. Her back was to them, her shoulders hunched and her head bowed. A sliver of panic slipped through Brenda.

Is she hurt? Is she even alive?

"Emily!" Matt shouted, louder this time, as they started up the slope toward her. Their feet slipped on the rain-soaked grass.

Brenda's pulse throbbed hard in her neck as she followed a step or two behind, and every time she inhaled, the cold, ozone-tinged air numbed her throat and chest. She couldn't shake the impression that her stepdaughter was dead, and that her lifeless body had been propped up against one of the gravestones.

Is that what I was afraid was going to happen? . . . What if

I killed the wrong man? . . . Or what if someone else has done this?

Her knees almost buckled under her, but she forced herself up the slope to the grave site. For an instant, when Emily turned around slowly to look at them, Brenda imagined that she—*Like I am*—was no more than a lonely ghost, lingering in the graveyard, waiting to fade away into the darkness. Forks of lightning split the night like hot wires, and the throaty grumble of thunder that followed made the earth tremble.

"Em! What are you doing out here?" Matt had to shout to be heard above the driving rain.

Emily's face was pale and drained of all emotion as she stared wordlessly at her father, who had stopped a few feet away from where she was kneeling.

"I came to see her," Emily said, her voice tight as she indicated the larger of the two gravestones with a quick nod of her head. Keeping her distance, Brenda squinted until she could make out the name that was carved there: Susan McKenney Ireland.

"It's her, isn't it?" Emily said, turning away from her father and staring at the stone, which glistened with silver streams of rainwater.

"Her," Matt echoed, his voice sounding so lost and alone it made Brenda's chest ache.

"The lady who tried to kidnap me. She said she was my mother. She died after the accident, and this is her grave, isn't it?"

Matt started to speak but could only stammer something unintelligible.

"Who's this, then?" Emily asked, glancing at her father as she raised her arm and pointed with a trembling hand at the smaller headstone beside Susan's. The name on it read: Alison Louise Ireland. Carved below that were the birth and death dates. January 10, 1990–August 14, 1990.

"Did I have a sister?" Emily's voice was flat, almost perfectly toneless, and her eyes were half-closed as though she were mulling over the idea.

Brenda saw Matt's shoulders droop as he raised his hands in a gesture of utter helplessness. His lips were moving, but the only sound that came out was a low, strangled groan.

"You didn't . . . I mean . . . She was . . ." He couldn't finish, and he just stood there with the rain beating down on him.

"Tell her the truth," Brenda said softly. She felt like an intruder, and was trying not to let the enormity of what was happening hit her. Still, she couldn't help but think, *He never even told me he lost a daughter!*

Matt was glancing back and forth between them and then, finally, he lowered his gaze and said in a soft, wounded voice, "Yes. You did. You had a sister, Emily. Her name was Alison. She . . . she died when she was a baby."

"I can see that by the dates, but how'd she die?" Emily asked simply. At her question, Matt turned and looked desperately at Brenda, their gazes locking. She could see in his eyes how much this was costing him, and her heart broke for him. She nodded her head, urging him on to tell everything.

"Your mother . . . your real mother was . . . was responsible," he said, shuddering and narrowing his eyes with pain as he spoke. "She . . . you see, she had a serious problem with drinking, and she had a terrible car accident. She was mentally ill, too. You were only a baby yourself, and Alison . . . it was too soon for another baby." His voice broke, and he almost couldn't continue, but he took a deep breath, and as lightning flashed around them, he forged on. "One day, she was giving Alison a bath. You were asleep in your crib, and your mother had been drinking. When she went to check on you, she forgot all about your sister, and she . . . Alison drowned. Your mother had a complete breakdown after that. The doctors said she was in total denial. She forgot Alison ever existed. She forgot what she'd done . . ." His voice trailed off.

"So she *was* my real mother," Emily said, indicating the larger gravestone with a nod of her head. "The lady who tried to kidnap me."

Matt didn't say a word. He simply stared at his daughter, his eyes blank, his face as white as bone.

"She really scared me," Emily said after a long pause. Rain had pasted her hair into dark curls across her forehead. Her jacket was soaked through and hung heavily on her frail shoulders. With a nod of her head, she stood up slowly and turned to face her father, her eyes wide and bright. Brenda could see that it was more than raindrops that were streaming down her face.

"Why didn't you tell me, Daddy?" she asked, her voice low and controlled. Brenda was surprised that she didn't scream.

"I . . . I don't know," Matt finally said, staring down at the ground and shaking his head. "I . . . I know I should have, but I . . . I just don't know. I guess I figured if I didn't talk about it, if I didn't acknowledge it, then maybe I would eventually forget that it ever happened." He took a deep breath that rasped in his throat. "But I didn't forget. . . . I couldn't. And when she came back, I had to do everything I could to protect you. You understand that, don't you?"

Brenda froze when Emily shifted her gaze away from her father and fastened it on her. They stared at each other so long, Brenda's vision began to shimmer, and she began to see dazzling diamond lights, dancing like a swirl of fireflies around Emily's head. Luminous shapes moved all around her, hovering in misty swirls that could have been ground fog, but Brenda knew they weren't. In that timeless instant, she saw Emily not as the fifteen-year-old girl she was, but as the mature, middle-aged woman she would become. She had come out here to pay her respects to the mother and the sister she had never known. And in that same instant, Brenda imagined herself as a much older lady, still with a disfigured face, who had lost her husband to a wasting disease and who would live out the rest of her life in the house where she now lived.

Once again, Emily turned to her father. "Why'd you lie to me? Don't you trust me?" she asked.

Emily's voice cut through the haze that had descended over Brenda's mind. Shaking her head to clear it, she watched as Matt stepped forward and, sobbing, stretched his arms out to his daughter.

"Of course I do, darling," he said just before thunder clapped overhead. "I love you, and I . . . I know I shouldn't have lied to you, especially now that you're so much older. I should have trusted that you'd understand, but I—" He sighed and shook his head. "I don't have any excuse except that I was afraid."

"She was telling the truth all along." Emily said as she started walking slowly toward him. She frowned as though the words almost didn't make sense to her, and she had to let them sink in before she could fully understand. Then, as another bolt of lightning flashed brilliantly overhead, illuminating the tombstones around them, Emily looked at Brenda again. Her expression was softer now, as tears welled in her eyes.

"I know who she was, Daddy," Emily said as she walked past him, her eyes still locked onto Brenda. "But she wasn't my mother. Not really."

Brenda couldn't hold back her tears any longer. She held her arms out to Emily and enfolded her, unable to keep from sobbing as she ran her fingers through the wet tangles of Emily's hair. A dizzying wave of elation filled her, and she clung to Emily as if she were the only real thing that kept her from fading away into the darkness of the night. Emily's body trembled violently as she pressed her face against Brenda and cried in her arms. After a while, with the rain still pouring down on them, they broke off the embrace and stared at each other in the perfect silence of understanding.

When Matt walked up to them and hugged them both, Emily looked Brenda straight in the eyes and whispered softly, "You're my real mother. Right?"

And in reply, all Brenda could do was hug her again and hold her as close to her heart as she could.

A. J. MATTHEWS is the pseudonym for national best-selling author Rick Hautala.